ZOMBICIDE BLACK PLAGUE
AGE OF THE UNDEAD

"So it begins," the man whispered, darkly fascinated as the graveyard pitched and heaved as its occupants dug their way out from below. First one plot disgorged its contents, the rotten husk of a milkmaid, her flesh pitted with decay and her forehead crushed by the cow that had ended her life. Another grave spat out the bloated bulk of a blacksmith, his hair burned away, and his skin charred. Others quickly followed until there were a dozen undead horrors shambling about the cemetery.

The disturbance in the graveyard was noted by the sexton. Unaware of the nature of the trespassers, he rushed from his shack to confront them. The undead converged upon him, dragging him down with their necrotic hands. Then the zombies turned away from their prey. As they stalked off, the mangled remains of the sexton stirred once more. Lurching to its feet, the chewed corpse staggered away to join its killers.

T0112100

ALSO AVAILABLE

AGE OF THE
UNDEAD

CL WERNER

ACONYTE

First published by Aconyte Books in 2022

ISBN 978 1 83908 112 5

Ebook ISBN 978 1 83908 113 2

Cover art by Daniele Orizio

Distributed in North America by Simon & Schuster Inc, New York, USA

Printed in the United States of America

9 8 7 6 5 4 3 2 1

ACONYTE BOOKS

An imprint of Asmodee Entertainment Ltd

Mercury House, Shipstones Business Centre

North Gate, Nottingham NG7 7FN, UK

aconytebooks.com // twitter.com/aconytebooks

For Kevin, who drew my attention to Zombicide: Black Plague and provoked the resultant backlog of unpainted miniatures.

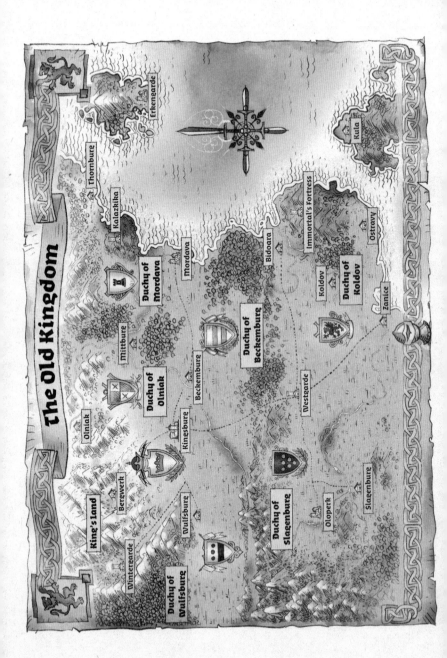

The Old Kingdom

King's Land

Erkengarde
Thornburg
Kolazkika

Duchy of Mordava
Mittburg
Mordava
Bidoara

Immortal's Fortress
Ostravy
Kula

Duchy of Olniak
Olniak
Beckemburg
Duchy of Beckemburg

Koldov
Duchy of Koldov
Zanice

Bergwerk
Kingsburg
Westearde

Winterearde
Wulfsburg

Duchy of Wulfsburg

Duchy of Slagenburg
Oloperk
Slagenburg

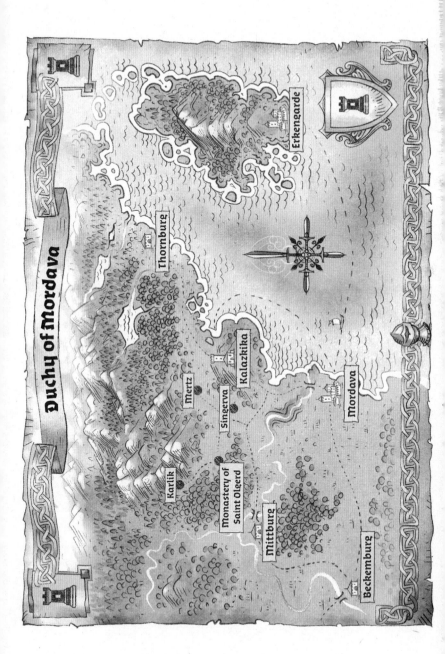

PROLOGUE

Darkness and the rancid stench of death lay thick within the underground vault. The scratch of rats' claws upon stone was the only sound that echoed through the gloom. What little light strove against the shadows came from a few tapers set into niches in the dank stone walls.

A shape flickered across the uneven paving, disturbing the vermin as they gnawed their charnel dinner. The hem of a heavy robe swished through the dust as the figure rapidly crossed the ancient crypt. Dull thuds resounded in the dark as the butt of a staff tapped against the floor.

The intruder hurried toward a plinth set at the very center of the vault. Eyes peered from beneath the hood that swathed the figure's head, fixating on the object that rested atop the pedestal. Leaning forward, a hand reached out and brushed away the patina of dirt that was caked about a fist-sized sphere. Where the fingers scratched it, the gleam of crystal caught the dim light and sparkled in crimson translucence.

A low chuckle rose from the intruder, and he threw back the hood revealing a lean and predatory visage. Straggly black hair spilled away from his scalp in long, greasy locks. His face, the skin drawn taut across high cheekbones, had a sickly pallor to it. The eyes alone were vibrant, deep pits that burned with a remorseless fire.

The man stared at the crystal sphere for a moment, then quickly swung the malachite-capped staff he carried. The knobby head, carved into a grinning skull, swatted one of the rats as it scurried across the floor. The macabre intruder dipped to the ground and with his free hand snatched up the stunned rodent. Stepping closer to the plinth, he raked a long, dirty fingernail across the rat's neck. Blood spurted from the animal and pattered down onto the ruby crystal.

"The Eye of Darkness," the man hissed, both avarice and awe in his tone. He clenched his fist and squeezed the bleeding rat as though it were a lemon. More of its blood splattered across the sphere. The crystal, in its turn, was stimulated by the gore. Its formerly transparent depths became cloudy.

The intruder tossed the dead rat aside, leaving it to the cannibal attentions of its fellows, and fixated his gaze on the scarlet fog billowing within the sphere. As he watched, the murk resolved itself into distinct images. He could see high mountains and rolling fields, walled castles and lonely hamlets. He recognized these scenes, for they represented the realm of King Heinrich IV, a monarch the great and powerful had christened "the Good" but who the majority of his subjects knew by another name.

"Heine the Indolent," the observer scoffed as he gazed into the crystal. The king had inherited a land largely devoid of conflict. Greater predecessors had driven marauding monsters like ogres and trolls from the land. Only on the western frontier, in the rain-swept moors and forests of the

Duchy of Wulfsburg, did the warlike orcs persist in such numbers as to be any manner of menace. True, the occasional dragon drifted down from the mountains to burn a farmstead or devour a herd of cattle, but for the most part, the kingdom was a peaceful one.

"But peace breeds strange ideas." There was bitterness in the voice, a malice that provoked the crystal. The man watched as the image shifted. The landscape narrowed, focusing upon a stone tower rising above a small village. Black-clad antagonists were dragging a battered old man from that tower. His robes were ripped, his white beard stained with blood, his face bruised and battered. The villagers watched in silence as the elder was carried into the square where a post had been raised and wood was piled. "A wizard accused of practicing the black arts, summarily tried and convicted by the king's agents."

It was a scene that had played out many times across the kingdom. The Wizards' Guild was often tardy protesting when the Order of Witch Hunters decided one of its members had turned to black magic. There were those in the court who used the strife to expand their own influence in the kingdom and to maintain their authority, the zeal of the witch hunters was never appeased. Always there was another magician or conjurer accused of delving into proscribed magics. Always there was someone else to be exposed and condemned to the pyre.

A sneer curled the man's face as he stared into the crystal. "Their fanaticism to destroy the necromancers only made their worst fears become reality," he muttered. Many an enchanter, fearful of death on a witch hunter's pyre, sought the quick power promised by the black arts. The necromancers they'd been created to destroy grew in number. Lone practitioners banded together into cabals for mutual protection.

The scenes within the crystal now displayed a coven of humans swathed in robes edged in arcane sigils. Runes, ancient and profane, were daubed upon their foreheads and cheeks in pigments ground from bone and blood. The skulls of murdered men topped their staves or hung from their belts. In their hands they bore the accouterments of their morbid sorcery; daggers fashioned from femurs, wands carved from tombstones, grimoires bound in the flayed skin of corpses. A gathering of necromancers.

The grim cabal was gathered in a dismal, fog-wrapped swamp. Ugly menhirs projected up from the dank earth, each stone caked in black mud and green scum. The ruins of a lost and ancient place, a last testament to a terrible and forgotten race. The observer squirmed uneasily as he contemplated the inhuman design of each monolith and the grisly hieroglyphs just visible under the muck. They bespoke a prehuman age of such remoteness that evil was a feeble word to describe the profane sensation it evoked.

Before the intruder's eyes, the crystal showed the necromancers performing a ghastly rite. Hideous sacrifices performed at a conjunction of the menhirs created a concentration of arcane energies that could be felt even across the gap of space and time. The cabal pooled their powers, drawing on the energies they'd invoked. The slime of the swamp rippled and undulated like waves on a storm-swept sea. Stagnant water and viscid mud rolled away, excavating a deep pit in the midst of the menhirs. Ancient stone blocks protruded from the sides of this depression, hints of some colossal ruin buried beneath the morass.

It wasn't the rubble of a forgotten city that interested the necromancers. Burrowing out from the sides of the pit as though they were living things, long-buried relics crawled into view. Apprentices, attendants, henchmen and thralls, such companions as the cabal had brought with them now dropped down into the slimy hole. Eagerly they snatched up the relics as they emerged and handed them up to their masters. Just as eagerly, the necromancers seized the relics, cherishing them against their bosoms as though they were long-lost children. Some of the objects resembled swords and daggers, though of a design never intended for human hands. There were things that looked like misshapen circlets and helms, others that might have been scepters and wands. Tablets of fossilized bone, etched with the same grisly hieroglyphs of the menhirs. Fanged skulls with reptilian contours and horned brows.

"The rewards of evil are death," the observer commented, as he watched on. The associates of the cabal, too low in the pit to climb out on their own, raised their arms in appeal to their masters as the last of the ancient objects were extracted. The necromancers stepped away, their eyes pitiless as they gazed down at their helpers. Frantic realization struck their minions then, but in their panic, none thought to aid the person next to them, instead pawing futilely at the slimy walls. Screams of horror rose as the muck that had been extruded came flooding back in. Soon the pit was filled and its occupants entombed beneath tons of mud.

The betrayed minions served as a final sacrifice in the infernal magic. Armed now with their prehuman relics, the cabal set themselves to a spell far greater than anything ever attempted before, magic of such ferocious malignity that it was beyond the power of any one of them to invoke. By pooling their energies, using the stolen relics to focus those energies, the necromancers called upon the forces of Darkness.

Even among the cabal there were those frightened by what they sought to harness. Some quivered in fear, others cried tears of terror. The most depraved, however, had only bitter satisfaction written on their cruel faces. They cried out in joy as shadowy tendrils of profane magic crackled into their bodies and flowed outward into the relics. From these foci, the dark magic was projected into the sunken menhirs.

"Magnified and defined by primordial curses." The man nodded to himself as he watched the process. He looked on as streams of shadow slithered away from each menhir, squirming through the swamp like great worms. With unbelievable swiftness, the conjured energies scattered from the site of the cabal's ritual. Through forest and over field, the magic spread.

The observer willed the crystal to fixate upon the village where the tendril of cursed energy alighted. He watched the slithering magic ripple through the community before darting into its graveyard. Fingers of necromantic power burrowed into each plot. Foul energies seeped into coffin and shroud. The dead stirred.

"So it began," the man whispered, darkly fascinated as the crystal showed him the graveyard pitching and heaving as its occupants dug their way out from below. First one plot disgorged its contents, the rotten husk of a milkmaid, her flesh pitted with decay and her forehead crushed by the cow that had ended her life. Another grave spat out the bloated bulk of a blacksmith, his hair burned away, and his skin charred from when he'd drunkenly fallen into his own forge. Others quickly followed until there were a dozen undead horrors shambling about the cemetery. The observer judged that every corpse that had been interred within the year had been reanimated. Those bodies that hadn't fallen utterly into dissolution had been revived by the necromancers' spell as zombies.

The disturbance in the graveyard was noted by the sexton. Unaware of the nature of the trespassers, he rushed from his shack to confront them. Too late did he notice the ghastly decay and hideous wounds, for by then he was in the very midst of the zombies. The undead converged upon him, dragging him down with their necrotic hands. Decayed jaws set their teeth in his flesh, relenting only when life was extirpated. Then the zombies turned away from their prey. As they stalked off, the mangled remains of the sexton stirred once more. Lurching to its feet, the chewed corpse staggered away to join its killers.

Drawn by the sexton's screams as he was slaughtered, other villagers now saw the pack of zombies lumbering through the graveyard. Cries of alarm from the villagers brought purpose to the zombies. The creatures turned at the sound and relentlessly marched on the village. They fell upon those who had been friends and family in life, dispatching them with the same bestial ruthlessness as the sexton. Only those too severely mutilated when they were killed remained as inert corpses. The rest rose again to join the ranks of the undead. What had started as a dozen soon became twenty and then thirty. Before long, the zombies outnumbered the living in the doomed village.

The man with the crystal was impressed by how completely the population had been overwhelmed. There had been times before when a necromancer would raise a small company of undead, but never had such a horde as this been unleashed, a menace far beyond the ability of the witch hunters to combat.

"So, King Heinrich sends his army," the observer muttered. "The king thinks he can stop the curse that now rises against him." The crystal showed armored knights in noble livery riding before massed ranks of spearmen and archers. An army greater than anything the kingdom had mustered since the orcs were finally driven across the frontier. The pennants of a hundred noble houses flew behind the heads of lances, the banners of powerful guilds were borne by the freebooters hired by their coin, even a few mages from the Wizards' Guild were in evidence, escorted by their acolytes.

On a day so overcast that the sun was blotted utterly from the sky and noon was no brighter than midnight, the army encountered the zombie horde. Ranks of archers let loose arrows into the shambling undead. Lances were lowered as the cavalry massed. At a signal from High Marshal Konreid, the knights charged ahead into their monstrous foe. Scores of zombies were ripped apart by the lances and trampled beneath the hooves of destriers, yet even mangled and crushed, the undead continued to fight. Broken bodies clutched at stirrups and clawed at fetlocks, pulling down the kingdom's chivalry by sheer weight of numbers.

Only a fraction of the cavalry broke through to the other side of the undead horde. As they wheeled about, the knights saw their comrades being slaughtered. Warriors were dragged from their saddles as their steeds collapsed from their wounds. Some managed to fight afoot for a time, but surrounded on all sides, it was inevitable that they'd be overwhelmed.

Afforded a far less clear view of the efficacy of his cavalry, High Marshal Konreid hurried his infantry forward to support the knights. When he did, the magnitude of the trap was revealed. The moment the infantry closed upon the horde and found themselves locked in battle, swarms of undead crested the nearby hills and began their relentless march onto the plain. Thousands of zombies, a tide of walking corpses larger than the king's entire army.

Pinned by the initial horde, the infantry struggled to retain cohesion while also seeking to disengage. Archers shot volley after volley into the oncoming tide of undead, but the casualties they inflicted did little to lessen the menace before them. Many lost heart and fled. High Marshal Konreid, desperate to restore order, charged down several bowmen. While his horse stomped the life from a retreating mercenary, an archer turned and loosed an arrow, piercing the general's neck. Without Konreid's guiding hand, his panicked steed galloped away, its master slumped over the saddle.

"The snake has lost its head," observed the man in the crypt, a thin smile twisting his face. The High Marshal was the only one who might have prevented the army from disintegrating into a rout. With him gone, the battle was lost. Now the massacre would begin.

The mages sent by the Wizards' Guild tried their best to wither the horde's numbers by loosing powerful spells on the undead. Clutches of zombies were immolated in arcane fire or frozen in blocks of enchanted ice, but the enemy weren't without their own magic. Several necromancers, set to supervise the walking dead, employed their own spells to counter those of the wizards. Sorcerous duels fought in the minds and wills of the combatants, the skill and discipline of the mages might have prevailed over the unrestrained recklessness of their opponents but for the fact the necromancers didn't need to overcome their adversaries. They needed only to keep the wizards occupied long enough for the tide of zombies to wash over them. With the morale of the archers broken, with the infantry too far away to protect them, the wizards and their retainers were unable to stave off disaster. One after another, they were brought down by packs of slavering undead.

"Carnage," the observer declared, as he gazed on the finish of the battle. Only a small portion of the army escaped the zombie hosts. Many of those who fell to the horde rose again to increase their ranks. In the end, far from exterminating the zombies, High Marshal Konreid had doubled their numbers.

"Now it's our turn," the man whispered. He willed the crystal to show him not things already past, but events that were still unfolding. Not all of the necromancers had gone to the southern swamps to participate in the great ritual, but these too had their part in the cabal's plan. With the army gone away to fight the horde, they now set upon their own conjurations. Many of them had received relics to facilitate their magic and allow their spells to draw upon the morbid Darkness. The observer had a moment of terrified uncertainty. The artifacts were by nature evil and their power unpredictable, ever ready to twist the desires of those who called upon them into unintended nightmares. For now, at least, the dread forces evoked by the necromancers were obedient. In hamlets and villages, towns and cities across the northern Duchy of Mordava, the dead stirred in their graves. From scores of graveyards, zombies emerged to attack the living.

"All the kingdom is beset," the man declared. He glanced around at the walls of the vault, his senses keyed to the least sign of motion. Even the rats were still now, as though the vermin sensed the hideous power at work in the land.

"Eye of Darkness, past and present you've shown." The observer leaned over the crimson crystal and set his hand across it. His body trembled as he fought to impose his will upon the orb. "Now show me those things which are yet to be…"

Red shadows flickered through the vault, sending the rats scurrying for shelter. There was a sharp crack as the staff clattered to the floor. The intruder clasped one hand to his chest and groaned in agony. The Eye of Darkness was a potent artifact… but its greatest powers demanded a price.

CHAPTER ONE

The armored rider crested the hill just as night fell upon the village of Mertz. He strained his eyes but not so much as the flicker of a rushlight shone from the community. He'd ridden long and far to reach this place, but it wasn't the homecoming he'd expected. A chill crept down his spine. There was something menacing, almost predatory about the darkened buildings. The only sound that rose from the place was the whistle of the wind through the thatch roofs and the groan of the waterwheel outside the mill. In vain did he try to pick out the drift of smoke rising from a chimney. Nothing... just the desolation of a forsaken place.

The rider urged his steed away from the village. The horse staggered as it turned onto the path that wound up the hill above the village. The walls and battlements of a castle reared up, dark shadows against the night sky. Even less sign of life exuded from the bleak fortress. No watchfires in the towers, no sound of activity from the keep, no moonlight shining from the helm of a sentry at the battlements. Just the same silent menace as the village.

From the castle, however, the rider would not turn. He'd

driven his horse hard to reach this place, crossing half the province to find his way here, sparing neither himself nor his steed. The knight was one of the few survivors of King Heinrich's army. Two days in the saddle since the disastrous battle with the undead. In that time, he'd passed through a landscape ravaged by evil, finding no succor in village or hamlet. From this castle, however, the knight would not turn. For his name was Alaric von Mertz, and this was his home.

The doughty warhorse, accustomed to carrying its armored rider into battle but not bearing his weight for hours on end, finally surrendered to exhaustion. The animal had no sooner started up the slope toward the castle than a tremendous shiver swept through its powerful frame. It wilted to the ground, giving Alaric just enough time to slip his feet from the stirrups before his mount rolled onto its side.

"Poor Thunderstrike," Alaric said, leaning over the horse and running his hand down its froth-flecked neck. The destrier had endured beyond any reasonable expectation. If he could have spared it time to rest he would have, but to linger even an hour in zombie-infested country was to court disaster. More, there was his fear for his family, a driving passion that pushed him on against all restraint. The long-serving Thunderstrike had paid for his determination. The animal would be helpless for days, if indeed it could recover from the exertion he'd demanded of it. Alaric looked back at the darkened village with its aura of malice. How many zombies might be hiding in those shadows, waiting to strike out at the living? Through his mind flashed images of steeds brought down during the battle and how they'd been torn apart by the undead.

"That much, at least, I can spare you old friend." Tears glimmered in the knight's eyes as he drew the dagger from his belt. He stroked the horse's mane, nerving himself for what he had to do. His dagger struck true. A shiver, and Thunderstrike was beyond the pain of its passing and the threat of zombie teeth.

Alaric turned away from the dead warhorse and climbed the path up to the castle. He tried to quell the dread that swelled within him with each step and cling to the last tatters of hope. Someone was alive! They had to be! The silence, the lack of light, it was all because the Baron was taking precautions against attracting any packs of zombies to the castle. Over and over, he repeated the idea in muted whispers. He was almost able to convince himself it might even be true.

It was the sight of the main gate that ended Alaric's happy illusions. The drawbridge was down and the portcullis raised. The castle's defenses would never be lowered if the Baron still held command. His noble father was strict and precise in his way of doing things. Habits honed by years on the frontier fighting orcs were ingrained into Baron Gerhoelt von Mertz so deeply that they formed the backbone of his character. Even when he'd been awarded a demesne far from the border, the Baron never lost the caution that enabled him to survive years of skirmishes and ambushes.

Alaric drew his broadsword as he approached the yawning gate. The darkness of night made it difficult for him to be certain, but it seemed the surface of the drawbridge was splotched and stained. He leaned down to get a closer look, but as he did, his eyes caught something floating on the surface of the moat below. It was pale enough to contrast with the murky water and there was no mistaking its distinctive outline. The object was a human hand, severed at the wrist.

Hope dies hard in a desperate man. Alaric could no longer delude himself that his home had escaped the plague sweeping the land. Still, it was just possible some of the household had managed to barricade themselves in one of the rooms. He didn't know how long any such survivors could hold out, but if they were in the castle, he would find them. He put two mailed fingers to his lips and whispered a prayer to the God of Justice that some of his family were still alive. It was too much to expect the old Baron to have run from a fight, but his mother, sister, and younger brother were a different matter. It took all his self-restraint to keep from shouting their names as he rushed into the courtyard.

The place was a shambles. Broken arrows and splintered shields were strewn about the paving stones. A flock of hideous black crows gamboled about the shattered remains of the stables, picking at the mangled carrion in the stalls. Slumped against the base of a watchtower, Alaric found the final proof to what had happened here. It was a corpse with an axe buried in its skull, but the advanced decay of the body told that it hadn't been truly alive when it suffered the blow that ended its existence. He'd seen enough zombies to recognize this carcass for one of them.

The door to the watchtower was broken down. A quick glance across the courtyard showed Alaric that the one opposite it had likewise been forced. He doubted if any of the inner doors would have withstood anything that could smash the steel-banded outer portals. If there were survivors here, he'd have to look elsewhere.

Warily, Alaric circled the courtyard and approached the keep. He saw the broken heft of a halberd and a horribly mangled body dressed in the von Mertz livery. The zombies had shown the man-at-arms such attention that there wasn't enough left of the soldier to join the undead. Not enough face left for Alaric to put a name to the warrior. Whoever he'd been, the knight prayed the man had given a good account before his finish and that he'd already been dead when the zombies tore into him with their teeth and claws.

The massive doors at the front of the keep had been torn from their frame and lay sprawled across the corridor beyond. There was even less light inside than there was in the courtyard, but Alaric didn't need illumination to pick his way through these halls. This was his home, the place he'd grown up. He knew it as well as he knew the back of his own hand. It took him only a moment to orient himself. He tried to think where the best place was for someone to try and hide from the undead and finally decided to start in the chapel. He'd seen for himself that the roadside shrines and village temples had offered no sanctuary from the zombies, but others couldn't be expected to know that. They'd try to seek protection from the gods when force of arms wasn't enough. If anyone had survived the initial onslaught, he expected to find evidence of them in the chapel. Perhaps even a clue to where they'd gone from there if, indeed, the zombies had left them anywhere to run to.

As he moved through the dreary halls, Alaric stumbled over the many objects strewn about the floor. Proof that there had been fighting here as well as outside. Some of the things he brushed against he thought must be overturned braziers and upended chairs. Others he was certain were discarded swords and helmets. Once he almost tripped over something that gave under his boot and made a sucking noise when he withdrew his foot. He tried not to think of what it was… or who it had once been.

Though he could find his route through the keep, his frequent encounters with obstacles wore on Alaric's nerves. What else might be waiting there in the darkness? The knight could find his way through the halls, but he had no way of knowing what else might be in those corridors with him. He strained his ears, listening for any sound that might betray the lurking undead if they lurched into sudden motion. So intense was his concentration that the slightest noise he made felt to him like the roar of a dragon. He paused, focusing on the blackness around him, trying to will it into surrendering its secrets to him.

Alaric's crazed wish seemed to be granted when a tiny light disturbed the gloom. He blinked, wondering if the strain had been too much on his eyes, but the light remained when he opened them again. Just the smallest glow, like a little firefly flitting across a meadow. If the surrounding darkness wasn't so complete, he doubted he'd have noticed it at all. Notice it he did, however, and a thrill rushed through him when he realized where the light was coming from.

It was in the chapel!

The knight hurried to the room, pushing open the barred gates. "Who's there?" he called out.

The light was somewhere down near the altar. He had only a momentary glimpse of a human shape, little more than an outline, before the illumination was obscured. "It's me,

Alaric," he said, trying to allay the fears of whoever was in the chapel.

"Keep your voice down," a scolding voice hissed at him from the shadows. Alaric winced at the reprimand, knowing himself to be in the wrong. There was no knowing what else might be within earshot.

The knight didn't call out again, but he speedily made his way down to the altar. He kept a firm grip on his sword as he advanced, wary lest his incautious appeals had been noticed elsewhere. Alaric was brought up short when he saw the light again, shining from the floor just to the right of the altar. It was a wax candle, like any of hundreds that would normally illuminate the keep's chambers. Something about it, though, excited his suspicions. He spun around to the left side of the altar. By the candlelight, he saw a figure brandishing a dagger. The shape drew back when his sword turned towards it.

"Now there's a hostile greeting for you." The voice was the same that had scolded Alaric earlier. It belonged to a stocky man with dark, close-cropped hair and a rough, haggard face.

Alaric kept the tip of his sword pointed at the man. He wasn't unknown to the knight. Neither was the burgundy doublet he was wearing or the dagger in his hand. The doublet was from his brother's wardrobe, the dagger was one he'd seen many times hanging from the belt of the castle's seneschal. He might have expected, if anyone in the castle would be slippery enough to escape the zombie horde, it would be this rogue. "Gaiseric," the knight said, finally putting name to the man. "The last I saw of you, the Baron had you locked safely away in the dungeon."

An awkward smile pulled at Gaiseric's face. "All a

misunderstanding," he insisted. "Your father thought better of keeping me chained after you left. I mean, after all, to imprison a competent, hale…"

The knight's eyes narrowed. "The Baron wanted to hang you," he reminded Gaiseric. "I persuaded him to be lenient. He didn't think too much of someone who'd steal from the village temple." Alaric's eyes darted to the rogue's other hand. He spotted one of the golden icons that should have been on the altar in the little man's hand.

"The deacon shouldn't have left the window open," Gaiseric protested. "It's tantamount to deliberately encouraging sin from people with compromised willpower. You'd not hold it against a fox for taking bait from a trap, would you?"

Alaric groaned deep inside himself. He couldn't explain even to himself why he felt so charitable toward Gaiseric. Maybe it was the unabashed boldness of the thief, a bravado more to be expected from a swordsman than a burglar. The knight always respected courage, and however larcenous Gaiseric might be, it was hard to deny that he was brave as well. Perhaps, had he been born to a higher station rather than the son of a cutthroat who was hanged for cattle rustling, he'd have proven himself a dependable comrade-in-arms.

"I wouldn't set the fox free to do it again," Alaric stated, reminding himself that Gaiseric was a thief just the same. He stepped forward, pressing the tip of his sword against the rogue's neck. "My father didn't let you go. What happened here?"

Gaiseric's visage grew somber. "You won't like what I have to tell you. I'm sorry about that." He glanced fearfully toward the entrance to the chapel. "We'd best keep our voices low and our eyes open."

"I'm keeping my eyes on *you*," Alaric returned. "Wotun's Scales aren't the only thing you've stolen from the castle," he added, plucking at the rich doublet Gaiseric was wearing.

The thief shook his head. "I took what nobody had use for," he said. There was an unexpected note of sympathy in his tone. Alaric could see the regret in Gaiseric's expression when he spoke. "You saved me from the hangman, and I wish it wasn't an ill coin I had to repay you with."

Alaric felt the last flicker of hope dying inside of him. "What happened to my family?" he demanded.

Gaiseric lowered his eyes. "They're dead. Everyone in the castle." A visible shudder pulsed through the thief. "I escaped only because I was in the dungeon."

The knight moved his sword away and grabbed Gaiseric by the collar instead. His fingers twisted in the rich cloth, tightening it around the rogue's neck. "What happened here?" he growled.

"Zombies," Gaiseric replied, horror in his face. "Even in the dungeon, I could hear the screams, the sound of doors being battered down. So much screaming…" He lost himself for a moment in the grisly memory. The scene must have been truly horrible to rattle the thief in such a manner. It took Alaric shaking him to draw him back into his account. "Eventually everything went quiet. Then *they* came down into the dungeon looking for me." Again, the thief shuddered. "There must have been dozens of them… zombies… each more horrible to look on than the next. Some looked almost alive but for some ugly wound where they'd been bitten by the undead. Others were so decayed I couldn't understand how they could be moving around. The worst was Otto

Grueber, the farmer they buried last spring after he fell under his own plow. His flesh was completely rotten with worms still crawling through it..."

Alaric shook the thief again as the horror of his experience threatened to overcome him once more. "How did you escape?"

The question caused Gaiseric to laugh, but he quickly checked his merriment and cast an anxious look at the corridor outside the chapel. "The hall between the cells is narrow," he said. "Only one zombie at a time could try to break down the door to my cell and it was too much for them to manage. While a zombie was scratching at the door, I made my own way out."

Alaric shook his head. Twice before Gaiseric had found a way out of the dungeons. They'd always thought he'd bribed the jailer or somehow picked the lock. Different jailers and new locks, however, didn't prevent further escapes. "How did..."

The question went unfinished. Gaiseric's face went pale, and his head whipped around, staring out at the hallway. Alaric felt the thief twist in his grip and in an instant found himself holding nothing except his brother's stolen doublet. The knight was shocked by the man's swiftness. Gaiseric slipped to the floor, but instead of running away, he dashed over to the candle and kicked it behind the altar.

"Get down, you idiot!" Gaiseric hissed at the knight. "They're back!"

Alaric didn't need to ask who it was the thief meant. Planting one hand on top of the altar, he vaulted over and joined Gaiseric behind it. Together, the two men peeped around the edges. Alaric still couldn't see anything, but he thought he heard the gate creak as something brushed against the bars.

"If we stay quiet and out of sight, they'll leave," Gaiseric told Alaric. "I've been dodging them ever since I got back into the castle."

"Got back *in*?" Alaric asked, but more sounds from the hallway gave him bigger concerns for the moment. From the noise, it seemed there was a considerable presence out there. He thought of what Gaiseric had said about seeing dozens of zombies when they came for him in the dungeon.

"Keep quiet," Gaiseric whispered, gripping his dagger so tightly that his knuckles were turning white. "It means our lives. They won't look long and if they don't find us, they'll go away."

Alaric nodded his understanding. He still had questions but getting torn apart by zombies wasn't going to answer any of them. He focused on the sounds creeping from the darkness. The clop of a bare foot against the stone floor, the creak of an oak pew as something stumbled against it, the drip of decay from rotten flesh.

The noises came closer and closer. Alaric hardly dared to draw a breath, his mind racing with the image of the zombie horde that had destroyed the army. He could picture a similar horde steadily bearing down on them in the chapel, rank after rank of animated corpses. Perhaps only inches away from him in the dark.

Gaiseric leaned down and snuffed out the candle as the sounds drew still closer. Alaric felt dread seize him as even that feeble light was extinguished. Now to his senses was borne the necrotic smell, a rancid stench of decay and corruption. He wondered again how near the zombies could be for their stink to be so overwhelming. If he dared to stretch out his hand, what would he find?

"They can't see us any better than we can see them," Gaiseric whispered. "They'll leave soon when they can't find us."

Alaric took some reassurance from the thief's words. After all, Gaiseric had escaped from the zombies before, had intimated he'd done so several times. The undead wouldn't find them in the dark...

Suddenly, an eerie green luminescence exploded across the chapel, bathing everything in light.

CHAPTER TWO

Gaiseric threw his arms across his face as green light burst across the chapel. He rubbed at his eyes, trying to clear his vision. When he could see again, he almost wished that he'd remained blind.

The aisle down the middle of the chapel was filled with zombies. Some wore shrouds, others the simple homespun clothing of peasants, but many more were in the blood-spattered livery of Baron von Mertz's household. Villager, servant, or soldier, the undead bore the same hideous expression on their faces, a vicious admixture of hatred and hunger.

"Snap out of it!" Gaiseric snarled at Alaric. The knight was staring in horror at a zombie toward the forefront of the mob. The thief recognized the flowing gown and jeweled necklace of the Baroness, though there wasn't enough left of her clawed face to be absolutely certain. "Snap out of it!" he growled again, pulling Alaric back. "Keep gawking and you'll end up like her."

The zombies shuffled forward with outstretched arms. Their groping hands were crusted over with dried blood and tatters of skin dangled from their nails. Gaiseric cringed when he saw shreds of flesh caught in their teeth as well. As he stepped back into the sanctuary itself, he spotted the source of the strange light. It was an orb about the size of his fist, a spectral globe that sputtered and flitted above the zombies. He felt a chill ripple down his spine. Black magic as well as walking corpses!

Just outside the chapel, standing to one side of the zombie throng, was a ghoulish-looking man in a cassock-like robe. His skin was of a jaundiced hue, mottled with leprous blemishes. The face was as cruel and evil as anything Gaiseric had ever seen, making the Baron's headsman seem as charming as a tipsy minstrel. Despite his cadaverous looks, the man's eyes lacked the dullness of the zombies. When he caught Gaiseric's gaze, the villain's lips curled back in a cruel smile. The thief took a step back, wondering with a touch of panic if he'd ever stolen something from the zombie master.

"Brunon Gogol!" Alaric suddenly cried out. The knight's eyes had strayed away from his undead mother and fastened upon the zombies' leader. It was clear he recognized the man, and with that recognition came a surge of rage. He brandished his sword at the necromancer and Gaiseric feared he'd plunge right into the zombie horde to reach his enemy.

The thief groaned and threw himself into action. Before Alaric could commit some reckless – and doomed – gesture, Gaiseric decided to provide a more immediate conflict to draw the knight's attention. Darting ahead of Alaric, the thief brought the heavy icon of Wotun sweeping around. The golden scales smashed into the head of an advancing zombie, cracking its skull and throwing it back into the mob.

•••

"Back!" Gaiseric shouted. "You're never going to get to him through these zombies!" He felt an obligation to the knight. Alaric had saved him from execution, now maybe he could save his life in turn. At least he felt bound to make the effort. In Gaiseric's peculiar ethics, it was one thing to steal and another thing to welch on a debt.

The knight glowered at the thief as he slashed his blade across a zombie's chest. "I've run once already!" Alaric whipped his blade around and cleft the pate of an enemy as it grabbed at him.

"Good, then you know it's better to live to fight when the odds aren't a hundred to two," the rogue grumbled, wondering why anytime he tried to do something noble it was never easy. Gaiseric hurled his makeshift cudgel into the face of the nearest zombie, causing it to stumble and trip up those following behind it. He scrambled back behind the altar and grabbed one edge. "Help me with this," he told the knight. For an instant it looked like Alaric would refuse, but after hacking the arm from a zombie arrayed in the von Mertz livery, he swung back around and took hold of the opposite corner.

"Heave!" Gaiseric grunted. Together they were able to tip the stone altar onto its side. The weight of the top caused it to break free as it struck the floor and it went tumbling down into the undead mob, breaking bones and crushing several of the zombies as it came to rest.

Gaiseric glared up at the wan light flitting through the chapel. He'd eluded zombies elsewhere in the castle without a spectral light showing up to betray him. "We need it dark to get away," the thief hissed. Alaric had his sword again and was thrusting at the zombies as they resumed their advance.

Gaiseric glared across at the necromancer. Gogol hadn't taken any active role in the fight, staying back while his creatures carried out his commands. "I'm betting you need to concentrate to keep that light going," he muttered as he flipped his dagger between his hands. His fingers pinched down around the tip of the blade. "Let's see if I'm right."

It was a long throw, and if Gaiseric had really weighed his chances, he'd have seen how low those chances really were. Maybe worse than Alaric's impulse to try and cut a way through the undead horde. The thief, however quick to disparage the risks someone else took, trusted in his own luck. In his profession, confidence and daring had to be instinctive rather than rational.

Instinct prevailed over reason, and he let the blade fly across the chapel. Nearly forty feet stretched between Gaiseric and his target, with both zombies and the bars of the gate providing cover for the necromancer. Despite all the impediments, Gogol's face twisted into a mask of pain, and he threw back his head in a shriek as the dagger struck his arm. Gaiseric had a fleeting impression of the villain turning and fleeing down the corridor before the gibbous light evaporated and the chapel was plunged into darkness.

"Did you kill him?" Alaric called out.

"I was lucky, but not so lucky as that," Gaiseric replied. He plucked at the knight's surcoat and drew him deeper into the sanctuary. The necromancer might have retreated, but in the blackness, they could hear the zombies shuffling towards them, murderous and remorseless.

"We're not getting out the way we came in," the thief warned Alaric. "Fortunately, we don't have to." Gaiseric pressed his hand against the stained-glass window at the back of the sanctuary, running his fingers down it until he reached its base and found the corner. The catch was almost perfectly hidden, but he felt the slight depression it made. Jabbing his finger into it, he triggered the concealed spring. There was a dull thump as a panel under the window flipped open.

"Drop to your belly and follow me." Gaiseric suited action to words. He felt like some sort of enormous lizard as he scrambled through the opening. The scrape of armor against the floor told him that Alaric was close behind. The thief pressed himself against one of the walls to let the knight pass, but in the cramped confines, it was too tight a fit. He muttered a curse against all armorers and his own lack of foresight. If he'd known Alaric would block the passage, he'd have had him go first. He shot a bitter look at his companion.

The knight gave Gaiseric a stern look of his own. "How did you know about that door?" Alaric demanded.

Gaiseric could sympathize with the knight's frustration. He'd grown up in the castle without ever knowing about the secret passage. Alaric wouldn't appreciate learning it had cost the thief only a few cups of ale to pry the information from a clergyman who'd been dismissed by the Baron. At the moment, however, the important thing was to make use of the other half of the secret. And that meant getting back to the opening. "I could tell you, but if I don't shut that door, it won't do either of us much good."

Alaric shifted his body and tried to press up against the far wall. The passage was cramped, too low to do anything but crawl and not much wider. Gaiseric had experience contorting his body to get through narrow spaces, but he couldn't recall any conditions more cramped than trying to squeeze past the armored knight. The sounds of the zombies back in the chapel gave him ample reason to try. If he didn't get back to the panel and close it, the undead would be scurrying after them.

"It's not going to work," Alaric hissed at Gaiseric, shoving the thief down the passage. "It's too narrow for both of us. Tell me what to do and I'll close the door."

Gaiseric frowned at the suggestion. "You'll never find it in the dark. You'd probably get stuck." The noise of the zombies as they stalked around the toppled altar echoed into the passage. There wasn't time to waste. Fumbling at his belt, he retrieved the tinderbox he'd salvaged from the lamplighter's room. Soon he had another taper lit, the flame casting a hellish flicker across the confined space. "Take this and look for…"

Alaric took the taper, but as the knight turned, Gaiseric could see past him. "Keep back!" the thief hissed in warning, his hand clutching Alaric's shoulder.

The knight recoiled when he saw what had alarmed Gaiseric. At the mouth of the passage, the gnawed face of a cook glared down at them. The zombie stretched its claws toward Alaric, its fingers sliding down his boots. The creature was unable to push deeper into the passage because another zombie was trying to squeeze past it and both undead were caught in the opening.

"So much for that." Alaric shuddered, drawing his feet away from the zombie's grasping fingers. "Wherever this tunnel goes, we'd better start. I wouldn't count on them being jammed up for too long."

Gaiseric could see the revolting reason for the last statement. As the zombies strained against each other, where their rotten bodies rubbed together, they sloughed away ribbons of flesh. By grisly attrition, they'd eventually squeeze through.

Gaiseric lit another taper. "The passage gets bigger in about a hundred feet," he told Alaric. Crawling on elbows and knees, the two men squirmed through the musty tunnel. After a few yards another passage connected to it from the right. "There's a whole network of these running through your castle. It would be easy to get lost in them."

"I knew about some of these passages, though never one that led from the chapel," Alaric said, surprising Gaiseric. "My governess warned against playing in them when I was a child. Of course, my sister and I did anyway after we found a few of the entrances. We used wax shavings to find our way back. My sister tried breadcrusts once but got lost exploring after rats gobbled them up. I managed to find her after mother started to panic when she'd been gone too long." While the knight spoke, his voice grew melancholy and wistful. It was easy to tell he was thinking of his slaughtered family and how some of them at least had joined the undead.

Gaiseric could appreciate the bittersweet pangs such memories provoked once the people who'd helped make them were gone. He'd lost his own siblings the winter after his rustler father was hanged. Recollections of childhood frolics inevitably collapsed into the image of burying their starved bodies in the snow. After so many years, the pain was a dull ache now. He imagined the knight's was much worse since he'd only just lost his family.

"But you never knew about the secret door in the chapel?" Gaiseric repeated as they went on, trying to refocus Alaric on something else. "This castle has stood here a long time. The Baron expanded it, but so did his predecessors. Each time they added something new they'd cover up something old. It stands to reason some things would be forgotten."

"Just see that you haven't forgotten where we're going," Alaric advised, a sense of authority stealing back into his manner.

"It's a bad thief who doesn't know all the ways in and out of somewhere he's going to rob," Gaiseric assured him. He didn't turn to look, but he could feel the knight scowling at him. That was good, it would keep Alaric focused. "Pride isn't exclusive to the nobility, you know. Anyone can take pride in their craft. A dwarf makes a magnificent jewel, an elf carves a splendid longbow, or a thief finds a way to pilfer for a wealthy and well-guarded prospect. Pride all around."

"The wolf howls about bringing down the ewe," Alaric shot back. "That makes him easy for the wolfhunter to find."

This time Gaiseric did turn his head. "When the forest's on fire, I'd think the wolfhunter has more pressing concerns than bothering with a wolf."

Conversation fell away as the pair reached the spot where the passage became wide enough to stand. Gaiseric felt relieved to be in the open again, but Alaric positively exulted in being able to stretch out. The knight was a big man, just straying into his third decade. His hair was cut close to his scalp, a deep brown in color. His eyes were a light blue, sharp as two chips of ice. His features were firm, with a knife-like nose and a squared jaw. Gaiseric could see the steel mail shining from rents in Alaric's surcoat. This heavy garment was ragged and weathered, stained by blood and mud to such a degree that the original blue was completely obscured in many places. Across the breast was emblazoned the coat of arms of von Mertz, a white field with a black dragon transfixed by a red lance. Gaiseric could see the same heraldry repeated in the pommel of Alaric's longsword.

"I see now why you thought you could fight your way through to that necromancer," Gaiseric said. "You put the lie to my notion that nobles prefer to let commoners do their fighting for them."

Alaric glanced at his sword and the rancid blood that stained it. "A knight holds his land because he's willing to defend it. That's what bestows the rectitude to exact taxes from those who live on that land. Only a blackguard holds that obligation cheaply." His eyes took on a bitter quality. "There were no blackguards who rode out with High Marshal Konreid. If twenty of us rode away from that massacre, I would call it miraculous."

Gaiseric gazed at the knight in shock. "The king's army is dead?" The words felt unreal even as he spoke them.

"Most of it," Alaric answered. "We forgot the hard lessons learned fighting orcs on the frontier. We let contempt of the enemy make us underestimate the adversary. We walked into a trap… and there was no hidden door to provide our escape."

The thief shivered as he listened to Alaric relate the disaster to him. Perhaps because he spent so much time trying to elude them, Gaiseric had imagined the royal forces as an unbeatable juggernaut. To learn otherwise shook him to the core. A stray sound from the passage they'd just emerged from spun him around, his eyes wide with fright.

"They're still following," he declared. "We've got to get moving." He gestured to the tunnel ahead of them. The close-set blocks that formed its walls dripped with slime and the cobwebs were thick on the vaulted ceiling, but at least there was no evidence of zombies here.

"I'm staying," Alaric said. He set down his taper and turned to face the passage. "I can kill each one of them as they crawl out."

Gaiseric looked at the man in disbelief. "And what happens when you tire? What happens if one does manage to get past you? You saw how many there were in the chapel, and who knows how many more are scattered through the castle!"

Alaric's face was grim, set with a cold fury that was terrible to see. "These aren't part of the horde the army fought. Someone else brought this blight to my home. That someone is Brunon Gogol."

"I know you want revenge, but this is throwing away your life," Gaiseric objected.

"If it means punishing Gogol, then I'll pay that price." Alaric champed his teeth together. A pained note crept into his voice. "It's my fault. Three years ago, my father's men caught Gogol practicing sorcery. I convinced the Baron to be lenient. Exile instead of execution." He gestured with the longsword at the passage and the noises emanating from it. "This is how the fiend repays that mercy."

Gaiseric could see the guilt pressing down on Alaric and knew that it was the foundation of the knight's fatalistic resolve. It wasn't a question of survival for him – Alaric wanted to die here. He felt it was the only way he could atone. There was no appeal to self-preservation that would sway him from his course. Gaiseric would have to take a different track.

"If the zombies kill you, Gogol will escape justice," he told Alaric, his mind racing as he seized upon the one argument that might sway the knight. "Have you thought of that? This task is too big for you to do alone, and you'll need more than my help."

"What are you saying?" Alaric asked, keeping his eyes on the opening to the passage.

Just the faintest hint of a smile played on the thief's face. He knew he had the knight hooked, now he just had to reel him in. "I'm saying we get out of here. Go someplace where you can recruit the help you need." Gaiseric patted one of his pockets, producing the sound of jingling coins. "I'll pay if it's necessary to hire the swords you need." A brief laugh shook the rogue. "In a sense it's your money anyway."

Alaric shook his head. "The land is overrun. Every hamlet and village I saw was plagued with zombies."

"Singerva," Gaiseric said. "The town's walls are thick and its garrison is hundreds strong. The zombies couldn't overwhelm such a big town. It's impossible." As he spoke the last words, he wondered just who he was trying to convince, himself or Alaric. He saw, however, that there was doubt in the knight's face now. He pressed the idea further. "If only a few escaped from the battle, it's possible they don't know what's happened in Singerva. They need to be warned. Surely that's a greater duty than revenge."

With a growl, Alaric turned to Gaiseric. "What concern is it to you? When did a thief know anything about duty?"

Gaiseric shrugged. "I don't, but you've said the countryside is teeming with zombies. If I want to put myself behind the safety of Singerva's walls, I'll need help getting there." He smiled at the knight's show of disgust. "An ugly truth is still the truth and we've got to trust each other." He nodded at the passage. The sounds of the zombies were drawing closer. "There isn't time to bicker. You asked me how I escaped the dungeons. Here's your chance to see for yourself." The levity left his tone and he gave Alaric a severe look. "I can't take warning to Singerva alone. Do you think they'd give credence to whatever I told them? But if they heard about the zombies from a knight, the son of Baron von Mertz…"

The last point decided Alaric. "All right, Gogol will wait." He turned from the opening and followed Gaiseric down the tunnel.

They had to navigate several turns through the forgotten corridors. At one corner they were suddenly set upon by a dark shape that lurched out of the shadows. Alaric froze when the figure came into the light. Gaiseric immediately saw why. The shape was that of the Baron.

Hesitant to strike his own father, Alaric was borne down to the floor by the zombie. His sword was knocked from his hand and went clattering across the ground. He caught the Baron by his shoulders, striving to hold him away even as the undead tried to sink its teeth into his flesh.

Gaiseric's first instinct was to flee, but he'd gone only a few steps before he turned around and scurried to catch up the knight's sword. Even if there were more zombies converging on the spot, he couldn't leave Alaric to be killed by his own father. Taking up the longsword, he thrust it into the Baron's temple, piercing its skull and stabbing the brain within. A dry groan rose from the zombie and it slumped to one side.

"Let's hope that was the only one," Gaiseric said, as he helped Alaric to his feet.

Alaric stared down at the twice-dead Baron. "He must have been wounded but slipped through a secret door before the zombies could finish him." The knight looked along the floor, spotting the trail of blood left by the Baron. He bent down and retrieved a dropped kite shield, its face painted with the von Mertz coat of arms. Gaiseric recovered a discarded sword lying nearby and thrust it beneath his belt. He wasn't used to swords, but it was a better weapon than the knife he had tucked away in his boot.

"We have to go," Gaiseric nudged Alaric. "If there are more in the tunnels, they're certain to have heard that racket." He pointed down the corridor. "It's not far to the dungeon. There's another tunnel that leads off from the cells, an old escape route in case the castle was besieged. It opens up half a mile past the moat. One of the old castellans must have been worried about being locked up in his own dungeon," he added with a chuckle.

Alaric seemed not to hear him, but kept staring at his father. "You will be avenged," he vowed.

Gaiseric nudged the knight again. "Come on. We've still got to warn Singerva, remember?"

The knight slowly nodded and followed after Gaiseric. "I think it's already too late, that this plague has struck every corner of the kingdom. You play long chances, thief. Pray to your gods that luck is still on your side."

CHAPTER THREE

Flesh and bone crumbled under the mace's flanged edge. A spume of rotted brain and clotted blood dripped down the zombie's face as the walking corpse crumpled to its knees. Its decayed hands reached out blindly for its destroyer, but before it could grab her leg, the fell magic animating it faded. Truly dead, the body slumped against the weaving stalks of grain around it.

Helchen Anders gave the fallen zombie scant notice. There were four others of its ilk still pursuing her through the field. From the wide-brimmed hat to the knee-high boots, everything she wore was black. Like a shadow, she drifted through the rows of wheat, her senses sharp for the least trace of her foes.

Yet it wasn't panic that stirred Helchen as she crossed the field. A determination as cold and hard as the brutal mace she carried filled her heart. She fled only so far as necessary to find a new vantage point, to gain the brief respite needed so she could turn on her enemy. After dispatching the zombie that had nearly caught her, she returned her mace to the hook on her belt and grabbed the crossbow looped across her shoulder by a leather cord. Her fingers dipped into a pouch on her belt and removed a stubby bolt with a broad iron head. A grim smile pulled at her pale features. She'd seen such a bolt punch through a knight's helm, she could imagine the havoc it would wreck on a zombie's rotten skull.

Helchen paused in her retreat to load the bolt and crank back the crossbow's string. It was a light weapon, designed to be easily concealed beneath a coat or cloak. A favorite trick of the Order of Witch Hunters and a nasty surprise for the heretics they hunted. There was only one downside to the small crossbows, and as she saw a zombie stagger out from behind the grain a dozen yards away, Helchen appreciated that flaw in full. Her weapon was designed for close distance and would rapidly lose both accuracy and penetration at range.

Biting her lip, Helchen took aim and forced herself to wait. She could hear the other zombies stumbling through the wheat but couldn't fix their positions. If they were too close, they might surround her before she could get off a shot. If the one she was looking at represented the enemy vanguard, she might be able to drop it and reload before the rest even knew where she was.

"Destroy them," Helchen told herself. "Fight until every last one of them is no more." She'd been remorseless against the Order's enemies, and she wasn't about to relent when there were foes who'd given her even greater cause to hate them.

The salty tang of blood dripped into her mouth, the tension in her body making Helchen's teeth tear her lip. She was grateful for the pain and reflected on its usefulness. Against spells and enchantments, a witch hunter was taught that pain was the best way to free the mind from distraction. Just now, she needed her focus to be keen, ready to shoot the very instant the zombie was near enough to be certain of hitting it.

The zombie lurched onwards, its gait so ungainly that Helchen thought it must trip over its own feet before too long. Yet somehow, the creature's clumsiness never brought it crashing to the ground. Closer it came, its arms flailing ahead of it as it sensed it was nearing the witch hunter. As it closed she could see details that had been obscure to her before. The blue-checked pattern of the apron, largely obscured by bloodstains, could be discerned. The wooden clogs on the feet, their tops decorated with painted flowers. The copper necklace that poked out from the gory ruin of a torn throat. All of these told Helchen that this was no stranger. In life, the zombie had been a milkmaid named Miranda, one of her brother's servants. The witch hunter used to help her churn butter on her infrequent visits to the farm. She'd shared Miranda's confidences, the servant's hopes to marry a fletcher named Fritz, her worries about an elderly father who lived in the village of Mertz.

All her memories of Miranda flashed through Helchen's mind. She could hear the milkmaid's demure voice, see that shy smile, smell the scent of lavender in her hair. She'd been one of the few people in the witch hunter's life who didn't regard her with suspicion and fear. She'd been one of her only friends.

Helchen squeezed the crossbow's trigger without hesitation the instant the zombie staggered into range. She watched as the bolt smashed through the corpse's forehead and shattered its skull. The undead spilled over onto its back and was still.

"That wasn't Miranda," Helchen whispered, as she fitted another bolt to the crossbow. "Not anymore." She glared at the fallen zombie. The milkmaid was far from the first monster wearing a familiar face that she'd dispatched since returning to her brother's farm. Nor would it be the last.

The witch hunter was still cranking back the crossbow's steel string when zombies emerged from the vast stretches of wheat and onto the narrow lane. Helchen whipped around and hastily shot one of the undead. The bolt crashed through the creature's hip and caused the leg beneath it to buckle. The zombie went sprawling in the dirt. Before it could rise, it was trampled by the rest of the pack.

The crossbow dangled from the strap looped over her shoulder as Helchen drew her mace once more. There was a sick feeling in the pit of her stomach now. The zombie she'd just dropped and the ones staggering towards her weren't from the initial group she'd encountered. As though to drive home that point, she spotted the remaining members of that original band walking past Miranda's remains. By accident or design, the zombies were closing in on her from two sides.

"Saves me the trouble of tracking you down," Helchen hissed. She swung her mace, smashing through stalks of grain to crush the clutching hand of a zombie. The undead gave no notice of its wound, but pressed on, wagging the gory stump at her. A second blow shattered its head and sent it pitching to the ground.

Three more from the initial group and what she judged to be at least five still mobile in the second. Helchen backed away, trying to put distance between herself and the undead. She needed room to work, enough vantage to whittle down their numbers with the crossbow. Reluctantly, she realized she'd need to fall back to the farmhouse. She had no great desire to look at what the zombies had left there… and the things she'd been forced to do.

"But it'll let me destroy more of you," Helchen rationalized. Her mace exploded through the knee of a zombie harvester, causing it to stumble and veer into the path of those following its advance. The undead collided in a tangle of rotten limbs and cadaverous faces. While they were extricating themselves, the witch hunter turned and sprinted down the dusty lane.

The sound of rustling grain to her left gave Helchen pause. The noise wasn't that of the staggering, clumsy tread of zombies. A flash of hope filled her heart. A survivor! Someone had escaped the slaughter! Images of her nephew flashed through her mind. She'd found no trace of the boy in her brother's house. It might be he'd escaped the slow-moving undead during the massacre.

"Over here!" Helchen called out. The running sound diverted from its original course, plowing through the grain directly towards her. "Over here," she said, but now there was uncertainty in her tone. Why wasn't this person responding to her?

Suspicion made her grip her mace more tightly and keep it angled in the direction of the rustling grain. Helchen took a step back just as a figure erupted from the field. Indeed, it was Gustl, her eldest nephew. Or rather, it had been. Gustl's clothes were caked in dried gore, his skin polluted with a gray, lifeless tone. The man's shoulder was exposed and bore a grisly wound. His eyes were hollow, devoid of any thought, only a pitiless hunger.

Unlike the other undead Helchen had fought, Gustl sprang at her with fearsome animation. She was stunned by the crazed ferocity of the thing, unlike any zombie she'd seen before. Gustl was like a rabid animal as it bared its teeth and ripped at her with clawed hands. Her caution, however, served her in good stead. In its initial leap, the creature slammed into her mace, crushing several ribs. The impact snapped her from her shock and she was able to push it back and keep it from coming to grips with her.

While the corpse of her nephew slavered and raged, Helchen noted the sounds of other undead hurrying through the fields. Runners, she thought of the things, comparing them to the plodding walkers she was accustomed to. Appreciating she had no time to waste, she brought her boot kicking against Gustl's chest. The blow pushed it free of the sharp flanges of her mace. Gustl didn't hesitate but lunged back to the attack. Helchen had counted on the thing's mindless ferocity. As it sprang for her, she twisted aside and brought the edges of her mace slashing across Gustl's neck. The zombie's own momentum provided the extra force to decapitate it. The body crashed into the field while its head went spinning down the lane.

Helchen turned and ran. The runners completely altered the situation. She couldn't rely on being quicker than the undead or depend on them just shuffling towards her in a mindless mob. It was doubly important now to get out of the fields and find a defensible position.

The noise of grain rustling now rose from both sides of the lane. Helchen couldn't tell how many runners were hurrying after her. It might only be four or five or it could be dozens.

A glance back down the dusty path showed her at least that many of the slower walkers in pursuit of her.

If she could reach the barn, Helchen felt she'd at least be able to hold her own. Grimly, she recalled evidence her brother had tried to make a last stand there. He had been lured down, no doubt to aid some member of his family. That vulnerability, at least, Helchen didn't have to worry about. Once she climbed into the loft, the undead were going to pay a heavy toll to get her to leave it.

The fields opened out to the cleared ground where the farmstead stood. The half-timber house with its turf roof was in ruinous condition, its windows and doors smashed down by the undead. A few bodies lay sprawled outside, zombies Helchen had dispatched when she'd first returned to her brother's home. She scowled at the corpses and tried to blot out the image of that hideous combat. At least she knew her brother was truly at rest.

Helchen started to turn towards the big stone barn away to the side of the house when she noticed movement in one of the windows. She could hear the runners in the fields behind her. If more of their kind were in the farmhouse, they'd be able to intercept her before she reached the loft. "Marduum," she invoked the stern God of Vigilance, patron of her order, "grant that they're walkers."

Having muttered her brief prayer, the witch hunter sprinted towards the barn. The moment she did, she saw a figure lunge out from the house. Focused on reaching the loft, she didn't delay to take in more than a quick impression. She heard footsteps racing after her, spurring her on. When she decided she couldn't outrun her pursuer, she stopped and spun around, slashing her mace at her adversary's neck the way she had Gustl.

Her pursuer came up short, falling backwards in his haste to avoid the brutal swing. The look of shock on his face was far too expressive to be that of a zombie, the howl of protest that rose from his mouth too articulate for one of the undead.

"Wait, now!" the man shouted, holding his arms out to his sides and dropping the sword he carried. "I'm not one of them! I'm alive!"

"Looter." Helchen let the epithet drip from her tongue. She fixed the man with an icy glare, then nodded to the sword he'd dropped. "If you want to stay alive, pick that up and follow me."

"Looter's a strong word," the man objected. "Scrounger is less hostile."

"Get that sword and hurry…" but Helchen's admonition for haste was already too late. From the field a pair of zombies jogged into view. They tarried a moment, but once they spotted the witch hunter and the thief, the creatures resumed their feral rush. Somehow, she thought, the rest of the pack must have sensed the eagerness of the first runners, for soon there were four more hurrying out from behind the wheat.

The man snatched up his sword and started to run back for the house. The witch hunter bit her lip in frustration. "Stay here! We can't outrun them, so our only chance is to fight!" The looter looked anything but pleased, yet to his credit he fell in beside Helchen. Perhaps, she thought, he was more fool than coward.

"Alaric! We've got trouble!" the thief shouted at the top of his lungs. The noise only agitated the zombies more. Like a pack of starving wolves, the runners hurtled towards them.

Helchen smashed the first zombie with a crippling sweep of her mace. One of its legs was shattered and it tumbled into the dirt. Her return caught the zombie beside it, staving in the side of its head. The creature veered off and managed a few more steps before it crashed to the ground.

The thief sprang forward as a third zombie charged for Helchen. His sword stabbed deep into the thing's gut, a mortal wound for anything truly alive, but less than a nuisance to the runner. The creature twisted around, widening the cut as it did so. Its clawed hands reached for the looter, and a hungry groan gargled from its gaping mouth.

"The head or the heart!" Helchen admonished the man. The zombie had turned to attack him, leaving itself exposed to her mace. She bludgeoned it from behind, cracking its skull. There was a spurt of stagnant blood and brains as she ripped the flanges free. The runner sagged to the ground, its animation broken. "Hit them anywhere else and you only slow them down."

"Take your own advice," the thief said, suddenly darting past Helchen. She turned to see the zombie whose leg she'd broken scurrying toward her on all fours. The looter brought his sword down as though it were an axe and split the creature's head in two.

Helchen gave the rogue a brief nod of gratitude. It was all the thanks she could show, for now the other zombies were upon them. She broke the arm of one, crushed the face of another, but there were too many to take more precise aim. The thief's swings were even more hurried than her own.

Their efforts were, at best, only delaying the moment when they'd be overwhelmed.

"There's too many of them," Helchen cursed as a zombie tried to claw through her brigandine. The reinforced leather resisted its fingers, but she wondered how much protection it would provide when the monster tried to gnaw its way to her flesh. It wasn't so much the thought of death that disturbed her, but the idea of being infected and rising again as one of the undead. *There* was a fate to send terror through her veins.

Suddenly, the runner was knocked away from her. It stumbled back, one arm snapped by a tremendous impact. The man who'd struck the creature didn't move to press his attack but brought his heavy kite shield swinging wide to collide with another of the undead that was assailing Helchen. The monster was sent sprawling, a broken rib jutting from its ragged clothes. A third zombie went down as the man's longsword sheared away the side of its head.

Helchen guessed that the swordsman must be Alaric, the confederate the looter had called out to, but she was surprised to see such a man in company with a thief. There was a strength to his face that was hard to reconcile with a slinking criminal, and a fearlessness in his eyes that was impressive even to a witch hunter. Moreover, he was arrayed in the heavy armor and surcoat of a knight. Of course, it was possible he'd stolen them, but the ease with which he bore their weight bespoke a warrior long accustomed to wearing such a burden.

"Bones of Belieth!" the warrior cursed, as one of the runners he'd thrown down leaped up and lunged at him. He brought his shield up to hold back its flailing claws. "You might have warned that these ones were so spry, Gaiseric!"

The other man, whom the warrior called Gaiseric, hewed the arm from a zombie that was attacking him. A kick sent the mangled creature stumbling. "I thought knights already knew everything!" The thief dodged the zombie's remaining arm and came at it from its crippled side. His sword jabbed into the monster's face, splitting its jaw as the steel dug into its brain.

"The lady here advises striking for the head or the heart," Gaiseric added as he pulled his weapon free from the inert corpse.

Helchen finished the creature with the broken rib, cracking its skull with her mace. "To destroy them, you must destroy the nexus points for the magic that animates them." She didn't know if either of them had the learning to understand, but she'd found that even an unintelligible explanation could spur someone into obedience. Witch hunters often had to recruit men-at-arms and peasants when finally confronting their quarry. They didn't need to understand either, only do what they were told to do.

The only zombie remaining in the vicinity was the one trying to claw its way to the warrior. The knight drove his opponent to the ground with his shield. While it was pinned to the earth, he smashed its skull with his armored boot. After the third stomp, the creature was lifeless. "Sound instructions," he said as he turned and looked Helchen over. His expression remained stern, and she saw a wariness creep into his eyes. "I won't ask how you know such things. It's obvious you belong to the Order of Witch Hunters."

Helchen gave him a thin smile as she cleansed the clotted gore from her mace. "I should expect such disdain from a peasant, but not from a knight. Not from someone tasked with defending the kingdom." There was just a hint of temper at the edge of her voice.

"The enemies I fight are real, not phantoms of an over-zealous imagination," the knight countered. "I've seen for myself how you fanatics operate."

"It is better that a hundred innocent suffer than the seed of evil be allowed to take root," Helchen retorted, quoting a favorite injunction of her captain in the Order. She gestured with her mace at the destruction all around them. "This is what comes from being permissive, of being so concerned about innocence that corruption is left unchecked!" She kicked the severed head of a zombie and sent it bouncing towards the barn. "This was my brother's farm. All the family I had left in this world." Her eyes blazed as she looked up at the knight. "You dare say my Order went too far? Had we gone still further, these people wouldn't be dead!"

Sheepishly, Gaiseric stepped between the two. "Much as I'd be amused to watch you two fight, I think we've bigger concerns." Having gained their attention, he pointed to the field. A lumbering mob of zombies was trudging down the path. Stalks of wheat waved and fell as more walkers marched through them. "These might not be fast, but I don't think that'll matter when there's a lot of them."

Helchen kept her steely gaze on the knight for a moment. "Your squire has more sense than you do. Get out of here while you can."

The knight shook his head. "He's not my squire. Gaiseric

was a prisoner in my father's dungeons." He tapped the coat of arms on his chest. "I'm Alaric von Mertz."

"Helchen Anders," the witch hunter said, trying to make it sound as impressive as the name of a baron's son.

"I don't think this is the place or the time for introductions," Gaiseric snapped. The thief was rapidly backing away and casting covetous eyes on the road leading past the farm.

"Take his suggestion and get moving," Helchen told Alaric. She hooked her mace and started to reload her crossbow.

"And what do you intend to do?" Alaric asked. He noticed her glance up at the barn and its loft. "That's foolish," he growled. "What do you think you'll accomplish?"

Helchen bristled at his tone. "I'll defend my brother's farm and destroy every zombie…"

"Look around you," Alaric said. "There's nothing left here to protect. Nothing to defend." His tone changed, and his gaze softened. "Believe me, I know. My home was destroyed by these things. I had to strike down a thing that had once been my father. I know you want to fight, to feel like you're doing something, but this isn't the way to do it."

The story gave Helchen pause. She'd been ready to argue with the knight, but the horror of his story was at least the equal of her own. It managed to pierce the admixture of anger and self-reproach that smoldered inside her. The conviction, the certainty that had gripped her, wasn't so absolute as it had been just a moment before.

Gaiseric dashed back to them and waved his hands. "How about this? We can talk over all of this someplace else. We find a safe place, somewhere that I'm not counting twenty-four… no, twenty-six, zombies walking straight toward us? Doesn't that sound like a good idea? Then, if you still want to, you can come back here or the castle or anywhere else."

"It does no good to kill zombies," Alaric said, adding his own force to the argument. "To really accomplish something, you have to strike at the ones who caused all this."

The knight's words broke through Helchen's resolve. "What do you mean?" she demanded.

Alaric nodded at the thief. "Let's first follow Gaiseric's lead. Find ourselves someplace we can talk without scores of undead dogging our heels."

CHAPTER FOUR

The winged reptile hopped from one beam to another in the old, ruined mill. It struggled to find just the right spot, one that would both give it a nice place to bask in while likewise serving the needs of its master. When his familiar was flying, Hulmul was able to smoothly adjust his senses and place them in harmony with Malicious, but when it kept hopping about, he found the abrupt shifts disorienting.

Stay still, the wizard sent the imperative to the reptile. Malicious was only a little bigger than a crow, but Hulmul had conjured demons that were less ornery. It crooked its lizard-like head back on its thin neck and flicked its tongue – a natural enough habit for a reptile, but the familiar had learned it was a derogatory gesture among humans and adapted itself accordingly. If its lips weren't rigid and scaly, it would have blown a raspberry for good measure.

Fine, have it your way. Hulmul pulled his mustache in frustration. It was poor form for a wizard to tolerate defiance from his familiar, but in the current situation he just didn't have the luxury to invest time and energy in curbing the reptile's willfulness. He needed to hear what was going on in the mill.

Malicious settled down, fanning its wings so it could draw the most warmth it could from the sun. The reptile was a bit higher up in the mill than Hulmul would have liked. From such a distance, he knew the familiar's own senses were very keen. Tapping into them, however, would be to limit himself to the creature's perception. He still remembered the awful moment when he discovered that Malicious could interpret only three numbers: one, two, and lots.

For the sake of understanding what he was hearing as well as seeing, Hulmul employed his own senses. Rather than observing the mill with Malicious's eyes and ears, he observed *through* them. His own myopic vision rendered the people sitting down around the millstone indistinct blurs and he had to strain to hear what they were saying. The alternative would have brought them into sharp – if monochrome – relief but limited their speech to unintelligible noise mingled with the few spoken words Malicious understood.

"… were supposed to stop this invasion in the south." The words came from the taller of the three occupants of the mill, a man Hulmul had heard addressed as Alaric. "The army rode out to keep the zombies from overrunning the province."

"It was already too late for that." This was spoken by the woman, Helchen. From the first, Hulmul had taken a dislike to her. Her next words explained that instinctive uneasiness. "The witch hunters have long hunted necromancers hidden throughout the realm. We simply failed to appreciate how many there were. While your army rode out to fight, the enemy already within the kingdom set to work, raising their own battalions from every graveyard and charnel house." Hulmul shivered to hear the intensity that filled her voice. "I was with Captain Dietrich at the monastery of St. Olgerd when the catacombs below burst and all the monks who'd died of the gray pox last winter came swarming into the temple. We tried to stop them... but there were just too many."

"So you went to your brother's farm?" Alaric asked. "Someplace you felt you could still do some good."

"I was too late," Helchen snarled. She threw a chip of the millstone she'd picked up and sent it clattering off among the mill's debris. "Zombies had already been there and killed everyone." She made a helpless motion with her arms. "This is more than a local outbreak of sorcery. It's an arcane plague that's rolling across the entire province."

Hulmul indulged in a bitter smile. He doubted the witch hunter knew the half of it. Though his mind was peering through the senses of his familiar, his body was hiding inside a haystack and surrounded by a hastily conjured protective circle – of questionable efficacy, he had to concede – because in every direction, for leagues around, there wasn't a hamlet or homestead that hadn't been overwhelmed by the undead. Wherever he sent Malicious flying, there was only death and destruction.

"The more reason why we must hasten to Singerva," Gaiseric, the last of the trio, said. "Whatever the plight of the countryside, the zombies won't find a town like Singerva so easy to conquer."

It had been the name of the town that first attracted Hulmul to these travelers and caused him to divert Malicious so that the reptile could learn more about them. He was interested in

Singerva for his own reasons, but it might just be that these three could be useful to him.

"St. Olgerd's monastery was an easily defended site, but we were powerless to stop the zombies," Helchen told the thief. "There's only so much fighting someone can do. There comes a breaking point even for the most determined."

Gaiseric shook his head and waved aside Helchen's objection. "Captain Dietrich had only a few witch hunters. The rest of your 'fighters' were nothing but monks and peasants. Singerva is a thriving town with guards and soldiers, hundreds of them!"

"Marshal Konreid had hundreds of soldiers too," Alaric pointed out, his voice hollowed by regret. "We couldn't stop the zombies."

"That was in an open field," Gaiseric said. "The soldiers in Singerva have walls and battlements, defensible positions from which they can strike down the zombies at their leisure." He smiled as he warmed to the subject. "I've heard the town withstood four sieges during the War of the Three Kings. You think a bunch of mindless undead can accomplish what catapults and sappers couldn't? I tell you, we'll be safe once we get inside Singerva."

Alaric inspected the pommel of his sword, running his fingers about the coat of arms depicted there. "I only care about the resources Singerva can provide," he said, his tone as sharp as his blade. "There's a debt I owe Brunon Gogol, and every hour I'm delayed is a dishonor I can scarce endure."

The discussion faded away and they began eating food Gaiseric and Alaric had scavenged from Helchen's brother's farm. As soon as they were finished, they set out again. Hulmul withdrew much of his awareness from Malicious, simply directing the familiar to follow them. It was enough to register things now with the limited comprehension of the animal. He needed to keep his focus on himself at the moment.

Hulmul carefully gathered up the polished bones and etched stones that formed the points of his protective circle. A sweep of his left hand cleared away the essential salts that made the design itself. Taking up his staff, the wizard used it to poke a hole in the side of the haystack. He put his eye to the opening and peeked out. He'd much have preferred to have Malicious check that there were no zombies around, but the familiar had other duties.

After a minute of seeing nothing more fearsome than a mongrel dog picking at a horse carcass lying in the road, Hulmul decided it was safe enough to emerge from hiding. He turned in the direction he sensed Malicious and those it was following. They would have to head east to reach Singerva. Taking that into consideration, the wizard calculated a point at which he could overtake them.

"Not that I'm eager for the society of a witch hunter," he grumbled to himself. "But I'm less keen on keeping company with the undead. If I run into trouble, I'd feel better knowing there were people nearby who could help."

When trouble came, however, it wasn't the wizard who walked into it. For two hours, Hulmul trekked across fields and pastures, every step drawing him nearer to that point when he'd intercept Alaric and his companions. He dallied when he got too close, still wary of Helchen. He considered that he could hang back and just let Malicious keep tabs on them.

That was when the reptile noted movement in the bushes on either side of the road. Malicious was a bad judge of color and useless with numbers, but it was alert for even the slightest motion. What it saw now was far more than the rustle of wind or the scurry of rodents.

Hulmul ducked behind a broken wall that edged up onto the road and poured more of his awareness into his familiar. At his urging, Malicious flew lower and took a closer look. There were people ducked behind the bushes, obviously lying in wait for the trio on the road. Hulmul saw several men who gripped cudgels and staves. A few others had bows with arrows nocked.

Ambush! Alaric and the others were walking into a trap.

Get away, Hulmul commanded Malicious, directing the winged reptile to the branches of a nearby chestnut tree. It wouldn't do to have a stray arrow hit his familiar. Any hurt dealt to the creature would be felt by its master. Indeed, any fatal wound had a good chance of killing the wizard as well as the animal.

Still, there remained the problem of what to do. Hulmul was intent on reaching Singerva and he'd rather not do so alone. So far, Alaric's group were the only people he'd found going to the town. Indeed, except for a few panicked farmers, they were the only people he'd seen alive in the past three days.

Through Malicious's watching eyes, the wizard saw the lurking men waiting as their prey drew near. Hulmul was about to have his familiar shriek in warning, but at that moment Helchen noticed movement in the bushes.

"Draw arms!" she shouted, snapping up the crossbow

looped over her shoulder. Alaric and Gaiseric had their swords bared in a flash and fell in to either side of the witch hunter.

From both sides of the road, a dozen men and women sprang into view. The fact that their adversaries were living people rather than zombies surprised the travelers. That instant of hesitation was all it took for the ambushers to surround them.

"You'll be dropping your weapons," a scar-faced man ordered, hefting a blacksmith's hammer.

A bowman dressed in the soiled ruin of a crier's livery took aim at Helchen. "You might get off one shot, but I promise you won't manage a second."

Neither Helchen nor Alaric showed a hint of submission. It was Gaiseric who lowered his sword and made appeasing gestures with his hands. "Now let's just all take a step back and try to keep things in perspective," he said. "You've got the advantage in numbers, but even if what you say is right and my friend here can only shoot one of you, do you really want to gamble on being the unlucky one?" He jabbed his thumb at Helchen. "In case you didn't notice, she's a witch hunter, so you attack her you're not just putting your lives at risk, but your souls too."

Scar-Face laughed at the thief. "You can't scare us with that kind of talk. After what we've seen, we're not afraid of kings or gods. None of them rule these lands anymore."

"There's only one law now," a pot-bellied matron carrying a club snarled. "Everyone for themselves."

From the vantage of his familiar, Hulmul could see that the situation was rapidly worsening. The ambushers weren't going to have things entirely their own way, but he didn't see how Alaric's group was going to survive unless they surrendered.

The knight put paid to that idea. "Brigands," he named the ambushers. "You'll take no plunder from us."

Gaiseric stepped forward, again making placating motions with his hands. "Let's not be hasty. We're on their road after all. They're entitled to compensation." His hands dug into the pockets of his coat and tunic, spilling an assortment of coins and jewelry onto the ground. "I'm sure there's enough here..."

Scar-Face spat on the glimmering gold and waved his hammer at Gaiseric. The thief simply blinked at him in disbelief, unable to comprehend anyone who wasn't interested in gold. "We want your armor, your weapons, and whatever food you're carrying." The statement brought sullen nods from the others.

The thief stirred from his stunned incredulity and gave the brigands a dumbfounded look. "Well, if you won't be reasonable and take the gold..." Quick as a flash, Gaiseric had a dagger in his hand and lunged at the scarred blacksmith. Catching hold of the man, he spun him around and brought the dagger to his throat. "Tell your people to leave," he ordered Scar-Face.

The captive chuckled. "You think they care about me? Kill me and there's just one less mouth to feed."

Hulmul could feel the situation about to explode. Capturing their leader had been the best chance for the travelers to extricate themselves. Now they would need help.

The wizard withdrew all but the last speck of his mind from Malicious. He unslung the pack he wore and hastily rummaged through its contents. Hulmul quickly unrolled a vellum scroll, his eyes roving across the cabalistic writing. He mouthed the incantation and pointed his staff to the spot where he desired the magic to manifest.

Hulmul hesitated. Once he acted, there was no turning back. These were the first people he'd seen going to Singerva, but one of them was a witch hunter. Even when conjured to render them aid, some witch hunters couldn't set aside their hatred of magic. Instead of welcoming the wizard's help, they might look at him as a worse menace than the ambushers.

"I'll take the chance," Hulmul decided, making the final gesture to work his magic.

A few yards from the ambushers, an enraged bellow sounded. The next instant, the bushes parted and a colossal figure charged onto the road. Twice as tall as a human, its muscular frame covered in black fur, enormous horns jutting from its bovine head, the minotaur stamped its hooves in the dirt. Each ambusher felt the burn of the monster's beady red eyes as it swept its gaze over them.

Fear gripped the attackers. The moment the minotaur started forward they were in retreat. Scar-Face twisted about, squirming free of Gaiseric's grip and joining the others in flight. The monster roared again, its predatory instincts roused by the sight of its fleeing prey.

As the beast hurtled after the ambushers, Helchen loosed a bolt at it. "Foul abomination!" she cursed the minotaur. Her eyes went wide with shock as the bolt passed harmlessly through the monster. It didn't so much as glance at her before it plunged into the bushes in pursuit of its initial targets.

"Maybe it won't shrug off cold steel," Alaric said as he started to chase after the beast.

"I can assure you it will," Hulmul called out to the knight. Alaric and his companions swung around, stunned to see the wizard calmly walking down the road toward them. The distance was great enough that he was forced to employ a cantrip to project his voice to them, but it was a minor conjuration beside the spell he'd just invoked.

"A crude illusion," the wizard continued, almost apologetic in his tone. "A more nuanced one would appear to react to anything that happened to it. This one was a bit hasty, real enough to frighten someone, but it wouldn't convince anyone who paused for a closer look."

Helchen reloaded her crossbow and started to crank back the string. Alaric motioned for her to lower the weapon. "We're grateful for your assistance, friend wizard, but you'll forgive us for being suspicious."

"Caution is ever its own justification," Hulmul said as he drew closer. He locked eyes with Helchen and added, "Though it's sometimes expected to be given the benefit of the doubt."

"Happy is the village that hangs its wizard," she returned.

"So, you've read *The Sword of Sorcerers*," Hulmul mused. He was gratified to see that Helchen was surprised he was familiar with the infamous witch hunting handbook. He pressed that momentary advantage. "I've recently seen several villages without wizards. None of them looked very happy."

The knight motioned for Helchen to desist. "Which direction did you come from?" Alaric asked. He nodded to Helchen and Gaiseric. "Between us we've traveled from south and north."

"And I came from the west," Hulmul provided. He held up his hand. "I know what you'd ask. The plague is at work there as well. Lifeless villages infested with zombies."

"But you were able to stay alive," Helchen interjected, her voice barely above a growl. "About what could be expected of a wizard, to save his own skin."

Hulmul shook his head. "I could say the same about you. All of you are alive when many are not." His face took on a sour expression. "I know it's an ugly fact your Order likes to ignore, but the Wizards' Guild is just as eager to root out and destroy necromancers as you are. We're just a bit more judicious about when we act. Accuse the wrong person and the real culprit is apt to sneak away in the confusion."

Alaric intervened again before the argument could go further. "Real or illusion, your spell was most timely. It would have gone hard with us if we'd fought those brigands."

"Yes, it was lucky you drove them off," Gaiseric agreed. The thief was down on his knees collecting the treasure he'd dumped on the ground. Hulmul noted a brooch that carried the same design as Alaric's coat of arms. It didn't need a leap of logic to know where Gaiseric had come by his wealth.

"Not entirely luck," Hulmul said. He tapped his shoulder and summoned Malicious to him. The reptile flew from its perch and soared past the knight's head before landing on the wizard. The effect would have been more impressive had his familiar not decided to nip at his ear once it was settled. Hulmul had to brush away the lizard's teeth.

"You've had a demon spying on us," Helchen snapped.

"My *familiar* has been watching you," Hulmul corrected her. "Keeping me advised if you got into trouble so I could intervene. Rather effectively, you must admit." He pointed to a few weapons the ambushers had dropped when they fled.

Alaric stared at the wizard, studying him carefully. "Why the interest in us?" he finally asked.

"I thought you could help me reach Singerva," Hulmul said. He shook his staff at the road. "This path leads to the town, so I presumed you were going there." He decided it would be unwise to reveal the full extent of his familiar's spying.

"What business do you have in Singerva?" Helchen demanded.

"Business even a witch hunter would endorse," Hulmul countered. "I'm going to consult my old mentor, Vasilescu." He smiled when he saw surprise on Helchen's face again. "Ah, you recognize that name. He's helped your Order many times in the past. He's far wiser and more learned than I am. I hope Vasilescu will have some understanding of this zombie plague that is scourging the land. Maybe he'll know a way that the undead threat can be contained and countered."

"Whatever your reasons for going there, you're welcome to join us," Gaiseric quipped as he finished stuffing his pockets. "You'd be mighty handy to have around if we run into more brigands."

Hulmul leaned on his staff and gave the thief an indulgent smile. "Oh, those weren't brigands. Did you ever hear of a brigand, however hungry, who turned his nose up at gold?"

A wary look entered Alaric's eyes. "If they weren't brigands, who were they?"

"Didn't you guess?" the wizard replied. "They're refugees. Refugees from Singerva."

CHAPTER FIVE

Gaiseric had once been bed ridden by Red Fever, unable to ingest anything more substantial than broth and scarce able to keep even that down. Yet, he could honestly say that his first sight of Singerva when they crested a nearby hill was the sickest he'd ever felt in his life.

"So much for a safe haven," the thief muttered, as he tried to reconcile himself to the grim reality before him. The great walls, those ramparts that had resisted orc hordes and rebel barons in the past, were as robust and mighty as ever, but what use were even the strongest walls when the gates hung open and unguarded? Plumes of smoke billowed up from the town itself, rolling across the gable roofs, too thick to merely be the product of chimneys. He could only just make out the spire of Singerva's cathedral above the veil. The road leading into the West Gate was strewn with debris, an assortment of carts and wagons littered the sides of the path. The bodies of horses and humans lay bloating under the sun, crows and dogs picking at the carrion.

"Even Singerva has fallen," Helchen groaned, a pained light in her eyes. "The town garrison numbered into the hundreds.

My Order maintained a temple-fort here with dozens of witch hunters…"

"And you might reckon on the men-at-arms and knights who served the noble families," Hulmul said, ticking off factions on his fingers. "The guards of the mercantile guilds, all the mercenaries and sellswords lurking about seeking work … Singerva probably had over a thousand fighters to draw upon, yet still it wasn't enough." His expression darkened. "The bigger the community, the bigger the graveyard. More bodies for this profane plague to raise as zombies."

Gaiseric spun around, clutching the wizard's sleeve. Of them all, Hulmul seemed to have the best grasp of what was going on. "Do you think the town's abandoned, or are there still people alive down there?"

"You can be certain that there'll be people who preferred to hole up than run away," Alaric stated. "The question isn't if there are people there, but rather how long they can hold out."

"Some places will be easy to defend," Hulmul added. "At least against such undead as we've seen." He nodded to Helchen. "I'm confident the temple-fort of your Order would be able to hold out for quite some time, though I wonder how much help they'd provide anybody else."

Helchen shot the wizard an icy glare, but surprisingly didn't argue his point.

"There'll be other strongpoints." Alaric focused on the watch towers that were scattered along the exterior walls and the immense gate house that straddled the West Gate. "Just because we can't see anyone on the parapets doesn't mean nobody got inside and barricaded themselves in." The knight paused, clenching his jaw. Gaiseric could tell he was thinking of his family's castle and how its defenses had been overcome.

"We might still rally some help," Gaiseric suggested. "Castle von Mertz would be easier to defend than some tower in the middle of a destroyed town." He smiled and jangled one of his overstuffed pockets. "If there's any mercenaries still looking for work, we can certainly pay them."

Alaric seemed to take some solace from Gaiseric's speech. "Let's see if there's anything here to salvage," the knight declared. His gaze swept across each of his companions. "Whatever we find, remember I'm only interested in getting back home and making Brunon Gogol pay for his crimes."

Gaiseric plucked a gold ring from one of his pockets and sighed. "I imagine all the fences have closed up shop anyway." He flipped the ring and caught it in his other hand before returning it to his pocket. He turned and clapped Hulmul on the shoulder, almost knocking over the wizard. "Since you seem to know Singerva better than any of us, maybe you should lead the way."

Hulmul shook his head. "I saw little enough of the town. Just my master's tower."

"Well, that's a starting place at least," Gaiseric said. He frowned when the wizard's familiar leaned forward and stared at him, its little tongue flicking from between its scaly jaws. "Do you think your mentor is still there?"

"Oh, of that I'm certain," Hulmul replied. "Vasilescu would never abandon his library. He'd die before letting that happen." Gaiseric noted a certain uneasiness in his tone. So did Helchen.

"There's something you're not telling us," the witch hunter accused Hulmul.

Hulmul bowed his head in contrition. "Nobody cares to have a wizard living near them. The Order has made our kind undesirable…"

"Your obscene magic has made you undesirable," Helchen interjected.

"Maybe we could save the hostility for the undead," Gaiseric suggested, darting the witch hunter a dark look before encouraging Hulmul to continue his explanation. "Is there something wrong with Vasilescu's tower?"

"Only where he was forced to have it built," Hulmul said, his voice uncomfortable. "You see, the town elders made Vasilescu take a plot nobody else wanted. His tower, you understand, is right next to Singerva's oldest graveyard."

"Oldest… graveyard?" Gaiseric sputtered, that sick feeling growing in his stomach again.

"Aye," Hulmul confirmed, his familiar letting out a low hiss. "The town's oldest graveyard… and its largest."

It was easy enough to gain entry to Singerva. The gates were both open and unguarded. Alaric could find no hint of life stirring in the fortified gatehouse, the iron shutters of its windows closed tight against the gray stone of its fortifications. The knight warily made his way down the covered gate, anxiously aware of the arrow slits in the walls to either side and the sinister murder holes above his head. He breathed a good deal easier once he stepped out into the square on the other side. A stable ran along one side of the square, its empty stalls open to the street. The fire-blackened bricks of a large warehouse were close by, its doors reduced to soot by the flames that had ravaged the interior. Alaric could make out the town's coat-of-arms amid the debris, a dripping axe set above the fanged heads of a mystical ettin. Clearly the warehouse had been used by the authorities to hold goods confiscated from those passing through the gate.

Nearby, Alaric spotted an overturned table and chair poised in the very shadow of the gate. A big wooden box lay beside the furnishings, its side smashed in, and a litter of coins strewn about it in the mud. The sight sent a chill through him. Nothing could better relate the speed with which disaster had fallen on Singerva than the obvious swiftness with which the exciseman had deserted his post... and that nobody had availed themselves of the abandoned taxes.

At least not until Gaiseric caught the glint of silver twinkling in the mud. "So easy it's shameful," the thief quipped as he ran over and started scooping up coins.

The knight tapped Gaiseric on the shoulder. "You might wonder why nobody else took advantage," he suggested, directing a meaningful look at the towers to either side of the gate. Alaric saw the thief blanch when he looked up at the windows and the arrow slits in their shutters. Hurriedly, he backed away from the broken box.

"You think someone's in there?" Helchen asked as she and Hulmul joined them.

"Only one way to find out," Alaric said. He prevailed on her to check the other tower while he tried the door at the base of the one closest to him. They found both barred from the inside. The knight started to call out to anyone within, but Hulmul quickly dissuaded him from trying.

"I dare say you've seen by now that zombies are attracted by noise," the wizard cautioned. He shook his staff at the gatehouse. "Anyone still in there can see us from the windows. If they had any interest in communicating, they'd have done so by now."

"A poor showing for soldiers." Alaric scowled at the towers.

"Disaster exposes everyone's true quality," Helchen told him. "A prince proves to be a coward and a peasant is revealed to be a hero." She used her mace to poke what looked like a pile of rags beside the gatehouse. It crumbled apart into the gnawed remnants of a body. "Anyone in there didn't come out to stop this. They won't come out now."

The knight nodded in agreement and motioned for Hulmul to lead the way. "We'll try for your mentor's tower."

"You did hear what he said?" Gaiseric objected, dropping the emptied tax-box on the ground. "You know, the part about being next to the graveyard?"

"Take comfort in that, burglar," Helchen said. "The graveyard is where the zombies would *start* from. They won't be there now. They'd have spread to where they could find victims."

"Well, there's just a chance a bunch of them felt lazy," Gaiseric protested. "Or maybe some of them started getting homesick and went back."

"I don't think that's likely," Hulmul assured the thief, oblivious to his sarcasm. "Besides, unless they caught him completely by surprise, Vasilescu knows how to protect his tower from worse things than zombies." He darted a cold look at Helchen.

Alaric waved them forwards. The animosity between wizard and witch hunter was understandable, but hardly productive. The odds against them were long enough without adding internal strife into the mix as well. Like a military unit, to survive they all had to work together. He wondered if he could get this rag-tag group to understand that.

The devastation to the town was greater the further they got from the West Gate. Debris was strewn about the streets. Gaiseric was forever lagging behind as he inspected valuables abandoned by the townsfolk as they fled the undead hordes. Some buildings they passed were partially collapsed from carts and wagons that had slammed into their walls, their plaster and timber construction unequal to such violence. Fire, untended and unchallenged, had wrought even more destruction. They passed many structures that had been reduced to charred husks, smoke rising from the glowing embers. Thicker plumes helped to steer them away from areas where fires continued to rage. The crackle of flames and the croak of carrion crows mingled as a consistent background noise.

At least until Alaric detected the distinctive din of combat. Raised voices and the sound of splintering wood, screams of fright and cries of protest. "Someone's near!" Alaric growled, turning in the direction of the sounds. "Someone in trouble!"

Gaiseric stuffed an ivory cameo he'd found into the breast of his tunic and frowned at the knight. "I know what you're thinking, but there's no sense getting ourselves into a fix we can't get out of."

"I won't abandon them," Alaric retorted, acid in his tone. He should have expected that attitude from a thief. Gaiseric might have his own brand of courage, but he had no sense of chivalry or duty. A knight did.

"Then let's at least see what we're getting into," Hulmul said. The wizard plucked his familiar off his shoulder.

Malicious snapped at his hand as he held the reptile aloft, drawing blood from his finger. "None of that," he scolded the animal. "I need your eyes." With a flick, he sent Malicious into the air. The reptile's wings snapped open as it took flight. It circled the group twice, then wheeled away in the direction of the noise.

Hulmul's hands tightened around his staff, leaning against it as his body began to tremble. "I can see the next street over. There's a square. A big stone building dominates one corner… a guildhall, I think. Barriers have been placed around the outside, barrels and crates and boxes. There are zombies… many zombies… tearing at those barriers. People are stabbing at them with spears and poles… whatever they can… trying to keep them away from the windows and doors." The wizard gasped and his face contorted in a grimace. "The undead have forced their way to one of the windows… they drag a man through the hole…"

"How many are there?" Alaric grabbed the wizard by his shoulder. "How many zombies lay siege to this place?"

Hulmul stirred from his trance. "Many," he replied. "Malicious is poor at counting, but I think there must have been at least a dozen."

"Too many for us to fight," Gaiseric insisted, shaking his head.

Alaric wagged his sword at the thief. "Alone, perhaps, but if we came at the zombies from behind and broke their attack it would give the people inside a chance to sally." Seeing he hadn't swayed Gaiseric, he looked to Helchen. "We'd have the undead caught between us."

"And if the people inside aren't inclined to help?" Helchen

frowned at the knight. "There might be a dozen zombies there now, as the wizard says, but all that noise is certain to bring more."

"At least we can give those people a chance," Alaric declared. "We can do that much."

"Fifteen hells of an unlucky gambler," Gaiseric grumbled. He removed the cameo and tossed it down the street, clearly considering it to be jinxed. "Let's try it. If it proves a bad idea, we can always run."

Alaric unslung his shield and smiled at the thief. "I'm glad there's some decency about you after all," he said.

Gaiseric's voice was sour when he replied. "You kept me from hanging. That's a debt I intend to repay." He caught the knight's arm as Alaric started to march toward the sounds of combat. "If it looks bad, we *are* going to run. No vainglorious heroics." He pointed at the von Mertz coat of arms on Alaric's surcoat. "Just remember, if you die here then your family goes unavenged."

Of all the things Gaiseric might have said to unsettle him, that was the one Alaric wasn't prepared for. The knight slowly nodded his head. "If it looks bad, we run," he conceded, even though he was revolted by the doubt that tore at him. When put to the test, would vengeance have a stronger hold on the knight than chivalry?

Helchen was close behind Alaric as the knight charged down a narrow side street. Holding his kite shield sideways, he was just about able to completely close off the passage. Any zombie trying to come at them would have to claw its way through the shield.

When the street opened onto the square, things were quite a different matter. The plaza was so wide that it would have taken a rank of knights forty strong to establish an unbroken line across it. There were a dozen other streets and alleyways that opened onto it, each a potential avenue for the undead. Indeed, she could already see walkers shuffling to the square from several directions, drawn by the sounds of conflict. She wondered how many more there were that she couldn't see from her vantage.

What she could see was the guildhall, the stone building where some of Singerva's citizenry had taken refuge. Hulmul's estimate about how many zombies were besieging the place was an understatement. There were nearer to two dozen of the creatures trying to batter down the barricades the townsfolk had raised. One of the windows and a side door were already smashed in, and it was at these spots that most of the zombies had converged, trying to overwhelm the defenders inside. As she watched, a man wearing the tabard of the town watch was pulled from the doorway by the undead. He was borne screaming to the ground where several of the creatures began ripping into him with their teeth.

"Marduum have mercy," Helchen prayed as she raised her crossbow and sent a bolt slamming into the doomed watchman's head. His screams were stifled and the zombies lost interest in his body once the spark of life was extinguished.

"Try to draw them away from the guildhall!" Alaric shouted to his companions. The knight banged his sword against his shield, making as much noise as possible. A clutch of walkers turned away from the barricades and ambled towards him. A runner wearing the gory tatters of a nun's habit sprinted past its fellows to spring at him. Alaric's sword caught the creature in mid-leap and struck it down. A second blow crushed its head and the corpse fell still.

Hulmul drew a roll of parchment from his pack and started to read from it, all the while rapping the butt of his staff loudly against the cobblestones. A mob of walkers clambered toward him, but when they got within a few yards of the wizard, he gestured at them with his palm. A bolt of arcane fire erupted from his hand and immolated several of the zombies. Some of the others were knocked back, flames licking at their ragged clothes and decayed flesh. Oblivious to the fact that they were still on fire, the creatures continued to advance on the wizard.

"There's too many of them," Gaiseric howled. The thief threw rocks at the zombies battering away at the guildhall's front doors, trying to distract them. He hastily dropped the stone he was holding and drew his sword when the badly mauled remains of a wagoner staggered out from an alleyway and reached for him with a clawed hand. The rogue jumped back and slashed at his assailant, felling the walker with repeated cuts to its head.

"Get out of there while you can!" Helchen shouted to the people inside the guildhall as she loaded another bolt into her crossbow. Better than half the zombies had been drawn away by the surprise attack. If the defenders could just concentrate their efforts and drive a wedge through the ones that remained, they might be able, as Alaric had said, to smash the enemy between their forces. Hopefully before too many more made it into the square.

It was at that moment that she saw a huge zombie come to

grips with Alaric. The creature had a leather apron partially covering its bloated bulk and from its belt an array of knives jangled when it walked. The butcher, for such she judged it to have been in life, grabbed the knight's shield and nearly wrenched it free from the warrior's grip.

"Lumbering knave!" Alaric cursed the creature as he swung his blade. The sword slammed into the brute's head, but failed to split its skull! Before the knight could recover, a decayed hand ripped at him, tearing his surcoat. Only the mail he wore prevented the zombie's claws from gutting him.

"Alaric!" Helchen shouted. She spun around and sent a bolt ripping into the butcher. She saw the missile pierce its head, but even this wasn't enough to bring it down. The monster simply continued trying to tear through the knight's armor.

"By Wotun, you'll not prevail," Alaric snarled. He threw his weight into the sword embedded in the zombie's head. With a vicious twist, he drove it still deeper, sawing through the rancid flesh and thick bone. Finally, he penetrated to the brain, delivering enough damage that the brute dropped like a slaughtered steer.

Other zombies were closing upon Alaric's position. Helchen thought there was no chance for him, but seeing the brute dispatched had inspired the defenders inside the guildhall. Fighters poured out of the building, cheering as they charged the walkers. Several of the creatures were destroyed in the initial rush. More than the zombies they brought down, the sally sowed confusion among the undead. They wavered between pressing their attacks on Alaric and Hulmul or turning back to engage the townsfolk.

Alaric took full advantage of that confusion. He became

an avalanche of steel, knocking down zombies with his shield and decapitating them with slashes of his longsword. Each foe he vanquished ignited greater ferocity from the townsfolk, and they set upon the creatures with spears and axes, strewing the square with their corrupt bodies.

"We're winning!" Gaiseric crowed. Even as he spoke, the joy drained from his voice. The thief gestured with a shaking hand at a fresh mob of undead that lumbered out from a side street only yards away.

Helchen felt dread pulse through her veins. At least ten zombies were entering the square, but more than their numbers, it was the monstrous figure at the forefront that provoked fear. It was far larger than the brute Alaric had killed, so large in fact that it was impossible for its proportions to be natural. Its limbs rippled with such a quantity of muscle that the skin had been stretched and split by the bulging tissue beneath. Its face was a frenzied parody of a human visage, devoid of all expression except the urge to destroy. There was a glimmer of awareness in its yellowed eyes absent from the other zombies, a mania of unbounded hate.

"Fires of Toa-komorgh consume you!" Hulmul shouted, pointing his hand at the hulking zombie and its mob. Once more, arcane flames rippled from the wizard's palm. Helchen saw a few of the walkers reduced to ash by the fiery blast, but the big monster's hide wasn't so much as scorched by the spell. The wizard paled when he saw the creature was unharmed and staggered back when the hateful eyes focused on him.

"Over here, dog!" Helchen yelled. She shot a bolt at the monster, horrified to see it glance off its skull. Surely the creature was saturated in black magic to shrug off both spells and steel. One thing she'd managed, however. She'd diverted the abomination's attention.

"It's turning this way," Gaiseric advised her. The thief's frightened words gave Helchen an idea.

"Alaric! Hulmul! Help these people!" Helchen began to back away as the abomination and the walkers with it turned and started towards her. She spun around and gave Gaiseric a shove. The thief scrambled ahead of her as they made for an alleyway. "We'll lead the zombies away!"

The witch hunter couldn't spare a backwards glance to see what the knight was doing. She hoped Alaric had sense enough to do what she told him. She didn't know if they could kill this monstrous abomination, but at least they could get it away from the other survivors. At least if nobody did anything to make it head back into the square.

"All right, it's chasing us," Gaiseric huffed, as he sprinted down the alleyway. "What's the plan now?"

Helchen shook her head as she hurried after the thief. "Keep running," she told him. She could hear the zombies behind them. For one thing, at least, they could be grateful. However strong it was, the abomination wasn't any faster than the walkers.

"Keep running," Gaiseric coughed. "That's your plan?"

"Keep running and don't get killed," the witch hunter elaborated. Helchen could hear Gaiseric grind his teeth.

"I liked it better the first way you said it," the thief grumbled.

CHAPTER SIX

The alleyway felt like it was closing in around Gaiseric. No cell he'd ever been thrown in had felt so confined. His breath came to him in short, desperate gasps and his heart felt like a hammer trying to beat its way out of his chest.

"Calm," he told himself as he scurried between the half-timber buildings. He repeated the word again and again to himself, as though it were a sacred hymn. If he could only stop for a second and try to collect himself, he'd be all right.

The sound of splintering wood farther down the alley disabused Gaiseric of that idea. The narrowing of the alleyway wasn't entirely imagination. It had grown too restrictive for the abomination's swollen bulk, but instead of abandoning its pursuit, the monster was bulling its way onward, ripping slats from the walls.

"At least that should slow it," Helchen told Gaiseric. "If we can just get out of sight, maybe we can lose it."

"There's an intersection ahead," Gaiseric replied. Somewhere he found the energy for another burst of speed. "This way," he directed Helchen as he darted around the corner.

When Gaiseric made the turn, he grabbed the edge of the corner and pulled himself back. There were zombies around the bend, shambling straight towards them. In his mad dash, he'd almost run into the foremost of the undead mob.

The thief brought his sword stabbing into the zombie's chest. He wasn't sure if he'd pierced its heart and destroyed it, but at least the blow sent it stumbling into the ones behind it. For a moment, at least, the walkers were stymied in their advance.

"This way doesn't look too healthy. There's so much smoke!" Gaiseric said as he backed out from the intersection. He glanced ahead and saw smoke rolling across the alleyway. He waved Helchen forward. "We'll try this."

"It looks like everything's on fire," Helchen objected.

"I'd rather get burned than get bit by one of those things," Gaiseric shouted as he plunged onward. He pulled the collar of his coat around and tucked his face into its folds, hoping to stifle at least some of the smoke as he dove into the sooty fume.

The thief's eyes were stinging almost immediately. He could feel an intense heat off to his left, so instead veered right and kept running. Any instant he expected to slam into a wall. When he didn't, he realized what had happened. Wind was blowing smoke across the mouth of the alley, concealing the wider street that it opened onto. As he sprinted onward, the cloud dissipated enough that he could see his surroundings. A row of workshops with residences above them. They had a shabby, dilapidated appearance, evidence that even before the zombie attack these places hadn't been in the best condition. In the panic of the undead invasion, windows had been smashed and furnishings thrown into the lane. A few bodies sprawled on the cobblestones were the only sign of the former inhabitants.

Or at least they were until Gaiseric saw a wretched figure rise from behind an overturned vegetable cart. Any doubt of the vendor's condition was removed when the thief saw the vacant eyes and a throat chewed down to the spine. The zombie started toward him with outstretched arms. Before it moved more than a few paces, there was a crunching sound and its head whipped around. It flopped back, its body sagging across the cart.

Gaiseric turned to see Helchen emerge from the smoke, already fixing another bolt to her crossbow. The witch hunter expelled the breath she'd been holding once she was clear of the cloud. "You get accustomed to working around smoke in my trade," she informed him. Gaiseric shivered at her grim humor.

"Unless you think one of those bolts can stop the big ox chasing us, we'd better get moving," Gaiseric said. He gestured at the smoke behind them and drew attention to the sound of splintering wood – a sound he was certain was caused by the abomination chasing them. "And I'm not eager to go stumbling around in that mess again."

Helchen quickly cranked back the crossbow's string. Her eyes were locked on the street ahead. The smoke had thinned into a brown haze, allowing them to see that a mob of walkers was lurching in their direction. "Forward is a bad idea, too."

"Eight… nine…" Gaiseric gave up counting the zombies when he reached ten. "Too many to fight, and too many to dodge." He tapped Helchen on the arm and drew her toward one of the workshops. "We duck in there and try to hole up until they go away."

The very moment they started toward the workshop, a hulking shape emerged from the smoke. The abomination glanced about for a moment, then its enraged gaze spotted Gaiseric and Helchen. With powerful strides, it lumbered toward them.

"New plan," Gaiseric said as he scrambled into the workshop, kicking over half-finished barrels. He waited only long enough for Helchen to duck inside before he slammed the door. He scowled at its battered condition and started piling barrels behind it.

"What's your new plan?" Helchen asked, as she helped the thief reinforce the door.

Gaiseric wiped his brow as he hefted an iron-banded keg onto the pile. "We get this solid enough that it might delay that monster more than a few heartbeats, then we find the back door to this place."

"What if it doesn't have a back door?" Helchen demanded, tugging a box of iron fittings over to the barricade.

Gaiseric picked up a hatchet from a workbench. "If it doesn't have one already, I'll make one," he promised. There was a loud crash against the door. Despite the weight pressing against it, the force of the impact caused the barricade to shift several inches inward. The thief could see the abomination pressing against the portal. He thought he saw more zombies behind it.

"I'd say the first part of your plan is a bust," Helchen stated. She drew back from the door, casting her eyes around the room. There was a door leading to another room and a ramshackle stairway leading up.

"If the second part doesn't work out, you won't have time to complain about it," Gaiseric said, nudging Helchen toward the doorway. As they hurried into the farther room, he cast a last look about the workshop. The abomination's brawn had pushed the barrier back almost a foot now. A few more shoves and the gap would be wide enough for the monster to get inside.

The room behind the workshop proved to be used for storage. Planks of wood of varying sizes were piled against the walls and stacked on the floor. A few completed barrels were lined up in the middle of the floor. These details Gaiseric took in at a glance, his attention quickly drawn to the feature that had commanded Helchen's interest. A wooden door at the back of the room.

"It won't budge," Helchen reported as she pushed against the door. She kicked a bar she'd removed and sent it skittering across the floor. "I think it's blocked on the other side."

Gaiseric could hear the barrier behind the front entrance being jostled as the abomination forced its way into the workshop. If whatever was blocking the back door was even half as robust, they were trapped.

"Get a running start," Gaiseric told Helchen. She stepped away and they counted down from three. When they reached two, they could hear the barrier in the front room collapse and the zombies start lumbering into the building. Another moment and the undead would be on them.

"Three," the survivors said as they ran at the door. Their combined weight smashed through the barrier and they went hurtling through the splintered panel.

Gaiseric had expected them to spill out into a street or alleyway. Instead, they were in a dark space that was rank with animal smell. The storage room was connected to another building!

The thief started to pick himself off the ground when a low snarl stopped him. In the gloom he could make out a hairy body and gleaming fangs. Gaiseric had broken into enough places to know a guard dog when he saw one.

Or did he? This looked to be bigger. A lot bigger. There was something else in the room too, something that had a weapon clenched in its hands. From the broad shoulders, long arms, and bandy legs, Gaiseric knew what he was looking at couldn't be human.

Even in the dark, he could see the reddish gleam of eyes staring at him. The sort of eyes that, once seen, no one could ever forget. How it could be, Gaiseric didn't know, but in their hurry to escape from the zombies, they'd fled straight into an orc.

Helchen froze when she heard the low, bestial snarl. She spotted a lupine shape crouched only a few feet away, its fangs gleaming in the little light that trickled into the room. Then her eyes fell upon the gruesome figure that stood beside the animal. She'd heard of orcs before, seen drawings of them, even saw the pickled head of one at a traveling sideshow when she was a child. But she'd never seen a live orc before. Even in this dim light, she could sense the brutal strength of that inhuman frame.

"Wutz der rumpuz?" The orc's voice was a deep rumble, his words twisted by fangs every bit the equal of the animal beside him. The brute ducked down and peered through the smashed door. He made an impatient gesture with the weapon he carried. "Dangle, ya mugz," he snarled.

Gaiseric caught at Helchen's arm. "He wants us to go inside," he told her.

"You understand that gibberish?" the witch hunter marveled.

"Of course," the thief answered, though there was a dubious note in his tone. He glanced up at the orc. "They're not known for patience," he said, urging her on.

Zombies behind her and an orc looming over her, Helchen saw no point in arguing. She scrambled alongside Gaiseric into the most miserable grog shop she'd ever seen. The smell of the liquor seeping from the barrels behind the bar would gag a rat. A scattering of rickety tables and stools made up the place's furnishings. There was more light though, courtesy of a jagged crack in the ceiling above.

Helchen spun around when she heard a loping tread behind her. The animal had followed them out from the back room. She saw now that it was a big gray wolf, its hide mottled with old scars. One of its fangs was capped with a sharp piece of iron and it had a spiked collar around its neck.

The wolf glared at the humans as it circled past them. A moment later, its master shifted into the room.

The orc was well over six feet in height, his arms longer than those of a human while his legs were shorter in proportion. His face had a pushed-in appearance, with broad, flaring nostrils and a low forehead. The red eyes were small and recessed deep in the sockets. His jaw bulged with yellowed fangs that projected past his lips. The orc's coloring was a deep green and the skin had a leathery texture to it.

The orc's vestments added to his savage appearance. His head was covered by a mail coif, rents in the sides allowing his pointed ears to project past the armor. He wore a kind of jerkin fashioned from hides, to which had been added strips of mail and patches of steel plate. His left arm was encased in greaves clearly forged for a human knight and then battered and smashed to accommodate an orc. About his waist he wore a wolfskin and the boots on his feet were fashioned from the same material. Helchen could see a curved scimitar thrust under the band of his belt. Its edge serrated like the teeth of a saw.

"Ya mugz gotz der cadavaz ta ruckuz," the orc snarled. He hefted the weapon he held, which Helchen now saw was a huge mattock with a spiked head.

"Uh… he's not happy we brought zombies to his hideout," Gaiseric said. Before he could add anything else, the sound of the creatures in question tearing their way out of the storeroom reached them.

"Dangle," the orc grunted, nodding impatiently at the street outside the grog shop. Without waiting to see what they would do, he hefted his mattock and brought it slamming against the frame of the door leading into the back room. Plaster pelted down from the ceiling and a violent groan shook the building.

Helchen's eyes went wide when she understood what the orc was doing. "That's the supporting wall! He's going to bring down the whole building!"

The pair scrambled for the door. Helchen flung herself out into the street, rolling as she struck the cobblestones. She just had time to look back and see the orc swat the wall again, to note the abomination stalking towards him from the inner room before the dilapidated structure came crashing down. The demolition sent a wave of dust spilling across the neighborhood and a thunderous roar booming across the town.

Helchen regained her feet, watching as rubble pattered down from the partly demolished structure. A great mound of broken wood and shattered tiles had replaced the room they'd so recently escaped. She watched for any sign of movement, uncertain which she feared most to see claw free of the pile: the abomination or the orc.

"I guess that's one way to kill a lot of zombies," Helchen commented as she glanced aside at Gaiseric.

Gaiseric shook his head, his eyes roving over the buildings around them. "The orc might have just brought every undead in Singerva headed this way," he advised. "We know they follow noise, and there isn't a chance they didn't hear *that*." He nodded at the collapsed grog shop. "At least he seems to have settled that monster that was chasing us." Curiously, it seemed to Helchen the rogue regretted that the orc had buried himself along with the zombies.

The witch hunter frowned as she looked at their surroundings. "I don't see how we'll get back to Alaric," she confessed. "After all the turns we've taken, I don't even know what direction to take."

"Anywhere that isn't here is fine to me," Gaiseric told her. "If the zombies think they just heard a dinner gong, I intend to get as far away from here as I can." He spat in his palm and clapped his hands together. "Luck," he said as he parted his hands and glanced at his damp palm. "That way," he pronounced, pointing to a side street.

"Why that way?" Helchen challenged him.

Gaiseric smiled. "Because it's better to trust in luck than random chance," he explained. "Just because the town's a shambles is no reason to be uncivilized."

The thief's reasoning left Helchen flabbergasted. That Gaiseric didn't try to explain further, but just started off in the direction he'd chosen agitated her even more. Just the same, she found herself falling in beside him as he hurried along the deserted street.

"I suppose it's better to be lost than alone," Helchen told herself. There was a sardonic satisfaction in knowing that if Gaiseric came to regret his capricious whim, at least she'd be there to see it.

The desolate street they followed led into another even more decrepit. Abandoned shops, looted warehouses, once they even came upon a granary, the doors smashed open and grain spilled across the street. Helchen saw even worse evidence of the chaos that had enveloped Singerva. From a tree she saw a body hanging by a rope, pinned to its chest a sign that read "Usurer". In its death throes, some of the citizenry had set themselves to settling old grudges.

"A bad way to go," Gaiseric commented when he saw the hanged man. He prodded the corpse, setting it to swinging. As he did, the body suddenly sprang into a far more lethal animation. It clutched at the thief with its hands, grabbing him by the hair and trying to lift him up toward its gnashing mouth.

Helchen leveled her crossbow and sent a bolt smashing into the zombie's face. The body lost its animation and Gaiseric fell onto the street. "Maybe I would be safer alone," she sighed, shaking her head.

"You know you'd be lost without me," Gaiseric said as he dusted himself off.

"It seems to me I'm lost *with* you," Helchen replied. "What do I need you for?"

"You…" Gaiseric's expression suddenly shifted from levity to deadly seriousness. He was staring past Helchen, at something behind her. "You need me as an interpreter."

Helchen let the crossbow drop and reached for her mace as she spun around. Only a few yards away she saw the orc and his wolf. They were covered in dust and dark blood oozed from a cut in the orc's forehead, but the two looked very much ready for a fight.

"Been snoopin 'bout fer ya mugz," the orc growled. "Not lampin ya stiff 'n der road. Noodl'd ya wan't cold."

Helchen glanced over her shoulder at Gaiseric. The thief's brow was knotted as he tried to decipher the orc's grunts.

"He was trying to find us. See if we were dead or not," Gaiseric translated.

Helchen kept her weapon ready, though it looked puny beside the mattock clenched in the orc's fists. "Why? He wanted to kill us himself? Take a few heads back to his cave?"

The orc glowered at her and Helchen realized that while she might not understand him, the same didn't necessarily hold true.

"Der haigh haht donna wash," the orc scowled at her. "Imma kroak ya, ya bein' buzzrd chow aready." He turned and looked at Gaiseric. "Ya der abrecrumby, wot lampz wotz wot. Der town gawn louzy from cadavaz. Cadavaz makin' all der bimboz inta slugburgah." He hefted his mattock and his eyes narrowed. "Biggah der mawb, betta der bulge."

Helchen shook her head. "Tell me that made sense," she defied Gaiseric.

The thief smiled at her. "He says because Singerva is overrun by zombies, it would make sense for us to join forces." His grin broadened. "He also seems to think I'm the smart one." He was less pleased with himself when he found both the orc and the witch hunter glowering at him. "That's not a direct translation. More of the gist."

Helchen looked over the orc again, and the huge wolf at his side. "Gaiseric... I think you'd better try very hard to tell me exactly what he has to say. Because I'm pretty sure the orc understands."

The orc took one of his hands away from his mattock and slapped his own chest. "Ya bein' call me Radabrag."

Gaiseric was quiet for a moment. Helchen could see him trying to work things out before speaking. "He says his name is Ratbag," he finally announced.

The orc's eyes widened and he stomped a foot against the cobblestones. "Booshwash," he growled. "Lissen, ickie! Radabrag!" He slapped his chest again. "Radabrag!"

"That's what I said," Gaiseric snapped at the orc. "Ratbag!"

Helchen rolled her eyes. "Yes, let's argue at the top of our voices. I'm sure there's no zombies who'd come over to check on the noise." She fixed Gaiseric with a stern look until she was certain he wasn't going to persist. To her surprise, she found Ratbag almost sheepish when she gave him the same look.

"All right, if that's settled, let's find someplace where we can figure out our next move," the witch hunter said. "We need to get back to Alaric. I'm sure he'll need our help." She pointed at the orc's mattock. "The more warriors, the better our chances of surviving."

Ratbag nodded to her. "Abrecrumby," he said, then gestured with his thumb at Gaiseric. "Twit," the orc grunted as he led his wolf down the street.

"What was that about?" Helchen asked the thief.

"Nothing," Gaiseric grumbled. "He just seems to have reconsidered who's the smart one."

CHAPTER SEVEN

Gaiseric kept a careful eye on Ratbag's wolf as it loped down the street. He'd abandoned trying to pronounce the animal's name in orcish, deciding instead to just dub it "Fang." As near as he could make out from the orc's speech, the wolf was able to smell "cadavaz" from a good distance – exactly how far was a detail that he'd also given up trying to decipher. Knowing there were zombies around before the creatures knew *he* was around, Gaiseric didn't think there was anything more advantageous.

Unfortunately, Ratbag was inattentive to Fang, taking little notice when the wolf became agitated. Twice now, the beast had alerted him to a pack of walkers lurking in a building or prowling an alleyway but its master had ignored the warning. Gaiseric had to concede that the orc's mattock made short work of the undead, but had the zombies been more numerous he didn't think things would have been so easy.

"Ya wantta miss der rumble," Ratbag chuckled when Gaiseric broached the subject. An orc's laugh was an unsettling thing, like listening to a lion licking its chops.

"He's more interested in fighting than he is surviving,"

Gaiseric confided to Helchen as they picked their way down the street.

"If that was true, he'd already have been killed," Helchen pointed out. "There's no shortage of zombies prowling Singerva."

"Maybe he has sense enough to run away if he thinks there's too many," Gaiseric suggested. He nodded as he warmed to his own idea. "That's probably why he demanded we join up with him. He figures with us along he can get into bigger fights."

"Only a madman would think like that," Helchen said.

"You seem to forget that he isn't human," Gaiseric replied.

"Neither are elves or dwarfs," the witch hunter countered. "Yet they're rational enough."

"I've been around orcs when I was a scout on the frontier," Gaiseric said. "They don't think the way we do."

Curiosity gleamed in Helchen's eyes when she looked at Gaiseric. "You were a scout on the Duchy of Wulfsburg?"

The thief squirmed under her scrutiny. "Years ago," he tersely replied. "I don't like to talk about it. It wasn't to my liking. I don't like being responsible for other people." He made a furtive gesture at Ratbag, desperate to turn the conversation away from himself. "Besides, we were talking about orcs. How their minds work. They see everyone and everything as either a challenge to be overcome or a possession to be controlled."

Helchen shook her head. "And you say an orc doesn't think like a human? You've never met someone who sees the world in just those terms?" For just a moment, a troubled look crossed her face, some connection she'd rather not have made that was stirred by her words.

"Whatever you think, I'm keeping my eyes on Fang," the

thief said. "Ratbag might not pay attention, but I'm going to. Next time that wolf picks up the smell of zombie, we're going in the other direction."

Ratbag suddenly turned. Gaiseric squirmed when the orc's eyes met his. More than just comprehension, his hearing was also keener than the thief had thought. "Gastric," he fumbled Gaiseric's name – deliberately, the rogue thought, "wotz der schnozz gonna sniff if'n der cadavaz bein' frontta der wind?" The orc gave him a toothy grin before turning back around and taking the lead again.

"So?" Helchen inquired.

Gaiseric only had a few words he understood, but he wasn't about to admit that to her. "Ratbag said if I was so interested in Fang, I could start feeding him." That made more sense than some prattle about noses and the "front of the wind." At least the explanation satisfied Helchen.

Abruptly, the wolf turned to the right, its nose lifted and its hackles raised. "There, see?" Gaiseric said. "Fang smells zombies." He glanced over at Ratbag, but once again the orc was unconcerned by the wolf's warning. "Come on, let's make sure this mob doesn't catch us by surprise."

Gaiseric had his sword at the ready as he came up to where the wolf stood. Fang gave the thief a threatening snarl. Its master might have taken up with the humans, but the animal was less certain of its new companions. Gaiseric made a placating gesture and took a step back.

"Where are they?" Helchen asked, unlimbering her crossbow.

The thief stared into the bleak courtyard Fang was looking at. "I don't know," he admitted. "But I'm certain they're near."

Ratbag ambled back down the street to join them. He peered at the courtyard, then aside at the humans. "Nah somuch cadavaz," he grumbled. "Nah somuch tuzzle." He squinted at Gaiseric, then at Helchen. "Ya wanna lamp der cadavaz?"

"Better we find them than they find us," Gaiseric chided the orc, remembering the last two times he'd ignored the wolf. He looked over at Helchen. "I'm not exactly eager for a fight, but if Fang is agitated, it means they're close. If they're walkers, all's well. We can avoid them."

"But you're thinking there might be runners," Helchen said.

Gaiseric rapped his finger against the hilt of his sword. "If there are, we won't be able to lose them so easily. Worse, they can keep us too busy to slip away from the slow ones." He looked at his companions, resenting the sense of responsibility that was coming over him. It was like being a scout all over again, trying to keep others out of harm. "We need to know what's coming this way. Hit them first and then determine if we can safely withdraw."

Ratbag shrugged and whistled to Fang. At once the wolf lunged forward, dashing off in menacing silence. "Ya gonna bashem der cadavaz?" he asked, pointing after the wolf.

"Ambush!" Gaiseric growled. "We were going to ambush them here!" He didn't argue with Ratbag but set off after Fang.

"Maybe you should have explained your plan to him," Helchen suggested as she ran after Gaiseric.

The courtyard acted as a kind of garden for the surrounding buildings. Gaiseric spotted a couple of dead hogs in a sty that stretched along one of the walls. A few rows of mostly trampled vegetables. A collapsed coop for chickens. A quick glance revealed nothing that could have set off Fang nor where the wolf had gone. Then Gaiseric noticed an open door, a kind of angled hatch, between the courtyard and the building to its left. As he hurried towards it, he heard angry snarls echoing up from below.

"Be ready," Gaiseric advised Helchen. "I'll try to draw them out after me. You shoot the first zombie you see." He gave the witch hunter a warning grin. "Just make sure it's a zombie."

"I hit what I aim at," Helchen responded. From her tone, Gaiseric wasn't sure he should be reassured by that.

The thief dropped down into what proved to be a root cellar. The light was sufficient that he could see Fang on the floor below. The wolf was pawing at a door set into the opposite wall. Gaiseric could hear movement coming from behind the panel. "Hello?" he called out. "Anyone in there?"

His answer came by way of a frantic pounding against the door, shaking it on its hinges. Fang snarled, its attention fixed on whatever was inside. Gaiseric started to back away. "Hello," he called again. "If you're in there, you'd better answer."

"Over here," a raspy voice replied. It surprised Gaiseric so much that he almost stumbled down the steps. That desperate, wasted voice hadn't come from behind the door, but from under the stairs.

The thief peered over the railing, noticing for the first time that there was a man in the cellar. He was huddled up in the corner. The floor around him was dark with blood. Gaiseric dropped down, ready to render what help he could to the invalid.

Before Gaiseric could so much as start for the back corner, however, the door exploded off its hinges and crashed to the floor. A grotesque, hulking zombie stomped out from a closet-like space. Fang lunged at it, but the wolf's teeth just nipped the flabby hide. The brute swung its arm and sent the animal tumbling across the cellar. Then it turned toward the thief.

Gaiseric thrust his sword into the zombie's chest, but he couldn't drive the blade deep enough to strike its heart. The animated corpse swatted him with the back of his hand and threw him halfway back up the steps. He landed hard, the breath forced from his lungs in a pained gasp. Stunned by the impact, he watched in numb horror as the brute started to climb up after him.

"Keep your head down," Helchen barked at him. The witch hunter leaned down into the cellar and shot her crossbow at the creature. Flesh and bone exploded from the side of its face, one eye rolling free from its shattered socket. But even this hideous injury wasn't able to do more than make the brute stumble.

Helchen grabbed Gaiseric with both hands and pulled him up into the courtyard. The hulking zombie was right behind them, its eye dangling down past its chin on a string of veins. The creature reached for them with its swollen hands, intent on tearing the life from their flesh.

Gaiseric's ears rang as a bestial war cry echoed through the courtyard. The next instant he saw Ratbag charge at the lurching zombie. The orc swung his spiked mattock at the brute's head. The impact pulverized its skull and spattered the wall with a mash of bone and brain. The headless body toppled backwards, sliding noisily down the steps back into the cellar.

"Keen ta lamp der cadavaz," Ratbag sneered at Gaiseric. He

tapped a clawed finger against his brow. "Dizzy az wingmauz." Being called crazy by an orc was a new experience for the thief.

"There's somebody down there," Gaiseric said as he struggled back to his feet.

"Quik orn cadava?" Ratbag grumbled.

"Alive," Gaiseric told his companions. "Or at least he was."

They hurried back down the cellar stairs. Gaiseric took the lead, alert for more undead as he descended into the cellar once more. Helchen kept her crossbow trained on the doorway the brute had broken through. Ratbag went over to check on Fang. It seemed the zombie hadn't done more than phase the wolf. It shook its head and snarled a greeting to its master when the orc approached.

"Nah chaw der cadavaz," Ratbag snarled as he picked up his wolf. Gaiseric watched as the orc squeezed Fang, forcing the animal to hack up the contents of its stomach. It was at once an impressive display of strength and a crude exhibition of wariness the thief hadn't considered before. What would happen if an animal ate zombie flesh?

The man in the corner was a different matter entirely. Gaiseric could see at once that he was quickly losing what little vitality he had left. He'd been badly mauled, his belly torn open and what looked like a bite taken out of his knee. It was difficult to be certain with all the blood that covered them, but Gaiseric thought his clothes were too rich for those of a peasant or tradesman.

"Listen to me," the dying man groaned when Gaiseric and Helchen crouched down beside him. "You… have to… help…"

Helchen shook her head. "Make your peace with the gods," she informed him. "You're beyond anyone's help."

"Not… not me…" he gasped. The man stared up at the ceiling. "They sent me… to get help…"

"Who are they?" Helchen asked him.

"At… at the… leatherworks…" the man muttered. He lifted his hand and pointed at the broken door. "Follow… the marks…"

"But who are 'they'?" Gaiseric pressed the man. Whatever answer might have been coming left the wounded man in a rattling burble. He sagged back against the wall, his hand flopping to the floor.

"So much for that," Gaiseric said, stepping away from the body.

Helchen gave him a sharp look. "He said someone needed help."

"He didn't say who," Gaiseric retorted. "For all we know, it's a bunch of corrupt old burghers he's talking about." He thrust an accusing finger at the headless zombie. "Don't forget that he pointed to the very place that lovely thing came from. Which means there's probably more of them."

"Propa bad cadavaz," Ratbag said, kicking the corpse. Gaiseric could swear the orc was grinning.

"Whoever it is, they need help," Helchen said again. "If that's not enough for you, consider that we could use their help too. We're strangers to Singerva, they probably aren't. We could use someone who knows their way around, who could lead us back to Alaric or over to the tower Hulmul was talking about."

Despite his distaste for the idea, the rogue had to admit she was right. "I hate it when something I really don't want to do makes sense," Gaiseric conceded. "Let's see what we can do for light in there. Some of the rails from that pigsty might be a good foundation for torches."

Gaiseric had just turned to climb back to the courtyard when he saw Helchen suddenly smash the dead man's skull with her mace. "What did you do that for?" he demanded.

The witch hunter shook the blood from the sharp flanges. "He'd been bitten," she said, gesturing at the injured knee. "From what we know of this damnable plague, anyone who dies after being bitten by a zombie becomes a zombie." Helchen hooked the mace back on her belt. "Why wait for the weed to grow when we can crush the seed?"

Gaiseric felt a chill crawl down his spine as he moved up into the courtyard. There were times when he could almost forget Helchen was a witch hunter, then she'd do something ruthless and remind him precisely what she was. Her proactive measures for destroying zombies were an example. Mutilating a corpse after it was dead was one thing, but he wondered if she'd wait until a zombie's victim was dead before taking steps to make sure they wouldn't come back.

The tunnel at the back of the root cellar appeared to fascinate Gaiseric. Helchen supposed the thief wasn't cosmopolitan enough to be familiar with the devious methods of city folk. Any community that grew to the size of Singerva was bound to be crisscrossed by subterranean passages and chambers. Helchen had seen enough in other settlements to know that smugglers often created vast networks to get contraband to their customers. Merchants would employ the same tactics to sneak goods past the excisemen. Dwarfs, never particularly interested in human laws, would often go to ground and return to their roots when they settled among men, maintaining only a token presence on the surface while most of their activity went on below ground. Then there were religious dissidents and heretical cults, all employing tunnels to conduct their proscribed meetings.

It was these last that made witch hunters inured to discovering such passages beneath the very streets of a city or town. Helchen herself had often accompanied Captain Dietrich on raids into places every bit as dank and sinister as the tunnels they were now traversing.

Though she couldn't recall any that smelled nearly so vile. The tang of urine was heavy in the air. The dying man had spoken of a leatherworks, but Helchen hadn't quite appreciated that the industry might be underground. A boon for Singerva, to be spared the stink of such an odorous trade, but it did trap the rank smell in the tunnels.

"If this can't kill someone, I doubt there's much zombies can do to them," Gaiseric said, his voice muffled by the cloth he'd wrapped around his face. He probed ahead with his torch, ready to jump back if one of the undead suddenly shambled out of the darkness.

"It does take some of the veneer away," Helchen said, glancing down at her leather boots, "to know this part of the process." She looked back at Ratbag and Fang. The wolf was continually stopping to rub its nose against the floor. The orc, by contrast, appeared more disturbed by the flicker of the torches than the stench in the air. She'd heard their eyes were especially good in the dark and suspected the torches spoiled his enhanced vision. It was something Ratbag would have to adjust to. She wasn't going to walk around blind in these tunnels just to accommodate him.

"How far do you think these tunnels go?" Gaiseric wondered. "I mean, how close are we to whoever that fellow wanted us to help? We still have to try and get back to Alaric and Hulmul. For all we know, we're getting farther and farther away."

"We'll stand a better chance of joining Alaric if we have someone with us who knows Singerva," Helchen reminded him. She sighed as she considered their best bet for doing so. "We know they'll try for Vasilescu's tower, we just need someone who can lead us there."

"But how long are we going to keep crawling about in this reek?" Gaiseric pressed. "Just how far did that guy go to look for help?"

Helchen considered the question. "It depends when that zombie caught up to him," she decided. "With such severe wounds, he couldn't have gotten far." She dipped her torch toward the ground and motioned for Gaiseric to do the same. "I think we're here," she whispered.

There was a subtle change to the atmosphere ahead. Not so much a brightening of the gloom but rather a lessening of the dark. Helchen could hear a dull, persistent roar, a sound she associated with swift-flowing water. An underground stream would explain why Singerva had put its leatherworks down here. The water would help carry away the waste from the industry without lugging it up into the streets.

There were other sounds as well, noises that were all but drowned out by the roar of the stream. That mix of shouts and screams they'd heard before when trying to break the siege at the guildhall.

"Datz gonna bein' a bulgin' sockdallapa," Ratbag stated, hefting his mattock.

"We probably want a better plan than just storming in there," Gaiseric told the orc.

Ratbag gave the thief a surly look. "Ya bein' der kroakjoy." The orc's tone was such that Helchen knew he wasn't happy hanging back, but at least he had sense enough to do so.

"We'll have to get up as close as we can," Helchen said. "See what the situation is, then decide what to do."

The witch hunter carefully advanced down the tunnel, motioning for the others to hang back. If there was a mob of zombies waiting ahead, there wasn't any reason they should all walk right into their arms.

Instead of the undead, however, Helchen found that tunnel opened into a big cavern ahead, lit by dozens of lanterns strung along the walls. She saw the vats where the tanners treated hides. Above the vats, suspended by posts, was a flue that snaked its way across the chamber to an enormous, odious reservoir. The smell told her what was in there wasn't water.

Away from the vats, a stream cascaded through the cavern, powering a series of mill wheels before shooting into a channel beneath one of the walls. Helchen didn't know what the wheels were used for, but she saw that they were connected to a tower-like structure. It was here that she spotted the people the dying man had implored them to help. When she saw them, she regretted the callous way she'd treated his body. He'd deserved better than that.

The people scrambling about the upper levels of the spire

were all youths, the oldest couldn't have yet seen his sixteenth summer. From the uniformity of the robes they wore, Helchen judged them to be students and racked her memory trying to recall if Singerva had a university. Whatever the case, the man they'd found in the cellar must have been their instructor, doing his best to save them from the zombie invasion. He'd brought them below ground to try to keep them safe.

Only the undead had followed them. All about the base of the spire, a horde of zombies had gathered, scratching and clawing at the structure, trying in their clumsy fashion to climb up to the students. Helchen watched as youths hurled bundles of leather, loose stones, even spare slats for the mill wheels down at the creatures, trying to hold them back. There was only so much such resistance could accomplish, however. While the walkers were too slow to pose an immediate threat, the runners were able to scramble quite high before being knocked down by some missile hurled at them from above. Once the students ran out of their improvised ammunition, the faster zombies would be all over them.

"Marduum, I won't leave them to be slaughtered," Helchen swore. If Dietrich had been here, he would have reprimanded her for being soft. He'd always tried to teach her that it wasn't a witch hunter's province to protect the innocent, but rather to punish the guilty. She'd never been able to reconcile herself to that mindset.

Yet what could she do? There were at least forty zombies around the spire. Too much for her motley collection of fighters. Helchen wondered if they could lure them away but abandoned the idea. The roar of the stream would drown out any noise they could make, and to get the undead to take their eyes off the spire would mean walking right up to them – hardly a viable plan.

Helchen took off her hat and ground her knuckles against her forehead, as though she could drive an idea into her brain by force. She closed her eyes, trying to visualize a way to save the students. It was difficult to concentrate. The roar of the stream was deafening. The stink of the reservoir…

The witch hunter opened her eyes and stared at the cistern-like fixture and the posts that supported it. A good sharp hit in the right place and the foul reservoir would burst. Granted, it would take incredible strength to deliver such a blow, but she had access to just the right person.

"Gaiseric! Ratbag! Get up here!" Helchen called to her companions. She smiled as the thief scrambled up to her, then nodded to the orc as he ambled over, his wolf whining at the smell from the reservoir. An eager gleam came into Ratbag's eyes when he saw the zombies below and she could hear his knuckles crack as he tightened his grip on the mattock.

"Listen carefully," Helchen said. She gestured at the mattock and then over to the foul reservoir. "Hit that in the right place, and you'll destroy every zombie down there with one blow." She wasn't sure how much of that Ratbag understood, but from his expression whatever he had gleaned was to his liking.

Helchen lowered herself to the little ledge that skirted the periphery of the cavern and beckoned to Ratbag. The orc shouldered his mattock and followed her along the narrow expanse until they stood beside the cistern. She gave it a careful study, trying to envision how the structure would react when its integrity was compromised. She needed a precise angle to achieve her purpose.

Ratbag shifted impatiently as Helchen inspected the reservoir. She wished she could be absolutely certain, but she didn't know how much time the students had left. "There," she said, pointing at one of the support posts that gave the reservoir its shape. She hurried out of the way as Ratbag stepped forward with his mattock.

"Dis'll bein' der swell rumpuz," Ratbag bellowed as he struck the post. The orc sprang back along the ledge as the impact wrought destruction on the reservoir.

Straining to contain thousands of gallons of urine for the leather-making process, the cistern needed only the slightest dint in its structure to bring disaster. The outer wall crumpled, bursting apart where the pressure was greatest. A deluge of liquid foulness slammed down into the cavern. The flues, the vats, all the tools and racks of the tanners and leatherworkers were smashed in an instant, broken into unrecognizable detritus as they were propelled into the underground stream.

The same fate befell the zombies. Uncaring of their imminent destruction, the undead continued to claw at the spire even as the flood carried them away. By the dozens they were bashed against the cavern walls and sucked down into the stream. Helchen could see a few of them clawing at the water before they were dragged into the subterranean depths.

Now came the worst uncertainty in her whole plan. Helchen watched the spire, praying that it could withstand the torrent. She held her breath as the fury of the cascade swirled about its base. Then the flood receded. The structure remained standing. Those who'd sought refuge there were safe.

Helchen turned her head when she heard Gaiseric picking his way over to her along the ledge. He drew the cloth away from his face, then hastily restored it. "Congratulations," he said. "Somehow, you found a way to make it smell even worse in here."

She looked across the cavern. The students on the spire were waving to her and cheering. "Right now, Gaiseric, I think you and the wolf are the only ones who care."

CHAPTER EIGHT

It took no great deal of persuasion for Alaric to convince the people who'd taken shelter in the guildhall to leave their compromised sanctuary. Commoners in the kingdom had been conditioned to defer to knights, however grudgingly, and in a crisis, it was almost instinctive for them to look to the nobility for direction. Leadership, however uncomfortably it might rest on his shoulders, was something Alaric simply had to accept.

Of course, simple fear made the survivors quick to accept Alaric's directions. The zombies had made a shamble of their refuge. It wasn't a question of merely reinforcing the place. There were too many doors and windows to defend, too many avenues by which the undead could converge on the building. Nor, after seeing the hulking abomination that Helchen and Gaiseric had drawn after them, did it seem even walls were a guaranteed barrier to the creatures.

As he urged the frightened survivors away from the guildhall, Alaric still hoped that his missing friends would circle back. That they hadn't been caught by the abomination. He delayed as long as he dared wait for them, but it wasn't only his own and Hulmul's lives he jeopardized doing so. Reluctantly he conceded the necessity of taking the survivors someplace that was truly safe, whether Vasilescu's tower or some other refuge. Only then could he entertain the idea of going on his own to look for Helchen and Gaiseric.

The survivors from the guildhall numbered fifteen. That number felt even smaller to Hulmul and Alaric as they led their charges through the streets. Though Malicious had spotted several bands of walkers, and helped them avoid running into the zombies, as yet there was no sign of anyone else alive in Singerva.

"I can't believe everyone else was killed," Alaric told the wizard, as they marched along what had been the town's main thoroughfare. There was something eerie about a place that should have been bustling with activity being so still and quiet.

"Don't despair," Hulmul said. "There are certain to be others. The same measures that would keep the undead from finding them will baffle our efforts as well." He frowned as a thought occurred to him. "I could send my familiar to investigate the tower. Protective wards will prevent Malicious from getting too near without Vasilescu's indulgence, but we may learn something."

Alaric shook his head. "That would leave us exposed or force us to seek shelter while Malicious was away," he said. "It would also distract your familiar from the other task you've given it."

Hulmul focused a bit more of his awareness into his familiar, reminding Malicious of what it was looking for. "So far there's been no trace of them," the wizard reported. "Which is maybe better than finding the *wrong* traces of them." When he'd first sent the winged reptile to find Helchen and Gaiseric, he'd been resigned to finding them dead, whether reanimated as zombies or simply carrion. But the longer Malicious prowled the sky without seeing them, the more he began to think they were still alive.

"They know where we're headed," Alaric said. "If they aren't dead, they'll try to find us at Vasilescu's tower." The knight considered the bleak vista before them. A mongrel dog and several lean rats were gnawing at the carcass of a horse pinned under an overturned coach. Carrion crows circled overhead, sometimes swooping down to peck at the dead animal before the cur's barking would drive them off. "I'd feel better with a few more swords with us." He lowered his voice and cast a furtive look at the townsfolk following them. "Whatever fight they had in them is just about spent," he confided to Hulmul.

"Some of them haven't had a rest in days," the wizard said. In his researches, he'd made a study of human anatomy and some of the afflictions that could vex the body. A mere look was enough for him to assess a person's fatigue and how long it had taken to reduce them to such a state. "It must have been very nearly the moment the king's army engaged the undead horde that the zombie plague broke out in Singerva."

"Which can't be coincidence," Alaric added. The knight's visage hardened. "I've seen with my own eyes that necromancers have had a part in all of this. Either causing this plague or else harnessing it. Whatever the case, it's certain they've helped to spread this dark magic. Now I wonder if they've been colluding with each other, coordinating so that their attacks happen simultaneously."

Hulmul pondered the idea. "Magic has its own laws," he stated. "Eldritch patterns and rules that it would take much too long to explain. It is enough to tell you that there are certain hours and days that are more auspicious than others for bending arcane energies to specific purposes. It may be that some terrible alignment of the constellations has produced a dark harmony which the necromancers have sensed and made use of. Like farmers who sense the ideal time to harvest their fields, it needn't be a wider conspiracy but simply a matter of those who know these things acting in accordance with that knowledge."

"That sounds..." Alaric stopped and turned towards a darkened alleyway. He made a warning gesture to the townsfolk. The survivors stepped back as the knight moved forward and put himself between them and the menace he'd detected.

A group of pale, disfigured creatures shambled onto the thoroughfare. Hulmul found them especially horrible to look upon, for their faces and arms were peppered with ugly lesions, as though they'd rolled across a bed of spikes before they died and returned as zombies. Strips of skin had peeled away from some of the wounds, exposing the meat underneath. The ghastliest feature, however, were the bloody holes that gaped in each lifeless face. Every single one of the undead was missing its eyes.

The zombies, however, didn't need eyes to sense Alaric's presence. They turned towards the knight, reaching for him with their clawed hands. Alaric lashed out, striking one a blow that split its skull and sent it toppling to the ground.

"Get back!" Hulmul yelled at him. The shout caused the zombies to turn towards the wizard. He quickly read from the arcane scroll, shaping its words into magic. Flames crackled across the walkers, burning away the foremost of the mob.

A half dozen were still standing in the aftermath of Hulmul's spell. The wizard staggered back, his energy sapped by the hasty conjuration. Magic was meant to be a careful and precise art, not something to be wielded like a sword. He tried to refocus his mind, draw up the reserves necessary to unleash the bolt of fire once more.

"Stay your sorcery!" Alaric roared. The knight drove into the zombies, smashing two to the ground with his shield while slashing his sword into the head of a third. Inspired by his fury, the townsfolk rushed in. The two walkers thrown down by his shield were obliterated by a fury of clubs and knives, one of the other zombies was impaled on a spear and pinned to the wall behind it.

Hulmul swung his staff as another creature staggered towards him. The stout wood cracked its scalp and set a stream of filth bubbling out of its skull. It took another few lurching steps, then collapsed at his feet.

The living, however, didn't have things completely their way. The last of the walkers managed to grapple one of the townsfolk, a lamplighter from the wealthy merchants' quarter of Singerva. He fell screaming as decayed teeth sank into his arm and worried his flesh down to the bone. Hulmul hurried to the man's aid, smashing open the zombie's head with his staff. The loathsome thing sprawled atop its victim for a moment until Alaric pulled it away.

"He's been bitten," a burly taverner growled. There was both fear and anger in his face, but not so much as a speck of pity. Hulmul saw that same expression in the other survivors.

"I'm alive," the lamplighter gasped, clumsily trying to bind up his wound with the bright sash he wore around his waist.

"You'll become one of them now," a gray-headed midwife said, turning to spit on one of the destroyed zombies.

"I'm still alive!" the lamplighter insisted, tears in his eyes as he implored the others for mercy.

"Wait!" Hulmul told the crowd. "We can take him to Vasilescu. My mentor is sure to know a spell that will cure…"

The taverner shook his head. "Helping him will slow us down," he declared. "We've got to think of ourselves."

"Who's going to stay by him, knowing any moment he could become one of *them*?" the midwife asked. The question brought angry nods from many of the survivors.

Alaric laid his hand on Hulmul's shoulder. "We don't know how long it will take, how long this man has." The knight's eyes became distant, staring into unpleasant memories. "I've seen for myself that the change does happen."

"We can't just let them slaughter this man," Hulmul objected. He felt responsible. After all, the lamplighter had been hurt trying to keep the zombie from attacking him.

"It might be the most merciful thing," Alaric replied.

"No!" the lamplighter screamed. Seeing the way things were going, he sprang to his feet and ran off, nimbly dodging the survivors who tried to grab him.

"Let him go," Alaric called to the townsfolk when they would have pursued. "If the gods are gracious enough to let him live, it would be churlish to deny him that chance. If he dies, it adds one more to the enemy's numbers." He let his steely gaze sweep over the survivors, locking eyes with each until they quailed before him "But if we waste time chasing him and run into another pack of zombies, how many more of us will be lost?"

The knight's words swayed the crowd. Hulmul continued to watch the lamplighter until he was lost behind the buildings.

"We'd better get moving," Alaric whispered to Hulmul. "Maybe you should bring Malicious in closer." He nodded at one of the fallen zombies. "Another surprise like that..."

Hulmul closed his eyes. During the fray he'd withdrawn his awareness completely from his familiar. It took a moment to reestablish that contact. When he did, a smile pulled at his face.

"Good news, at last," Hulmul said. "Malicious has spotted Helchen and Gaiseric. They're alive, and it looks like they've taken some people under their wing the same as we have. I can tell Malicious to dive down and get their attention. He can guide them to us."

The knight was thoughtful for a moment. "We need your familiar close to keep watch and give us warning," he said, regret in his voice.

"I'll have him get their attention and show them the direction we're in," Hulmul insisted. "That much we owe them at least." Alaric nodded his assent. The wizard closed his eyes again as he sent commands to the winged reptile. Through the familiar, he was able to see Helchen's group, but not many details about them. He had it swoop low, then circle repeatedly overhead once it had gained Helchen's attention. Once he saw the witch hunter staring up at Malicious, he had the reptile divert and fly off back towards its master. He had no liking for members of her Order, but he was confident Helchen knew enough about the ways of magic to understand what the reptile was doing.

"It's done," Hulmul reported. "Malicious has shown Helchen the direction we're in. Now I have him hurrying back."

"Good," Alaric said. "We'll take it slow until your familiar can scout ahead for us... with more precision than he did before."

Hulmul paid no notice to the knight's reproach. He was instead feeling the excitement of his familiar. The winged reptile had spotted something that agitated it and it was conveying that disturbance to the wizard. Sinking his mind back into Malicious, Hulmul didn't see what could upset it so. There weren't any zombies in the streets below...

The wizard gasped when he saw what Malicious was trying to warn him about. His fright was such that his full awareness snapped back into his own body. He ignored the sickening pain that went with the hurried transition. "We need to move... Now!" Hulmul told Alaric. He looked over at the townsfolk and their anxious faces. There wasn't any time to spare their fear or hold back. "Run!" he commanded, gesturing with his staff down the street.

Alaric started to object, but Hulmul cut him off. "Run! Don't worry about whatever might be ahead of us. Worry about what's coming from behind!" He pointed at a black cloud above the distant buildings. A cloud that was moving against the wind. A cloud that was speeding their way.

"That isn't smoke," Alaric said, the first hint of alarm creeping into his voice.

"No," Hulmul assured him as he urged the knight to flee with the townsfolk. "It isn't."

Alaric sprinted after the rest of the group. It wasn't the weight of armor that held him back. Even with that burden, he could have outpaced Hulmul and many of the townsfolk. He'd have liked to say it was a sense of duty that kept him to the rear – the direction from which they could now expect an attack.

The truth was, since spying that sinister cloud that wasn't a cloud, fear had steadily been mounting inside him. Fear that Alaric refused to submit to. If only to prove it to himself, he wouldn't let his courage falter. Whatever came, he would know there was still valor in his heart.

He almost swung his sword at the shape that flew past him before he realized it was Malicious. Alaric saw the reptile briefly land on Hulmul's shoulder before taking off again. He wondered what the wizard and his familiar had communicated, but there were other concerns that were much more immediate. Keeping himself and those in his charge alive.

"Help!" The cry rose from the old midwife. She had fallen in the street, losing her footing on a slick cobblestone. None of the other townsfolk did more than glance back at her. Alaric took it on himself to pick her up and get her moving again. There were tears of gratitude, almost adoration, streaming down her face when she felt the knight's armored hand close around her own.

"You came back for me," she wept. It struck Alaric that even so slight a display of compassion was something the desperate survivors had come to regard as remarkable since the destruction of their town.

As he lifted the old woman out of the gutter, Alaric happened to look back down the street. His blood went cold at what he saw. The 'smoke' was now close enough to make out what exactly it was. Crows! A murder of hundreds of crows!

Yet these weren't the raucous, noisy birds he was accustomed to. They flew without vocalizations, the only sound coming from them was the flapping of their wings.

Through Alaric's mind filtered the image of vanquished zombies lying in the courtyard of his castle, in the fields, in the streets of Singerva. Carrion crows picking at the flesh of the undead, drawing down into themselves that corrupt meat! If a zombie could pass the plague with a bite, what would happen to an animal foolish enough to eat even the smallest part of it?

"This way!" Hulmul shouted. "Malicious has found a place we can take shelter!" The wizard waved his arm, beckoning everyone to follow him. The familiar circled around his head before darting away again.

The structure to which Malicious led them was a squat, stone-walled building of two floors. Alaric thought it looked as stout as a fortress and the heavy door at its front appeared thicker than that in Singerva's gatehouse. A sign swung from a hook above the door, its surface painted with an image of a purse and a gold coin.

"Fluchsbringer, the money-lender," the taverner growled as they neared the place.

Alaric pushed his way through the townsfolk. "I don't care if it's the assassins' guild," he scolded the man. The knight tried the door, unsurprised to find it barred from within. "Open! We need shelter!"

"There's no shelter for you here!" a wizened voice snarled back at him.

"We've no time for this," Hulmul hissed. The wizard drew Alaric away from the door, then set his palm against its thick oak panels. There was a momentary chill in the air and a burst of energy surged from Hulmul's hand. The force of his invocation blasted the door back, snapping the bar that held it and nearly tearing it off its hinges.

"Catch him!" Alaric ordered the taverner as Hulmul collapsed. The conjuration, it seemed, had sapped the wizard's stamina.

The knight surged into the room. It was a narrow chamber, dominated by a counter towards the rear on which stood a set of large bronze scales. Behind this a little man in a rich burgundy tunic was poised, a feather cap scrunched on his head. He had a sharp, ferret-like face, and an expression in his eyes that somehow managed to be both imperious and craven.

"Get them out! Get them out!" the little man yapped.

The order was directed to the other occupant of the chamber. He was much taller and younger than the money-lender. His features would have been handsome but for their harshness, a kind of sneering arrogance had set its stamp upon the visage. The man had a pantherish build, powerful without the appearance of brawn. The most notable aspect, however, was that from his shoes to his tunic, every article of clothing he wore was white. Even the scabbard from which he now drew a slim rapier was dyed to match his outfit.

"If we waste time crossing blades, we're all dead," Alaric warned the man in white. Without giving him a second thought, the knight turned around and helped the townsfolk push the door back into place.

"Get them out! Get them out!" the money-lender continued to howl. "Do what you're paid for, Drahoslav!"

Drahoslav! Alaric was surprised to recognize the name. The most notorious duelist in the kingdom! He should have made the connection the moment he saw that white raiment, a uniform the swordsman chose to wear because it made it easier for a spectator to see that he'd won a fight without taking so much as a scratch.

"You'll have real sword-work if you don't help secure this door," Alaric snapped. At that moment, the door was struck from the other side. It wasn't much of an impact, but it was only the beginning. One or two crows ahead of the rest of the flock. He could hear the flutter of their wings as they pecked and clawed at the panel.

The next impact was more forceful, causing one of the survivors to lose his grip and stumble to the floor. Through a gap near the hinges, Alaric could see the black beak of a crow trying to scratch out an opening. It pushed its head through and presented the grisly sight of its dead eyes and balding feathers. Where its skin was bare, it was necrotic and squirming with maggots. Feeding on zombies, the crows had become what they'd eaten.

"Get them out!" the money-lender shrieked, terror overcoming any semblance of authority in his voice.

"If I do, something worse will get in, Ernst," Drahoslav snarled at his employer. The duelist rushed over and pressed up against the door, adding his weight to that of the knight and the few townsmen helping him. "Some of you drag the counter over here," he ordered the other survivors.

Alaric felt the door sag back into place. The head of the crow that had managed to work its way in was severed by the thick panels, popped from its neck like a dandelion. The rest of the flock continued to batter and peck, but once the counter was dragged over to act as a buttress, the threat of the birds forcing their way through was eliminated.

At least for the moment. Alaric could hear the crows flying around the walls, circling the building as though it were a carcass lying in a field. He could see their black shapes blot out the light creeping in from the shuttered windows.

"They know we're here," the knight told Drahoslav. "They won't give up."

"But they can't get in!" Ernst scrambled over to Alaric and grabbed his arm. "They can't get in!"

"You should know," Alaric told the money-lender. "This is your place." He ignored the little man and went back to watching the walls. Tense moments passed as they listened to the crows scratching at the exterior, trying to find any weak spot that would afford them entry.

"It looks like it'll hold," Alaric finally said. The words brought visible relief to the townsfolk. Ernst clapped his hands and tried to recapture at least a veneer of dignity.

Drahoslav, however, discerned a facet Alaric hadn't mentioned. "Maybe we're safe from the crows, but what happens when all this noise brings other zombies? They've left this place alone because we've kept quiet. What happens when they know there's food here?"

Alaric nodded at the duelist's blade. "Then, I think, we're going to see if you're as good with that sword as your reputation says."

CHAPTER NINE

The sound of crows swirling around the money-lender's shop intensified. Alaric thought more of the zombie birds must have joined the first flock. If so, it meant other undead would be drawn to the scene.

"We must rest and regather our energy," Hulmul said. He was sitting with his back against the iron chest Ernst kept coinage in. The money-lender tried to get him to move, but as soon as he came close, Malicious hissed and nipped his finger.

"What we need is a plan," Drahoslav said. "A way to get past those fiends without being overwhelmed the second we open that door."

Alaric glanced around the room. He pulled down a heavy curtain behind where the counter had stood and threw it to one of the townsfolk. "Start cutting that into strips," he ordered. "We'll try to make torches."

Ernst snatched the curtain away, hugging it protectively to his chest. "I paid two crowns for this!"

Drahoslav walked over and glowered at his employer. "That means it's worth at least ten," he said as he pulled the curtain from his grip and returned it to the townsfolk. Ernst trembled under the duelist's cold gaze and was visibly relieved when his bodyguard turned his attention back to Alaric.

"You think fire will keep the crows away?" Drahoslav asked.

Alaric was looking at the door the curtain had covered. "It might," he speculated. He opened the door and peeked his head into a little sitting room. The chamber was stuffed with furnishings that would have looked ostentatious even in a castle. "We'll need to break up some of this to wrap the cloth around." He pointed to a glass-fronted cabinet filled with wine bottles. "We can use that to soak the rags."

Ernst scrambled ahead of the knight, blocking the doorway with his arms. "You can't do that! This is worth a fortune!"

Drahoslav tapped his finger against the money-lender's chest. "How much will it be worth to you if you're dead?" He pushed Ernst into the room. "Here's a compromise. Pick your best chair and a bottle of your best wine and sit down and get drunk."

"But… I pay you to protect me!" Ernst sputtered.

The duelist shoved Ernst into one of the chairs, then walked over to the cabinet. It was a matter of a moment for him to smash the locked door and pluck out a bottle at random. He went back to his employer and gave him the wine. "You can pay a man enough to risk his life, but not enough for him to throw it away."

The warning ended Ernst's protests. He sank back in the chair and clung to the wine bottle as though it were a holy relic.

Alaric waved the townsfolk in to start breaking up the furniture. A tapestry with gilded details and silver tassels along its edges would provide additional cloth if they needed it. As the knight gave them directions, he noted the stairs at the side of the room. "Where do those lead?"

"Sleeping quarters," Drahoslav replied. He nodded at Ernst. "One for him, one for me. He doesn't trust any servants to be here overnight, but he wouldn't sleep without a guard in case a burglar got in."

"Blankets and linen might soak up the wine better," Alaric suggested. He started up the steps. Drahoslav followed after him.

"You think this will work?" the duelist pressed him once they were out of earshot of the others.

"I don't know," Alaric admitted. He peered down the narrow hall at the top of the steps, noting five doors opening into the corridor. He gave Drahoslav a quizzical look.

"Empty," the swordsman stated. "All except the two nearest the stairs. I imagine at one point Ernst considered starting a family, but ended up deciding he didn't want the expense."

The knight turned towards the door Drahoslav indicated was Ernst's room. If the money-lender was as miserly as he seemed, he would have kept the majority of linen for his own use. His room was the best place to start looking for supplies. From what he'd seen, the commoner surrounded himself with more ostentation than his father's castle had enjoyed. Then, he supposed a man like Ernst didn't have estates to finance and farms to maintain, obligations that went hand-in-glove with a noble title.

"I've known barons who didn't live in such luxury," Alaric said when he opened the door and saw the massive bed with its silk canopy and curtains. A washstand with gold basin and crystal accouterments was nearby, a large silver mirror looming above it. Delicate rugs, their intricate patterns proclaiming them to be elf-work, were thrown about the floor. An enormous wardrobe dominated one corner, its sides carved into the semblance of roaring lions. There was a desk with a staggering array of different inks and quills, even a box that Alaric recognized as containing materials for acid-etching and a stack of thin copper sheaves beside it – necessary tools for conducting business with dwarves as they never trusted anything recorded on something so transitory as parchment or vellum.

"Your employer has done well for himself," Alaric commented, as he paced about the room.

"My employer is a petty, frightened little weasel," Drahoslav corrected the knight. "So afraid of being robbed he can't enjoy the things he owns. Thus, he hires the best sword in…" The duelist suddenly stopped. He held his hand up, motioning for Alaric to be quiet.

Alaric listened for a moment, then whispered to Drahoslav, "I don't hear anything."

"Exactly," Drahoslav said. "Where'd the crows go?"

The knight cursed himself for not noticing. When had that clamor from the zombie birds stopped? Moreover, why had it stopped?

Then a new sound intruded upon the silence. A dull, persistent tapping followed by the crackle of splintering wood. Alaric dashed back into the hall. "That's not coming from downstairs. That's up here!" He took a few steps and turned to one of the doors. "You said these rooms were empty."

"They should be," Drahoslav said, his rapier at the ready.

Alaric kicked the locked door, sending it crashing inward.

As it was flung back, his eyes fixated on the opposite wall. There was a barred window there, but only a few rays of sunlight streamed into the room. Most of the vantage was blocked by feathered bodies. A swarm of crows, their sharp beaks pecking away at the shutter. Before he could make a move, the shutter lost its battle to block the window and fell to the floor.

"They found a way in!" Alaric shouted. The moment the shutter fell, crows careened into the room. Several of them rushed past the knight and into the hall before he could pull the door closed and seal up the room again.

"Seven or eight got past me," Drahoslav snarled. One of the birds was stuck on his rapier, battering him with its wings as it tried to free itself. He shook the crow off, then stamped on its head before it could pick itself up.

Shrieks of terror rose from below. Alaric pushed past Drahoslav and hurried for the stairs. "Stay here and call out if more get in!" he yelled as he dashed down to the sitting room.

The room below was a shambles. The old midwife was stretched out on the floor, three of the decayed crows picking at her flesh. Another man was pressed up against the wall, struggling to keep one of the black birds from pecking out his eyes. The taverner had managed to fell one of the creatures, smashing it so forcefully that it was plastered against the wall, but another crow had its claws in his shoulder and had gouged a hole into his cheek with its beak.

Alaric rushed to the midwife, using the flat of his sword to scatter the zombie birds. They hopped only a few feet away, then sprang at him. One got its claws caught in his mail as it dove for his chest, frantically twisting and turning to try and sink its beak into his face. Another slammed into his shield when he raised it. When it fell to the floor, he fell after it, pressing it with his shield and pulverizing the creature with his armored weight.

The third crow came at his back, flapping its wings about his head as it strove to peck through his helm. Blinded by the feathers slapping at his eyes, Alaric dropped his sword and reached back to grab the bird. It tried to stab him with its beak, but his mail glove withstood its attack. Sinking his fingers into the creature, he twisted its avian body until he felt its bones snap. When its strength was spent, he threw it across the floor. Tilting his head, he glared down at the crow with its claws caught in the chain links of his armor. A blow from his mailed fist knocked it free, a kick from his steel boot sent it slamming into the wall.

The knight didn't even have a moment to catch his breath or to see how the others in the sitting room were faring. From the shop itself, he heard Hulmul yelling. "Stop! You'll kill us all!"

Alaric spun around and ran into the front room, but it was already too late. Overcome by panic, Ernst had fled the sitting room when the zombie crows flew down. Terror drove reason from the man's brain, but also poured strength into his body. He seized hold of the counter barricading the door and managed to shove it aside.

"No, you fool!" Alaric shouted. He tried to seize Ernst, but it was too late. The money-lender whipped the door open and darted out into the street.

Dread seized the knight. He expected to see the entire flock of crows stream into the shop. Instead, the birds dove away from the building and pursued the money-lender as he fled down the lane. He continued to run when only a few landed on him, but at last the screaming wretch was toppled by the black-feathered swarm. He slammed against the cobblestones, and the next instant was completely smothered by clawing, pecking birds.

"Wotun have mercy," Alaric gasped as he pushed the door close again. In trying to escape, Ernst had only quickened his own death.

The knight shifted the counter back into place, one of the townsfolk helping him set it tight behind the door. He turned from the labor to see Drahoslav emerge from the sitting room, raking a cloth along the gory length of his rapier.

"They stopped trying to get in upstairs," he told Alaric. The duelist nodded at the room behind him. "These ones are accounted for. The old woman's dead. The others…" He shrugged.

Hulmul noted the grim expression that came on Alaric's face. "Wait," the wizard enjoined him. "We don't know if the crows carry the plague. They may not be able to infect their victims, or perhaps they can only pass the contagion to other crows."

Alaric nodded slowly. He had no taste for killing wounded men. "Bind their wounds," he decided. "Bind their arms also and gag them. If they do become zombies, we can render them helpless to inflict harm."

The townsfolk hurried to carry out the knight's instructions. Alaric turned back to Hulmul. "The dilemma remains. Once those crows are finished with Ernst, they'll be back." He sighed, feeling the full burden of leadership and the agony of watching those he led die. "How do we get away from them?"

Alaric's question was one that Hulmul had been pondering since the moment they'd become trapped in the building. It wasn't until he saw Ernst's terrible death, however, that an idea started to form.

"We can't depend on force of arms," Hulmul said.

"There speaks someone unversed in the sword." Drahoslav scowled at the wizard.

Hulmul gave him an indulgent smile and gestured at the rapier. "Indeed, and how many of those creatures do you think you can kill before their sheer numbers overcome you? Your blade will be as useful against them as it would be against a raging torrent. These aren't natural animals, not anymore. They can't be frightened off by killing a few of them. You'll have to destroy them all to win that way."

"Is there another way?" Alaric asked.

"Use their own nature against them. Exploit what we already know." Hulmul stroked the scaly head of his familiar. "The undead are many things, but they aren't versatile. Once you understand how a zombie will react, it will do the same thing every time with little variation." Malicious uttered an angry hiss and nipped at the wizard's hand.

"I don't see how that helps us." Drahoslav nodded at the ceiling. "The crows will just come back and now that they know they can get in upstairs, they're sure to try again. We don't have enough people to watch every window and door."

Hulmul stared thoughtfully at Malicious for a moment. The familiar was irascible and mean-tempered, but even so he shared a connection with it that few except a wizard would understand. It wasn't an easy thing to send it into danger. Yet he could see no other way.

"I was speaking of their other reactions," Hulmul explained. "How they all swarmed after Ernst the moment he ran out into the street. They'd pursue other prey if it appeared."

"Another illusion?" Alaric wondered.

Hulmul shook his head. "An illusion must be maintained by a mind active enough to be deceived. No, the zombies won't be tricked that way." He waved his hand at the ceiling. "You'll have to open one of the windows upstairs. Be as quiet as you can. While the crows linger in this vicinity, any noise could bring them swarming back to this building. You make a mistake, Drahoslav, thinking they can remember how they got in before, but they are certain to find their way in again if they're reminded that there's food here."

"Why the window? What's your plan?" the knight pressed him.

"I'll send Malicious to draw them away," Hulmul answered slowly. "If he can get the crows far enough, we can make our escape."

"If the wizard thinks it'll work, we should try it," Drahoslav said. "It beats waiting here for the place to be surrounded again."

The duelist and the knight hurried back upstairs. Hulmul sent part of his awareness into Malicious and compelled the reptile to follow them. He could see the lavish bed chamber the men stepped into through his familiar's eyes. He watched as Drahoslav forced open the iron shutters that sealed one of the windows.

The instant it was open, Malicious darted to the sill. It took the creature a moment to squeeze past the bars, but then it was dropping away towards the street. Its leathery wings snapped open and it arced up out of its dive. The familiar circled above the building. Hulmul could feel the creature's agitation as it sensed danger all around.

Rooftops and lampposts for dozens of yards were black with crows. The avian zombies were as still as stone gargoyles, waiting and watching for the first sign of prey. Ernst's corpse was like a pile of bloody rags in the street, picked down to the bone in many places by the undead flock.

On its own, the winged reptile didn't present itself as something the zombies would notice. For his plan to work, Hulmul knew he'd have to change that. *I'm sorry*. He sent the thought impulse to Malicious, hoping it would understand. Then he sent into his familiar a commanding compulsion it could not defy.

The dewlap under Malicious's throat expanded into a bright fold of red scales. From its maw issued the raucous, strident mating call of its species, a sound that could crack glass if the proximity was too near.

The loud ululation instantly disturbed the zombie crows. The undead birds leaped up from their perches, taking wing as Malicious's cries struck their senses. Hulmul compelled his familiar to make one wide circle, then sent the reptile soaring off to the north, away from both Vasilescu's tower and where Helchen's group had been spotted. The grisly flocks of crows sped after Malicious.

"When… I say… take to the streets," Hulmul muttered as Alaric and Drahoslav rejoined him. He didn't dare risk withdrawing too much of his awareness from Malicious. The moment he did, the reptile would stop screeching and might lose the attention of the crows. The best chance any of them had of reaching Vasilescu's tower was to draw the murderous birds as far away as possible.

Down narrow streets, darting around corners, diving beneath archways, Malicious led the crows on a desperate chase. Left to its own, the reptile could have easily outpaced its pursuers, losing them in the confused warren of Singerva's alleyways. Hulmul, however, didn't allow his familiar that luxury. Always there was that compulsion to give its raucous cry and prevent the birds from losing its trail.

Other crows took to the sky as Malicious drew near to them. The original swarms were increased as other flocks joined the hunt. It was these lurking zombies that gave Hulmul the most concern, for there was no telling where and when they would suddenly appear.

Malicious flew onward. Now the great cathedral of Wotun was visible, an imposing edifice of white marble that stood upon a small hill. Hulmul shuddered when a veritable cloud of crows rose up from the spires and sped towards his familiar. There was nothing more to be done. He'd given the survivors as much opportunity as possible.

The reptile stifled its cry the instant Hulmul permitted it to. The dewlap folded back against its throat and it dove for the chimney of a bakery to seek refuge. Before Malicious could reach safety, it was struck from the side. One of the crows had found it and torn the leathery wing with its beak. The wizard screamed in pain and crumpled to the floor, feeling as though someone had slashed his arm.

"What is it? What's happened?" Alaric demanded, hovering over the gasping wizard.

"Get… everyone out…" Hulmul stammered between agonized grunts. He was trying to draw his awareness out of Malicious, but the pain made it difficult to concentrate. Too much of himself was still within the reptile as it crashed to the roof of the bakery. He felt the delicate bones of its wings snap with the impact.

Then the crows were diving down on him. Hulmul shrieked, feeling the beaks tearing into his body, stabbing out his eyes, ripping away his flesh.

"They… they have… Malicious," Hulmul groaned as his mind snapped back into his own body. With his familiar's destruction, there was nowhere else for his consciousness to be.

Alaric lifted him off the floor. "Can you walk?"

Hulmul gave a brief shake of his head. "Someone… must help… me." He knew he couldn't explain to this knight, or indeed any of them, what it cost a wizard to lose his familiar in such a manner. A portion of his very life force had been stripped away, a wound to the soul itself far more debilitating than the cut of a sword or the thrust of a spear. At the moment, he couldn't tell the severity of his injury, or whether it would heal at all.

"Get moving," Drahoslav ordered the townsfolk. The survivors awkwardly moved away the barricade and started into the street. "Be quick about it, before those crows come back."

If Hulmul had the energy, he could have reassured the people on that last point. Zombies, however frenzied they might be, lacked the comprehension for memory. The crows wouldn't remember the people hiding in the money-lender's. They'd linger around the cathedral now, fanning out from its vicinity only by the most gradual degrees unless some new stimulus attracted their attention and excited their predatory instincts.

No, the crows wouldn't be back. As Alaric helped Hulmul out into the street, the wizard had to wonder about his own state. Would he recover? Would *he* be back?

CHAPTER TEN

Helchen kept looking up at the narrow ribbon of sky she could glimpse from the street. The buildings had grown closer together after crossing the grand thoroughfare and created a more confined atmosphere. She preferred such a route. It felt much less exposed. A witch hunter was always wary of who might be watching.

At the moment, she was hoping for an arcane observer. When Hulmul's scaly familiar had circled them, it was obvious the creature wanted them to follow. The winged reptile offered the only way of finding Alaric and the wizard again. She still had her suspicions about Hulmul, but she was pragmatic enough to know the presence of a former pupil would make Vasilescu more likely to lend his aid. If, of course, the mage was still alive.

"Naht lampin' der slinkie-bat," Ratbag gruffed. The orc held a hand up to shield his eyes as he followed Helchen's example and tried to spot Malicious.

"He says–" Gaiseric started to translate.

"I figured it out," Helchen cut the thief off. She gave him a sharp look. "I thought you were going to keep herd on those students?"

Gaiseric glanced back at the group they'd rescued from the leatherworks. They were keeping close together, staying in the middle of the street. "Oh, none of them are going to wander off," he assured her. It had been a recurrent problem that as they moved through the town, one student or another would want to go away to check on their family when they passed near their home. "I just told them about that abomination that chased us away from the guildhall. I don't think any of them wants to risk running into that monster." The thief was thoughtful for a moment. "For that matter, neither do I."

"Be bulgin' rumpuz," Ratbag said, slapping his hand against the heft of his maul.

"I think that's one fight even you wouldn't be walking away from," Gaiseric warned the orc. "I'm still praying it didn't manage to dig itself out the way you did. I'm much happier thinking that thing is buried under a pile of rubble."

Helchen shook her head. "I doubt that abomination is still on our trail. Out of sight, out of mind. Or at least such mind as a zombie still has." She frowned as she considered that last point. While she wouldn't really define the look in the abomination's eyes as intelligence, there had certainly been an awareness there far in excess of the other undead they'd encountered.

The witch hunter shrugged away that worry and instead expressed a different one. "Out of sight out of mind seems to apply to the wizard's familiar as well." She removed her hat and ran her hand through her hair. "I'd have expected the thing to come back by now, at least to let us know we're still on the right track."

"Maybe Hulmul doesn't want it roaming around," Gaiseric suggested. "I've always heard that it's serious business if a wizard's familiar dies."

"A wizard binds a fragment of his own soul into his familiar," Helchen told him. "A dangerous and abominable practice. It's always been theorized that when they do so, a part of the animal is likewise absorbed into their own spirit. That makes their thoughts… abnormal. A wizard who makes a rat his familiar develops the verminous morality of a rat, that sort of thing." She replaced her hat and looked back at the sky. "At least such is the theory. What is undeniable is that a wizard's vitality is impacted if his familiar dies. It can leave him weakened for months or years, sometimes even cripple mind and body permanently. It's one reason witch hunters always try to unmask whatever familiar a renegade sorcerer might be employing. If it can be destroyed, the enemy is much easier to defeat. Or have you never wondered why so few of those charged with heresy use their magic to escape the Order's dungeons?"

Gaiseric gave her an uncomfortable look. "To be honest, I always figured it was because they didn't have a good set of lockpicks."

Helchen couldn't tell if Gaiseric was being flippant or combative. He was a difficult character to evaluate, and frustratingly it seemed the longer she was around him the more enigmatic he became. Almost like *he* was the one reading *her* and figuring out how to conceal things from her. It was a pity he was so contemptuous of authority. His kind of skills would be useful to the Order.

Ratbag's wolf was loping up ahead, still sniffing for any

lurking zombies. Fang went on alert, its tail straightening and its ears perking up. Helchen noticed that the animal wasn't snarling and its fur didn't bristle as it had before when it came across the undead.

"Wez gotta der quik wunz, nah cadavaz," Ratbag told them before marching over to join Fang.

"Ratbag says whoever Fang smells isn't a zombie," Gaiseric translated. "At least not yet."

"Doesn't look much like he cares," Helchen said. "He's spoiling for a fight." She looked back at the students. A few of them had armed themselves with clubs and bits of debris they'd found in the streets. Even with proper weapons, she didn't know how good they'd be in a fight. "Keep back a bit," she advised. "At least until we know what's happening."

Helchen checked her crossbow and kept it at the ready as she and Gaiseric walked up to Ratbag and Fang. The wolf was watching a side street at the next intersection. Clearly it had caught the scent before there was anything to see. "You hold back too," she told the orc. "Let me see who they are."

"Yer gotta der buddafly bootz," Ratbag grunted at her. "Whatcha noodlin'? Deyz goofz, goonz, er bimboz." He gave his mattock a meaningful pat. "Ready ta rumpuz."

"He's of the opinion anybody still alive around here is going to be crazy, bad, or both," Gaiseric said. "Ratbag might be right. We don't know what kind of people they might be."

Helchen nodded. She pointed to an overturned tun across the way. "Get around there and wait for my signal." She snapped her fingers to get Ratbag's attention and waved him over to a cart someone had abandoned at the corner. It was just large enough to hide the orc's bulk if he crouched down. "Wait until I give the signal," she emphasized.

"Yer der darb," Ratbag said. Fang trotted off with him as he took up his position.

The witch hunter found a spot behind a divan some looter had dumped in the street. She didn't think it was sturdy enough to provide cover, but at least it would afford concealment. She took off her hat and set it on the ground beside her. The crossbow she leaned against the back of the divan within easy reach. Keeping just her eyes above the splintered back of the furnishing, she watched the side street.

Helchen's vigilance was soon rewarded when a man appeared. He moved too warily to be one of the undead, and she doubted a zombie would have been able to keep the white vestments he wore as pristine as he'd managed. Still, as Ratbag had warned, just because the fellow was alive didn't mean he wasn't a threat. There was a villainous stamp about his visage, something that marked him as not only someone accustomed to killing, but someone who enjoyed it. Helchen reached for her crossbow and started to lift it. When she shot, it would give Gaiseric and Ratbag leave to spring into action.

She hesitated when she saw the people following behind the man in white. They seemed just ordinary people, not some band of ruffians scavenging the ruins. Then again, in desperate situations, what would be unthinkable to someone in better times could quickly become necessity. The group might yet be a band of robbers and killers.

Only when she saw the figure at the back of the ragged procession did the witch hunter begin to relax. "Alaric!"

she called to the knight, stepping out from her place of concealment.

Her sudden appearance startled the unknown man in white at the procession's front, whose hand flew to the hilt of the sword he wore. Alaric turned in her direction, a smile drawing at his features. Helchen saw now that the knight was supporting – all but carrying – Hulmul. The wizard was pale, his entire being had a withered appearance. It was a symptom she could recognize even from a distance, and it explained why Malicious had failed to reappear.

The swordsman in white was tense when he saw Helchen appear, and had his rapier drawn when Gaiseric stepped into view, but Alaric's assurances that the thief and the witch hunter were friends kept him restrained. The real crisis was when Ratbag came into view. The townsfolk recoiled from the orc and his wolf. Alaric sprang away from Hulmul, leaving the wizard to support himself with his staff. The knight unstrapped his shield from his back and curled his fingers around the grip. Sword drawn, he advanced on Ratbag.

"Stop!" Helchen called out to Alaric. "He's not an enemy! He helped us against the zombies!" The witch hunter dashed toward the two warriors, but she could see she'd be too late. Neither knight nor orc was going to give ground. They seemed determined to fight.

Gaiseric was closer than Helchen and ran over to prevent the fray. He grabbed the edge of Alaric's surcoat and pulled him back. "That's brilliant!" the thief snapped. "Let's just kill each other and save the zombies the trouble!"

"That's an orc," Alaric growled at Gaiseric.

"Now's not really the time or place where you can pick your

friends," the thief told him. He twisted around and shook his fist at Ratbag. "And you can calm down too. If he can't stab you, you can't bash him with that over-sized hammer either!"

"Giffer der frosh der turn ta lamp wotz wotz," Ratbag bared his fangs at Alaric. The wolf snarled and started to circle the knight.

Helchen let the bolt from her crossbow slam into the cobblestones between the antagonists. Both of them turned towards her. Under their gaze, she loaded another bolt and started to crank back the string. "Gaiseric told you how things stand. You two want to kill each other, how about you let it wait until we've gotten these people to safety?" She saw the point she raised was one that punctured Alaric's stance. Whatever animosity he held for orcs, it wasn't greater than his sense of duty.

"A little fight now, or a big one later," Gaiseric addressed Ratbag. The orc was more impressed with that line of reasoning. He took a step back.

"They're killers," Alaric said, wagging his sword at Ratbag. "Monsters without honor or decency."

"Sounds like someone damn helpful to have around in the current circumstances," Helchen stated.

Alaric pointed at the steel plate Ratbag wore on his arm. "Ask him where he got that! I'll tell you. He stripped it from a fallen knight before a bunch of orcs hacked up the body and roasted it over their campfires."

Ratbag scowled at Alaric's speech. "Hooey. Der glad ragz iz upanup. Kale fer lampin' ginkz fer bullz."

"He says that was a reward for scouting," Gaiseric explained. The knight's expression only soured more. "A renegade," he spat. "Spying on his own people to make gold. You're going to trust *that*?"

"I hardly think the zombies are going to try to bribe him," Helchen told Alaric.

"Naht stuckon wotz ginkz be noodlin', naht stuckon wotz der frosh be noodlin'." Ratbag hefted his broad shoulders in a rude approximation of a shrug.

"He doesn't care what other orcs think, why should he care what… well, you think?" Gaiseric translated.

Alaric glowered at Ratbag. "Just keep him away from me," he said, before stalking off.

Helchen watched him cross the street, then glanced over at Ratbag. The orc was tapping the pommel of his scimitar with one finger, a vicious gleam in his eyes. "As though I needed more problems," she grumbled.

"Sorry to add… another." Hulmul coughed, each word intoned as though he had to dredge it up from deep inside. "But… I need help… just now." He rapped the staff on which he was leaning.

The wizard swept an anxious gaze along the street. "I'd rather… not be… stuck here… when some zombies… decide to investigate all that racket."

Helchen looked over at the white swordsman, but it was clear from his haughty expression that he'd no intention of helping the wizard. She didn't know if she could trust the townsfolk or students not to abandon Hulmul if they were attacked by zombies. For that matter, Ratbag was a poor prospect, though in the orc's case he'd be running toward, not away from the enemy.

"Gaiseric, lend your shoulder to Hulmul," Helchen said as

she finished cranking her crossbow. "Let's hope your teacher's tower isn't too far off, wizard."

"I suppose it would be a stupid question to ask if that's the place?" Gaiseric said to Hulmul as they crouched down within the stalls of an abandoned stable.

There were wide gaps in the slats of the wall to ease the flow of air within the stables. They also afforded an easy view of the imposing structure across the way. Colossal was the only way Gaiseric could describe the tower. It was hundreds of feet high, taller than the castle back at Mertz, even including the promontory on which it stood. Enormous buttresses anchored the foundations and stretched up along much of the facade. They seemed too thin to actually support the immense construction, and Gaiseric felt his skin crawl when he considered that it was Vasilescu's magic that made such architecture possible.

Away from the tower, as Hulmul had warned, there stretched a vast graveyard, so overcrowded with markers and monuments that, at a distance, it looked like a big jumble of stone. Nearer at hand, only a hundred yards from the stables, was the broad ditch that surrounded the tower, and it was this feature that truly troubled the thief. Flames crackled all along the moat. Fire where a mundane fortress would employ water!

The flames were needed. All about the tower zombies had gathered. Gaiseric thought there must be hundreds of the undead. The creatures moved with the same mindless lurch they'd seen before, but whenever they got too near the moat, the heat would cause them to divert and turn back.

"Looks like a secure place," the swordsman Drahoslav said. "But how are we supposed to get in there?"

"That should be your specialty," Alaric told Gaiseric.

The thief shot the knight a dirty look. "If I was considering that place from a professional angle, I'd abandon the idea the moment I knew a wizard lived there." He nodded in apology to Hulmul, just in case the dazed man was following the conversation.

"But if you did decide to tackle it?" Helchen pressed him.

Gaiseric gave the tower a closer study. "If I wasn't worried about some spell giving me away or turning me into a newt, I'd think about getting onto that roof over there." He pointed to a funerary chapel several dozen yards to the left of the stables. Though dwarfed by the tower, it was a large building with a belltower about fifty feet off the ground. "I'd try to shoot an arrow – with a rope attached, naturally – into that window." He indicated a narrow opening that was roughly at the same level as the steeple.

"And then?" Alaric inquired when Gaiseric fell silent.

"And then nothing," the thief replied. "It would be wasted effort. If I did get inside, I wouldn't be able to get all these people in." Gaiseric waved back at the stalls behind them where the other survivors were doing their best to keep quiet.

Helchen directed Gaiseric's attention to the immense drawbridge in the face of the tower. "No, but you could open the door for us. Lower the drawbridge and I guarantee we'd waste no time getting across it." She pointed at the iron-banded oak of its construction. "Unless Vasilescu has put enchantments on it, which is likely, all things considered, we'd only have a few minutes before it started to burn in any event."

"We'll need a way to get past the zombies," Alaric mused. "Draw them away long enough to get through." The knight thought for a moment. "Someone would have to divert their attention."

Hulmul coughed out a reply. "When… the drawbridge is… lowered… I might… be helpful…"

Gaiseric scratched his chin. *If* he could get the drawbridge lowered… "It still wouldn't work," he decided. "You'd need an expert archer to make that shot."

Drahoslav smiled at the thief. "The sword isn't the only weapon I've mastered," he bragged. "Get me a proper bow and a decent arrow to shoot, I could make that shot."

Gaiseric had only known the duelist a little while, but he was already finding the man's haughtiness bothersome. "That's the other problem. We don't have the tools. We need a bow, some thin cord, a stout rope…" He ticked off each item on his fingers as though taking inventory.

"I know where we could get the bow," one of the townsfolk offered. Like the rest of the survivors, she'd been paying close attention to the discussion. "There's a bowyer who had a shop not far from here."

Drahoslav turned to the woman. "Take me there," he said. "I'll see if there's anything in the fellow's inventory that looks suitable."

"We also need…" Gaiseric started to say. His words were drowned out by Alaric as the knight marched through the stables.

"Does anyone know where to get rope?" the knight engaged the survivors. "A grapple? Some strong cord?" As each item was called off, someone replied to Alaric, recalling a blacksmith or a ropewalk where the needed implements might be found.

Ratbag swaggered over to Gaiseric and slapped the thief on the back. The orc chuckled at his distress. "Yer shudda noodl'd," he grunted. "Der goofz der sap as squawkz 'steada stayin' dumb."

Gaiseric shook his head. "You're right. If I was half as smart as I think I am, I'd have kept quiet."

Still inwardly berating himself, Gaiseric followed Drahoslav and the woman who had offered to guide them – a student named Ilona – out into the street. The trio cautiously picked their way down the lane, frequently glancing back in the direction of the plaza. The thief didn't know what they would do if the horde of zombies noticed them and started their way.

"We're the first group to leave," Drahoslav advised Gaiseric. He wagged a finger to indicate a couple of the other students stealing away from the stables. "The zombies will go for whoever's closest."

Ilona directed a look of disgust at the duelist. Gaiseric shared her sentiment. "Is that why you volunteered? Found yourself the safest place?"

Drahoslav gave him a thin smile as they circled through the shambles of what had been a corner smithery. Except for the huge forge, it looked like everything inside the place had been smashed to splinters or bent out of usable shape. "I don't stick my neck out for anybody," he said, a note of pride in his callous words.

"Coward," Ilona scowled.

The duelist's hand clenched the hilt of his rapier. "There's an ugly word I don't like to hear twice."

"It suits a man who tries to stay safe," Ilona retorted, defiance in her expression.

Gaiseric sighed and darted back to peer out of the broken facade into the street. He now had a new appreciation for Helchen's anxiety when he'd let himself get into a shouting match with Ratbag. "Safety isn't something to shy away from. We're hoping Hulmul can provide a distraction, so there's no need for us to start one now."

Ilona glanced over at Gaiseric. "I know you're brave, but by his own speech, this foppish knave says he has no stomach for a fight."

"She has a point," Gaiseric said, addressing Drahoslav. "The way Alaric tells it, you were helpful at the money-lender's, but maybe that's because you didn't have anywhere to run..."

The words caught in Gaiseric's throat. In a blur of motion, Drahoslav whipped out his sword and had its point tickling the rogue's neck.

"Call me a coward again, cutpurse, and you won't need to worry about the undead." Drahoslav spun around and stung Ilona's hand with the flat of his blade as she started to raise a club she'd found as a means of defense. The bludgeon clattered on the floor. The duelist regarded them both for a moment, then sheathed his sword with a theatrical flourish. He smirked as he brushed dust from his sleeve.

"I've killed many foes," he announced. "Always in open combat. I've left outraged counts and hired assassins alike as carrion for the corpse-carts. Forty duels since coming to Singerva and I've never taken a scratch." Drahoslav smiled and smoothed the front of his immaculate tunic. His gaze swept from Gaiseric to Ilona. "You're right, I do play it safe, but when it's a question of swordplay, there's no danger for me. It's whoever... whatever... has decided to stand against me that takes all the risk."

Gaiseric swallowed the knot that had grown in his throat. Maybe Drahoslav was boasting, but the speed with which he moved wasn't a pretense. "I could, of course, be in error," he said, his voice sheepish.

Drahoslav gave him a slight nod by way of acknowledgment, then looked over at Ilona. "You said there's a bowyer. Lead on, and let's hope there's a weapon there that's worthy of my talent. Let's hope the others have had better luck."

As they moved through the debris and exited onto a street behind the smithy, Gaiseric hoped the duelist was as skilled as he was insufferable.

It took a few hours before the rest of the supplies were gathered. Gaiseric wasn't sure if he should be pleased or horrified that the gear the other survivors had collected looked to be exactly what he needed. Briefly he debated claiming otherwise, but one of the groups had run into a pack of zombies while out gathering rope. Two of them had been killed to further this plan. Gaiseric felt obliged to make sure their sacrifice wasn't in vain.

Gaiseric, Drahoslav, and Ratbag carefully made a circuit over to the funerary chapel, the orc's wolf present to warn of any zombies. At least that was what Gaiseric hoped it could do. He wasn't sure if the presence of the horde surrounding the tower would make it difficult for Fang to sniff out any undead inside the building.

At the best of times, a funerary chapel was a grim place. The dour effigies of Khaiza, Mistress of the Tomb, weren't such as to really comfort anyone. Her robed figure and crone-like visage didn't reassure mourners that there was tranquility in the grave, but rather reminded them of their own impending mortality. That was a reminder Gaiseric could have done without, considering what he was about to do.

"There's the stairs to the bell," Drahoslav commented. He had the bow, a masterfully crafted weapon of elven make, slung over his shoulder and a ready hand on his rapier. The arrows in the quiver had been placed with the heads up and the feathers inside. This was to accommodate the iron cross-pieces that had been tied a little behind the arrowhead. Gaiseric was worried that the added weight would interfere with Drahoslav's aim, but after holding one in his palm, the duelist insisted it wouldn't be a problem.

"Ratbag, stay here and keep watch," Gaiseric told the orc. He gave the darkened steps a worried look, then followed Drahoslav up into the belltower.

The stairs curled back onto themselves as they ascended, creating a squared spiral. Drahoslav roved ahead of Gaiseric, climbing at a much more rapid pace. The thief lingered behind, nerving himself for what was to come.

"They're all depending on you," he reminded himself, then groaned at the reminder. "That's the worst part." It was one thing if he broke his own neck, but he agonized over the fix that would put the other survivors in.

The sudden rasp of steel scraping free of a scabbard startled Gaiseric. An instant later he saw something small and black plunge down the middle of the stairway. Drawing his own sword, the thief hurried upward. He glared at Drahoslav when he found the duelist standing over half of a dead crow.

"You gave me a fright," the thief snapped. "Scaring me over a blasted crow!"

Drahoslav wiped the gore from his blade. "You weren't around the last time I saw crows." He returned the rapier to its scabbard and continued up. "We're here," he announced.

The top of the belltower was a narrow platform. The priests of Khaiza were either foolhardy or contemptuous of death, for there wasn't a railing around the platform, only the posts that supported the roof from which the bell hung. The bell, a monstrous thing that must have weighed a ton if it weighed a pound, left little room on the platform for the two men.

"That's the window I need," Gaiseric stated, pointing at the slender opening in the tower's facade. He tried not to look down, but the flicker of flames compelled his gaze. The fiery moat, the masses of zombies… either one would mean certain doom.

Drahoslav unslung the bow and poised himself at the very edge of the platform. He plucked one of the arrows from the quiver and nocked it to the string.

"Now, take your time," Gaiseric encouraged him. "We made plenty of arrows. If you miss the first time…"

The arrow flew from the bow, speeding across the plaza and the moat, the rope fitted to it playing out as it went. To Gaiseric's wonder, the shot sped straight through the window.

"I never need to do something twice," Drahoslav boasted. He stepped back and motioned Gaiseric to take his place.

Gaiseric grabbed the rope and gave it a tug. The danger now was that the arrow, with its crosspiece, would fail to find purchase inside the tower and pull free. If that happened, Drahoslav would need to try again. Yet, to the thief's surprise, even in this the duelist's shot had been true. Pulling on the rope, he was pleased to find it held fast. He motioned to Drahoslav and together they took in such slack as there was. There'd been little room for error in the length. Too much slack and it would have dropped down where the zombies could grab at it. As it was, several of them noticed the movement above them and tilted their decayed heads back to see what was going on.

"Secure the other end to the bell," Gaiseric directed Drahoslav. Whatever happened, he was certain that bell wasn't going to budge. Once the rope was taut between the bell and the tower window, Gaiseric reached into his pockets and removed a pair of calfskin gloves. Thick enough to protect his hands, but thin enough that he'd lose none of his dexterity.

"If I succeed, I'll get the drawbridge lowered halfway," Gaiseric said, reiterating the plan the survivors had developed. "When it is, that's the signal to make for the tower. It'll be down all the way before you reach the moat."

Gaiseric turned back and stared at the rope. There was a good sixty feet between the chapel and the tower. A good distance to cover, climbing hand over hand. One slip, and even if he didn't break his neck in the fall, the zombies were certain to finish him.

"A great plan," Gaiseric muttered as he lowered himself over the side and began pulling himself along the rope. "I just wish there was somebody else around to take over for me."

Low moans rose from the zombies below. They'd clearly noticed him climbing above them. Gaiseric resisted the urge to see what they were doing. He'd cleared about thirty feet before the compulsion was too great to deny. He at once wished he hadn't. What was below him was a lake of rotten faces and outstretched hands. Some of the runners were making wild leaps, trying to grab his legs and pull him down. They were well short of reaching him, but the dogged persistence with which they tried sent a shiver down his back.

Nearer now was the tower and the flames of the moat. Sweat dripped from his forehead as the heat washed over him. Gaiseric had intended the gloves simply to keep the rope from chafing his hands, but now he could feel his palms sweating and was even more thankful. If he lost his grip he'd plunge into the fire and burn. A death only marginally better than being ripped apart by the undead.

At last Gaiseric reached the end of the rope. He swung his leg over the windowsill and tried to slip inside. Instantly a hideous revelation came to him. The opening was too narrow. He might get a leg in, but he couldn't squeeze his body through.

"Ten curses on misfortune," Gaiseric hissed. He unwound the trim cord wrapped about his waist and unhooked the grappling iron from his belt. He craned his neck back, staring up at the expanse between the window and the roof of the tower. "I was hoping I wouldn't have to do this. Just once, I wish someone wouldn't be so worried about burglars breaking into their homes."

The thief swung the grapple in a loose circle, careful not to play out so much cord that it dipped into the flames. As he built up momentum, Gaiseric cast it up at one of the buttresses. The hook caught on one of the carvings that adorned the support. He tested to make sure it was secure, then scrambled up the cord to his new perch.

"Cast and climb," Gaiseric said once he had a firm footing. He withdrew the hook and repeated the process. "And make damn sure not to look at how far you have to fall," he ordered himself.

By slow, arduous process, the thief finally reached the roof. Gaiseric scowled when he found that the parapet was edged with broken glass. "He honestly expected someone to climb up here," the thief marveled as he cautiously pulled himself onto the flattened roof. He was surprised to find that it resembled a garden. Potted flowers, a fishpond, marble benches.

"I guess I can see why Vasilescu would try to keep people out," Gaiseric said as he scrutinized his surroundings.

"I'm glad you're so understanding."

The voice rose from nowhere. As far as Gaiseric's eyes could tell, he was alone on the roof. Yet something more primal than his senses warned him that he was anything but alone.

"Vasilescu? Who is that?" he demanded, suddenly full of fear. He could see no one.

The voice chuckled. "I should ask you the same. Breaking into a wizard's tower, many would think you had ill intentions. Perhaps I should render you immobile until you confess your true purpose…"

"Please, no!" Gaiseric begged, knowing time was of the essence and terrified of being spellbound. "My companions are fighting for their lives outside the tower. We've come to seek aid. You have to help us."

Silence. And then the voice said, "Tell me why."

Gaiseric took a deep breath to calm his nerves and began to explain, knowing each moment brought his companions closer to their fate.

CHAPTER ELEVEN

Alaric kept careful watch on the drawbridge from the stables. It had been nerve-wracking to see Gaiseric climb across the plaza, and even worse to observe while he ascended the face of the tower. Several times, he was certain the thief would fall to his death, but at last he clambered onto the roof.

That had been several minutes ago. Alaric tried to picture what the interior of the tower might be like. How long it would take Gaiseric to reach the windlass that raised and lowered the drawbridge. He wondered what kind of reception he'd receive from Vasilescu or the wizard's servants when and if they discovered him. If Hulmul wasn't so weak, he'd have asked him more about his mentor. Vasilescu had a reputation as a great man, but it was Alaric's experience that the great and the good were not always the same. Would the wizard even deign to help?

Commotion at the back of the stables drew the knight's attention. He started back, sword and shield at the ready, but relaxed again when he saw it was Drahoslav and Ratbag returning from the chapel. For just an instant he held the orc's brutish gaze. At least the renegade made no effort to hide his hostility. It gave him the impression that if Ratbag decided to fight, the knight would at least know the attack was coming first.

"Get them ready," Alaric told Helchen, as he turned back to his vigil. "When we get the signal, we'll have to move fast."

"What about drawing off the zombies?" Helchen asked, pointing at Hulmul.

The wizard glanced over at them. "I'll… try something. A spell to… draw them off."

Alaric didn't think Hulmul could stand on his feet, much less conjure a spell. "We'll need whatever you can manage," he assured him.

They'd also need every blade. With Gaiseric gone and Hulmul incapacitated, there were only four among them Alaric felt he could depend on. There was an irony in Ratbag being someone he considered dependable, but if there was one thing an orc could be counted on for, it was violence. He was certain the brute would hold his own when the time came to charge across the plaza. Indeed, Alaric's plan was to form a wedge, with Helchen and Drahoslav at the center and himself and Ratbag anchoring the sides. The witch hunter and the duelist were finesse fighters, while the knight and the orc were brawlers, better able to sustain themselves in a protracted melee. If it came to it, they could try to distract the zombies while the rest of the wedge pushed on to the tower. He only hoped Ratbag would follow his lead if it became necessary.

The long minutes dragged on and still there was no movement from the drawbridge. Alaric's worries increased. Gaiseric had been discovered and met a hostile reception. Vasilescu wasn't going to let them in.

Then, the knight saw a quiver pass through the drawbridge. He thought at first it was a trick of the eyes, an effect of keeping his gaze focused on it for too long. The creak of chains and the groan of timber spoke otherwise. The drawbridge was indeed being lowered.

"Gaiseric did it," Alaric hissed to the others in the stables, careful to keep his voice low lest any zombies be drawn to the sound.

"Everyone's ready," Helchen said. A glance back showed the survivors assembled in rough formation. Hulmul and the wounded were at the center. Ratbag stood to one side, waiting to throw back the main doors.

Alaric watched the drawbridge start to creep downward. To him, it seemed to take an agonizingly long time, but he knew his impressions could hardly be considered impartial. The chain continued to spool outward as the timber span was lowered. When it halted, that would be the signal to start across the plaza.

The rattle of the chains didn't go unnoticed by the zombies. To Alaric's horror, he saw the undead start to converge on the sound. Scores of zombies, shambling directly to where the survivors needed to go! Too many to have any chance of fighting their way through.

The sound of shattering glass rang out from another part of the plaza. Many zombies turned and staggered off after the noise. Alaric lifted his gaze and saw a fat-bellied alembic come sailing down from the roof of the tower. It exploded against the cobblestones, the noisy impact drawing zombies away. Other bottles, full and empty, went hurtling to the plaza. The undead masses thinned out as they were drawn away.

Alaric looked down again and saw that the drawbridge projected at an angle over the fiery moat. Flames licked up at it but failed to so much as char the wood. Helchen's speculation about enchantment appeared to be true. He waited, but it didn't descend any further.

"Now!" the knight snapped the command. Ratbag shoved open the doors and the wedge of survivors dashed out into the street. The orc and his wolf ran to anchor the left side while Alaric hurried to his post on the right.

There were still some zombies in the hundred yards between the survivors and the tower. Alaric felt disgust when they turned their dead faces toward the refugees and reached toward them with groping hands. Helchen snapped off a shot and dropped one with a bolt through its skull, but there were at least ten still standing in their way. Worse, the ones that had been drawn off by breaking bottles were now turning back. He looked over at Hulmul, but the wizard's condition looked worse rather than better. There was no distracting the zombies now that they sensed living prey was near.

"They're not all so slow," Drahoslav shouted as a runner charged at him. His rapier pierced its heart, spilling the creature to the ground.

Alaric could see more of the runners hurrying toward the wedge. The slower walkers impeded their progress, but he knew the ravenous zombies would force a way through.

"The bridge is dropping!" Helchen cried. The drawbridge had again resumed its descent, but far too slow to suit Alaric. By the time they reached it, he was certain the runners would be upon them. He'd have to try and pull the undead away from the main body. Give them the time they needed to escape. But first they had to clear away the ones blocking their path.

"Hurry to the moat!" the knight commanded. "Don't bother trying to kill them, just push them into the flames!"

Everyone in the wedge picked up their pace. Though more comfortable fighting from a horse, there were times when Alaric had led men-at-arms into moors and forests to engage brigands and the odd orc raiding party that had strayed down from the frontier. Even with the bridge still up, at least they'd have the moat to keep them from being completely surrounded.

The zombies were tireless, relentless, but they had no concept of unity. When the survivors closed upon them, it was as a single mass. The undead were thrust back when the living smashed into them. There wasn't a townsman or student who hadn't picked up some loose board or broken box to use in lieu of a shield. They now used these to drive against the zombies. Many were raked by the claws of their cadaverous enemy, but they were able to keep the decayed teeth away from their bodies.

"Into the fire!" Helchen cried. At the head of the formation, she and Drahoslav plied their blades relentlessly, battering zombies with their pommels, anything to force the undead back. As they met resistance, the wedge fanned out into a line.

"Sizzlin' der cadavaz!" Ratbag howled. The orc's mattock struck a zombie with such force that the creature was thrown through the air to slam into several of its fellows and send them all stumbling closer to the moat.

Alaric used his shield to bash the undead before him. His

sword slashed at the creatures that tried to slip around him, hewing rotten limbs from their decayed bodies. He risked a glance over his shoulder. Several runners had broken through the mass of walkers and were now charging straight at them.

A cheer went up from the survivors. Alaric turned back to see the first zombies pushed back into the flames. It was eerie watching them fall, for even as they pitched down into the fire, no screams rose from them.

The survivors were close to the drawbridge now. Alaric evaluated their chances. A dozen yards, perhaps less, but it was still too far. They needed more time. For an instant he felt bitterness swell up inside him. Who were these people to him anyway? He'd come to Singerva to find the resources to avenge his family and kill Gogol, not rescue some rabble. He could leave them behind and reach the tower. Live to see the necromancer dead.

But duty was an even stronger force within Alaric's heart than revenge. Instead of making a dash for the drawbridge, he drew back and prepared for what he had to do. "Ratbag! Draw the zombies away!" He clanked his sword against his shield as he pivoted and faced the horde. "Over here! See what you can do against a von Mertz!" He couldn't see if Ratbag was following his example, for at that moment a runner diverted from its rush toward the survivors to charge at him. His sword cleaved its decayed head from its shoulders.

The knight pushed on, forcing the few zombies before him into the flames. Then he was himself sent stumbling forward. A runner was on Alaric's back, mindlessly struggling to tear through his mail. He tried to dislodge the zombie, but then a second ravening undead sprang at him. He managed to turn his shield towards it, fending off its lunge. From the corner of his eye, he saw a third runner sprinting at him, its necrotic mouth open in a soundless shriek. Alaric just managed to drive his sword into the creature, splitting its leg and dropping it to the ground.

The zombie on Alaric's back continued to flail and tear at him. He felt the mail around his throat pull tight as the monster worried at the coif, trying to chew its way to his neck. Foiled by his armor, the creature remained a deadly menace, for its rabid fury was pushing the knight towards the moat. He tried to free himself, but the runner he'd struck with his shield came lunging back.

Alaric twisted around. This time he dipped his shield, catching the zombie on it. He quickly turned the kite shield and used the runner's own momentum to pitch it over into the moat.

Something snatched at his leg when Alaric tried once more to wrest the zombie from his back. He knew it was the creature whose leg he'd shattered. The mangled corpse clung to him and tried to pull itself up his body. He stabbed down with his sword, splitting its skull. The now lifeless claws continued to cling to him, weighing him down and unbalancing him still further.

Alaric slashed at the runner on his back, but he wasn't able to deal the thing a telling wound at such an awkward angle. If he could only free himself of the zombie before it sent them both into the flames!

As he struggled with the runner, Alaric saw two more charging for him. The drawbridge was down now, and the other survivors were clambering onto it. His diversion had succeeded. Being the nearest living thing to them, the knight became the natural target for the zombies.

Burdened by two zombies, Alaric didn't see any way to fend off two more. He was resigned to casting himself into the moat and preventing his own return as one of the undead when he suddenly saw Ratbag barrel into the runners. The orc's mattock struck one with such force that its chest caved in, leaving it a writhing mass on the ground. The other managed to champ at Ratbag's arm but broke its teeth on the steel enclosing it. Ratbag shifted his grip on the mattock and grabbed the biter by the neck. With one hand, he hefted it up off the ground and threw it into the blazing trench.

Alaric shook his head in wonder. If anyone had ever told him his life would be saved by an orc, he'd have called them mad.

More runners were rushing towards the scene now. Ratbag stood ready to meet them, a sadistic grin on his brutal face. "Cmon ta der rub, yer bimboz!" The orc smashed the first of the zombies flat with his mattock.

Singly or in small groups, the runners might pose small threat to the orc, but Alaric could see that the horde of walkers were now closing in. Ratbag would need to cut and run or be overwhelmed. Either way, he wouldn't be able to help the knight more than he already had.

If Alaric was going to free himself, he'd have to take desperate measures. Unable to pull or cut the runner free, he chose the course left to him. Kicking out his feet, Alaric dropped backwards. He heard the crack of bones as the zombie was crushed by his armored weight. The problem lay in how much damage he'd been able to do. If the creature had the strength to hold him down, he'd be helpless when more zombies came.

The knight rolled onto his side, feeling the crushed zombie peel away from his body as he did so. A glance showed him that its head had been crushed. Free to act now, Alaric swiftly pulled away the dead hands of the other creature.

"Ratbag! Move!" Alaric called to the orc. The occupants of the tower saw the walkers closing in and were starting to raise the drawbridge again. Everyone but himself and Ratbag had made it across. If they didn't hurry, they'd be left alone against the massed undead.

Alaric sprinted to the rising drawbridge. He threw his sword and shield ahead of him, watching them sail over the edge and into the tower. Then he leaped for the timber. His hands just caught the edge as it continued to rise. He grabbed at one of the iron bands that reinforced the span, using it to help pull himself up. He felt the drag of his armor as he hung suspended for a moment, then with a herculean effort, he swung one of his legs over the side. He now found himself on the incline. Looking down, he could see Helchen and several others watching him from the entryway. The witch hunter made frantic motions to someone inside. All at once, the motion of the drawbridge stopped. It was still a precarious climb down to the entrance, but at least the prospect of plunging the whole distance was mitigated.

A dull impact against the timbers nearly made Alaric lose his hold. He looked back to see if any of the zombies, possibly some of the runners, had tried to leap the moat. What he found was Ratbag clinging to the middle of the drawbridge.

The orc gave him a toothy grimace that could be either a grin or a snarl.

Whether it was a friendly or hostile look, Alaric's sense of chivalry made him crawl along the top of the drawbridge to reach the orc and help him over. After all, Ratbag had come back when he could just as easily have left the knight to the zombies. He told him as much as he pulled the renegade over.

"Why'd you come back for me?" Alaric asked.

"Naht gonna letta dolledup frosh hawg der rumpuz," Ratbag said. He looked back at the zombie-infested plaza. "Hadda lam. Ditch'd der ritzy sockdallaga." Alaric guessed he was talking about the mattock, which the orc must have left behind.

"Gotta shiv fer der cadavaz," Ratbag added, patting the scimitar hanging from his belt.

"You're bound to get the chance to use it soon enough," Alaric assured the orc as they climbed down the half-raised drawbridge. It was certain Singerva had no shortage of undead still prowling its streets. Enough, maybe, to make even an orc tire of battle.

Hulmul's entire body ached, and his head felt as if a goblin had been using it to crack snails open. His thoughts had an indistinct feel about them, as if they were a jumble of abstracts that were struggling to find a cohesive structure.

Questions bubbled up through his mind. Who was he? Well, that one was easy enough to answer, though it took him a moment to *feel* he really was Hulmul the Magician. Where was he? Ah, now that one refused to come into focus. With considerable trepidation, he opened his eyes.

"He's awake." The voice was familiar to Hulmul, but it took him a moment to connect it to the armored knight leaning over him, a little longer to identify the man as Alaric von Mertz.

Hulmul found that he was lying in a bed with a hillock of pillows piled up behind him. The room around him was richly appointed, with wood paneling on the walls and thick rugs on the floor. He smiled when he saw the bookcases arranged in every available nook and cranny. Helchen was inspecting the shelves, a sour look on the witch hunter's face. Nearby was Gaiseric, making his own study of the quills and inkpots that sat on a small writing table. It was easy to guess that the thief's interest had been attracted by the golden shine of the gilded implements. Away to one side was the duelist Drahoslav, sitting in a high-backed chair while he used a brush to restore the pristine condition of his white tunic. There was an orc off in a corner, sitting on the floor while he teased a large wolf with an old bone. Hulmul vaguely attached the name Ratbag to him.

Another person was in the room, and he turned when Alaric spoke, quickly moving toward the bed. He was a tall, lean man, arrayed in deep red robes. Hulmul recognized the arcane sigils that were embroidered into the hem of the garment. They were intended to both enhance the efficacy of spells and protect against inimical arcane energies, though in practice they had little influence over either. It was more tradition than utility that caused wizards to don such clothes.

The man, then, was a fellow practitioner. Hulmul felt he should know him, but it wasn't until the wizard spoke that full recognition came to him.

"It's a good sign," Vasilescu said. "I was worried that he'd be insensible for days yet."

Hulmul blinked in disbelief, trying to reconcile the man in red robes with his memory of his mentor as he'd last seen him several years ago. Then, Vasilescu had been a robust, almost vivacious personage, a thin black mustache over his lip, his hair dark and vibrant. He'd affected an air of sophistication and nobility, a poise that enabled him to engage the society of the kingdom's elite. The diffident magnetism of the connoisseur and the dilettante had been his.

Such a change! The man he looked at now could have been the father – or grandfather – of his old mentor. The mustache had thickened and grayed, joining a scraggly growth of beard that coated his cheeks and chin. His hair had faded almost to pure white and now fell down past his shoulders when before it had always been kept to the nape of his neck. His skin was cracked with deep wrinkles and had taken on a thin, almost leprous look. His eyes, however, retained the remembered keenness, so sharp that they seemed to peer through flesh to the soul itself.

Vasilescu sighed and gave a sad nod when he saw the shock in Hulmul's expression. "Yes," he admitted, staring down at one of his hands, "I fear I've changed a great deal since you last saw me. I must confess to possessing a vain streak and not being above using a bit of magic to fend off the years that are my due." He frowned and shook his head. "Lately I've not had the leisure to squander any of my power on frivolities." He gave Hulmul's arm a squeeze. Despite the friendliness of the gesture, Hulmul squirmed under his mentor's touch as though a serpent had slithered across his skin. "The Duchess of Mordava wouldn't fret about being too old to entertain me now, would she?" Vasilescu laughed as he stepped back from the bed.

Hulmul sat up, still shaken by the horrible change his mentor had undergone. "You look as though you've aged fifty years…"

"Vasilescu had to use his magic to replenish your vitality," Alaric told him. The knight set his helm down at the end of the coverlet. "He was afraid that you wouldn't revive otherwise."

"He had to ink a rune of healing into your arm," Helchen said. There was a curious inflection to her speech, an unspoken question behind her words. Hulmul wasn't sure if it was his imagination, but he thought he saw the witch hunter dart a wary look at Vasilescu.

"Your old master put his entire tower into the effort to save us," Gaiseric stated as he moved toward the bed. "After he caught me on his roof and I had a chance to explain everything, that is. I have to admit, when I heard his voice coming out of nowhere, I took such a fright that I almost started climbing down again."

The elder wizard chuckled. "It is unwise to disturb a mage in his meditations." He laughed again and gripped Gaiseric's shoulder. "You took me by such surprise I barely had time to cast a pall over your vision to hide myself from your eyes."

Hulmul smiled at his mentor's remark. "That was a spell I recall you were fond of when an errant husband…" He found he lacked the strength to continue the reminiscence and sagged back down among the pillows.

Vasilescu folded his hands together, assuming the scholarly attitude Hulmul remembered from so many lectures when he was a mere apprentice. "To suffer the loss of a familiar is a wound many wizards do not survive. Yet I am told you sacrificed yours to save the lives of others." He looked over as Helchen and Gaiseric walked toward the bed. "I hope you appreciate the risk Hulmul took on." A grave tone entered his words. "You owe him your lives."

"And I owe you mine," Hulmul declared. He agonized over the physical deterioration of his mentor and the thought that he'd reduced Vasilescu to such a condition.

The elder wizard tried to put his mind at ease. "I will not make light of the powers I drew upon to restore you, but don't think they're so severe as what you see." He chuckled as he indicated himself. "This toll has been exacted on me since this black plague fell upon Singerva. Only by my arcane exertions have I been able to keep this tower safe."

Vasilescu's expression grew grim. "The people you led here are not the first to seek refuge in my tower. Including them, I am now the unexpected host of some two hundred people. The greatest single concentration of life in all Singerva. The very success of offering sanctuary to so many threatens that sanctuary. Every hour more zombies are drawn here, lured by their hideous appetite." He shrugged. "At some point their numbers will be so great that the press will shove those closest into the moat down into the flames. Not a few, but hundreds. Enough to smother the alchemical fire and give them a way across to the tower."

"Is there nothing that can be done?" Hulmul asked, sickened by the resignation in his mentor's tone. A man who accepted doom was already beaten. Vasilescu himself had taught him that.

For just a moment, a sparkle came into Vasilescu's eyes. His gaze swept across the room. "There might be," he admitted, almost as though afraid to express the hope. "If you feel well enough, I can show you."

Hulmul swung his legs over the side of the bed. "Even if I don't," he insisted.

The depths of the wizard's tower might have been reared by giants rather than humans, Helchen thought, as they descended into the vaults below the main floors. The blocks were of incredible size and fit together with a precision a dwarf might have envied. They rose in great pillars that met in an arched ceiling some twenty feet overhead. Braziers were placed at the base of each column, rising from mere embers to bright flames as Vasilescu passed them. Their light sent eerie shadows flitting along the walls to keep company with the ghostly echoes of their footsteps.

"I've made a study of these creatures since they appeared," Vasilescu announced, leading the group past a series of what looked to be glass caskets. Helchen saw that each contained a body, corpses in varying stages of decay. However fresh they seemed, there was a foul sense of corruption about them, the tang of black magic. There were a few that had the lean, rabid look she associated with the runners, and one that had the swollen bulk of the hard-to-kill zombies they'd taken to calling brutes.

"It's not only people who change," Vasilescu, said as they passed some smaller cases. Helchen saw the carcasses of crows and rats beneath the glass coverings. "Animals that feed on flesh that has been tainted by the plague run a risk of drawing that corruption into themselves."

"So we've learned," Hulmul replied, scowling as he looked down at the necrotic crows. The wizard leaned on Gaiseric for support. Sometimes, as he moved, Helchen was afforded a glimpse of the rune Vasilescu had put on his arm. It might be precisely what the old wizard claimed it to be, but she couldn't shake the impression it was something else entirely. She knew the mage's reputation with the Order, that he was held beyond rebuke, yet she couldn't stifle a sense of disquiet. This morbid collection only added to her suspicions.

"We've seen many scavengers since entering Singerva," Helchen informed Vasilescu. "Many of them looked like they were still alive. Why didn't they change?"

Vasilescu paused beside a large glass box, his hand resting on its top. "I cannot say for sure. My research hasn't gone quite that far. I can only theorize." He steepled his fingers and smiled at the witch hunter as he lectured. "A human zombie can only pass the infection along to another human. Perhaps a dwarf or an elf could be infected as well, but I've seen no proof of it." He glanced over at Ratbag, studying the orc for a moment. "Your friend is perhaps immune," he speculated, excitement coloring his voice as he broached the possibility.

"But what about these crows and rats?" Gaiseric reminded Vasilescu. "It's certain they've changed into zombies."

"To be sure," Vasilescu said, returning to the topic. "You see, when the undead inflict too much damage on a victim, the body doesn't rise again to join their ranks. It is merely a corpse." He raised his finger to emphasize the point. "But a corpse that still burns with the black plague. When scavengers arrive to unwittingly feed on the tainted meat, they run the risk of drawing into themselves too much of that dark power. At some critical level, the magic acts as a poison and kills them only to revive them as zombies."

Helchen glanced aside at Ratbag and considered the savage way he forced Fang to spit up whatever it had eaten after fighting the undead. Was it possible that an orc had reached the same conclusion by sheer instinct that Vasilescu was still only theorizing?

"And once the first crow becomes a zombie, it can pass the plague to other crows." Helchen followed Vasilescu's logic.

"Precisely," Vasilescu said. "Unless, of course, there are unexpected complications." He glanced down at the glass box. "*This* we caught in these very vaults before the moat was ignited. It might demonstrate more eloquently than I can, the severity of our situation."

Helchen stepped forward along with the others. She felt the icy hand of fear tighten around her heart when she saw what was inside.

"Derez der goon wotz gotta der bulge." Ratbag shook his head, his lips pulling back to expose his fangs. His wolf bared its teeth and backed away from the box.

The orc had cause to be impressed, Helchen thought. The thing in the box was bigger than an ogre, so immense in scale it made the abomination that had chased her and Gaiseric look like a child. The form wasn't humanoid, but rather that of a colossal rodent. It was almost completely devoid of fur, exposing its raw, naked hide. The skin was a light gray, mottled with white scars and red sores. The tail was scaly and cut off abruptly after a few feet of its length. The wound where it had been severed was black with decay. The same necrotic erosion was present around the claws on each of its hand-like paws and also around its muzzle. Four enormous orange fangs, chisel-shaped and long as daggers, protruded from its jaws, recalling to the witch hunter travelers' tales of giant tigers in far off lands.

"You couldn't pay me enough to even look at that thing if it was still alive," Gaiseric commented as he backed away.

Helchen tore her eyes away from the verminous carcass. "That's just the problem. While this plague savages the land, are you sure there aren't any more like it roaming around?"

The group followed Vasilescu on through the vault. The underground halls seemed to stretch on for miles, though common sense made Helchen appreciate they couldn't be farther than the foundations of the tower itself. The mage directed them away to the left where two servants were tending a huge mechanism unlike anything Helchen had seen before. It was something like a metal furnace, but even that similarity was scant. A crazed array of pipes rose up from the main body to drive up into the ceiling in every direction. It was like looking at some weird octopus hugging the bottom of the tower.

One of the servants operated a windlass set beside the mechanism, pumping it at a constant, measured pace. The other man took big flasks from racks arrayed all around this part of the vault. There was a reddish liquid inside, but it looked to have a syrupy consistency about it. Helchen was certain it wasn't wine, or any liquor she'd ever heard of. The man carrying the bottle brought it to the machine. Knocking away the metal stopper with a mallet, he hefted it up and poured its contents into a funnel-like opening. At once, the witch hunter noticed the pipes overhead shiver and realized whatever the substance was, it had been pumped through those tubes.

"The alchemical mixture that feeds my moat," Vasilescu pronounced, answering Helchen's unspoken question. The old wizard pointed at the ceiling. "Those pipes will send the mixture out of drains in the walls. While my supplies hold out, the moat will keep the zombies at bay. At least for now."

Helchen looked across the racks where the flasks were held. Two of them contained only empty bottles.

"How long can you hold?" Alaric asked Vasilescu, the tactical part of his mind already thinking in terms of siege.

"For now, two bottles each hour are enough," the old wizard answered. "When the horde grows larger, it will take much more of the mixture to burn them before their bodies can smother the flames."

"Is there a way to make the supply last longer?" Helchen wondered.

Vasilescu turned to her. The smile on his face was withering. "Indeed, I know that the mixture could be strengthened. A simple enough process. If the secret were known." He pointed an accusing finger at the witch hunter. "Your Order, in its fanatical zeal, has destroyed much knowledge. In your mania to destroy necromancers, you've executed many innocent scholars, students of other schools of magic."

Hulmul drew away from Gaiseric and stepped over to his mentor, trying to temper the elder's anger. "What has been done is done. There's no changing it. What we need now is a way to make the tower safe."

Vasilescu shook his head, snapping free of his rage. He gave Helchen a brief nod of apology. "There was an alchemist, a genius of his profession, who was arrested a few years ago and condemned by your Order. Along with the man himself, the witch hunters confiscated his books." He turned and let his gaze sweep across each member of the group. "Those books are still held in the Order's inquisitorial temple. All the arcane tomes they've seized are held there, in guarded vaults." A bitter laugh echoed through the gloom. "Of course, the guards are unlikely to still be at their posts."

"You need this alchemist's book?" Drahoslav asked.

"If I am to refine the potency of this mixture, it is essential," Vasilescu told the duelist.

"Even if the guards are gone, the catacombs will still be protected," Helchen pointed out, thinking of the temple-forts she'd seen elsewhere. "It is the Order's policy to never trust to any one safeguard. Guards can be bribed or bewitched, so traps will have been laid to dispose of intruders. Every witch hunter in the temple might be gone, but the traps will remain."

"So, you understand the dilemma," Vasilescu said. "It will need brave souls to recover the book." He tapped his hand against the side of the pump. "Nor can I lend my magic to the effort. I must stay here to manage the level of the moat. If you would do this thing, you must do it on your own."

Hulmul shook his head. "It seems we have no choice. If something isn't done, then the tower is doomed."

"There's too many survivors to try and move them all

safely away from Singerva, even if we knew a safe place to lead them," Alaric agreed.

Gaiseric paced between them. "I've some expertise with breaking into places and evaluating the risks. So I hope you'll listen to me when I say this is a bad idea. Witch hunters are inventive enough devising tortures to exact confessions, just imagine what they came up with when they didn't need to worry about keeping their victim alive."

"On that, at least, you can set your mind to rest," Vasilescu said. "The traps under the temple were designed and built by dwarfs. Ironshield and Company, the most renowned engineers in Singerva."

Drahoslav scratched his chin as he considered that bit of information. "Ernst had plenty of dealings with Gilri Ironshield. The dwarf was obsessed with keeping meticulous records. It's likely he kept track of whatever he built for the witch hunters."

Helchen nodded. It troubled her, this plan that would ultimately lead to violating the security of her Order, but she saw nothing else that could be done if the people in the tower were to be saved. "Then the first thing we need to do is find Ironshield's records and see what they can tell us about the traps."

CHAPTER TWELVE

"The things you talk yourself into," Gaiseric hissed under his breath as he crept along one of Singerva's desolate streets. He glanced down at Fang and thought the wolf sympathized with his view. The worst part was that it made sense for him to range out ahead of the main group. He had the sharpest eyes and the keenest ears of any of them, except Fang. But the wolf couldn't exactly communicate what it spotted, only that it had spotted something. Gaiseric could drift back to the others and let them know exactly what was ahead of them.

"It isn't that you shouldn't be here," the thief reminded himself. "It's that you should have stayed in the tower and let them handle it." After ducking several mobs of zombies already, the relative safety of Vasilescu's fortress was something to pine for.

That option had been lost when Vasilescu arranged a big distraction to draw off the zombies so the drawbridge could be lowered. The moment Gaiseric ran out with the others across the plaza, there was no turning back. He was committed now.

"Loaded dice and marked cards," he berated himself. "You know you wouldn't have been able to sit back there either.

Not when you know they'll need somebody who knows how to spot a trap." Gaiseric wasn't as confident as Drahoslav that the dwarves had a guide to the traps they'd built for the witch hunters. It just didn't seem the thing anybody paying to stop thieves would let the builder record, however fanatical Ironshield and Company were about keeping an account of their labor.

Gaiseric recalled the time he was in Karlik and he'd tried to burgle the storehouse of a dwarven weaponsmith. He was much younger and naiver then, cocksure in his innate talent and deaf to the advice of far more experienced thieves. He knew the market value of a dwarf-made sword, and that was enough to make him intent on pilfering the wares. The trap he'd found on the window was contemptuously easy to spot and disarm. It hadn't dawned on him that it was too obvious. It was naught but a ploy to draw him in. He'd nearly lost his fingers when a steel shutter came slamming down after he tripped a pressure plate just behind the sill. Luck and the swiftness of youth kept him from being maimed. After that he maintained a healthy respect for dwarves.

Turning the next corner, Gaiseric spotted the building Drahoslav had described. It was a broad stone building, only a single floor high, with a flattened roof and no windows. A squared arch, carved extensively with runes, framed a pair of immense bronze doors. A plaque bolted to the side of the building proclaimed, in both dwarfish runes and letters legible to Gaiseric, that this was Ironshield and Company.

The thief was so thrilled at finally reaching the place he didn't notice that Fang was hanging back a few paces. The wolf's ears were flattened against the sides of its head, its lips curled to expose sharp teeth. Gaiseric spun around to see what had provoked the animal. The excitement of a moment before became horror as a pack of zombies shambled out of a ruined warehouse. Among them was a creature of unspeakable foulness, its body bloated to such a degree that the folds of fat dripping off its frame were rigid from the pressure inside its body.

Gaiseric scrambled back. "Fang! Here!" he called to the wolf. He didn't know what kind of monster the bloated zombie was, but it seemed unlike anything he'd yet come across in Singerva. Something about it set off an instinctive warning deep inside him.

Fang didn't respond. The wolf lunged at one of the walkers as the undead got close, tearing open the zombie's throat with its teeth and knocking it down with its paws. A second creature grabbed at Fang, impaling its hands on the spiked collar.

And still the bloated zombie was lurching its way nearer. Gaiseric hesitated to go to Fang's aid seeing that swollen corpse closing in. The wolf, however, ignored his calls. Then he tried a different method. Pulling the sound from the pit of his stomach, he mustered his best approximation of Ratbag's bellow. "Gitta outta dat, yer simprin' cur!"

The imitation of the orc was close enough for the wolf. Fang released the walker it had tackled and dashed over toward Gaiseric. The creature with its hands embedded in the collar was dragged along with the animal. Gaiseric finished it with a slash of his sword once Fang brought the zombie within reach.

Across the way, however, the rest of the pack was still active. The zombie Fang had tackled stood up, oblivious to the gory ruin of its throat. The bloated corpse pushed past the others, using its corrupt mass to shove them aside. Its dead eyes stared back at Gaiseric.

Gaiseric grabbed the steel loop at the back of Fang's collar. There wasn't any question of forcing the wolf to follow him, it was much too big for that, but he was able to guide the animal. Given direction, Fang wasn't against hurrying back down the street toward the rest of the group.

"Hold it! That's Gaiseric!" Helchen's voice rang out as the thief turned the corner.

Drahoslav lowered the elven bow he'd appropriated. "You came close to…"

Gaiseric waved away the duelist's reprimand. "Zombies!" he gasped the warning. "A big one with them!" He shook his head when Helchen shot him a worried glance, trying to assure her it wasn't the abomination they'd faced before. He was too winded to say anything.

Nor was there time to. The thief had just rejoined his companions when the zombies turned the same corner. Immediately, Drahoslav let an arrow fly and dropped one of the walkers. Helchen shattered another undead skull with a bolt from her crossbow.

"The big one," Gaiseric cautioned as the bloated zombie came into view. It had fallen behind the others, but with living prey again at hand, the creature shoved aside the rest of the pack.

"Derez der bimbo wotz good fer der rumpuz," Ratbag growled. The orc started forward with his scimitar. Again, that nebulous warning made Gaiseric hold him back. There was something indefinably wrong about the bloated zombie.

Something that made him feel it was more dangerous to be near than any of the undead they'd so far seen.

"Don't get close," Gaiseric said when Ratbag glared at him angrily.

"Then let's keep them where they are," Hulmul said. The wizard drew a scroll from the bag Vasilescu had given him. Quickly he recited the incantation on the parchment and waved his staff at the approaching undead.

At once the air took on a ghastly chill. Gaiseric felt the sweat on his forehead freeze, saw Ratbag's breath turn to mist. Hulmul's magic was far more potent where the wizard had actually focused it. The pack of zombies were coated in ice, as though the Queen of the Frost Giants had breathed over them. Two of the walkers at the front of the mob were frozen so solid that they crashed to the ground and shattered into grotesque fragments. The bloated corpse and the others were immobilized by the icy coating that encased them.

Hulmul sagged against his staff. "A rare spell," he told the others. "Be grateful that Vasilescu gave me access to it."

Alaric started forward. "Most effective," he commented as he looked over the flash-frozen undead.

Worry still nagged at Gaiseric. At his side, Fang remained tense. It was only when he felt something dripping down his face that he realized why. His sweat was thawing. He looked at the mob of frozen corpses. Helchen had joined Alaric now in examining the icy bodies.

"Get away!" the thief called to them. Nothing alive could survive being frozen like that, but the zombies hadn't been truly alive to begin with. "They're not dead!"

The warning was given just as the first walker cracked free

of its icy casing. Its clutching hand snagged Helchen's coat. She twisted around and smashed its hand with her mace, the frozen limb snapping off at the wrist. Alaric delivered a more permanent resolution, cleaving the creature's head in two. The warriors hastened back, watching as the thawing zombies resumed their shambling march.

Gaiseric still sensed a great menace from the bloated zombie. They couldn't let that monster get close. "Drahoslav, shoot the big one!" he told the duelist.

Drahoslav nocked an arrow and let fly in one smooth motion. The missile slammed into the zombie's head, but merely quivered in its flabby skin. "I still hit my mark," he declared. Quickly he put another arrow to the string.

The second arrow pierced the zombie's eye, tearing so deep that the feathers sank into the socket. The bloated corpse crashed to the ground. In that moment, Gaiseric discovered that his fears were anything but unfounded.

The swollen flesh burst when it slammed against the cobblestones, splitting open like a wine-skin. Only instead of wine, it was a sizzling green muck that exploded from the zombie. The caustic filth showered the walkers around it, rapidly corroding their decayed flesh. In a matter of only a few moments, the entire mob collapsed, eaten away by the acids.

"Wotun, if I'd struck that thing with my sword." Alaric shuddered.

Helchen shook her head and looked over at Gaiseric. "Did you know it would do that?"

"I didn't," the thief confessed. "It just looked so much like a dead toad after a hot day, it seemed the thing would burst any moment."

Drahoslav looked across the group. "It may have escaped your notice, but it was my shot that killed the thing."

"Your *second* shot." Gaiseric couldn't help but try to deflate the duelist's pomposity.

"When it exploded, it took six others with it," Drahoslav said. "That makes it seven for two."

Helchen rolled her eyes. "Let's hope there aren't more like that. Otherwise, his ego might burst."

The doors to Ironshield and Company looked like they could withstand a drunken troll with a battering ram. Alaric had seldom seen anything so robustly built. The building around it was more like a fortification than a business. He knew dwarves built with an eye to durability, but he hadn't expected anything like this.

"There'll be no forcing our way in there," Alaric declared. He looked over at Gaiseric. "Well, you've broken into places before. What do you think? Can those locks be picked?"

"Fortunately, they don't have to be," Hulmul said. The wizard rummaged in his pack and withdrew an iron flask. He motioned for the others to step back as he unstoppered the bottle and stepped to the door. Dipping what looked like a tiny femur into the flask, he slathered the door in a pungent, gooey blue muck. When he'd covered a section two feet across and about five feet high, Hulmul stepped back and threw away the empty vessel.

"Avoid looking at the door," Hulmul instructed. He ran his hand down his spade-shaped beard. "You'll have no problem knowing when it's safe to look."

Alaric turned his back on the building, as did the others,

while Hulmul began to conjure. The strange inflections of the eldritch chant were unsettling, causing the hair on his arms to prickle. Yet it wasn't nearly so disturbing as the sizzling sound that soon followed. The smell of hot metal soon reached his nose while the wizard continued to chant.

Finally, there was a loathsome, slopping sound and Hulmul fell silent. Alaric spun around, ready to confront whatever had interrupted the ritual. When his eyes fell upon the doors, he nearly dropped his sword in amazement.

The ritual hadn't been interrupted. It had been completed. The portion of the immense metal doors that Hulmul had treated with the blue paste was gone, reduced to a mass of steaming slag at the base of the doorway.

Helchen stepped forward, gingerly testing the edge of the opening with the flat of her sword. The corrosive force appeared to have dissipated, for the blade was unmarked when she withdrew it. "The bile of a beithir," the witch hunter mused, as she gave Hulmul a sideways glance. "More of mummery than magic in this trick."

"Agreed," the wizard conceded with a bow. "Anyone accustomed to the right cadence could have agitated the stomach parasites into activity." He raised his finger for emphasis. "But is there not a certain magic in being able to mimic the gastric rumble of a cave wyrm?"

Gaiseric whistled as he checked the gap for himself. "Now there's a trick I wouldn't mind learning."

"You'd have a hard time finding something valuable enough to warrant the expense," Helchen told him. "There's a short list of people who've managed to harvest bile from a live beithir." She glanced back at Hulmul. "It does have to be alive to collect the parasites?" The wizard answered in the affirmative with another slight bow.

Alaric drew Gaiseric away from the door and stepped through. "Whatever its provenance, it worked. Let's find those records and get out of here." He looked over at Drahoslav. "Do you have any idea where the dwarves would keep their accounts?"

The duelist shook his head. "I only know the room they escorted Ernst to when he had business with them. It could be that's where they kept their records, but it's also possible they have an archive somewhere else."

"At least it's someplace to start," Alaric said. He peered into the chamber beyond the doors. Or would have, had there been one. There was only a broad landing followed by a stairway plunging down into the earth. He could just make out the glow of lights below. "Drahoslav, take the lead with me. The rest of you follow. Ratbag, stand watch here. If Fang detects any zombies, let us know about it *before* you start chopping them up." It was a good excuse to keep the orc away. Alaric might have developed a grudging acceptance – even respect – for the renegade, but he didn't think the dwarves would be so understanding.

Keeping close so he could guard Drahoslav's left flank, Alaric followed the duelist down the stairs. Only a few steps down, they were greeted by the sight of a mangled body. The stocky build and short legs indicated the corpse was dwarven rather than human. Sword at the ready, Alaric turned the corpse over with his shield. He let out a sigh of relief when the body remained inert.

"At least it doesn't look like the contamination has passed

into him," Helchen commented as she peered down at the dwarf.

"He was clearly bitten though," Alaric said, indicating the ugly wound on the dwarf's thigh. The flesh was charred and blackened, but at the edges there were still the distinct marks of teeth. "Looks like he tried to burn the wound to kill the infection." The knight shook his head and stepped back. "The cure might have been what killed him."

Gaiseric glanced over the dwarf, then pointed at the illuminated hall below. "Doesn't it strike you as odd that the dwarves would leave him like this?" The thief fingered the hilt of his sword. "I don't think he's the only one we'll find who's dead."

The thief's logic was hard to refute. Alaric had seen the reverence dwarves paid to their dead. They wouldn't leave one of their own lying around without good reason. "Something happened here," he said. "Until we find out what it was, stay vigilant." He didn't need to stress the warning. The mangled dwarf at their feet did that for him.

The steps led down to a vaulted hall, somewhere between a mine and a royal palace in appearance. The dwarves had spared no effort on the decorative carvings that covered every archway and column. The walls were of granite but polished to such an incredible sheen that they shone like marble in the flickering light. The illumination, Alaric noted, was provided by glowing crystals housed within iron cages that hung from the ceiling at intervals of thirty feet or so. The hall, as far as he could see, stretched away for hundreds of feet. Intermittently, doorways opened into the main passage, at least a dozen within the immediate proximity.

All of this, Alaric noted in passing, for his attention was quickly commanded by the carnage strewn about the hall. Bodies and blood were scattered throughout. The corpses of dwarves gnawed and dismembered. The remains of humans, corrupt with decay, smashed and pulverized as though they'd been caught in an avalanche.

"So who won here?" Drahoslav commented. "Whatever else you can say about them, the dwarves gave a good accounting of themselves. They must have destroyed hundreds of zombies down here."

"Maybe the survivors fled," Alaric proffered, though he sounded uncertain even to himself.

"There couldn't have been many left then," Drahoslav said as he marched through the havoc. "Otherwise they'd have seen to their own dead." He shook his head and pointed to a doorway some fifty feet ahead. "That's where they brought us when Ernst had business with Ironshield."

Alaric started toward the doorway, then stopped. He looked down at one of the destroyed zombies. Its chest had collapsed from a terrific blow. It wasn't the nature of the wound that disturbed the knight, but rather the suggestiveness of the outline. The zombie might have been crushed under an enormous boot.

Alaric looked up, staring ahead not at the doorway but a little farther down the hall. On either side of the corridor, poised upon pedestals set before each wall, were two massive statues. They were each ten feet tall and were some abstract representations of a dwarf warrior in design. Both stood with their hands folded over the peen of an enormous warhammer, leaning over the weapons... as though standing vigil.

"Drahoslav, wait," Alaric said. The duelist, however, was already moving toward the doorway. Alaric's gaze remained fastened on the statues. He thought of Gaiseric and the subconscious realization about the bloated zombie's menace. He was experiencing a similar sensation. He was seeing something, but not recognizing its importance.

Then it came to him. There was blood on the warhammers, more blood on the stone boots! "Drahoslav, come back," Alaric hissed.

It was too late. With a rumbling groan, one of the statues turned its helmeted head, staring at the duelist.

"Golem!" Hulmul shouted from back down the tunnel, fear in the wizard's cry.

Golems. As Alaric backed away, he realized this was the answer to who'd prevailed in the battle of dwarf against zombie. Ironshield had brought stone automatons to guard his hall, mindless sentinels that had been roused to battle when the undead attacked. They'd prevailed, though too late to preserve the lives of their masters! Now, without anyone to command them, they were ready to attack any intruder, living or undead.

Drahoslav ran back, his arrogant poise broken by the heavy footfalls of the golems as they stepped down from their pedestals. One after the other, they raised their hammers and lumbered towards the humans.

"I think we have a problem," Drahoslav said.

Alaric looked at the doorway where Ironshield's records might be held. "We can't run," he declared. "Too much depends on getting that tome for Vasilescu."

Helchen shot a bolt into one of the animated statues. It

merely glanced off the golem's chest. "I'd like to know how we fight solid stone!" she snarled.

Alaric continued to back away, racking his brain for an idea. Solid stone. In a siege, sappers would use fire to undermine castle walls and bring them crashing down. He turned his head. There was a burnt smell to the air. It wafted out from one of the nearby doorways. He couldn't read dwarf runes, but he recognized the image of an anvil etched into the cornerstone.

"Drahoslav, lead them in here!" Alaric told the duelist. "Hulmul, come with me!"

The knight and the wizard ran into the anvil-room. It was as much a shambles as the hall outside, bodies strewn in every direction. From the furnishings that remained intact, it looked to have served as both forge and workshop. Alaric smiled when he saw what the burnt smell had led him to hope would be here. A great stone pot hoisted over a smoldering fire. Within was a bubbling mass of molten bronze.

"Get to cover and be ready with that ice spell," Alaric told Hulmul. He dashed around to the side of the fire, his longsword clenched in both hands. He'd only have one chance. He wasn't going to waste it.

Drahoslav backed into the room, loosing arrows from the elven bow. Close behind him came the golems, mindlessly fixated on the antagonist who had first drawn their attention. Alaric could feel the floor tremble as the hulking statues marched.

"Drahoslav! Get clear!" Alaric shouted to the duelist. The man didn't need to be told twice. Spinning around, he sprinted for the back of the chamber. The golems stomped after him, but they didn't get far.

"Now, Hulmul!" Alaric swung his sword at the chain holding the pot of boiling bronze.

The pot slammed to the floor, its molten contents flooding toward the golems. The statues stepped through the boiling metal without regard, intent only on their quarry.

Then Hulmul's spell swept through that corner of the room. Alaric dove for cover as the icy blast spiraled in his direction. The golems were quickly covered in frost. Their stony bodies were unphased, but not so the molten metal on the floor. It was instantly hardened by the arcane cold, tightening around their feet, fastening them to the floor. Not comprehending why they couldn't move, the automatons strained to free themselves and continue their remorseless march. The strain finally told, and it wasn't the clinging bronze that finally yielded.

A loud crack echoed through the room as the first golem broke its own foot off at the ankle. It stumbled forward and its body slammed against the floor with a thunderous impact. The statue tried to raise itself with its hands, but the vicious fall had sent cracks throughout its monolithic frame. As it tried to move, the cracks became even greater fractures. Bit by bit, the golem crumbled away, still trying to reach Drahoslav as it disintegrated.

The second golem, without the initiative to learn from its companion's destruction, mindlessly copied the other statue. Soon both were naught but a heap of rubble.

"Give me a horde of zombies any day," Drahoslav commented as he wiped dirt from his coat.

Alaric shot him a grim look. "That's a wish this town is certain to grant," he said. The knight looked over at Hulmul. "Are you all right?"

The wizard nodded back. "I just need a moment to recover. That spell's power isn't so simple to evoke as others. I'll be fine though."

"Good," the knight said. "Then let's go search for Ironshield's records and get out of here."

After their encounter with the golems, it was a plan of action that brought no argument from his companions. It was a matter of moments before they were in Ironshield's office. Here, as elsewhere, the struggle between dwarf and zombie had left many grisly reminders.

"If you see anything, let Gaiseric check it first," Alaric advised as they started to search the room. "If Ironshield designed traps for the witch hunters, he's certain to have kept a few for himself."

Gaiseric sighed. "If he did, they won't be easy to find," he cautioned.

The thief's warning quelled the haste Alaric wanted to conduct the search. The urgency was still there… and the fear that there were more golems somewhere in the hall. But they'd be just as dead if they triggered a hidden trap as they would under a statue's heel. The knight was judicious as he inspected the tables and shelves that dominated the room. The others were equally cautious.

"How will we know it when we find it?" Drahoslav asked, turning from a desk in frustration.

"Any transaction with the Order is sure to bear our seal," Helchen reminded everyone. "Look for the emblem of a skull impaled by a wooden stake."

"It seems to me there's not room here for the accounts Ironshield and Company must have acquired," Hulmul suggested as he set down a sheet of copper he'd been examining. "Certainly, it would be a weighty collection if everything is etched into copper."

Alaric nodded in agreement. As he did so, he stumbled over a thick rug lying on the floor. Recovering, he saw that the corner had been kicked back by his tripping feet. There seemed to be a faintly larger gap between the paving stone beneath it and the one next to it compared with the rest of the room. "Gaiseric, help me move this," he said, leaning down and gripping the rug. When it was drawn away, they could all see the outline of a trapdoor. Under normal circumstances, it probably would have been nigh impossible to spot, but just now, the severed arm of a zombie was pinned beneath its edge, propping it up ever so slightly.

"Take a look," Alaric said, nudging Gaiseric.

The thief pressed himself to the floor, circling around the trapdoor like a dog sniffing at a bone. His hands hovered around the edges, his eyes peered into the cracks. Finally, he pressed his ear against the surface, listening for better than a minute for the murmur of a hidden mechanism. "I can't find anything, but that isn't a perfect guarantee there isn't something there."

Alaric took a moment to nerve himself to the implied risk. "I found it, it's my job to open it."

Gaiseric gave him a respectful nod. "Step back and I'll show you where the catch is." A wry smile curled his face the moment the knight withdrew. His hand dipped to a particular spot on the slab, depressing a concealed button. He closed his eyes and clenched his teeth, but the only result was the stone popped a few inches up from the floor around it.

"I said *I* would do it," Alaric admonished the thief.

"Can't have you paying for my mistake," Gaiseric replied. He gripped the trapdoor and swung it up. "Besides, it's safe ..."

Before the thief could say anything else, something lunged at him from the darkness below. He was bowled over by a figure that pinned him to the floor. Alaric started for the attacker but was warned back when he saw a knife at Gaiseric's throat.

"Explain yourselves, or he meets his ancestors." The threat was made by a bedraggled-looking dwarf, her clothes torn and her ruddy skin darkened with dirt and blood. She had a wild look in her eyes and a firm grip on Gaiseric's neck.

"Mistress Stonebreaker?" Drahoslav asked, stepping forward. His rapier was sheathed, but he had one hand resting on its pommel. Alaric had already seen the lightning speed with which he could draw the blade when he had to. "You remember me, I came here with Master Fluchsbringer."

The dwarf gave him a sullen look. "The foppish bodyguard. That is hardly a recommendation."

"Then how about this," Alaric said. With all the other hazards they'd endured to get this far, he'd little patience for the dwarf's paranoia. The longer they tarried, the worse things might be for the survivors at Vasilescu's tower and the more time Brunon Gogol was denied the retribution he so justly warranted. "Except for you, we found nothing else alive down here. Your people are dead. You can't be choosy about your friends right now."

The knight's words pierced the dwarf. She sagged back, stunned by his words. Her eyes roved across the room, moistening when she saw the dead bodies of other dwarfs. "All of them?" she asked.

"We didn't see any sign anyone got away," Alaric said. "How did the zombies get into your halls, Mistress Stonebreaker? It looks like this place is fortified to keep anyone out."

"Yet somehow you found your way in," the dwarf retorted, her sullen stare sweeping across the humans.

"It wasn't easy," Gaiseric gasped while her hand squeezed his throat.

"It should be impossible… for humans," she growled. "The doors above were sealed. None of your people know how to unfasten doors locked by dwarfs."

"Be grateful someone did, or you might have stayed in that hole." Alaric drew her attention back to himself. "It seemed to me the mechanism was blocked by this." He kicked the severed zombie arm across the room. "If we hadn't found you, you'd have been forgotten. Your name lost to your kinfolk." He thought that last part might touch a chord with her, knowing the importance dwarves placed on family and ancestry. He could see from the change in her eyes that he'd had some impact.

The dwarf relaxed her hold on Gaiseric and let the thief scramble away. "Ursola. My name is Ursola Stonebreaker," she said. She pivoted and looked back at the cellar she'd been hiding in. "My cousin Nilfir ordered me to hide down there when the fighting began. Told me I was being entrusted with guarding the company treasury."

Helchen crouched down beside the dwarf. "How did the zombies get in? What happened?"

"They came up through the cistern. Bubbled up from the water like dead fish. They must have gotten into the underground stream that fed our well," Ursola said, suspicion still in her voice.

The witch hunter shot Gaiseric a guilty look. Alaric had heard their account of fighting in the underground. Now wasn't the time to tell them, but judging by how many undead were strewn through the hall, there were certainly more of them than those they'd rescued the students from. The zombies had found some other way into the stream. What really worried him was if the creatures had discovered that route... or been shown it by someone like Gogol.

Alaric set his hand on Ursola's shoulder. "We regret what has happened to your people, but we came here to try to save others." He nodded at Helchen. "Some time ago, Ironshield did work for the witch hunters. Drahoslav tells me there might be a record of what was done."

Ursola studied his face for some time. "What would you want those records for?"

"Several hundred survivors have taken refuge in Vasilescu's tower," Hulmul interjected. Alaric could see the dwarf recognized the mage's name. "A moat filled with alchemical fire has kept the zombies at bay, but he's worried the defense can't last. He needs a book taken by the witch hunters to strengthen the flames."

Alaric nodded. "The few people still alive in Singerva are depending on us to get that book for Vasilescu. We need your help. The record of the traps built for the witch hunters will let us navigate their dungeons safely."

Ursola was silent, pulling at her hair as she digested everything she'd been told. Finally, she reached a decision and pointed at the cellar. "Down there. To a dwarf, the record of our deeds is as precious as gold. The archives are there with the rest of Ironshield's treasure."

Alaric sighed with relief. "Can you show us the documents we want?"

"Naturally," Ursola said. "The work done for High Inquisitor Elza and the Order will be recorded, just like any other transaction." A shrewd look came over her face. "You will be fighting the undead?"

"Any and all of them that get in our way," Gaiseric assured her as he massaged his bruised neck.

"Then before I agree to show you, you must come to an agreement with me," Ursola said, fire in her eyes. "You must let me come with you." She paused before adding a sentiment with which Alaric could empathize. "I've kinfolk to avenge."

Hulmul smiled at her. "Of course, an engineer would be as useful as any record of the traps your kin built."

Ursola smiled back at the wizard. "Oh, you're mistaken. My forte isn't building things, but demolishing them." She patted a large satchel that hung at her side. Dipping her hand inside, she brought out an iron globe about the size of an apple.

"A firebomb." Helchen paled, instinctively leaning away from the dwarf. "Captain Dietrich used one against the Witch of Unterhoff."

The dwarf casually replaced the incendiary in her satchel. "With the right materials to work with, I could make much better. But you won't find those this side of a dwarfhold." Ursola's eyes roved across the group, before settling on Alaric. "Is it agreed then?"

"It's agreed," Alaric said, extending his hand to her. Ursola spat in her palm, then shook his hand. The knight didn't know if there was any insult implied or if it was simply a dwarf custom.

"She's going to love Ratbag," Gaiseric groaned.

Ursola darted a dark look at the thief. "Who's Ratbag?"

One crisis at a time, Alaric thought. "He's watching the entrance," he said. After a pause, he added, "When you meet him, try not to blow him up."

CHAPTER THIRTEEN

The Order's temple-fort was an imposing structure, coiled like a stone viper across from the secular Halls of Justice where bewigged magistrates held court over more mundane crimes. Helchen knew there were detractors of the Order who'd point out the proximity to the courts rather than the cathedral as an indicator of where their priorities lay. Of course it was simple pragmatism. Those accused of sorcery and witchcraft were often charged with other crimes as well. The witch hunters had to act in concert with the king's law, allowing these secular transgressions to be tried, either in tandem with the more mystical violations or prior to the prisoner being turned over for an entirely separate inquisition.

Helchen had never been to Singerva before. She knew from Captain Dietrich that a woman named Elza held the position of high inquisitor here, with a reputation for being a harsh disciplinarian who demanded total obedience from the witch hunters under her command. So the moment she saw the doors at the front of the temple-fort hanging open, she knew everything had gone wrong here.

"At least we won't have to blast our way in," Ursola said, a note of disappointment in her tone. The dwarf presented a much different figure than she had in the cellar of Ironshield and Company. Though there hadn't been time to attend the dead, she'd availed herself of the opportunity to gather equipment for the trials ahead of them. Her ragged clothes had been replaced by a hauberk of bronze-colored mail, some exotic alloy known only to her people. A helmet with a wide nasal encased her head, leaving only part of her face and a long braid of golden hair exposed. She was draped in a wide array of satchels and bags in which she carried the destructive tools of a 'demolisher' as she termed herself. Bombs and explosive powders, fuses and acids, and other things to which Helchen couldn't put a name. Finally, there was the massive warhammer she carried. Ursola had started out with a smaller weapon, but one look at Ratbag had sent her back down into the dwarf halls to retrieve the bigger sledge.

"That much noise would bring every zombie in this quarter staggering over to investigate," Alaric told Ursola.

"Noodlin' der stumpie brewzup der soup," Ratbag laughed. "I long fer der carumpuz."

Gaiseric looked over at the dwarf. "Ratbag agrees with you. He'd like to fight some zombies."

Ursola scowled at both the thief and the orc. "I didn't come along to amuse morons."

Helchen wondered exactly why the dwarf *had* come along. Ostensibly, she claimed it was to avenge her dead kinsfolk, but the witch hunter was dubious if that was all. Certainly, self-preservation played its part. Ursola had better chances of survival in a group than she did on her own. But she couldn't help thinking about the possessiveness she exhibited toward the records regarding the work the engineers had done for the witch hunters. She'd shown Drahoslav where they were but had quickly appropriated the copper sheaves before anyone could examine them. The only inspection she'd permitted was Helchen's quick glimpse at the Order's seal to verify that they were indeed the right ones.

Worries about the dwarf and what secrets she might be keeping made Helchen think about Vasilescu and her nagging doubts about the mage. As far as the Order was concerned, Vasilescu was a valuable asset, one of the few dependable wizards. If she expressed concerns about him to her superiors, they'd have dismissed her fears with a wave of their hand. Yet she couldn't silence the suspicions she harbored. There was that curious rune he'd placed on Hulmul's arm and that grisly collection down in his vault. She felt in her gut there was something wrong about it all. She had to keep her own counsel on the subject, certain the others would simply chalk it up to the prejudice of a witch hunter towards spell-casters in general.

Helchen set aside her concerns. Right now, she needed to focus on the temple-fort.

"Well?" Hulmul asked, visibly disturbed by being on the threshold of a place no wizard regarded without fear. "Where do we start?"

The witch hunter was pensive a moment. "If Singerva's temple-fort follows a similar layout to others I've been in–"

Gaiseric interrupted her with a hollow laugh. "I doubt the Order would be so predictable as to use the same architect wherever you set up one of these… venues. Your people don't exactly…"

"There will be rooms that naturally complement each other," Helchen stated, annoyed by the thief's tone. "It makes little sense to put the kitchen distant from the larder."

Alaric nodded. "That follows. But we aren't looking for the kitchen."

"No, but there'll be a pattern we *can* follow," the witch hunter explained. "The cells, for instance, will be near the interrogation theater."

"And catacombs for disposing of suspects who expire under torture will be close by for ease of transport," Hulmul growled, anger straining through his fear.

Helchen gave the wizard a stern look, refusing to let any hint of doubt show. "So will those executed by the Order. The corpses of any necromancer or suspected necromancer are far too dangerous to consign to a normal cemetery." She pounced on the subject, raising a point she knew Hulmul would have to concede. "The body of Marius the Damned was stolen and no one knows where it was taken. They say his disciples built a secret crypt for him somewhere under Singerva."

"So, the temple-fort has catacombs as well as dungeons beneath its foundations." Gaiseric shook his head. "As though this place could be more sinister. Even when you die, they don't let you leave."

"The catacombs and dungeons will be the most heavily defended areas in the temple-fort," Helchen said. "Both to keep prisoners from escaping and to guard against unruly spirits rising from the catacombs."

"Being the best guarded, that's also where the Order would keep anything of value," Alaric added.

"Many inquisitors keep the artifacts confiscated by their

witch hunters, securing them in a protected vault." Helchen pointed her finger at the ground. "Somewhere down there."

Ursola looked through the documents she'd brought from Ironshield's archives. "High Inquisitor Elza must have figured that dwarves are the best engineers to employ working underground, so maybe she had a bit more sense than most of you tall-legs." She pointed at Helchen. "You've the right of it. What we're looking for will be below, not above. I'd suggest trying to find some stairs going down."

"So, we look for some stairs," Alaric stated. He motioned the group forward but had only taken a few steps before he immediately stopped before reaching the door.

"There's an ominous sign," Hulmul said, gesturing with his staff at a wide streak of blood that spread away from the temple-fort's doors. It looked like the trail of some sanguinary slug.

Helchen stepped nearer and pointed out something even more ominous. "Whatever left all that blood didn't stay where it fell," she said. A line of crimson footprints led away from the outline of a body picked out in dried gore. They turned back into the temple-fort.

"Cadavaz," Ratbag growled. Helchen thought he was referring to the footprints, but the orc indicated Fang. The wolf's ears were pressed back against its skull, its fur bristling. It was staring ahead at the doorway and the darkness beyond.

"I guess we won't be finding this place as deserted as Ironshield and Company," Gaiseric muttered. Immediately he turned and offered Helchen an apology. "I forgot these people were your colleagues."

The witch hunter shook her head. She'd learned long ago

to avoid emotional attachments. Helchen was stuck with the ones she'd brought with her when joining the Order, like her brother and his family, but Dietrich had impressed on her that it was weakness to form new ones. Even with other witch hunters. At all times, she was taught to strive only for the convictions of the Order, regardless of who had to be sacrificed for those convictions.

"What's done is done. There's no changing it," Helchen said. She inspected her crossbow and walked toward the gaping doors. "Make torches. It's dark inside." Her eyes roved across the shadowy threshold, almost hoping for a zombie to show itself. There was nothing she could do about slaughtered initiates of the Order, or the murder of its officials, but she could put a stop to the profanation of the temple-fort.

The undead would discover there was nothing so brutally impersonal as the vengeance of a witch hunter.

Hulmul's skin crawled and he felt a heaviness constricting his chest the moment he entered the temple-fort. *Your nerves*, he told himself. If there had been any anti-magic wards or similar protections, they'd have been much more definitive about pushing him out.

No, it was the mere fact that he, a wizard, was walking into a place that held such terror for those of practiced magic. However meticulous and scrupulous a wizard was about what was learned and how it was used, there always remained the fear. The fear that the Order would latch onto some spiteful rumor or a black lie spread by an enemy. The merest accusation, at the right time and in the right ear, might see anyone investigated by the witch hunters. Put to the question in their torture chambers. Perhaps a great man like Vasilescu was immune to such worries, but for Hulmul, the dread of being dragged into the dungeons of the Order had always been there.

"Be concerned about zombies," Helchen told the wizard as the group filed into the bleak entry hall. "Singerva's witch hunters won't be accusing anyone of necromancy any time soon." While she spoke, she glanced meaningfully at the walls and floor. By the crackling torches, Hulmul could see that there was blood everywhere, sometimes with a grisly, more substantial reminder of the human form.

"There are no bodies," Hulmul said. "That means whoever left all that blood must have risen again as one of the undead."

Drahoslav paced along one side of the hall, careful to anchor his flank with a solid wall. "It would have taken a lot of zombies to overcome the witch hunters," he objected, nodding at Helchen. "They wouldn't have gone down without a fight, and people in your profession know how to kill a zombie and make it stay dead."

Hulmul thought over the duelist's remark as they marched deeper into the building. The witch hunters hadn't been exactly austere when they furnished the temple-fort. The floor, where it wasn't spattered with blood, consisted of checkered tiles of white marble and malachite. The walls were covered by lush tapestries depicting scenes from the *Ten Heroic Classics*, the most revered of the kingdom's literary works. Gilded lamps hung from sconces along the walls. They were dull now, their oil consumed in the long hours since calamity struck the temple-fort.

Alaric moved to the first door that opened out into the hall, the rest following behind while Drahoslav kept watch in the corridor. The room within looked to have been a guardroom of some sort, little larger than an alcove, with a few chairs and a broken table. A rack of halberds rested against one wall while a shelf with several bundles of arrows was on the other. Here too, Hulmul saw the evidence of bloody battle but no bodies.

"Something's taking the dead away," the wizard declared, expressing what he thought they all must be thinking.

"Zombies aren't that clever," Gaiseric protested. He crouched near the broken table and started plucking silver coins off the floor from amid a litter of playing cards and broken flagons.

"At least not any we've seen," Helchen warned. "This plague has already created forms of undead not mentioned in any text."

Alaric's face took on a vicious quality as he added another thought. "It might also be that someone's been around to give them instructions." It was clear he was thinking about the necromancer who'd led the attack on his family's castle. Much as Hulmul didn't want to admit it, the notion was entirely possible.

"Necromancers can exert control over all but the most willful undead," Hulmul stated. "How great that control and over how many at any moment depends on many factors, not the least of which is the knowledge and power of the necromancer."

"Why take bodies?" Gaiseric asked. "I mean, any zombie killed by someone is finished, isn't it?"

Hulmul used his staff to tap a grisly object clasping one

of the halberds still in the rack. A severed hand, chewed off at the wrist, fell to the floor. "Magic, light and dark, is the realization of possibility. Harnessing arcane formulae to turn imagination into reality. Every wizard experiments with the art he's learned, trying to turn it down different paths. Evoke it by different methods. Refine and enhance."

"A typical wizard is constrained by the laws of the Guild," Helchen added. "Bound by a code that limits how far to go. The morality of the methods used. A necromancer recognizes no such restraint. That is what makes them such a menace."

Hulmul was surprised to hear Helchen express the matter with such nuance. Perhaps she was disabusing herself of the absolutes she'd been taught. Willing to admit there were wizards who didn't abuse their powers.

"One thing is certain," Alaric said. "The removal of the bodies can only be an ill tiding." He marched back into the corridor. "Let's find our way down to these vaults and get out of here."

Hulmul could hear the conflicted note in Alaric's voice. The knight's valor urged him to confront danger, but his duty to the people taking shelter in Vasilescu's tower forced him to turn away from it. He could appreciate the dilemma, torn between what he wanted to do and what he needed to do.

They proceeded through the temple-fort, checking each room they passed. Everywhere were the signs of battle, but always with the absence of bodies. Far from lessening the horror of the situation, Hulmul felt the lack of corpses contributed still another sinister overture. The temple-fort took on an atmosphere not merely of being abandoned, but a feeling of desolation. Here, he felt, the evil that had ravaged

Singerva had been far more than mindlessly capricious. Here, in this place, it had focused its full malevolence.

Yet was it as abandoned as it seemed to be? Hulmul noticed that Fang remained agitated, the wolf's attitude unchanged since they first entered the building. The animal knew something they didn't. He wished he'd at least dabbled in the sort of magic that could let him read Fang's mind, but the wolf was far different from a familiar. A familiar like Malicious wasn't merely an animal, but a part of the wizard himself, an extension of his own being. He still felt an emptiness within his soul where the winged reptile's presence should be, a psychic wound Vasilescu's spells might have healed but couldn't erase.

"Stairs," Gaiseric reported, jogging back from a bend in the corridor.

The group tensed as they rounded the bend. Ahead the corridor continued onward for forty feet, but one side of it was given over to a staircase with broad marble steps and a carved balustrade. Ursola sighed and said what all of them were thinking. "Those go *up*, not *down*. The traps Ironshield and Company built will be under our feet, not over our heads."

"Take it up with the architect," Gaiseric said, his tone sour. "I just find 'em, I don't build 'em."

"We can ignore the upper floors, for now." Helchen turned away from the stairs. "What we want shouldn't be there…"

The witch hunter spun around, her eyes narrowing as she stared back at the stairway. They all heard what had alarmed her. It was the sound of someone on the steps. A lot of people.

"Survivors?" Ursola wondered as some of the sounds resolved themselves into footsteps running down the stairs.

Ratbag stepped to the base of the stairway, a savage grin on his face. "Cadavaz," he hissed, slapping the flat of his scimitar against his palm.

Helchen raised her crossbow. The first runner that charged down the stairs was knocked back as a bolt slammed into its body. She was visibly relieved that the creature wore the rags of a valet rather than the vestments of a witch hunter. The zombie servant was far from alone. Six more undead townsfolk hurtled toward them, their eyes alight with that terrible, feral hunger.

Drahoslav dropped one of the creatures with an arrow through its skull, then he whipped out his rapier to join the melee at the bottom of the stairs. Ratbag slashed at the first runner to reach him, the strength of the orc's strike breaking the creature's spine and nearly cutting it in half. As the runner slid across the floor, it still struggled to claw at its foe. Gaiseric darted in and ended its animation with a chop to its head.

Alaric blocked another zombie with his kite shield, fending it away while he struck at it with his longsword. The runner's frantic, rabid motions made it difficult for him to strike a telling blow, but he was able to finally chop away enough of its leg to drop the creature. While it was prone, he collapsed its skull with the edge of his shield.

Fang bore another of the zombies to the ground, ripping and tearing at its decayed flesh. Ursola prevented another runner from rounding on the wolf. Her hammer struck it under the chin with such force that its jawbone was driven up through its face.

In the swirl of battle, Hulmul didn't dare to use his more

devastating spells. He instead read from a less intricate incantation and pointed his finger at the zombie Helchen had crippled. A blob of searing blue light leapt from the condemning finger and slammed into the valet as it started back down the stairs. It toppled back again, its face steaming where the arcane bolt struck it.

"Here's another one for them to carry away," Drahoslav bragged as he pierced the last runner's heart and let the zombie drop to the floor. Somehow, he was able to turn himself so that the blood spurting from its chest failed to stain his white vestment.

"Good, because I think they're here to collect," Gaiseric quipped, wagging his sword at the stairway. They could all hear the relentless tromp of many feet descending the steps. The runners had merely ranged ahead of a much greater company of undead.

"That answers where all the zombies went," Alaric said. The knight gave an appraising look to the breadth of the stairway. "This is the nearest thing to a chokepoint we're apt to find. We can hold them here, if we stand our ground."

Ursola motioned for Hulmul to hold her hammer and torch. While the wizard tried to manage them and his staff as well, the dwarf reached into her satchel and withdrew one of the firebombs. "I have a better idea," she said.

Hulmul was impressed by the dwarf's calm when the zombies turned the bend above them and the size of the horde became apparent. Ursola didn't care that there were scores of the undead, she just kept watching their progress. He realized she was gauging the distance to the landing above them, the last stop before they would start down to the corridor below.

Judging how much time it would take the zombies to reach that point.

"Light the fuse," Ursola asked Hulmul, holding the bomb towards him. Not without a little anxiety, he dipped the torch towards the weapon. Magic was something he knew and understood, but these dwarfish devices were another thing. For a horrible moment, he expected the bomb to explode in his face. It was almost a pleasant sensation compared to the nausea of watching the fuse burn while Ursola simply held it in her hand, eyes darting from the fuse to the landing. Would the bomb simply spread fire, or would it bring the entire structure down about their heads? The wizard shuddered. Whether they perished in the collapse or by the zombie horde, they'd still be dead.

Throw it! Hulmul could tell he wasn't the only one who wanted to shout at Ursola. None of them dared, lest they should distract the dwarf from her purpose.

"There," Ursola said with satisfaction as the foremost of the zombies shambled onto the landing. With a heave she sent the bomb sailing upward. It smashed into the walkers, engulfing them and everything nearby in orange flames.

Hulmul watched in wonder as the zombies collapsed amid the fire, their fearful animation consumed by the flames. Certainly, there were spells that could accomplish such a feat, but better than most, he knew the complexities of wielding such magic. Ursola had achieved the same results with a device that, he imagined, anyone could be taught to make and use. The… casualness… of such power was frightening in its possibilities. He was grateful the dwarves were so protective of their secrets and didn't share their knowledge with outsiders.

"Der cadavaz naht gonna scarpa," Ratbag growled. Hulmul thought he understood the orc's meaning. Unlike the moat around Vasilescu's tower, the zombies weren't driven back by the flames. Instead, they continued to march with mindless determination. More of them were consumed by fire, but with each addition to the pile, the fire burned a bit lower.

"We'll run out of fire before we run out of zombies," Hulmul declared.

Ursola patted her satchel. "No, we won't," she assured him.

At that moment, Helchen cried out. She pointed to a side passage that opened into the corridor. "More of them!"

Hulmul felt a shiver run through him when he saw the second horde plodding toward them. It wasn't merely the size of the mob, or even the fact that several wore the tattered remains of the Order's uniform. It was the ghastly thing that was in their lead. In life it had been a middle-aged woman. He couldn't make out much of her features, for half her face had been eaten away down to the bone. What was distinct, if bloodied, were the robes she wore. The black and crimson robes of the high inquisitor!

"Caught between the anvil and the hammer," Ursola grumbled. She nodded at the wood that lined the side passage. There was little fear of fire spreading from a marble stairway. The same couldn't be said for the route the second zombie mob was using.

"More trouble behind us," Gaiseric cursed. A third pack of zombies could be seen staggering into the temple-fort from the street outside.

"This way!" Alaric shouted, directing them down the corridor beside the stairway. "Before they encircle us completely!"

There wasn't time to question the knight's choice. Hulmul ran alongside the others as they hurried down the only avenue left open to them by the converging undead. But as he ran, he couldn't shake a dark feeling. An impression that they were *intended* to flee in this direction.

What the wizard's intuition couldn't tell him was why.

CHAPTER FOURTEEN

"They're herding us," Alaric snarled as the group hurried down the corridor. A few runners broke from the pack of zombies following them, charging down the hall. Ratbag and Fang quickly disposed of the creatures.

"They're witless," Drahoslav scoffed. "They can't plan a strategy." The duelist whipped his rapier at one of the zombies Ratbag slashed with his scimitar. The slender blade pierced the skull. "They're dead. They're all–"

"They're using some sort of strategy." Alaric cut him off. Two more runners came sprinting toward them. Ratbag chopped one almost in half with his blade while his wolf bore the other down and decapitated it after tearing out its throat. "Or do you have another explanation for their restraint?"

The knight could see that Drahoslav didn't. Ahead of them, another mob of zombies emerged from a doorway. Again, only a brace of runners broke away from the pack to charge them. Helchen dropped one with a bolt. Alaric met the other, catching it on his shield and using it to pin the creature against the wall. He chopped the top of its skull away with his longsword and the zombie's dreadful animation was extinguished.

"We can't get through that," Hulmul declared, shaking his staff at the mob blocking their path. It looked to be dozens strong, and any time spent hacking a path through them would allow the pursuing horde to close in.

"We'll have to take this hallway," Ursola said, pointing at a connecting passage midway between themselves and the zombies ahead.

Alaric nodded and motioned the others to follow his lead. No more runners came at them from the mob in front, though he could hear Ratbag and Fang fending off more of the creatures drawn from the horde behind them. The knight's uneasiness increased when he noticed that the mob at the end of the corridor appeared to have slowed their already shambling advance. Exactly as if some controlling force had ordered them to. He thought again of Gogol and the way the necromancer had commanded the zombies in the chapel. Let whatever blackguard was leading these undead show themselves for even an instant and he'd bury his sword in their heart!

The knight rounded the corner, almost hoping to see a necromancer waiting for them. Instead, Alaric found only an empty hallway. "Hurry!" he yelled to his companions. "The passage is clear!" He didn't know how long that last statement would hold true, so he urged the others on, waggling his shield at them.

"I don't like this," Helchen commented as she darted past Alaric and into the hall. "It's like they're pressing us just enough to keep us moving."

Alaric nodded. "My thoughts exactly." He glanced at the mobs of zombies at either end of the main corridor. "But I don't see there's anything we can do about it."

Everyone reached the side passage. A set of runners followed them, but again proved unable to bypass the orc's blade and the wolf's teeth.

"If we move fast enough, maybe we can get past whatever they're driving us towards," Helchen suggested. "Get there before they're ready."

Drahoslav shot a reproving look at the witch hunter. "Zombies can't devise tactics," he insisted. Alaric noted that the duelist quickened his pace just the same.

"If they're trying to trap us, I'll make sure to take them all with me," Ursola vowed, one hand slapping the satchel of bombs she carried.

Gaiseric ranged ahead of the group, holding his torch before him to illuminate the passage ahead. Alaric was puzzled that they'd yet to see any doors or hallways connecting to the one they were in. Then the thief stopped and called back to them. "More stairs," he said. "And this time they *do* go down."

Alaric came up beside Gaiseric and found himself staring at a narrow flight of stone steps that plunged into darkness. The thief waited until Hulmul came up with another torch, then tossed his own into the gloom. It sailed downward some thirty feet before crashing onto the floor at the base of the steps. Alaric could make out rough stone walls and a heavy oak door that had been battered off its hinges. Blood as well, though no bodies were visible.

"What we want's going to be down there," Helchen said as she joined them. She laughed grimly. "It doesn't look it now, but that would be the most secure part of the temple-fort."

"The traps Ironshield designed are down there," Ursola provided. She pointed to the copper sheaves she had bundled under her belt. "Some of the plans call for more space and stouter anchoring than you'd get above ground. Whatever High Inquisitor Elza was trying to protect, it'll be down there."

The sounds of combat were renewed. Alaric turned to see Ratbag and his wolf engaged with another clutch of runners. This time there were four of the rabid zombies. The knight hurried to help, striking down a creature before it could sink its fangs in the orc's arm.

"Clam yer booshwash, an' lay inta der cadavaz," Ratbag snarled, raking his scimitar across the shoulder of another zombie and leaving its arm lying on the floor.

"He says your talk is interesting," Gaiseric translated as he chopped into a decayed leg and sent a zombie to the ground. Ratbag bared his fangs at the thief. "Or words to that effect," he added in an apologetic tone.

Alaric took Drahoslav's torch as the man came up. Leaving him to help finish off the runners, the knight jogged a short distance back down the hallway. He stopped the moment the light he was carrying showed him a file of zombies slowly marching up the corridor. He recognized the ragged robes of the high inquisitor. The horde from before had joined up with the one that had forced them into this passage.

"Only one way to go," Alaric reported as he ran back. He dashed down the stairs toward the torch Gaiseric had thrown. After all the effort the zombies had shown pushing them this way, he expected an ambush when he reached the bottom.

Instead there was only gloom and shadow. Even whoever had bled all over the walls and door was gone.

"It's all right," Alaric called up. Helchen and Gaiseric were already halfway down the steps. The others quickly followed. Hulmul, as he descended, paused to lay his torch down to illuminate the top of the stairs.

Not long after they were all at the bottom, Alaric saw several zombies rush into the area illuminated by the wizard's torch. One fell down the steps, Drahoslav's arrow in its head. Another was thrown back by a shot from Helchen's crossbow.

Despite the proof that these were runners, the rest of the pack made no move to descend the steps. Another of Drahoslav's arrows pierced an undead head and knocked the creature down.

"What are they waiting for?" Gaiseric wondered.

"As long as they stay where they are, I can keep picking them off," Drahoslav laughed, letting fly with another arrow. Again, the duelist's precision dropped a zombie.

Helchen grabbed Drahoslav's arm as he reached for another arrow. "Have you thought what you'll do when you have no ammunition? Better conserve what we have until we need it."

Alaric saw Elza's zombie again, leading the slower walkers. Just like the runners, they stopped at the top of the stairs.

"It's as if they're afraid to come down," Alaric said. He glanced over at Helchen. "Would the Order have some sort of defense to hold back the undead? Keep them from straying down here?"

"Not anything I've heard of. At least not in a permanent sense," Helchen replied. She nodded at the bloodstains. "Besides, it looks like they were down here before."

"Something is holding them back," Hulmul said. "Maybe because this is where they wanted us to go."

Alaric scowled up at the mass of undead above them. "Whatever's going on, there's little we can do about it. At least right now." He considered the stone walls and floor. "If they do descend, Ursola's firebombs will give us an edge."

"It doesn't matter what's going on," Gaiseric declared. "Just as long as we get what we came for and get out."

As usual, Alaric reflected, the thief was taking the pragmatic view.

The tunnels beneath the temple-fort lacked the comfort and ostentation of those above. Here all was cold, bare stone. Sconces for torches were bolted to the walls, but the brands they'd held had burnt down to charred stubs hours – if not days – ago. Blood was everywhere, testament to the fighting that had unfolded here in the murk of the dungeons.

Helchen watched as Ursola took the lead, carrying one of the remaining torches. The dwarf was meticulous in her progress, exactingly studying the walls and floor – even the ceiling – every five feet or so before deciding to press on. The threat of the zombie horde at their backs, an undead tide that might come rushing after them at any moment, appeared to make no impact on her. The witch hunter studied the dwarf's every move, wary for anything suspicious. She didn't like being forced into a position where she had to trust the skill of someone else. It was one thing to make use of expertise to be expedient, but quite another to know success depended entirely on their ability... and their fidelity. In such circumstances, Captain Dietrich had always insisted that intimidation was the key to compelling loyalty, but that tactic simply wouldn't work with Ursola. Nor, did she suppose, would it have been agreeable to Alaric. The knight's sensibilities were much different from her own when it came to the use of authority.

"You'll be just as dead if we trigger one of Ironshield's traps," Ursola reminded them when Drahoslav urged her to hurry. The warning didn't need to be repeated.

Despite her vigilance, Helchen didn't see what made the dwarf suddenly stop in the middle of the passage. She thought she saw Ursola's eyes linger on the wall to her left, but couldn't detect whatever it was. What was certain was the dwarf removed the bundle of copper sheaves and quickly thumbed through them.

"She's found a trap," Gaiseric whispered, just a hint of wonder in his voice.

"Naht lampin' nuthin'," Ratbag grumbled.

"Just because you don't see it, doesn't mean it isn't there," Gaiseric told the orc. "That's kind of the point of a trap."

Helchen still couldn't see what had alerted Ursola, but now the dwarf was on her hands and knees, crawling across the floor and peering at the paving stones in front of her. Finally, she stopped and fixed her gaze on one stone in particular. She set her hammer and torch down. She rubbed her fingers across her palms, twitching as she tried to nerve herself for what she had to do.

For what seemed hours, the tableau held, Ursola staring at the paving stone, rubbing her hands. Finally, she scurried backwards, creeping like some cave lizard. When she was a few feet back, she turned to the rest of them.

"Well? What's wrong?" Helchen asked, not realizing until she spoke how tense she'd become.

Ursola wiped away the sweat that beaded her brow. "I can't do it." The confession appeared to come hard for the dwarf. "I'm not an engineer. I'm a demolisher. If you wanted me to blast it with powder and fuse, that I could do, but it would collapse the tunnel."

Alaric shook his head. "A fine time to tell us this," he reproached her. He gestured at the dark hallway behind them. "We've probably covered a hundred yards since the stairway, and now you tell us you can't disarm the traps?"

"I can find them," Ursola snapped back. "None of you would know the marks..." At once she closed her mouth, her face reddening. Helchen thought she understood now why the dwarf had been so cagey. The engineers had left secret marks to denote the location of each trap, marks that corresponded to the designs etched into the copper sheaves. She was trying to protect the trade secrets of her kinsfolk.

"You can find them, but you can't remove them," Helchen said. She looked over at Gaiseric. "Well, it seems in your line of work."

Alaric nodded at Gaiseric. "Far too much in his line of work. There wasn't a house in the whole of my father's domain that was safe if he showed an interest in it. Not even the Baron's castle. And we had some expert trapsmiths try to ensure that didn't happen twice." The knight smiled. "As it turns out, Gaiseric was too slippery to catch until his fifth excursion into the castle."

The thief licked his lips nervously. "Much as I appreciate the acknowledgment, I'm afraid you don't understand a dwarfish trap. They're the most complicated cockamamie things you'd never want to see." He nodded in apology to Ursola. "What I mean is a human tinkering up a trap is straightforward in how it's handled. A pressure plate or a spring or whatever other trigger and straight back to whatever surprise you want to leave for somebody. A dwarf makes a trap, though, and it's a maze of gears and pinfalls, all interconnected like a spiderweb. Break a single strand… just tease it too much, and you wake up the spider."

"At least you know your limitations," Drahoslav chuckled.

Gaiseric rounded on the duelist. "I'd like to see you take a crack at it," he told Drahoslav. "Might get that sparkly white outfit of yours mussed up if you caused an axe to drop from the ceiling or acid to spray from the walls." His face quivered with anger. "On second thought, I wouldn't like to see you try, because whatever you set off might miss you and hit me."

Still fuming, Gaiseric walked over to Ursola. Helchen glanced over at Drahoslav. The duelist winked and a cunning smile flashed across his features.

"All right, tell me what to look for," Gaiseric said as he inched toward the paving stone the dwarf had studied for so long. "You can coach me that far, at least."

Ursola sat down beside him and studied the copper sheet with the trap's design. "You just pry up the–"

Gaiseric held up his hand. "Before we start, what's it supposed to do and how is it triggered?"

The dwarf had to tone down her initial explanation, which strayed into too many technical aspects, but after a while explained it with such clarity even Helchen was able to follow what she was describing. It didn't make the witch hunter any easier. The paving stone they were looking at was the key to an entire chain of stones that would trigger an array of steel darts to spray out from the walls. It went without saying that they were tipped in venomous resin brewed from scorpions. The least scratch could kill an ogre. There was a way to safely disarm the trap, but since the Order maintained guards deeper in the dungeon and this trap was intended to stop people breaking *in* rather than *out*, the place it could be disarmed was on the other side.

Helchen had to credit Gaiseric's composure as he listened to the details. The thief really was in his element, she thought, whatever protests he might make otherwise. Learning the nature and purpose of the trap appeared to calm rather than excite him. She thought of something Dietrich had drummed into her during her training: the first terror of the human mind is the unknown.

"We've seen signs the zombies got this far," Alaric said. "Wouldn't that mean the traps have already been triggered?"

Ursola nodded, but her expression was dour. "There's a docket of darts that feed into the mechanism. It could be triggered scores of times before the ammunition was exhausted. A dwarf builds things to endure, not to be used once and discarded."

"Hulmul, you have any sort of spell that might knock away a dart?" Gaiseric suddenly asked.

"I could guard you with my shield," Alaric offered.

Gaiseric shot him a stern look. "A dwarf trap might punch through even steel. Besides, your shield can only cover one angle. Our other side would still be exposed."

Hulmul rummaged in his pack and withdrew a scroll. "The

Bellows of Thrynych," he announced proudly. His face soon dropped into a frown. "Of course they're very strong. The gust of wind would blow both you and the darts down the tunnel."

"Keep it handy anyway," Gaiseric said. "Better to be knocked around by your spell than poisoned by the trap. If you hear me swear, don't hesitate, just cast away." He reached to a pouch on his belt and withdrew a silver coin. Helchen had noted the thief availing himself of coins and other treasure, but hadn't seen him put any of it in that pouch. She started to think it was a lucky piece, but if it was, Gaiseric still had a more practical use for it.

Fascinated, the witch hunter watched as Gaiseric used the coin, which had one edge filed down to a sharp sliver, to pry up the stone. As he eased it up, he replaced the coin and produced a set of small iron triangles. Holding the stone up with one hand, he eased the wedges under until they were so firmly set that they could support the burden on their own.

"All right Ursola, tell me what I'm looking for," Gaiseric said. He started setting more tools on the floor next to him, picks and blocks of wax and things Helchen couldn't begin to give a name to.

Tense minutes followed as Ursola directed Gaiseric. The thief poked and prodded at the mechanism under the stone, sometimes breaking a corner from the wax to apply to some small lever or spring and prevent their movement. Each time he stopped, Helchen expected to see darts shoot from the wall and pepper the thief's body. The feared moment, however, never came.

"That was almost easy," Gaiseric declared as he stood up, wiping his hands on his leggings. He smiled at Ursola. "New experience having the design of the trap to work from. Feels almost like cheating."

"No wonder you look happy," Alaric told the thief. "Didn't you say the only game worth playing is one you've rigged in your favor?"

"It depends on the stakes," rejoined Gaiseric. "When the reward's slight, the risk isn't worth the effort."

The knight laughed. "The Baron never understood why I asked him to be lenient with you. It's hard to bear someone malice who takes such pride in being a rogue, and even a noble should concede when someone's good at their trade. However larcenous it might be."

Helchen didn't join in the laughter. She was thinking of what was ahead of them… and a point on which Ursola had so far been evasive. "How many more traps did Ironshield and Company build?"

The dwarf bowed her head. "I can't tell you that." She hurried to explain why, waving the bundle of copper sheaves. "I only know how many designs were used, not how many of those designs might have been constructed. They might have been used only once, or they might have been built many times."

Gaiseric turned toward her, all levity drained from his face. 'How… how many different designs did your people use?"

Ursola slapped the copper sheaves, producing a metallic warble. "Seven."

The thief was anything but happy with that answer. Half in jest he posed a question to his companions. "What do you say we try to cut our way through the zombies?"

"What we need to get is going to be down here," Helchen

said. She had a sour taste in her mouth as she thought about the purpose of their mission. They were, in essence, looting the treasures of the Order to fetch something for a wizard. Even if her concern about Vasilescu's integrity was baseless, it came hard for the witch hunter to reconcile such an action now that she was actually beneath the temple-fort. It felt almost tantamount to sacrilege. "This is the most secure part of the building."

Gaiseric gathered up his tools from the floor. "I don't know why anyone thinks playing hero is so great. The pay's lousy and the risks are absurd." He stuffed all of his implements back into the pouch. "Well, let's hurry along before I come to my senses and decide to sit this one out."

"It's all right," Helchen told him as they started back down the tunnel, Ursola resuming her place in the lead. "If you need to take a rest, we'll wait for you. You don't need to worry about Drahoslav stepping on your toes."

The thief slapped his fist into his palm. "You know," he mused, "I think he set me up."

"You're a suspicious man," Helchen told him. She smiled. "You'd have made a good witch hunter."

Gaiseric didn't even try to hide his relief when they finally reached the chambers at the end of the tunnel. True, there had been a few diversions along the way, guardrooms and storerooms where the group had hurriedly replenished their supplies. They continued to find bloodstains until they reached the fifth trap. This, as Ursola explained, was a mechanism that released a gout of fire into the tunnel. Knowing the trick of its operation, it was safely disarmed and the group bypassed it. Try as she might, however, Ursola couldn't get it rearmed. An ill omen in his opinion. As they pressed beyond the fire-trap, the sudden lack of bloodstains informed them that the zombies hadn't gotten further into the tunnel.

Six more traps followed afterward, one was a complex design that had to be manually disengaged just like the first one had, a last surprise for anyone trying to break into the dungeons. Its mechanism, if activated, would have sent a corrosive cloud rolling down the tunnel until it was sucked up through vents near the stairs. Gaiseric was sick after disarming it, aware that one slip would have doomed them all.

But now, at last, after seven hundred feet of perilous hallway, they were past. Gaiseric might have been happier about that had their surroundings been less grisly. They were in the torture chamber, the place where the witch hunters put their suspects to the question. A cistern with a dunking chair set above it on a long wooden beam. The terrible rack, with its chains and winches at either end. The infamous iron maiden, its exterior sculpted to resemble a praying woman, its inside ringed with cruel spikes. There were other implements, each ghastlier than the next. Just looking at them made Gaiseric shiver.

The thief looked over at Helchen, seeing her in a far different and more sinister light. It was one thing to know the extremes witch hunters went to in an abstract sense, but to see the evidence with his own eyes was a thing too grave to be ignored.

Hulmul glared at Helchen. "The monster's lair," he pronounced, trembling with fright and fury. The wizard stalked toward the barred gateway on the left side of the torture chamber. "The cells would be this way, wouldn't they?"

Until that point, Helchen had been quiet, but now she hurried after Hulmul. "Stop! We don't know who's in there... or why."

The wizard stopped and fixed her with a defiant stare. "It doesn't matter, I'm going to set them free. You'll have to kill me to stop me." Hulmul held Helchen's gaze, daring her to act.

Alaric ran over, trying to defuse the altercation. "We've got to do what we came here to do," he scolded them.

"And leave these victims of the Order to rot?" Hulmul waved his fist at Helchen. "I won't do it!"

"Free them, and set loose more necromancers," Helchen said. "I'm sure that won't make things worse."

The others looked on, uncertain what to do. Which side to take. Gaiseric was just as divided, but he couldn't stand idle and do nothing. "Isn't there some sort of test? Some way to see if the prisoners are..."

His words trailed off. At that moment, Gaiseric noticed Fang. The wolf was staring at the gateway, exhibiting all the signs that it detected the undead.

"But they couldn't get past the trap," Helchen said, noting where Gaiseric was looking, and why.

Alaric picked up on something else. He glanced around the torture chamber. "The trap was armed from this side. So where are the guards?"

The knight had just made the observation when sounds billowed out from the passage beyond the barred gate. The noise of flapping wings.

"Not again," Drahoslav grumbled.

"Crows!" Hulmul shouted, scrambling away from the gate and diving behind a torture rack.

Gaiseric saw black-feathered bodies squeeze through the bars on the gate before launching themselves into the chamber. He'd been wrong to think no zombies had slipped past that last trap. These undead crows had flown over the pressure plates without setting off the corrosive cloud. It was easy to guess that the guards had tried to barricade themselves in the cellblock only to be slaughtered along with their prisoners by the hideous birds.

"Guard your eyes!" Alaric shouted, swinging his sword at the birds swarming around him. It was like trying to swat flies with a mallet. The crows dodged his strikes and darted back for another attack.

Gaiseric howled as one of the birds tore his shoulder with its beak. He saw Fang dive into the cistern to free itself of the crows plaguing it. The wolf was soon joined by Helchen, her cheek bleeding from a crow's claws.

"There's too many of them!" Drahoslav yelled. The duelist was pressed up against a niche in the wall, availing himself of a situation where the crows could only dive at him from the front.

"Hulmul!" Gaiseric called to the wizard. "Make ready with that wind spell!" A wild idea had set upon the thief, but it would need cunning, magic, and a lot of brute force to work.

Brute force was near at hand, slashing away with his scimitar. "Ratbag!" Gaiseric shouted to the orc. When he was certain of the renegade's attention, he pointed at the iron maiden. "When I say, throw that into the tunnel."

"Yer goona daft, yer twit?" Ratbag growled back.

"Just do it," Gaiseric told him. "You'll kill lots of zombies," he added, hoping to encourage Ratbag the way he had down in the leatherworks. The renegade smiled, clearly recalling the same thing.

"Everybody, grab something and hold tight!" Alaric shouted, guessing Gaiseric's plan.

Gaiseric took hold of the counterbalance to the dunking chair. "Hulmul, do it now!"

At the thief's order, Hulmul stood up, his robes whipping around as though a cyclone were swirling around him. Several crows dove down, but the birds went spinning away as they struck the whirlwind that surrounded him. Then he lifted his staff in both hands and the whirlwind expanded.

Gaiseric felt the arcane tempest dragging at him, threatening to tear his fingers loose and send him careening through the air. Only by exerting every last speck of strength was he able to retain his hold.

The crows, with nothing to anchor them, were knocked about the torture chamber until, finally, they were sent tumbling out into the tunnel. Gaiseric watched as more and more of the birds were pushed from the room. When no more of the creatures were buffeted by the wind, he shouted to Ratbag. "Now!"

The orc had used the iron maiden to anchor himself. Now he stood up, hefting the insidious metal cabinet in both arms. Ratbag's body was blasted by the tempest, but still he managed to slowly march to the end of the tunnel. With a heave, he sent the iron maiden crashing into the corridor and rolling down the tunnel. In its tumble, the face of the sculpture triggered the pressure plate and caught. From hidden reserves, a great gout of corrosive gas was sent billowing into the tunnel.

Gaiseric could see the crows, struggling against the wind, trying to return to the torture chamber. The birds were caught in the cloud of gas, their feathers sizzling away from the bodies. One after another they dropped to the floor, flesh dripping from their bones. None could escape the deathly fog. Hulmul's spell hurled every wisp at them, and the pressure of the iron maiden kept the trap expelling gas until its reserves were finally exhausted.

Hulmul waited until no more gas bubbled up from the trap before he dismissed his spell. Exhausted, the wizard sagged against the torture rack. "Malicious, you are avenged."

Gaiseric started over to see if Hulmul needed aid, but an excited shout from Drahoslav turned him around. The duelist had taken shelter in the alcove, bracing himself against its sides. In doing so, he must have pressed a hidden latch, for now the back of the alcove stood open.

"I think this is what we were looking for," Drahoslav declared. "The witch hunters' vaults!"

CHAPTER FIFTEEN

The temple-fort's vault reminded Hulmul of a wizard's laboratory, though he'd never seen one so well stocked, not even Vasilescu's. There were several shelves of material components with everything from unicorn horns to the legs of colossal spiders, virtually any exotic substance the student of the mystic arts might need to further his research. Granted, much of the material had rotted from age and neglect, some of it was almost unrecognizable for the patina of dust that clung to it, but the sheer quantity of it all was impressive.

One side of the vault might have been an alchemist's shop, tables piled with potions and elixirs of every color and consistency, the motley variety of vessels of every size and shape that could be imagined. Hulmul saw narrow-necked amber bottles cut with elven glyphs on the sides, hollowed horns with hidebound seals painted with orcish symbols, and even bronze flasks branded with dwarven runes.

There were racks of miscellaneous apparatus. Hulmul noted ebony wands and crystal balls, skull-topped staves and athames with ripple-blades, devilish jade idols and waxen effigies. The shrunken heads employed by goblin shamans to commune with spirits. Dismembered hands coated in pitch that were used to bring unnatural sleep upon a household. Wolfskin belts with clasps fashioned from human fingerbones, the province of the sorcerous shapechanger. A veritable menagerie of arcane devices.

The wizard felt cold inside when he considered that all the items in the vault had been seized from people suspected of necromancy. How many of them, Hulmul wondered, had truly been guilty, and how many more had been innocent victims of inquisitorial zeal? It was the old argument between the Wizards' Guild and the Order of the Witch Hunters. Was it better that one necromancer go, free rather than unjustly condemn ten innocents? Or was it, as the witch hunter maintained, acceptable to sacrifice ten innocents lest one necromancer remain loose to spread evil in the kingdom?

Before the black plague, Hulmul could have answered that question. Now, having seen the magnitude of destruction visited on the land, he wasn't sure. It wasn't merely the ten innocents caught in the hunt, but all the potential victims of a free necromancer.

"The books," Gaiseric gasped. The thief dashed forward to a wide array of bookcases lined along the wall. He was careful to keep his torch well away from the musty tomes as he tried to read the letters on their spines.

"The library of the lost," Hulmul whispered as he went forward to help the thief. The volume Vasilescu was interested in had belonged to Arnault Kramm, titled *Metaphysical Investigations into Paranatural Studies*, a long-winded and not particularly illuminating title. Certainly, it wasn't one of the twelve books deemed so dangerous that the witch hunters would burn them the instant they were discovered, but as Hulmul looked over some of the illustrious and even renowned magical treatises that had been collected, he feared it might have been judged too mundane by Kramm's captors and thrown out rather than interred in the vault.

Alaric whistled appreciatively at the sheer scope of the collection... and the task ahead of them. "Like looking for the loose scale on a dragon's belly," he commented, shaking his head.

"If we each take it in sections," Hulmul suggested. He indicated a spot for Gaiseric to start, then motioned Alaric and Drahoslav to other bookcases. He looked over at Ratbag, finding him cleaning bits of flesh from between Fang's teeth with a nail he'd ripped from one of the torture implements. No, he didn't suspect reading, at least anything other than orcish symbols, was among Ratbag's talents.

"Some help here," Hulmul called to Ursola. Like iron filings to a lodestone, the dwarf was examining the collection of bottles and flasks, sloshing the liquid about in some, unstoppering others so she could sniff the contents.

"Busy," Ursola said, dismissing the wizard out of hand. She smiled and set one jar aside. It appeared to Hulmul that she had specific items in mind. He remembered her talk about crafting better explosives. He wasn't sure how pleased he should be if she did find what she needed.

Helchen was looking over the racks of assorted arcane implements. Hulmul watched her for a moment before calling her name. When he did, he thought he saw her slip something under her coat. "The book," he reminded her. The witch hunter nodded and walked over to one of the bookcases, carefully scrutinizing the titles. Hulmul wondered what, if anything, she might have surreptitiously removed from the collection… and why. If possible, he resolved to keep an even closer watch on her.

After what felt like hours, Alaric finally found the tome they were seeking. It was a battered folio bound in the hide of some reptile. When the knight handed it over, Hulmul leafed through its pages. It seemed a fairly straightforward alchemical treatise, but somewhere among its pages Kramm must have written down the unique formula Vasilescu needed.

Hulmul looked up from the book to find that his companions were all watching him. Even Ratbag had an expectant look. The wizard couldn't help but delay for a moment, teasing out that extra bit of tension, enjoying the rapt attention of his audience. After all, those who delved into the arcane sciences were showmen at heart.

"This is it," Hulmul finally declared, nodding to Alaric as he confirmed the knight's find. "This is the book Vasilescu was looking for."

"Thank Marduum for that," Helchen said.

"I'll thank any god you care to name if this means we can leave." Gaiseric started toward the vault entrance. He'd just gotten near the doorway when an arrow went whistling past his nose, missing him by a mere hair. The thief leaped back with a moan of horror, diving behind one of the shelves.

Drahoslav and Helchen scrambled forward, bow and crossbow at the ready. Hulmul tucked the book into his pack and followed them. When he reached a point where he could see into the torture chamber, the two were already shooting. Sight of the enemy sent an instinctive thrill of fear through him. Arrayed about the room was a file of fleshless skeletons, bloodied strips of armor and uniform hanging off their bones. Each skeleton held a bow and had a quiver of arrows strapped to its frame. With slow, methodical motion, the creatures drew and loosed in perfect unison, sending a volley of arrows flying into the vault. Missiles slammed into shelves and racks, shattering bottles on the table and sending everyone diving for cover.

"Is anyone hit?" Alaric hissed.

"I'm all right," Gaiseric replied, "but what in blazes are they? And where did they come from?"

A voice answered the thief, calling out from the torture chamber. "For you, they are emissaries of the grave." There was such contemptuous mockery in the tone that it was more an audible sneer than speech.

Hulmul was shocked to see the change that came upon Alaric. The knight's visage, strained but in control a moment before, became flushed with a raging fury. His eyes were like specks of fire. He drew his shield off his back and strapped it to his arm. Pulling his longsword, he marched toward the doorway. The wizard could just hear the name that left his lips in a hateful rasp.

"Gogol."

Helchen tried to stop Alaric as he charged toward the doorway, but the knight shoved her aside. "Gogol!" he shouted as he rushed from the vault. The skeletons outside concentrated their shots on him, but the arrows glanced off the heavy kite shield.

"Dis bein' der rumpuz!" Ratbag howled, his face full

of savage glee. The orc rushed after Alaric, Fang hurrying alongside him.

"Reckless or not, better than being trapped in here," Gaiseric declared, drawing his sword and following the others. It was a sentiment that made all too much sense to Helchen. To stay bottled up in the vault was to simply invite destruction.

The witch hunter plunged back through the alcove. The scene in the old torture chamber was chaos and confusion. Alaric was in among the skeletal archers, hewing their naked bones with broad sweeps of his blade. Ratbag had been foiled in his drive to reach the bowmen, a pack of less decayed zombie walkers intercepting him. Before he could be completely surrounded, Ursola was at his side, smashing skulls with her hammer. Fang leapt upon a large brute, sinking its teeth into the throat and worrying at the creature until its head went rolling away.

Drahoslav set down the elven bow, deciding a shot was too risky in the swirling melee, even for him. The duelist drew his rapier and engaged the zombies trying to encircle Alaric. He stabbed a walker, burying his blade in its ribs, then with a smooth motion sent the enemy toppling into the cistern. Unable to swim, the walker sank to the bottom.

Helchen had her mace out now, but before she rushed into battle, she spotted the necromancer. Gogol was keeping safe behind a cadre of his zombies, overseeing the fight like a general. In her experience there were two kinds of necromancers – crazed fanatics who practically worshiped death, and cowards so terrified of their own mortality that they resorted to the darkest magic to prolong their longevity.

Looking at Gogol, she'd place him in that latter camp. Why then had he risked himself by appearing now?

Helchen grabbed Hulmul's shoulder and drew him back toward the alcove. "We can't let him get into the vault," she told the wizard. "That's why he's here. That's why he dared to show himself – he wants to plunder the vault!"

It was clear to her now, the strange manner of the zombies in the temple-fort. They'd been directed by Gogol, used to drive the companions down into the dungeons. From the evidence in the tunnel, it was clear there were some traps that the undead were immune to, such as the poisoned darts, but there were others that could annihilate even them. The necromancer had used the heroes, sent them down to clear the way for him, gambling that they could succeed where his creatures had failed! Helchen shuddered to think what use Gogol could make of the materials confiscated by the Order. He could set loose horrors unimaginable, things such as the mutant rat they'd seen in Vasilescu's collection, monsters beside which the rotten hordes infesting Singerva would seem pleasant.

"I need a clear shot to target Gogol," Hulmul told her. "He's keeping zombies around him to prevent that." The wizard struck his staff against the wall in frustration. "I'm not even certain the Bellows would budge those brutes he has around him." To emphasize his words, he pointed his finger at the cadre around the necromancer. A bolt of arcane energy seared into one of the zombies, but only charred its meaty bulk.

Helchen realized the spells at Hulmul's disposal had their limitations. If Drahoslav felt hitting Gogol was so uncertain, she knew the wizard's aim wouldn't be better. "Marduum have mercy," she hissed. "We'll just have to hope we can destroy enough of his zombies that he decides to retreat."

Even as she said the words, Helchen repented them. It was as if Gogol had heard her. An enormous figure lumbered into the chamber from the tunnel. She felt her breath catch in her throat when she saw the thing. It was the abomination that had chased them away from the guildhall, a creature that had been not merely resistant but impervious to their weapons.

Hulmul, however, didn't know that. Hurriedly searching his pack, he drew out a scroll and invoked its spell. A sheet of flame billowed away from his palm. Several zombies were ignited by the wizard's magic, toppling to the floor in charred heaps, but the abomination, the real target, remained standing, uncaring that its skin had been blackened or that its clothes were smoldering.

Gogol glanced in their direction, an impish grin on his cruel face. Helchen expected him to send the abomination charging at them. Instead, the necromancer did something even worse. He pointed to the gateway leading to the cells.

The abomination stormed across the torture chamber, moving with a speed that seemed impossible for something of its bulk. Helchen looked on as its huge hands closed about the bars. With a jerk, the monster ripped the entire gateway free from its moorings and sent it crashing to the floor. From inside, a file of walkers shambled into view. Guards and prisoners, their eyes gouged out by the crows, their flesh torn by beaks and claws, marched into the room, animated by the foul energies of the zombie plague. Reinforcements for Gogol's hideous army.

Nor was the necromancer finished. Imperiously, he

gestured to a grating in the floor. Helchen paled when she saw the decayed hands reaching up through that grating, roused by Gogol's summons. She knew what it was that lurked below. Many suspects expired under torture. With their innocence in question, they couldn't be interred in a normal grave, so instead they were disposed of in catacombs beneath the dungeons alongside the remains of the guilty executed for practicing dark magic. The plague had reached down even into these blighted crypts and now the damned dead were answering the necromancer's call. Hundreds, perhaps even thousands of bodies rising from their unhallowed graves! Helchen tried to quell the dread that coursed through her veins.

The abomination stomped its way over to the grating. Ratbag broke through the walkers around him and rushed at the gigantic zombie. The orc's scimitar ripped into the monster's body, shearing through layers of flesh and muscle. Without breaking its stride, without even really looking at its attacker, the abomination struck out with its fist. The blow landed with such force that the big orc was sent flying back, spinning through the air to crash against the wall on the other side of the chamber. He sagged to the floor, stunned by the collision. Walkers started to amble towards him, but found their path blocked by Fang's frenzied efforts as the wolf defended its master.

Unopposed now, the abomination reached the grating. Much as it had with the gate to the cellblock, the creature's mighty grip tightened around the bars. There was a terrific scraping sound as the zombie strained against the locked trapdoor.

"Idiot!" Gogol snarled at it. "Remove the bar! Remove the bar!"

At the necromancer's command, the abomination shifted its focus to the steel bar that lay across the grating and secured it to the floor. Taking hold of the barrier, the creature's grip twisted the metal. When it pulled, Helchen saw the staples that held it to the floor rip free. Indifferent to its feat of strength, the abomination flung the bar aside and returned its attention to the grating itself.

This time the trapdoor's resistance was overcome in an instant. The grating was lifted away in a single piece, mortar crumbling from the frame. The abomination heaved it across the room, uncaring that it smashed a pair of walkers beneath it when it landed. The enemy hardly needed to worry about such losses, Helchen realized. There were plenty of replacements below.

A moment after the grating was gone, the undead started to emerge from the catacombs. They were even more hideous to behold, their desiccated flesh coated in a fungal fuzz. The dry conditions below acted to preserve the bodies, but until they dried out the fungi would try to draw nourishment from them. Now, as they moved, green powder drifted off the zombies as their sheen of dead mold flaked away.

Helchen felt a horror unlike anything she'd experienced before, watching the zombies climb up from the pit. Every one of them had been killed by the Order, whether by torture or execution. Now, to her, it was like the condemned were rising again to take their revenge.

And she was the only living witch hunter in the temple-fort.

•••

Every skeleton Alaric struck down only increased his rage. "Coward!" he snarled as his sword shattered the skull of another enemy and sent its bones clattering against the torture rack. "Face me, coward!"

Brunon Gogol simply sneered at him. The necromancer waved his hand and a pack of the moldy zombies rising from the catacombs moved toward him, setting another line of guards between himself and the knight. Then the villain gestured at the abomination, summoning the monstrosity to his side. It seemed he wasn't taking chances that Alaric might yet fight his way clear and charge him.

Alaric ripped his blade through the chest of a decayed walker, hewing through its heart and disrupting the profane energies animating it. He kicked the dying body aside and pressed on, stabbing at a creature wearing the frilled costume of a minstrel.

Gogol! The guilt Alaric felt was like a knife twisting in his gut. If not for him, the Baron wouldn't have shown Gogol mercy. The necromancer would have hanged long ago… and then maybe Alaric's family would still be alive. The only way he could atone for his misplaced compassion was to see the villain's blood dripping from his sword. To know that he, Alaric von Mertz, had sent the scum on his way to hell.

The knight was blind and deaf to everything else except coming to grips with Gogol. Alaric paid attention to the influx of undead only as it represented an impediment to his vengeance. The necromancer would die! Nothing else mattered, not even his own survival.

"Don't be a fool!" Ursola's gruff voice berated him. Alaric felt his surcoat caught in a firm grip. "You'll never reach him," the dwarf scolded as she tried to draw him away from the mass of zombies.

"Gogol must die!" Alaric snarled back, trying to twist free.

"Then use your brain, long-legs," Ursola said. With her free hand she smashed the knee of a zombie with her hammer. "Keep at it and all you'll do is add one more body to his horde. I have a better way."

Through the red haze of his anger, Alaric knew the dwarf was right. When he looked at her, Ursola could tell she'd pierced his rage. "Fall back and keep them off me," she said.

Alaric defended Ursola as they withdrew across the torture chamber. He nearly lost such composure as he'd regained when he saw the victorious smirk on Gogol's face, but he recognized that rushing back in was only going to get him killed.

The dwarf backpedaled toward the torture rack, swatting any zombie in her way with the hammer. Gaiseric fell in with them, panting from the strain of battle. "Mind if I tag along? Getting too much trying to watch my own back."

"Help me keep the zombies off her," Alaric said. "Ursola has a plan." He looked across the room. Drahoslav was up on the beam of the dunking chair, balancing himself above the cistern so the undead couldn't surround him as he stabbed them with his rapier. Helchen and Hulmul were back in the alcove, holding off the zombies with a combination of steel and spell. Ratbag, still looking stunned, was back on his feet and helping Fang against the creatures converging on them.

They were on the precipice of being overwhelmed unless Ursola's strategy worked.

With Alaric and Gaiseric to protect her, the dwarf dropped

her hammer and hopped up onto the torture rack. "Now that you're out of the way," she scolded Alaric, "let's see if we can make these accursed things regret climbing out of their graves." She snatched the torch from Gaiseric's off-hand. "Sorry, but I need this."

Alaric felt hope rekindled. The firebombs! There weren't any wood panels and lush rugs here to feed the flames and send them out of control. Only Gogol and his obscene minions.

"This is for Ironshield and Company!" Ursola shouted as she lobbed one of the incendiaries into the horde. Fire engulfed several of the zombies, dropping three of them instantly while many more continued to burn.

"The necromancer," Alaric directed Ursola. "Aim for Gogol!"

The dwarf lit another of her bombs and waited for the fuse to burn down. When the timing was just where she needed it, Ursola sent it sailing over the heads of the decayed horde and straight towards the villain.

"That's for Castle von Mertz and my family!" Alaric shouted as the bomb landed and flames whooshed up around Gogol and his cadre of zombie guards.

CHAPTER SIXTEEN

Gaiseric was blinded for a moment when Ursola threw the firebomb, so intense were the flames. He slashed out wildly and felt his sword chop into flesh... and become caught! Before he could pull the blade free, cold hands seized him and he was knocked to the ground. A body pressed down against him, the rank taste of decay seeping into his mouth as a zombie loomed over him.

Frantic, he let go of his sword and flung his hands outward, trying to keep his antagonist away. Gaiseric connected with his enemy and tried to push the zombie off. Terror filled him when his fingers brushed against teeth. He whipped his hand away before the walker could bite him. As his vision started to clear, he saw the grisly figure of the high inquisitor above him. The thing that had been Elza snarled and tried to lean into him, struggling to bring its necrotic mouth to his throat.

"No, you don't," Gaiseric snarled back, landing a fist against the zombie's chin. Elza's jaws cracked together and bits of broken tooth dribbled down onto the thief. Pushing against the creature with one hand, he continued to pummel it with the other, cracking more teeth with each hit. The zombie, however, was quite oblivious to pain. There wouldn't be any knocking it out and his bare hands couldn't deliver enough damage to destroy it.

"Black cats and broken ladders!" he cursed, fear racing through him. Gaiseric couldn't free himself of the high inquisitor and it was only a matter of moments before other zombies were drawn by his helplessness. Exerting all his strength, he strained against the walker, trying to lift it away from him. All he managed to do was push the thing a few inches higher.

To his marvel, a few inches proved to be all Gaiseric needed. A flicker of blue light slammed into the zombie, burning a hole straight through its head. All resistance ended at once and he flung the corpse onto the floor. Gaiseric sprang after it and ripped his sword free of the body.

"I always dreamed of doing that to a high inquisitor!" Hulmul laughed. The wizard pointed his finger at a zombie that was approaching the alcove, scorching a hole through its skull the same way he had Elza.

"I hope saving me was part of the idea," Gaiseric called to the wizard.

"Bit of a bonus, really." Hulmul smiled.

"Less talk, more killing," Helchen chided them as her mace exploded the head of a mold-covered zombie.

Gaiseric didn't like being told what to do, but he knew when to make an exception. His sword chopped into a zombie dressed in the sackcloth of a prisoner, ending the wretch's unnatural animation with a second slash that spilled its brains. The walker toppled back into a creature wearing the leather hood of a torturer, knocking them both down. Before the hooded zombie could free itself of the dead weight, Gaiseric stabbed it through the forehead.

The melee in the torture chamber was beginning to favor the living rather than the undead. Ursola's firebombs had decimated the zombies, leaving piles of smoldering bodies scattered about the room. Many more had been cut down by the warriors, the corpses strewn about the floor proving obstacles to the shambling walkers that yet remained active. Those zombies that tripped found it awkward to get back on their feet. They became easy prey when they sprawled within reach of Fang and Ratbag. Holding their positions, whether to guard the alcove, protect Ursola, or use the cistern for defense, the others didn't have the freedom to capitalize on the havoc the way the orc and his wolf did.

Gaiseric wasn't the only one who noted the changing tide. Looking past the thinning ranks of the undead, he spotted Gogol. The necromancer's cadre of brutes were burning heaps, but he himself had survived the firebomb with little more than a singed robe. The abomination itself exhibited even less effect from the flames. Gaiseric could see Gogol cast a longing look at the alcove, then an appraising glance across his diminishing forces. Finally, the villain stared at Alaric and watched the knight cutting down his zombies. Fear flickered across the man's face.

"Alaric! Gogol's trying to escape!" Gaiseric darted around a walker as it reached for him and ran to the mouth of the tunnel to block the necromancer's retreat. Alaric struggled to reach the thief and help him keep his enemy in the room.

Gogol, however, had a different escape in mind. The necromancer didn't turn to the tunnel, but instead rushed for the pit leading to the catacombs. The instant they realized his intention, Gaiseric and Alaric pivoted and charged toward the villain.

"Kill them! Kill them all!" Gogol snarled before dropping down into the pit. At his command, the last of his retinue turned and lumbered towards the heroes. Dread prickled Gaiseric's scalp as he saw the abomination coming towards him.

"You'll not keep me from him!" Alaric swore as he dove at the hulking zombie. His blade chopped into the creature but failed to do more than scratch the muscular mass. He whipped the sword free and swung his shield around to catch the monster's fist as it tried to punch him. There was a loud crash and Alaric was sent tumbling across the floor. Gaiseric could see the impression left by the abomination's knuckles on the shield's face.

The thief scrambled over to the staggered knight, protecting him from the walkers that moved in to finish him. Gaiseric chopped through the arm of one as it tried to grab Alaric, then stove in the skull of a second with the pommel of his sword. Before he could deal with a third zombie, the knight had recovered sufficiently to see to his own defense. An upward sweep of his longsword split the creature's face and sent it crashing to the floor.

"It's no good," Gaiseric told Alaric, catching his arm and trying to hold him back when he would have charged the abomination again.

"Gogol's getting away," Alaric snarled, trying to twist free. Gaiseric wondered if he shouldn't let him go. The creature was coming for them anyway.

"Keep away from it!" Ursola shouted by way of warning. She sent a large jar sailing toward the abomination. It looked like one of the concoctions she'd been examining in the vault. When it shattered against the monster, it coated the zombie and the floor around it in thick, greenish slime. The dwarf hurled her torch after the jar, but this time her aim was wide. The brand landed well away from the creature.

"Allow me," Hulmul shouted from across the room. The wizard stretched out his hand and sent a burst of fire searing into the slime-coated abomination. Flames engulfed the monster as the ooze covering it was ignited. A glottal wail of anguish, the first sound Gaiseric had heard it make, rang out as the burning abomination slumped to its knees. The slime on the floor ignited, surging up the legs of those walkers who'd shambled into or through it.

Unlike the firebomb or the wizard's spell on its own, the blazing slime burned with an intensity the abomination couldn't shrug off. Gaiseric watched in morbid fascination as meat and muscle dripped free of its bones. The monster's limbs gave out from under it and it slopped to the ground in a puddle of fire. The half dozen walkers also caught in the conflagration soon followed suit.

"Whatever that was, I hope she has more of it," Gaiseric commented as the zombies burned.

Alaric, however, was focused on something else. Skirting around the flames, decapitating a walker that staggered into his path, the knight was intent on reaching the pit and pursuing Gogol. Without hesitation, he dropped down into the hole.

"Damn fool," Gaiseric hissed under his breath. He glanced

across the chamber, finding that the others were very much still busy battling the remnants of the horde. He glanced back at the pit. Alaric would be all alone down there.

"More fool me for following him," the thief berated himself. Before he could reconsider his choice, Gaiseric dropped into the pit.

There was a fine line between heroic and reckless. As he dropped down into the catacombs, Alaric wondered which side of that line he was on. It wouldn't matter. As long as he got Gogol and put an end to the necromancer. Not just for the sake of avenging his family, but for the sake of all those who might be future victims of the man's evil.

The catacombs reeked of neglect and decay. The walls pressed in close, and from the light trickling in from the torture chamber above, Alaric could see they were even more roughly constructed than the dungeons were. The walls were of raw stone, jagged and uneven. The floor was dirt and might have provided a good way to track Gogol had it not been trampled by all the undead he'd summoned from this blighted place.

The tunnel ended just below the grating, so there was only one path to follow. At least at this point, the knight reflected, not knowing what sort of warren he was plunging into. Alaric started down the passage, then stopped, letting his eyes adjust to the murky gloom. Away from the light streaming down from the room above, he became aware that the walls had a ghoulish glow to them. He slid his hand down a section and discovered that the same greenish light now emanated from his fingers. In the brighter light above, it hadn't been noticeable, but the dried-out mold coating the catacomb zombies was luminous. It appeared the stuff covered everything down here, lending the place a weird and eerie brilliance.

Alaric could see about fifty feet ahead, but there was no sign of Gogol. He stood still and tried to listen for the sound of the necromancer running away, but the din of battle above his head made it impossible to tell if there were footfalls or not. He felt a pang of guilt, leaving his companions to fight alone, but reasoned that preventing Gogol from rallying another host of undead would be more help to them than staying behind.

The knight began to march into the deep when the sound of a body dropping down behind him made him spin around. He was ready to smite any zombie that had followed after him and only narrowly stayed his hand when he saw it was Gaiseric.

"What are you doing?" Alaric demanded.

The thief shook his head. "No, the question is, what are *you* doing?"

"Hunting Gogol," Alaric said. He turned and resumed his march through the macabre passage.

"And you thought you'd try that on your own?" Gaiseric trotted after Alaric. "Look, I don't much enjoy playing squire to you, but somebody has to watch your back."

The thief's show of loyalty caught Alaric off guard. It made him consider the danger he was putting Gaiseric in, and that made him face which side of the line he was on when it came to recklessness. Caution, not bravado, was why he'd survived when so much of Marshal Konreid's army had been slaughtered. For the sake of vengeance, he was casting aside caution now. It was well enough for himself to take that risk, but it rested ill with him to let another share the danger. "You should go back. I can hardly worry about being surrounded when there's only one way…"

Alaric's words trailed off as the tunnel ahead formed a junction, with connecting passages leading away to left and right. He could see niches cut into the walls, rotten shrouds and jumbled bones scattered about each opening. He'd thought in terms of dozens when it came to how many dead the witch hunters had interred. Now, seeing the corridor was but one of a network, he wondered if hundreds might not be a better gauge of how many victims of the Order were down here.

"You were saying?" Gaiseric chided him. The thief pushed past Alaric. "On second thought, of the two of us, I'm the one who has the better chance of picking out Gogol's trail. So you watch my back." He hurried to the junction and began to scrutinize the floor and walls.

Alaric didn't like it but was realist enough to let the thief work. He posted himself at the middle of the junction, ready to meet any enemy that approached. He glanced again at one of the niches with its scattered bones. They must have been too old and fragmentary to be reanimated by the black plague, but it didn't exclude the possibility there were fresher corpses which had revived. The moldy zombies that reinforced Gogol's horde were proof that the dark magic percolated even into these catacombs.

"Someone's been this way," Gaiseric said, indicating where luminous mold had come away from the wall.

"Maybe one of the zombies Gogol called up," Alaric suggested. "It might have brushed up against the wall."

"Perhaps," the thief mused. His attention shifted to the niche beside where the mold had come away. Gaiseric scowled. "As if this place couldn't get worse, rats have been gnawing at the bodies."

"Be grateful," Alaric suggested. "If not for the rats, there would have been more zombies to answer Gogol's summons." The knight gestured with his sword at the passageway. "Stick to trying to find the trail."

Gaiseric gave the gnawed bones a final look, then resumed his inspection. He turned his head and gave Alaric a sharp look. "The zombies from down here, they were all barefoot, weren't they?"

"I was trying to smash their skulls, not their toes." Alaric was impatient with each delay. Every moment, Gogol was putting more distance between them. He forced himself to be calm. Things would be much worse if they went into the wrong passageway.

"Someone came this way, and they were wearing shoes," Gaiseric declared. He glanced again at the niche. "The zombies from down here only had shrouds. The witch hunters wouldn't remove the rest of the clothes and then leave them with shoes."

Alaric's enthusiasm grew as he listened to the thief's reasoning. "Then Gogol did go that way! We might still be able to catch him." Now, at least certain of the direction his quarry had taken, the knight took up the lead again. Gaiseric struggled to keep up as the knight rushed ahead. At least until they reached another junction two hundred feet along the tunnel.

Knowing what he was looking for this time, Gaiseric found the footprints easily. So easily that his face was grave when he turned to Alaric. "Have a look," he said, gesturing to the print. It was close against the wall and fairly deep in the dirt. "Notice that little rise where the dirt has been pushed up? This wasn't an accident. It was done deliberately." He showed the knight what he meant. Stepping away from the wall, he stamped his foot close to it, pressing it in at an angle and shifting his weight so the mark would be deep.

"He's leaving a trail for us to follow," Gaiseric said. "He wants you to chase him."

"He'll rue that mistake," Alaric vowed. Whatever danger the necromancer was trying to draw them into, he was determined to plow through it and see justice done.

Gaiseric looked back at him and gave him a worried look. For a moment, the thief seemed like he would turn back and leave Alaric to proceed alone, but at last he sighed and started onward.

Over the next two hundred feet they came to three more junctions, but the trail was clear enough now that Alaric could have followed it even without Gaiseric's help. The niches they passed were entirely empty, evidence that they were in the more recently used section of the catacombs, where the bodies had been complete enough to be animated by the plague. Alaric was hopeful that they were drawing near to the end of their hunt. Gogol must be running out of places to run.

"He hasn't doubled back. I can swear to that much," Gaiseric assured him, when Alaric expressed concern that they had been going in circles. "We've yet to come upon our own tracks. If Gogol's idea is to get us turned around and lost, he's doing a poor job of it."

"Then we have him," Alaric declared. "These tunnels can't run much further."

Gaiseric was dubious on that point. "We're no longer under the temple-fort, so the witch hunters cared nothing about the boundaries laid on them up there." He nodded at the ceiling. "That could mean these catacombs run under the whole of Singerva, or connect to the caverns we found before."

"Then…" Alaric stopped, his attention drawn to movement in a niche to his left. Except for some tatters of shroud, it was empty, or at least so it seemed. The rags themselves were moving. From underneath, a loathsome shape emerged. It was a rat about the size of his hand. The creature was like one of those they'd seen in Vasilescu's laboratory, withered and decayed by the corrupt meat it had fed on. The animal was clearly undead, the flesh of its head rotted away to expose the skull beneath. The zombie rodent stared at Alaric with beady eyes, then sprang at him!

The rat's claws caught hold of Alaric's mail. It scurried up his torn surcoat, its muzzle jabbing against his armor, trying to find a gap into which it could sink its fangs. The knight stabbed his sword down into the dirt and tried to snatch the zombie vermin with his open hand. After several futile attempts, he finally caught hold of it and pulled it free from his mail.

The rat twisted about in his grip, scrabbling at his fingers with its claws. The scaly tail whipped at him. Alaric tightened his hold and bashed the creature against his shield. The bare skull split apart on impact and the zombie went still in his hand.

Alaric let the thing drop to the ground. He noted that its fur was coated in the glowing mold. Then his ears caught the sound of scratching claws from up ahead.

"Alaric, the floor's moving!" Gaiseric hissed in horror.

The thief's observation was monstrously accurate. To a distance of fifty feet the passage ahead of them appeared to be undulating like the surface of the sea. Alaric saw a few glowing specks leap down from niches and join the surging tide. The motion was made by the mold-coated bodies of hundreds of rats. A swarm of zombie vermin was flooding toward them.

This was the destruction Gogol had drawn them into!

"Run!" Alaric shouted. The thief bolted back the way they'd come. Nor was the knight tardy about following him. He'd been prepared to fight zombies, but not this seething wave of undead rats. He might butcher dozens of the creatures and still be overwhelmed by their sheer numbers.

"This way!" Gaiseric turned at the first junction without pause. The crossing was still fresh enough in Alaric's mind that he knew it was the same way they'd turned before. He was less certain at the next turn, and even less so at the third. The thief, however, took each corner without hesitation. Either he had an unerring map in his mind of the way they'd come, or else he was simply choosing a tunnel at each junction.

Alaric felt a sick feeling at the pit of his stomach. If it was the latter, then they'd soon be lost in the morbid maze. Lost, with a horde of undead rats at their heels, hungry for their flesh!

CHAPTER SEVENTEEN

Helchen looked over the vault one last time. She was certain she was making the right choice. She only hoped the Order would decide the same when her superiors reviewed her decision. Either way, it was her responsibility.

"Alaric and Gaiseric might still catch the necromancer," Hulmul told her. His tone was almost pleading. His reasons might be different from hers, but the wizard had no desire to see the vault's contents destroyed.

"Even if they do, we don't have the ability to fortify this place," Helchen said. "The Order locked these things away because they're dangerous." She wasn't going to argue that point with the wizard again. "We can't take the chance that someone else will find them. We have Vasilescu's book. That's all we needed to take."

The wizard trembled with emotion as he watched Ursola and Drahoslav pour more of the same liquid that had destroyed the abomination all over the vault and its contents. The dwarf had referred to the substance as dragon bile and claimed it produced the fiercest fire known to her people.

Helchen hoped they'd be able to turn the vault into an oven and burn everything inside to ashes.

"The books," Hulmul objected. "At least save those. There's no telling what secrets could be contained within them. Spells that could turn back the plague! Think about what you might be doing!" It was the point on which he was the most adamant and the issue on which Helchen was the most uncertain. She knew witch hunters often had cause to reference the grimoires and tomes they seized. To recognize patterns and predict the intentions of those they pursued, it was sometimes necessary to know something of the spells they were trying to cast. She herself had done so on occasion at other temple-forts.

"Magic is behind this plague," Helchen reminded him. Whether that magic was caused by necromancers or some other provenance, it was the same to her. "The same kind of spells might be in those books. They have to be destroyed. It is safer that way."

Hulmul scowled at her. "The mantra of the witch hunter. Better to kill ten innocents than risk a single necromancer remaining free." The wizard composed himself, his expression becoming desperate. "You can't just destroy all this knowledge. You can't burn generations of wisdom on a whim. For mere convenience."

Helchen bowed her head. "You can take what you can carry," she conceded. "They can be secured in Vasilescu's tower if everything works out." She didn't tell Hulmul that if it looked like the tower would fall, she'd be burning his mentor's library before she fell to the undead.

"Thank you," Hulmul gasped. The wizard's enthusiasm made Helchen worry. They still had to get out of the temple-fort and reach Vasilescu's tower. She couldn't risk Hulmul trying to carry more than he could reasonably handle. She patted her tunic where she'd hidden her own souvenir from the vault and wondered if it wasn't better left to the flames.

"Three," the witch hunter amended her decision. "Pick out three books. If we run into more zombies, I need you able to move." Hulmul gave her a sullen nod but knew better than to argue. He probably felt that she was right, and he would overburden himself with books in his desperation to save them.

"Bit o' der bulge 'n burn." Ratbag grinned. The orc could scarce contain his excitement. His attitude toward Ursola had transitioned from open hostility to grudging respect after seeing what she could do with her firebombs. Like all his people, Ratbag had a penchant for destruction and admired those who could cause a lot of it.

Helchen's heart sank. The endorsement of an orc was hardly going to ease the onerous nature of her responsibility here. Though they'd been taken from practitioners of the black arts, Hulmul was right when he said there were things in the vault that could be harnessed for good as well as evil. Ursola's employment of the dragon bile was just one example. When they set the place alight, they'd be destroying the useful along with the dangerous.

Loud noises from the torture chamber had her turning around, her crossbow raised. Helchen stared across the room, looking for any sign of motion. After killing the last of the zombies, they'd been careful to ensure none of the creatures would rise again. Between Ursola's hammer, and a set of iron tongs Ratbag had found, she doubted there was a complete head among the entire throng. But it was always possible one of them had been missed.

The sounds came again. This time Helchen was able to fix their source. "Something's down in the pit," she called into the vault. The others immediately turned from what they were doing and dashed across to the hole. Soon it was surrounded, anxious faces peering into the catacombs.

"It might be Alaric and Gaiseric," Drahoslav cautioned Ursola when she drew a firebomb from her satchel and made ready to cast it into the hole.

The duelist's prediction proved out. Helchen felt a surge of relief when she saw Gaiseric scramble into view. The thief didn't so much as pause, but the instant he was under the opening, he reached up and grabbed the edges to pull himself out. Ratbag reached over and hefted the man by the back of his tunic into the room. Gaiseric spun around and turned back to the hole. There was such an expression of panic on his face that it spread to the rest of them.

"Alaric!" Gaiseric shouted into the catacombs.

The knight's battered kite shield came sailing up from the pit. A moment later and Alaric tried to copy the thief's stunt of leaping up from the hole. His armored hands clutched at the edge, but the greater weight of his mail threatened to drag him down again. Both Helchen and Ratbag seized him by the arms and lifted him clear.

It was only then that the witch hunter saw the zombie rats crawling on Alaric's back. One of them launched itself at her, catching her arm. She could feel its claws scratching against her brigandine. The vermin circled around to the unarmored underside and Helchen felt its chisel-fangs rip into her flesh.

Before it could do more damage, she seized the rat and threw it to the floor, stamping out its hideous life with her foot.

Other rats had lunged onto Ratbag. The orc stumbled back, swatting them off his body. As each rodent hit the floor, Fang pounced on it, seizing the tiny zombie in its jaws and shaking its head so savagely that its prey fell to pieces.

Alaric struck at the rats still clinging to him, but only in a rough and uncoordinated fashion. His mind was on something else. "Ursola! Throw it!" he fairly screamed at the dwarf when he saw the bomb in her hand.

Distracted by the knight's plight, the dwarf had taken her eyes away from the pit. Helchen didn't have to guess what Ursola saw down below, for samples of it leaped from the hole and into the room. A dozen zombie rats, perhaps two dozen, scampering over the corrupt undead corpses to seek fresher prey.

Ursola cast down the firebomb then. There was a loud whoosh and flame billowed up from the pit. A few more rats emerged from the catacombs, stumbling about as fire consumed them. Helchen could only imagine the verminous swarm that was burning below.

The dwarf ripped away a rat that was climbing her leg, tossing it down into the pit to burn with the rest. A second zombie, its muzzle smeared with blood, was tearing into her thigh. Ursola struggled with it a moment before she plucked it free. Holding it in one hand, she twisted the thing's head off with the other.

Across the torture chamber, they hunted the remaining rats. It was an easy, if painful, hunt. If they failed to spot the vermin first, the creatures would announce themselves by springing at them and trying to gnaw their flesh. By the time the last one was destroyed, all of them except Drahoslav were bloodied. Somehow the dapper warrior had managed to keep himself unhurt.

"Looks like you took on more than you could handle this time," Alaric stated, nodding at the soiled state of the duelist's raiment.

"All of that belongs to someone else," Drahoslav remarked, indicating the bloodstains on his clothes. "Not much room to maneuver when you're poised on a beam," he elaborated, his tone defensive.

Helchen bound a rag around the spot the rat had bitten. She'd have liked to cleanse it with water first, but the only water to hand was in the dunking well. Not needing to breathe, the zombies Drahoslav had pitched into the cistern were trapped rather than destroyed. She decided not to risk having one grab her and pull her in.

"I hope Vasilescu's right about these rats and crows not being able to make someone into a zombie with their bite," Gaiseric groaned as he tended his hurts.

"My mentor appeared to have made quite a study of this plague," Hulmul said. The wizard had suffered the worst hurt among them, with a finger bitten down to the bone. A bloody strip of his robe was wrapped around his hand. He looked pale, but then his skin never had the most robust tone to it. Helchen hoped it was shock and blood-loss that affected Hulmul rather than anything more necromantic in nature.

As she studied the wizard's hurt, Helchen's gaze was drawn once more to the mark Vasilescu had inked on his arm. The sleeve had been torn by a rat, exposing the flesh beneath.

More than before, she felt she knew this sort of sign, though an effort had been made to alter or disguise it. Suspicion came crawling back, but in a confused manner. Why would Vasilescu lie and what cause would he have to mistreat his own protege? She'd seen Kramm's book and it appeared innocuous enough. Helchen shook her head and tried to disabuse herself of the idea that was taking root. A witch hunter had to be wary of jumping at shadows born from sheer imagination.

"Beards of the Forgefathers!" Ursola held a torch to her thigh, gritting her teeth as the flame cauterized the wound. She kept looking back at the hole. A firebomb rested beside her on the floor. It would need only a moment to light it and kick it into the catacombs.

Confident the dwarf would alert them if more rats appeared, Helchen approached Alaric. "That was stupid," she told him, lowering her voice so the others wouldn't hear. It was only in the knight's absence that she fully appreciated how much all of them, even herself, looked to him for leadership.

"Worse than that, it was a failure," Alaric said. "Gogol got away." The bitterness in his voice made it clear to Helchen that nothing could make the man feel worse than he already did.

"We found the book Vasilescu needs," Helchen said, trying to rekindle Alaric's flagging hope.

The knight's eyes narrowed. He looked back toward the vault. "What about the rest of it? I'm sure it was something in there Gogol was after."

Helchen thought she saw a craftiness in that glance back at the vault. She could guess what Alaric was thinking. "I intend to destroy it." She raised her hand to try to fend off any argument. "We're not equipped to lay a trap for him. We're too few and he's certain to come back with a bigger force. The only way to spoil things for him is to burn it all." She looked over at Hulmul as she said the last. The wizard had been listening to their talk. When he met Helchen's gaze, he gave her a reluctant nod.

"I want to see that swine dead more than anything," Alaric told her. For a moment his eyes blazed with repressed fury. Then he lowered his gaze and clenched his fists in frustration. "But I won't risk innocent lives to take my vengeance. And it will please me to know Gogol's been cheated of something precious to him."

"Ursola, I need one of your firebombs," Helchen called to the dwarf. Ursola left the bomb sitting beside her and drew another one from her satchel. With one hand, she tossed it to the witch hunter. Even knowing the incendiary was harmless without a flame, Helchen felt queasy when she caught it. So much destructive force in such a small thing.

The witch hunter took only a few steps toward the alcove when she noticed Ratbag sitting on the ground. She smiled at the orc and tossed him the firebomb. The renegade looked confused as he caught it. Helchen explained in terms she was sure he'd understand. "Burn it," she said, pointing at the alcove and the vault beyond.

The glee on Ratbag's face was the sort of thing Helchen imagined settlers on the frontier had nightmares about. "Yer der abbercromby," the orc grunted, as he surged up from the floor and hurried to the alcove.

"He says you're the smart one," Gaiseric translated. He shook his head. "I'd say crazy. You gave a firebomb to an orc."

The sound of the bomb igniting the dragon bile in the vault

was like the howl of a mighty wind. The glow of flames rippled out from the alcove and the tang of smoke drifted into the air. At the entrance, Ratbag capered in delight, clapping his hands against his chest in a vicious display.

"Anyone else would be thinking about the value of what's burning up in there," Helchen said, regret creeping into her tone. "Ratbag's the only one here who wouldn't hesitate. Sometimes the more civilized the mind, the less wisdom it retains."

The witch hunter stared back at the blazing vault. Useful or dangerous, there would be nothing here for Gogol when the necromancer returned.

It was a great relief to be back behind the thick walls and burning moat of Vasilescu's tower. Until he was able to relax, Hulmul hadn't appreciated the strain and stress he was under. Stealing across the zombie-infested ruins of Singerva and back again was hardly what a sane mind would call recreation.

The return was accomplished much more easily than their first arrival. Servants on the roof of the tower had watched for the group. Once the survivors were seen, the drawbridge was lowered to the midpoint, copying the signal arranged by Gaiseric. Vasilescu's retainers were better prepared to distract the zombies and pull them away from the entrance. Hulmul didn't think there were more than three zombies that had to be destroyed when the group made their rush from the stables to the tower.

Within, the building was bustling with activity. The refugees Vasilescu had taken in, the people Hulmul and his companions had brought through the undead hordes, were well aware of the mission the heroes had set out to achieve. Their dread was an almost palpable thing until Alaric assured them that everything was going to be all right. The alchemist's book had been found. Then the tower's halls echoed with the people's jubilation. Servants brought out victuals and wine from their master's stores and an impromptu celebration began.

"Before we celebrate, I need to get Kramm's book to Vasilescu," Hulmul informed Alaric as the great hall began to resemble a carnival.

"You will find the master below," the tower's chief steward interrupted to tell Hulmul. The dour-faced man looked about at the celebrants around them and lowered his voice. "He has been supervising the moat's pump almost from the moment you left. He will be most relieved to see that you've returned."

"I've had enough of cellars and dungeons," Drahoslav said. "You see to getting the wizard his book." The duelist plucked at his stained vestments. "For myself, I'm going to find a bath and someone to wash my clothes." He started off through the crowd, disentangling himself from those who tried to thank him for his heroics.

"I think I'll go with you, Hulmul," Helchen said, surprising him. "I'd like to see if getting that tome was worth the price." He'd only partly believed her when she expressed regret for destroying the things in the vault. Now he understood that she was sincere, and not merely because she'd be held responsible by the Order when everything was over.

"We'd like to tag along too," Gaiseric informed Hulmul. The thief slapped his hand on Ratbag's chest. The orc attempted a poor approximation of a human smile as he nodded his head.

"Been noodlin' der darb'z gonna pony up der kale," Ratbag chuckled in a show of yellowed fangs.

Gaiseric shifted uncomfortably when the orc spoke. "Yeah… well… there's that too. We were thinking Vasilescu might show his gratitude in a more substantive way."

"Der goodz," Ratbag emphasized.

Hulmul looked them both over and shook his head. "I'd think having a safe haven from the zombies would be reward enough," he told them, making little effort to hide the disappointment in his voice. When he saw his disapproval didn't faze the pair, Hulmul added something that did. "Even if Vasilescu does pay you, where are you going to spend it?"

Gaiseric and Ratbag looked dumbfounded, as though they hadn't considered that facet of their avarice. The wizard felt some satisfaction seeing them nonplussed by so obvious a flaw in their scheme.

Hulmul turned to find Alaric talking with Helchen. He caught only one word of their subdued exchange. Witchmark. He imagined it was something to do with helping Alaric overcome Gogol. A witchmark was something the Order often used to render a necromancer helpless so they might stand trial.

As he walked over to the pair, the knight gave Hulmul an apologetic look. "I'm going to stay up here," he said, then glanced quickly at the witch hunter, "and there's no use trying to change my mind." He gestured to the other side of the room where Ursola was draining flagons of ale as quickly as they were brought to her. "She has the right idea. Enjoy what you can, while you can."

The wizard didn't like Alaric's tone. He caught the knight's arm. "I'd think that you of all people would want to see this through." He thought for a moment, then added in a tone that was almost reverential, "You're our leader."

Alaric shook him off. "I didn't ask for that, and I don't want it." There was bitterness in his eyes as he turned away. "Find someone worth following if you have to, but let me be for now." He grabbed a bottle of wine from a passing servant and vanished into the crowd.

"It isn't you," Helchen told Hulmul. "I tried to talk sense to him, but he won't listen. He blames himself for letting Gogol get away. For failing to avenge his family."

"But it isn't his fault," Hulmul said. "He did everything he could." The wizard tapped Kramm's book. "We went out to get this, not hunt necromancers. He succeeded in what needed to be done."

"Give him time," Helchen suggested. "Right now, all he can think about is what he failed to do." She pointed at the alchemist's folio. "We'd better get that to your mentor. The sooner he has it, the quicker he can bolster this place's defenses."

The subtle reproach in her voice was a reminder to Hulmul that he was confusing his priorities. He'd just reprimanded Alaric for not seeing things through, yet here he was doing the same. "Of course," Hulmul said. "Let's get the book to Vasilescu." He nodded to the chief steward. "Take us to the master."

Once again, they were led down into the foundations of the tower and into the vast vault. Each passing moment set Hulmul's nerves on edge. Alaric wasn't the only one who could torture himself with his own thoughts, and now the wizard was berating himself for allowing even the slightest delay upon returning to the tower. He knew enough about the vagaries and inconstancy of magic. A spell that had performed a certain way a hundred times might suddenly become capricious and behave differently on its hundred and first casting. There were no absolutes with magic, only educated estimations. What was alchemy except magic distilled into physical state and bottled for later use? The system that fed the moat might even now be failing and he'd wasted time!

The wizard's sense of alarm only mounted when they passed the grisly collection of zombies Vasilescu had collected for study. Hulmul couldn't keep his eyes from fixating on the enormous rat-beast. It looked more menacing than the abomination Gogol had set upon them in the temple-fort. He could only imagine the nightmarish power this ratbomination had possessed when it had still been animated by dark magic.

The collection had been expanded during their absence, or else materials had been brought from some other part of the vault. Hulmul certainly hadn't seen the jar-laden rack that stood near the cases before. Each vessel was filled with a greenish liquid and contained some necrotic piece of human anatomy. When he saw the faint stirrings of animation each portion retained, the wizard realized he was looking at a vivisected zombie. The mixture in the jars was enabling the segments to retain their activity even away from brain and heart. He shivered when he saw the eyes in a severed head open and glare at him. The decayed jaws snapped at the glass, trying to sink their teeth in his flesh. Sickened, Hulmul turned from the awful sight. He was ready to find his mentor and leave this morbid menagerie.

Vasilescu was seated at a table only a short distance away, keen in the study of papers laid out before him. Hulmul was surprised to see that they were drawings, autopsy sketches of the verminous monstrosity in the glass coffin. The elder wizard looked up and smiled when he saw his visitors.

"You made it!" Vasilescu beamed, coming around from behind the table. "I'll confess I made auguries after you left and the omens were dire." His laughter echoed through the cellar. "But I never gave up hope that you'd succeed." He arched an eyebrow and stared at Hulmul. "You have succeeded?"

Before Hulmul could answer, Helchen stepped forward. "We were given the impression you were supervising the apparatus for the moat, not down here playing with monsters." Hulmul winced at the accusation in her tone.

Vasilescu appeared unsurprised by the witch hunter's suspicions. "Trust comes hard to someone in your profession, doesn't it?" He chuckled. "Would it help you to know that not an hour past I was most rigorously engaged in adjusting the mixture? Or would you prefer to think I've spent all my time making sketches of this menagerie for some nefarious purpose?" He shook his finger at her. "Whatever I say, you'll devise some way of twisting it into an admission of guilt, whatever it is you've decided I'm guilty of. Your kind is very good at that sort of thing."

"She meant no offense," Hulmul spoke up. He was as stunned as Vasilescu when he found himself defending a witch hunter to his own mentor.

"Fortunately, her intimations are of no consequence," Vasilescu declared. He smiled at Hulmul. "Tell me, did you bring the book?"

Hulmul reached into his robe and brought out the slim folio. Vasilescu nodded his head as he took the volume from his former apprentice.

"The Order is responsible for executing far too many people," Vasilescu said, glancing across the little group. "But when they hanged Arnault Kramm, they made a serious mistake."

CHAPTER EIGHTEEN

"I suppose you're going to tell us that Arnault Kramm was innocent?" Helchen asked Vasilescu.

The elder wizard leaned back against the edge of his table. "Innocent? Hardly. Kramm was quite the monster, if you want to know." Vasilescu gestured at the glass coffins with their morbid contents. "More of a monster than any of those, or your orcish friend here," he added with a nod at Ratbag. The renegade glowered back at the wizard and Gaiseric hastily tried to curb the orc's annoyance.

"Kramm was a murderer and a fiend," Vasilescu persisted. "He funded his researches in alchemy by murdering his entire family to gain their wealth." The elder wizard shook his head and smirked. "It's quite easy to get away with murder when you're familiar with poisons so exotic they're unknown even to the Assassins' Guild." He wagged a reproving finger at Helchen. "Your Order never suspected Kramm of that. He only ran afoul of them when he started abducting subjects to conduct his experiments on. A few managed to escape over the years. Commoners were easy enough to ignore, but not a high-ranking courtesan. It was her testimony that set the witch hunters on Kramm's trail. Their relentlessness drove him into hiding."

"If he was such a murderous fiend, why do you want his book?" Hulmul wondered. Helchen detected the first trace of uncertainty in the wizard's voice.

Vasilescu gave his old apprentice a patient look. "Genius always rails against the constraints imposed upon it by society. Kramm sought to penetrate beyond the borders of human understanding, to devise potions and elixirs never imagined before." The elder wizard caressed the book he'd been given. "If you truly understood what's in here, you'd be amazed."

It was Helchen's turn to smirk. "I've looked through it," she said. She gestured at Hulmul. "We both have. It's a rather mundane, even dry, treatise on alchemy. Frankly I had my doubts there was anything of value in there. Hulmul was certain you couldn't be mistaken, and that closer study would reveal what was so important."

Gaiseric stepped forward, an incredulous look on his face. "You mean the book's worthless? After all we've been through?" The thief's hands twitched, as though he could feel the reward he'd expected slipping through his fingers.

"Not worthless," Vasilescu assured Gaiseric. "Not to those who know what to look for." He turned back to Helchen. "Kramm worked in cipher, but such a cunningly contrived system that the finished text looked like, well, as you say, a dry and unremarkable treatise. He didn't want any of his revelations being read by those without the proper understanding."

"A lot of work to conceal alchemical formulae," Helchen opined. She removed her hat and shifted a stray lock of hair from her forehead. "But I suppose he also detailed the experiments that led him to those findings. A record of abduction and murder."

Vasilescu bowed his head in recognition of Helchen's perception. "Indeed, Kramm was most thorough documenting his research. The Order would have been quite interested in this book, had they been able to understand its true contents."

Hulmul stepped forward, his attitude one of anxiety. Doubt was in his eyes. "How do you know so much about Arnault Kramm?" he asked. His voice was timid, as though frightened by what the answer might be.

Helchen answered for Vasilescu. "It's because your old mentor was in communication with Kramm before he was arrested." The witch hunter shifted her hand so that it rested on the hilt of her sword. "Isn't that so?"

"Quite so, though not so much as an allegation fell on me," Vasilescu replied. He slapped his hand against the book's cover. "I numbered Kramm among the few brains keen enough to be considered a colleague." He glanced over at Hulmul. "You showed promise, at one time, but I discovered there were limitations to how far your abilities could be honed." He shook his head. "Such a disappointment. You could go as far as I could teach you, but never any farther."

"What he means is you were too decent to go where he would take you," Helchen informed the crestfallen Hulmul. "Vasilescu wanted someone as unscrupulous as himself. Someone like Arnault Kramm."

"Oh no," Vasilescu laughed. "Kramm was a monster long before I ever spoke to him. My contribution was to develop and refine what was already there. I had to merely point the way. Kramm found the path on his own."

"A path of evil." Hulmul looked as though his entire world had suddenly shattered.

Vasilescu stabbed his finger at his former pupil's chest. "No," he snarled, anger rising in his voice. "Knowledge is never evil! The uses to which it is put may be good or evil, but knowledge never is. Knowledge is the only pure thing in an impure world!" He rapped his knuckles against the book's cover. "Would you call the fire that protects this tower evil? It could be used for murder, but it is also responsible for keeping all these people safe. Which aspect defines whether it is a good thing or bad? The mixture that sustains it was discovered by experiments that would have shocked the Order's torturers and disgusted their sensibilities. And yet without it, we would all be dead."

Helchen railed at the comparison, as though the Order was on the same level as a sorcerous killer. "We don't kill indiscriminately," she told Vasilescu. "Those put to the question…"

"Ah yes, those put to the question are always guilty, aren't they?" Vasilescu's voice dripped with scorn. "Ten innocents is a fair exchange for one necromancer, but why stop there? Why not a score? Why not a hundred? After all, if they were so innocent, why did they bring suspicion on themselves? Why did they waste the valuable time of witch hunters?"

"You've only to look outside your own walls to see the menace we opposed," Helchen countered, refusing to show any doubt before the wizard. "How many thousands have already perished because of the necromancers?"

"Ah yes, there is always that scapegoat to justify your cruelties," Vasilescu said.

"It's true," Hulmul interjected. "We saw for ourselves that the zombies, if they weren't created by necromancers, are at least being controlled by them. There was such a villain who tried to stop us in the Order's dungeons."

Vasilescu gave Hulmul a disappointed look. "If you were in those dungeons, did you also see what the Order has done to people who sought knowledge? People like ourselves? Tell me, which is the greater villain?"

"Yer booshwash countin' der darb 'erez der hayburner?" Ratbag grunted, licking his fangs. The wolf at his side caught the agitation of its master and snarled at Vasilescu.

Gaiseric's mood was little better than the orc's. "He wants to know if you've been lying to us."

Vasilescu laughed. "You don't lie to people who are already deceived. You just let them keep believing what they already think they know."

"I trusted you." Hulmul gaped at his old mentor.

Helchen could sympathize with how the wizard felt. It was a horrible thing to learn your teacher wasn't who they pretended to be. "He used that trust," Helchen told Hulmul. "Another layer to the veneer of respectability he clad himself in. Tell me, Vasilescu, how deep does your treachery run?"

"Traitor?" Vasilescu rolled the word on his tongue. "I have been true to my loyalty. True to knowledge. That is the only thing any of us should aspire to. The only thing that can free us all from the chains of ignorance and the cruelty of despots."

"But you lied to us," Hulmul said. "By your own admission."

He waved at Kramm's book. "Do you really need that to maintain the moat, or for some other purpose?"

"You spoke of Kramm's experiments with admiration," Helchen accused. She unhooked the mace from her belt and slapped it against her palm. "Tell me, Vasilescu, did you copy his methods?" She advanced on the elder wizard, putting him within easy reach. "Did you stoop to murder to pursue your *knowledge*?"

When Helchen made her move, Ratbag swung around and seized the chief steward. The servant squeaked in fright as the orc wrapped his powerful hand around the man's throat. "Naht noodlin' nathin', goon," he warned his captive.

Gaiseric had his own sword out, uncertain what to do but determined to be ready for whatever would happen next. It was Hulmul who made one last, futile appeal for calm.

"This is wrong," he said. "It has to be. He's opened his tower to the refugees. Gave the people sanctuary."

"More subjects for his experiments," Helchen growled, keeping her eyes fixed on Vasilescu. The first hint of conjuring, she'd smash his skull and she could tell that the wizard knew it. "Convenient to have them coming to you instead of you needing to find them."

Vasilescu smiled at her. It was an arrogant smile. "Subjects?" he scoffed. "Oh, I'm well beyond needing subjects. Living ones, at least."

"Necromancer." Helchen spat the word at Vasilescu.

"Your Order has much to be proud of," Vasilescu told her. "Your paranoia created necromancers where there were none before, forcing wizards to seek protection beyond the unreliable support of the Guild. As your pogrom escalated, simply learning the dark arts wasn't enough. The necromancers had to come together and find strength in numbers."

"No!" Hulmul protested. "You can't be a necromancer!" The younger wizard looked as though he would be sick from the betrayal of such a revelation.

"Knowledge," Vasilescu told his protege. "It's the only thing that matters." He set a withering stare on Helchen. "It's the only thing that separates us from *them*. Knowledge is pure. Anything the mind learns can be used for good. Believe that."

Helchen realized now what Vasilescu was trying to do. Kramm's book wasn't enough. He wanted to bring his old pupil back into the fold. "You want to draw him into the same madness as yourself. Teach him to become a necromancer." Dietrich's training would have had her think Hulmul would leap at the chance, but she wasn't surprised to see horror on Hulmul's face at the idea.

"One of many," Vasilescu said. He stared at Helchen. "We number more than you could imagine. Your packs of hunters hounded us, so we joined in cabals. In the crypt of Marius the Damned, I've seen it! The cabals have harnessed the greatest feat of magic the kingdom has ever seen. The black plague that will reshape the world." He laughed at Helchen. "All because of your Order, your unreasoning persecution and zealotry."

"You lie," Helchen snapped, wishing she felt as certain as she sounded. She raised her mace, ready to bring it crashing down on Vasilescu's skull.

"I have no reason to lie," Vasilescu replied. "As I told you, there's no need to lie to those who will soon be dead."

"I've heard enough!" Helchen brought the mace down into Vasilescu's skull. Or rather, *through* Vasilescu's skull, for there was no resistance to her steel. She stumbled forward, crashing into the table. An illusion!

A snarl from Fang turned her around. She saw the wolf's fur bristle, its eyes fixated on a darkened doorway a hundred feet away. A musty, noxious smell that was strangely familiar drifted out from the opening. It took her a moment to realize it was the decayed stench of the catacombs. Two motes of greenish light shone in the darkness, low to the ground. As they came nearer, she realized they were shoes coated in phosphorescent mold.

"Why do you waste time talking to them?" Gogol asked, as he stepped into the cellar.

Beside her, Vasilescu's image smiled at Helchen. "After all I have suffered to conceal my activities from the witch hunters, am I not allowed my little amusements?" The illusion cast its gaze across her companions. "You're all going to die," it pronounced.

There followed a sound that, in the circumstances, was the most horrible Helchen could imagine.

It was the sound of glass breaking.

The sounds of frivolity wore on Alaric. He didn't begrudge the refugees their joy – with the destruction of Singerva there was little enough for them to cheer – but it was a celebration he could take no part in. His mind was still down in the catacombs, wondering where Gogol had escaped to.

The knight leaned back in his chair, his eyes straying from the dancing townsfolk to the pommel of his sword. He ran his fingers around the engraving, the von Mertz coat-of-arms. He'd vowed to avenge his family on their killer. It was the entire reason he'd been swayed by Gaiseric to make the journey to Singerva. Alaric uttered a bitter laugh. He'd come to the town seeking help and had instead been the one giving help, saving whoever could be salvaged from the devastation. Perhaps another could appreciate that irony, but he couldn't. The urge for vengeance was too strong.

Alaric's mood darkened further when he considered Helchen's whispered words. The witch hunter had tried to convince him that Vasilescu had deceived them in some way. She maintained that the master wizard hadn't been forthright with them and had some ulterior motive. The knight dismissed those suspicions, chalked them down to her prejudice against all practitioners of magic. Helchen had been trained to view all wizards as little more than undiscovered necromancers, thus it was only to be expected that she'd develop paranoia from such indoctrination. He had little sympathy for the attitude. Meeting Ratbag had made him take a hard look at his own hatred of orcs and he'd been less than pleased with what he found. If he could rethink his stance on orcs, surely Helchen could realize that not all wizards were monsters-in-waiting. He'd thought she was coming around to that notion from the way she'd started to accept Hulmul, but this resentment of Vasilescu made Alaric reconsider the impression. Her talk of witchmarks and manipulation wasn't exactly tolerant.

"If she wants a magician to burn, she can help me find Gogol," Alaric grumbled to himself. He was so deep in his thoughts that he only became aware of the man standing beside him when he heard a cough at his elbow. Turning his head, he found a tall, white-haired servant arrayed in a velvet doublet and curl-toed shoes waiting to attend him.

"Compliments of my master," the servant said, extending toward Alaric a silver platter on which stood a dusky wine bottle and a crystal goblet. "In gratitude for your daring exploits."

Alaric took the bottle and gave it an almost adoring scrutiny. The Baron's cellars had been extensive, the collection of wines being one of his father's favorite indulgences. Seeing a rare vintage sent a wistful nostalgia trickling through his heart. To think of all that was gone, never to be reclaimed.

The servant stood by, ready to pour the wine. Alaric noted the man's impatience and deduced he was eager to rejoin the frivolity. He started to hand the bottle back so he could perform his task when he noted something amiss. He stared at the label again. It was a Rheinwald, and of a vintage his father had sampled many times. The glass and the label were as they should be, but the cork lacked the ivory-pigmentation proper to a Rheinwald. He darted a questioning look at the servant.

If the servant had maintained his poise, Alaric wouldn't have thought anything more untoward than someone sampling the Rheinwald and putting the wrong cork into the bottle. Vasilescu's man, however, wasn't so accustomed to perfidy to stay composed. That questioning look was all it needed to unnerve him. Dropping the platter, he snatched a dagger from his belt and sprang at the knight.

Alaric swung the bottle around, smashing it across the servant's face. The man screamed as glass slashed his cheek, but ghastlier was the effect of the spilled wine where it splashed him. Every drop sizzled on his skin, sending up a greasy steam. All thought of attack vanished as the poisoner writhed on the floor, shrieking as the liquid burned through his flesh.

The celebrating refugees backed away in alarm, their eyes riveted to the man on the floor. Suddenly, they began to scream. Not because of the dying poisoner, but because of the armed men who rushed toward Alaric.

"Treachery!" Alaric roared, hoping his voice would be loud enough to carry to Ursola and Drahoslav, wherever they might be. The four men converging on him were some of Vasilescu's guards. It was obvious to him that they'd been waiting, keeping themselves in reserve should the poisoner fail. As he whipped up his longsword and made ready to meet the enemy, Alaric swore he'd attend Helchen's suspicions more closely in the future.

If there was a future.

The first of the guards went down when Alaric sprang forward and attacked. The man had no chance to recover from his surprise before he dropped his blade and clutched at his slashed throat. While he pitched forward and fell, the knight swung around and crossed swords with a second foe. The wizard's tower was a place protected by its fearsome reputation more than the quality of its soldiers. Perhaps the guard had been skilled once, but his edge had been worn away by too many years of idleness and indulgence. Two strokes and Alaric slipped past his defenses and made a thrust up and under his opponent's arm. The guard wilted, coughing up blood from a stabbed lung.

The other two soldiers backed away, no longer confident about dispatching the lone knight. Alaric seized on their hesitance. He feinted an attack against the one, then spun and struck at the other. The guard staggered away, blood gushing from a cleft hand.

"Is the wizard's coin worth your lives?" Alaric growled. Injured, the soldiers started to retreat, but found their path blocked by the refugees. The crowd was confused, shocked, but many owed their lives to Alaric and his companions… and they were becoming angry. A goblet sailed out from the crowd to shatter against the wounded man's helm. A plate of boiled potatoes and steamed greens was thrown at the other guard. A furious murmur rose from the survivors.

Alaric was about to demand the surrender of his enemies when screams broke out from the crowd. Like a flock of startled birds, the civilians scattered through the hall. Storming into the room was another squad of guards, pikes clenched in their mailed fists. Alaric cursed the fickle ways of fate. From the verge of victory, he was brought to the cusp of defeat. He was certain he could outmatch these men sword to sword, but the pikes would run him through before he could get close.

The remaining guards joined the newcomers and together they started into the hall, a fence of sharp points closing in on Alaric. The knight stood his ground, determined to meet his end with the bravery befitting his name. The confrontation, however, wasn't to be.

"Hold your ground, tall-legs!" Ursola's cry sailed across the hall. Alaric spotted her at the edge of the crowd, a flagon in one hand, a bomb in the other. She lobbed the missile into the advancing guards. They screamed in horror as they were enveloped in flames. Accustomed to seeing zombies immolated by the dwarven incendiaries, it was a far different thing to see the agonies of living men as they burned. It was the kind of death even a warrior couldn't become accustomed to.

"Extinguish those flames!" Alaric shouted to the crowd. "Use tapestries, rugs, whatever you can, but don't let the fire spread!" The refugees hurried to carry out his command. The last thing anyone needed was to have the tower gutted by flame from the inside.

Ursola shook her head as she walked over to join Alaric. "There's nothing to worry there. This place is good stonework." She stamped her foot on the floor. "At best, you might lose a room or two." Her eyes narrowed and she jabbed a thumb at the burning corpses the survivors tried to extinguish. "What got into them? They go crazy or something?"

"Following orders," Alaric grimly answered. "Vasilescu's orders."

"Vasilescu? Then he's betrayed us?" Ursola growled, color rushing into her face.

"Yes," Alaric said. He grasped Ursola's shoulder, thoughts racing. "We've got to find Drahoslav and then we've got to go after Helchen and the others! They're walking into a trap!"

"Treachery," she snarled, tossing her flagon of beer to the floor, as they turned to find the duelist.

Betrayal! Hulmul's very soul sickened at the word. His mentor, his teacher, a man he'd looked up to with admiration and fealty for most of his life, was proven a blackguard by his own words. By his own actions.

The stink of the catacombs wafted across the wizard's senses, and with it came the understanding of how deeply they'd been manipulated by Vasilescu. It was clear now that the tower's cellar and the order's catacombs were connected underground. Hulmul wondered how long it had been so. Since he'd studied under his mentor? Had the master wizard been burrowing his way into the Order's dungeons even then? How long had Vasilescu been planning to steal from the witch hunters? How long was it since the man became corrupt? The barred grating had prevented the zombies from breaking through from beneath and the traps in the tunnel had thwarted their efforts to reach the vault from above. So Vasilescu had availed himself of the opportunity to exploit his old apprentice one last time and let Hulmul and his companions press their way through to the vault.

Kramm's book! Knowing now that Vasilescu was simply an illusion, Hulmul tried to reason how it had taken the book from him. He noted how the image's hands were at the same level as the surface of the table. He clenched his teeth at the simplicity of the deceit. While the illusion reacted as though taking the book from him, in truth he'd reached through it and set the tome down on the table.

The sound of shattering glass rumbled through the cellar. Hulmul swung about, already knowing what he would see. The 'inert' specimens collected by Vasilescu were now animated and breaking free of their coffins. The motley menagerie started to shamble towards Ratbag and Fang. The orc lifted the chief steward, clamping a hand on his leg as well as his throat. He hefted the screaming man over his head and hurled him straight into the cadaverous collection.

Whether a willing helpmate of Vasilescu or a hapless dupe like Hulmul, the steward was merely living meat to the zombies. Without pause, the creatures converged on the doomed man, raking his body with their claws and tearing his flesh with their teeth.

Hulmul dug into his pack and removed the scroll Vasilescu had given him. He took a sardonic pleasure using the spell on the zombies, turning his mentor's gift against the necromancer's minions. The icy blast caught the entire pack, freezing them solid and silencing the steward's screams. The smaller undead, the crows and rats, crashed to the floor, their quick-frozen bodies shattering into gory fragments.

"Hulmul! More of them over here!" Helchen shouted. She'd lowered her mace and was unlimbering her crossbow. It took the wizard only a moment to spot her target.

Gogol. The sneering necromancer had emerged from the catacombs, but the zombies he'd brought with him were only now shuffling into view. For the moment, the villain stood exposed. Hulmul didn't think he could manage another ice spell so soon, but a bolt of arcane energy through Gogol's heart would settle the fiend just as well.

No sooner had Helchen fit a bolt to her crossbow and Hulmul pointed his finger at Gogol, than they were both caught by a fearsome wind. The tempest bowled them over, tossing them across the cellar along with the table Vasilescu's image had been sitting behind. As he was buffeted towards one of the pillars, Hulmul saw his mentor's image still poised as though leaning against a surface that was no longer there.

Hulmul struck the stone column hard. He thought the impact had dislocated his shoulder as pain rippled through his body. His vision blurred when he saw Vasilescu's image shimmer, then vanish entirely. He groaned when he saw the traitor step out from behind a column a hundred yards away. No longer needing his illusion, he'd simply stopped expending concentration to maintain it.

"Everything you know, you learned from me," Vasilescu laughed. He pointed his finger at Hulmul.

Dazed by his collision with the pillar, Hulmul was barely able to dodge behind the obstruction before a bolt of arcane energy flew at him. He heard it collide with the stonework, felt the tiniest portion of its power crackle down his back.

"You can't hide forever!" Vasilescu snarled.

Hulmul knew his mentor was right on that point. There was no spell he could call up that Vasilescu didn't already know. The villain knew everything he did.

Or did he? Hulmul wondered if Gogol knew Helchen had torched the vault, or if he'd dared to relate that intelligence to Vasilescu. His mentor might have wanted Kramm's book, but he probably also coveted everything else that had been seized by the witch hunters.

"You don't dare destroy me!" Hulmul shouted back at his old master. He reached into his robes and brought out the handful of books Helchen had permitted him to save. Now, if he was lucky, they would save him.

"She burned everything in the vault, Vasilescu," Hulmul taunted the betrayer. He stretched out his arm, displaying the tomes he held. "This is all I could save when she wasn't looking! Any magic strong enough to kill me is strong enough to destroy them!"

When Vasilescu answered, Hulmul knew he'd judged the situation correctly. "Give them to me!" he shouted. "Give them to me and I'll spare your life!"

It was Hulmul's turn to laugh as he drew his arm back behind the pillar. "You disappoint me, Vasilescu. I thought you said you didn't need to lie." Stuffing the tomes back under the breast of his robe, the wizard clenched his teeth. It was time to see just how much the necromancer wanted those books.

Hulmul darted out from behind the column and sprinted for another that was a dozen yards away. He knew he was exposed to Vasilescu's vision. The traitor could strike him down with any one of a battery of spells. When he reached cover, he breathed a little easier. His bluff had worked. Vasilescu wouldn't use magic to destroy him.

Of course, that didn't mean the necromancer wouldn't command a pack of zombies to rip him apart. Hulmul had taken a weapon from Vasilescu's arsenal, but he was far from safe.

Gaiseric dove behind one of the pillars the instant he heard glass shattering. His first instinct was to look back at the glass coffin that held the gigantic rat-creature. The relief he felt when he saw that the thing hadn't awakened along with the other zombies was as joyous as finding an unlocked jewel box in a courtesan's boudoir.

The other zombies started toward Ratbag and Fang, but before they could get close, they were frozen by one of Hulmul's spells. Then things really descended into chaos. A whirlwind whipped through the vault, bowling over Helchen and Hulmul. The rack of jars was upended, shattering on the floor and spilling noxious contents, which were in turn sent tumbling away into the darkness. Gaiseric managed to get a grip on the column he was sheltering behind and keep from being blown away.

When the tempest abated, he spotted Ratbag with one arm around Fang and the other with a death-grip on a corner of the ratbomination's coffin. By sheer brute force, the orc had anchored himself and his wolf.

Gaiseric turned to look back at the door to the catacombs. He paled when he saw the host of zombies that were following Gogol out of the tunnel. With the necromancer to give them commands, the creatures would be twice as dangerous. "Besides, you've a debt to pay Alaric," Gaiseric whispered to himself.

The tempest suddenly evaporated and the air within the vault fell calm. Firming his grip on his sword, Gaiseric charged out from cover and made for Gogol. The necromancer swung around, his eyes widening with surprise. Imperiously he waved his arm at the thief. The zombies emerging from the catacombs turned in Gaiseric's direction.

If all the creatures had been plodding walkers, Gaiseric was certain he would have caught Gogol before the undead could reach him. But mixed among the throng were two of the ravenous runners. The zombies sprinted straight at him, their clawed fingers ready to rend and tear. Gaiseric backpedaled. If he had to fight the runners, he wanted to do so well away from the slower walkers.

As he met the charging runners, a sly grin crept onto Gaiseric's face. Gogol had played himself! By sending so many zombies after the thief, he'd left himself exposed to a much deadlier enemy.

Ratbag and Fang rushed for the necromancer. Gogol

gesticulated madly, calling back his undead. While Gaiseric blocked the slashing claws of the runners, he saw the walkers turn to defend their master. Some of the closest ones he thought might reach the necromancer before Ratbag could, but none of them were going to be in time to intercept Fang.

The wolf sprang at Gogol, spilling him to the ground and snapping at him with its jaws. The necromancer kept his throat from being ripped out only by throwing up his arm and letting Fang champ down on it. Savagely, the wolf shook its head back and forth, as though it would rip the limb right out of its socket.

Then Gaiseric saw the dagger in Gogol's other hand. Viciously the villain drove the blade into Fang's side, stabbing over and over until the animal's ferocity ebbed and it fell still.

"Yer gonna get der bump yer rummy piker!" Ratbag raged as he drove toward Gogol. As Gaiseric had feared, before he could reach the necromancer, the walkers attacked. The orc lashed out with his scimitar, hewing limbs from his undead foes and cleaving skulls with each swing. Fast as he decimated them, more zombies shambled over to replace the ones he destroyed.

"Loaded dice and marked cards," Gaiseric cursed. He managed to pierce one of the runners in the chest, but the zombie remained active so he knew he'd missed its heart. The other creature raked its claws down his side, tearing his skin and drawing blood. He was fortunate that Gogol's panic had caused the walkers to withdraw, but the rabid pair he still had to deal with were proving more than enough to handle.

Gaiseric forced himself to ignore Ratbag's plight and concentrate on his own enemies. A dodge to the left caused one of the runners to spring past him. While it was recovering, Gaiseric thrust the point of his sword into the face of the other zombie. The creature's own momentum drove it further along the blade, deep enough to penetrate to the brain and disrupt the hideous magic animating it.

Gaiseric cried out in pain as the remaining zombie latched itself onto his back, digging its claws in his flesh. He struck out with the heavy pommel of his sword, smashing the runner's head as it leaned in and tried to bury its teeth in his neck. The blow caved in the side of the skull and foiled the creature's assault. A second strike expanded the damage and the lifeless zombie slipped to the floor.

"Ratbag," Gaiseric hissed. He didn't give himself a moment to recover from his fight, but started back toward the orc.

The ground around Ratbag was strewn with butchered zombies. Only a few more walkers stood between him and Gogol. The necromancer, however, wasn't inactive. He held the bloodied dagger over Fang's body and invoked a strange, slithering litany. The words, if words they were, made Gaiseric's stomach churn.

Suddenly the dead wolf kicked its hind legs. Awkwardly, Fang rose to its feet. Blood dripped from its fur where Gogol had stabbed it, but the animal gave no notice to its wounds. Instead, the zombie wolf turned toward Ratbag.

"Set your cur on me?" Gogol sneered, cradling his mauled arm against his chest. He pointed at Ratbag. "I repay you in your own coin!"

The zombie wolf lunged for its former master, but before it could tear Ratbag with its fangs, the creature was jerked back. To Gaiseric, it seemed as if an invisible leash had been pulled.

"We need the orc alive," Vasilescu warned Gogol. The traitor stood several yards from the other necromancer, a vicious scowl on his face. "The cabal wants to know how this one resisted the spell."

It was clear to Gaiseric from the way Gogol deferred to Vasilescu that the duplicitous wizard was the senior member of their partnership. Before the betrayer could issue any further commands, however, he cried out in pain and staggered back, blood streaming from his side.

"Next time you trick a witch hunter, make sure she's dead," Helchen jeered, lowering her crossbow. She ducked back behind a pillar before Vasilescu could send a spell sizzling after her.

"And be careful who you betray," Hulmul cried out. The wizard appeared to have been inspired by Gogol's talk of being repaid in the same coin. A vicious gale swept down upon Gogol, knocking both him and the zombies back. The wind, however, didn't so much as stir a hair on Vasilescu's head. He seemed more worried about another shot from Helchen than Hulmul's conjuring.

Gaiseric hurried to Ratbag and helped the orc finish off the few walkers that hadn't been blown back by Hulmul's spell. "We've got to regroup," he told the orc.

"Dat gink's head iz mine," Ratbag snarled.

"You won't get a crack at him now," Gaiseric warned, staring at Vasilescu as the traitor took cover behind a pillar. "That scoundrel will burn you down with a spell if you try anything."

Gaiseric was relieved when Ratbag relented and followed him back across the cellar. The thief had some idea of where

Hulmul had called out from. He spotted a big stone bench and dove behind it. True to his guess, the wizard was there.

"Do you think it's a bad time to ask him about rewarding us for the book?" Gaiseric quipped.

Hulmul gave him a thin smile. His brow was beaded with sweat and he was deathly pale. A glance at the wizard's shoulder told Gaiseric that it had been dislocated. It was no wonder his spell had missed Vasilescu. The incredible thing was that he could ignore the pain enough to work his magic at all.

"I… don't…" Hulmul gasped in pain. "This might… have been a bad… idea… coming here."

Ratbag rounded the bench and ducked down behind it. The orc studied Hulmul for a moment, then gave Gaiseric a questioning look. "Wotz der mummerz beef?"

Gaiseric nodded at Hulmul's shoulder. "He's hurt."

The orc glanced back at the wizard. "Dahtz all?" Without further preamble, he seized Hulmul and in one twist, popped the shoulder. The pain was enough that the wizard collapsed against the bench. "Der mummer gonna blotto," Ratbag commented.

The entire spectacle shocked Gaiseric. He checked Hulmul, but found the wizard was only stunned. The thief looked back at Ratbag. "If I ever get hurt," he told the orc, "do one thing for me."

"Wotz daht?" Ratbag asked.

Gaiseric clutched at his own shoulder. "Absolutely nothing."

CHAPTER NINETEEN

Helchen set another bolt into the crossbow and cranked back the string, disgusted with herself that she'd only wounded Vasilescu. It was true enough that her main intention had been to keep the treacherous wizard from killing Gaiseric and Ratbag, but if she'd managed to drop the villain their problems would be almost over.

"Instead, they look to be only beginning," she commented. Peeping from behind the column, she could see more undead shambling out from the catacombs. Few of them were coated in glowing mold, so she knew they hadn't been there long. The necromancers must have been using the catacombs as a staging area, hiding their obscene army in the murk beneath Singerva. It could be that they'd started long before the black plague descended on the kingdom. Certainly, by his own admission, Vasilescu had been a practitioner of the dark arts for many years.

She watched as Gogol emerged from cover to give commands to the zombies. Helchen debated trying a shot, but the distance was considerable. If she missed, all she would accomplish would be to give away her position.

Besides, Vasilescu represented the greater menace. He'd

displayed subtlety and craft, ingratiating himself with the nobility, the clergy, and the Order. He'd covered his tracks well and who could say how many secrets he'd managed to ferret out of those who trusted him? Certainly, someone had told him about the vault under the temple-fort and some of the things locked away there.

"At least that should appease the Order," Helchen considered. It was clear that the entire collection had been Vasilescu's objective. The necromancers had been able to slaughter the witch hunters but had been stymied by the traps and fortifications in the dungeons. They'd needed living, thinking agents to clear the way for them, because neither of the fiends was about to jeopardize his own life. And just at the right time, Alaric brought them all to the traitor's tower. Dupes to be lulled by Vasilescu's reputation as a stalwart defender of the kingdom.

Helchen eased away from the column, intent on working her way around to where she'd seen Vasilescu last. She knew a wizard needed to focus to cast spells, and the more complicated the magic, the greater the concentration required. With one of her bolts poking his ribs, she didn't think Vasilescu would be invoking any more illusions. The next time she was ready to bash his skull, she could be certain it was the man himself.

Creeping across the cellar, Helchen realized the grim irony of the situation. Unlike the dungeons under the temple-fort, the vaults below Vasilescu's tower were well lit by the torches arrayed about the pillars. Instead of lessening the danger, the light made things worse. Though their senses weren't those of the living, zombies could still see after a fashion and the light would help them spot her. At the same time, if she extinguished the lights, the necromancers would know where she was and redirect the undead accordingly.

Helchen grinned as an idea formed.

The witch hunter looked back at Gogol as he sent his zombies fanning out. He had only the roughest idea where his enemies were. To all intents, he was giving directions blindly and hoping for the best. Helchen decided to give Gogol something more substantial to follow.

Lifting her crossbow, she aimed at a torch only a few columns away. She shot the bolt and snuffed out the brand. The area around the column was instantly plunged into darkness. Gogol at once noticed the occurrence and waved several of the undead in that direction. Helchen hastily reloaded the weapon and cranked back the string. Aiming again, she picked out a column in line with the first but even further away. Unlike the first shot, she didn't have a clear view of the torch. If she hit it but didn't snuff it out, the deceit that someone was there would be lost. Worse, if she hit it and only knocked it to the ground, she might arouse Gogol's suspicions.

"Marduum guide my aim," Helchen prayed before sending the bolt hurtling across the cellar. She sighed with relief when the torch went out.

Now, certain that someone was there, Gogol sent nearly all the zombies off in that direction. Helchen saw the undead frame of Fang bounding ahead of even the runners, moving with almost as much speed and fluidity as the wolf had when alive. There was an added horror, seeing the animal's face pulled back in a perpetual snarl, yet making no sound other than the scratch of its claws on the floor.

Confident her ruse had worked, Helchen dashed away in the other direction, ducking behind a marble basin. She froze for a moment, listening for any hint that she'd been spotted before peeking back toward the darkened area she'd decoyed the zombies to. The undead continued their relentless march, unaware that they were chasing shadows.

Helchen turned around and started for a nearby column. She was midway between the basin and her goal when Vasilescu stepped out from behind the pillar. His side was wet with blood and she could see the bolt poking out of his flesh. "Aren't you clever?" the traitor hissed, lifting his hand.

The witch hunter tried to twist aside and scramble back to the cover offered by the basin. Helchen cried out as a powerful force slammed into her and sent her sliding across the floor. She could tell from the flash of blue light that Vasilescu had sent an arcane bolt into her. She was amazed to still be alive. The mangled wreckage of her crossbow provided the explanation. The spell had hit the weapon and it had absorbed the brunt of the energy.

Helchen scrambled back behind the basin just as Vasilescu sent another blast searing after her. "You're just delaying the inevitable," he told her.

Sounds of conflict erupted from across the cellar. Gogol's panicked shout rang out. "Alaric von Mertz! The others are here!"

The witch hunter smiled. She'd been suspicious of Vasilescu after seeing the strange "healing rune" he'd inked on Hulmul's arm. She'd expressed her concerns to Alaric, but after losing Gogol, the knight had been in no mood to hear her out. To see him now, hurrying down to help them, almost felt miraculous to her. She didn't know what had made him change his mind, but she was thankful he had. It gave them a fighting chance.

Helchen decided to play off events as though they'd been planned all along, just to rattle the necromancers.

"I delayed you just as long as I needed to," she shouted at Vasilescu. "And the only thing inevitable is the judgment you've eluded for far too long."

Alaric brought his longsword shearing through the walker's cranium. He kicked the zombie free of his blade and used his shield to fend off the attentions of a second creature. Before it could press his defenses, it collapsed with Drahoslav's rapier through its eye.

"Finesse is more elegant than chopping away like a woodsman," the duelist declared. He'd swapped his stained raiment for a loud yellow tunic and crimson breeches. Alaric suspected they'd been selected more for their ability to reveal injuries – or the lack thereof – than any other reason.

"Right now, I'm concerned about results rather than technique," Alaric said. The knight looked across the cellar, trying to spot any of their friends.

"Over there," Ursola said, gesturing with her hammer. Alaric at once saw what she was pointing to. Amid the litter of smashed coffins stood an assemblage of zombies covered in frost. Clearly Hulmul's handiwork.

Alaric struck down the last of the walkers close to them and started toward the frozen dead. He was half afraid of what he might find. He hoped the witch hunter and her companions hadn't become sacrifices to Vasilescu's treachery.

Nearing the quick-frozen zombies, Alaric spotted the

book they'd gone into the Order's dungeons to find. He took its abandonment as an ominous sign. He looked around, but all he could see were the shattered coffins and the glass sarcophagus where the gigantic rat-beast was entombed.

"Helchen!" Drahoslav called out. Alaric shot him a warning look, but the duelist simply shrugged. "You want to find them, don't you?"

There was no need to explain his agitation to Drahoslav. At the sound of the warrior's voice, the flash-frozen zombies began to move. Frost crackled and flaked off their limbs as they turned toward the heroes.

"Make yourself useful and get me a torch," Ursola snapped at Drahoslav. The duelist shot her a sullen look but hurried to take a brand from one of the pillars. The dwarf used it to ignite the fuse of a firebomb. She waited a moment for it to burn down, then lobbed it into the midst of the zombies as they started in their direction.

Alaric thought the detonation sounded different. Certainly, there was less flame than there had been with her other bombs. Then he realized that what was billowing from the undead bodies wasn't smoke, but steam.

"Brilliant! You thawed them out!" Drahoslav whipped out his rapier and met the rush of a runner as it charged for them. His blade pierced its heart and he stepped aside as the corpse's momentum carried it past him. "Finesse," he declared.

Alaric didn't have the luxury of being annoyed by Drahoslav's bravado. The rest of the thawed pack was lurching towards them. He cleft the skull of one creature as it swung at him with its necrotic hands. A second collapsed with its face caved in by a strike from the pommel.

"For Ironshield!" Ursola cried out as she swung her hammer at an obese brute. Alaric knew from experience how difficult it was to land a telling blow on the hulking zombies, but the dwarf connected with such force that even its blubbery bulk couldn't cushion the blow. The head shattered like an egg, spraying brains and bone in every direction.

"Von Mertz!" The hateful voice of Brunon Gogol struck at Alaric as though it were a physical blow. The knight spun around to see the necromancer once again surrounded by a pack of his zombies. The villain pointed at him with one hand while the other he kept curled close to his chest. "You surprised me last time we met. Now maybe I can surprise you."

"There won't be another time," Alaric promised Gogol.

"No. There won't." The necromancer grinned back at him.

From behind the knight the crack of breaking glass sounded. Too late Alaric realized why Gogol had been so bold. The necromancer needed to get close to give commands to the ratbomination!

The gigantic monstrosity erupted from its coffin in an explosion of glass. Alaric felt a sliver embed itself in his cheek as he saw other pieces slice his companions. The pain of their cuts went unnoticed beside the terror that gripped them as the verminous colossus surged into motion. It didn't climb from its sarcophagus; it simply swayed its weight and collapsed the side outward. The beast's body rippled with a loathsome, crawling animation, its very skin creeping and squirming as it stalked toward the heroes.

"Die, von Mertz," Gogol sneered. "Last son of a wretched pedigree."

The rat-beast turned toward Alaric and slashed at him

with its claws. He raised his shield to block the attack, but the enormous talons latched onto it. The monster drew back, shifting its obscene mass. As it did, the knight was drawn back with it. He felt as though his arm was going to be ripped from his shoulder, so strong was the creature's pull.

Ursola dove in to help Alaric. Her hammer cracked against the beast's side. The skin split under the impact, peeling away as though it were dry parchment. A foul, putrid odor exuded from the necrotic horror's innards. From his vantage, Alaric saw the dwarf recoil in disgust, but it was more than a mere stench that repelled her. Out from the mash of exposed organs, a swarm of undead rats emerged. The creatures sprang at Ursola, tearing at her with their claws, snapping at her with their fangs. She staggered back, trying to tear the vermin from her body.

Alaric's own peril was magnified as he was lifted into the air by the ratbomination. Its dull, lifeless eyes stared at him as it opened its reeking maw. He could see more normal-sized rats crawling at the back of its throat, ready to rip into the fragments he'd be reduced to once those immense jaws bit down on him.

Before the monster could bring him to those jaws, Alaric heard a squeal of fright. He managed to turn his head just enough to see one of Gogol's zombies drop with an arrow through its brain. Drahoslav cursed as he nocked another arrow to the elven bow. Of all the times for the braggart to miss! Yet by missing, he threw the necromancer into a panic and it was that panic that saved the imperiled knight.

Callously, the ratbomination tossed Alaric aside as it turned toward Gogol. He slammed into the floor, landing on his shield-arm. His body throbbed with anguish, but the knight fought back the pain. He struggled to his feet and looked back toward Drahoslav.

The duelist had nocked another arrow, but he didn't have a chance to send it speeding into Gogol and make good on his miss. Fearing for his life, the necromancer diverted the ratbomination away from Alaric and sent it after Drahoslav.

Drahoslav saw his peril and fought to the very last. He let fly with the arrow, pivoting to strike the charging brute. The missile punctured the lower jaw and flew on into the upper, transfixing the monster's mouth. When the beast seized Drahoslav in its enormous paws, it had to struggle to open its maw, succeeding only when it ripped away part of its mandible.

Alaric staggered toward the combat, his battered body resisting the demands he made upon it. He knew he would be too late to help Drahoslav, but he was determined to try anyway.

Help came from a different quarter and in the form of an enraged orc.

"Yer fried piker! Noodlin' yer gonna lamit?" Ratbag roared into the cadre of zombies surrounding Gogol. His scimitar hacked through two of the brutes, pitching them to the floor in a welter of dismembered limbs.

Gogol fled before the orc's onslaught. "Kill it!" he shouted to the ratbomination. "Kill it!"

The hulking beast employed the same attitude with Drahoslav as it had with Alaric, casting its captive aside so it could pursue new prey. The duelist landed ahead of the monster, stunned by his impact with the floor. Alaric could only look on as the ratbomination trampled the man lying in its path. Drahoslav didn't even have time to scream before the life was crushed out of him. It was a miserable death, the knight thought, for such a master of arms.

Ratbag had nearly carved a path to Gogol before the giant vermin could intervene. It was just as indifferent to zombies as it had been to Drahoslav. Several of the brutes were squashed by the monstrosity as it lunged at Ratbag.

The orc met the beast's attack, chopping a claw from its paw as it tried to grab him. The other paw caught him between its claws, but as it started to raise Ratbag toward its mouth, he slashed its belly. The smell that billowed from this wound was even worse than when Ursola had struck it with the hammer. The outpour of rats was likewise greater. The orc kicked and snarled as several of the zombie rodents leapt onto him and bit into his flesh.

Gogol skirted around the combat. With nearly all his brutes decimated by Ratbag or crushed by the ratbomination, he'd clearly decided to stop being bold. The necromancer was falling back to a dark doorway in the wall.

"No, you don't," Alaric swore, forcing himself on. It wasn't just vengeance for his family. Twice now, he'd seen the control over the ratbomination Gogol exerted. If he came to grips with the necromancer, he could force him to call off the beast.

The knight used the pillars to cover his advance as he closed in on Gogol. Like himself, the necromancer kept glancing back at the struggle between Ratbag and the monster. As the creature lifted its prey toward its mouth, the orc kicked out with both legs, snapping one of its orange incisors. The beast seemed confused by the attack, and for an instant it didn't move. In that brief quiet, Ratbag chopped into the arm holding him, sinking his blade deep into the rancid flesh just behind the paw A few undead rats squirmed out from beneath the damaged skin and fell to the floor.

Suddenly, the beast became animated again. It squirmed around, snapping at the orc with what remained of its fangs. The incisor grazed his arm, knocking free a rat that had been gnawing at his flesh. The pain incensed Ratbag, and with a vicious tug, the serrated edge of his scimitar sawed through so much of the monster's wrist that its paw fell away from the bone.

Alaric saw Ratbag drop to the floor, but then his attention became fixated on Gogol. The necromancer was only a few yards away now and still unaware that the knight was closing in on him. Firming his grip on the longsword, Alaric ignored the pain pulsing through his body and rushed the man who'd brought about the destruction of his family.

The knight's tackle sent both men crashing to the floor. Rage propelled Alaric to recover first. His mailed fist struck Gogol, tearing open his cheek and fracturing the bone. "Call off your monster," he snarled as he grabbed the man by the neck.

"How do I know you won't kill me?" Gogol objected.

Alaric's eyes were like a cold fire as he glowered at the blackguard. "I *will* kill you. How slowly you die, that's your choice to make." He struck the necromancer again, this time breaking Gogol's nose. "Call it off while you still have a face."

Gogol spat a tooth at Alaric. "Goodbye, von Mertz," he sneered.

Alaric was thrown off the necromancer when something slammed into him from the side. He tumbled across the floor, his senses reeling. For an instant he thought the ratbomination had somehow reached across the cellar to strike him down. Then he saw a low, lupine shape circle him. He was puzzled why Fang should attack him, then he saw the dead emptiness in its eyes. The wolf was now a zombie.

"Kill!" Gogol snarled. At his command, the wolf lunged at Alaric. The knight's sword chopped into its flank, nearly severing a hind leg, but the zombie's mass crashed into him and knocked him to the ground, his sword flying away from his fingers. Standing on top of him, Fang snapped at his throat.

Instinctively, Alaric grabbed at the animal's neck and tried to pull it away. Pain in his fingers made him jerk his hands away. The spiked collar, its sharp points so fine that they passed through the links in his mail. There would be no getting a grip on the animal that way.

Fang had the same problem as it tried to tear at his throat. Its teeth couldn't reach the warm flesh the zombie sensed beneath the cold steel. It was able to snare a damaged link in its jaws, however. Tugging furiously, the wolf began to widen the rent in Alaric's mail.

Desperation seized the knight. Once the gap was open enough, Fang would rip out his throat. Worse than such a death was the knowledge that he would rise again the way the Baron had, an undead thing enslaved to the whims of necromancers like Gogol. Unless he acted fast, there would be no avoiding such a grotesque fate.

Unable to grip the wolf's neck, Alaric instead took it by the ears. He didn't try to drag the zombie off, but instead tried to hold it steady. Closing his eyes, the knight slammed his head into that of the wolf, bashing it with his steel helm. Over and again he repeated the attack, trying to smash the unnatural life from his foe before it could strip away his protection and rip out his throat.

On the fourth strike, he felt the wolf's skull fracture. Two more hits, and he drove a splinter of bone into the zombie's brain. Alaric heaved the truly lifeless body off him and threw himself at the longsword lying only a foot away. When he had the weapon in hand, he rolled over and looked for Gogol, but the necromancer was gone. Alaric glared at the dark doorway that exuded the repulsively familiar stench of the catacombs. He'd learned a hard lesson before. It would be folly to chase the blackguard back into that necrotic maze again.

Yet even so, the urge to avenge his family was strong. If he hurried, perhaps he could still catch the fiend. It wouldn't matter if he died in the effort, just so long as he took Gogol with him.

The sounds of conflict echoing through the vault quenched the fires of vengeance blazing within Alaric's mind. His companions still fought for their lives. If he left them, it would be more than just himself who would be put at risk. It was better to fight here where he might help his friends. Dragging himself back onto his feet, Alaric headed back to help Ursola and Ratbag against their gigantic adversary.

The ratbomination had been slashed in several places by Ratbag's blade. One paw was gone, the other was missing a claw. Its fangs were cracked and broken. Despite all these injuries, the beast kept coming. Whenever it moved, zombie rats would drip from its wounds and lunge at its enemies. Alaric understood now why the thing's skin squirmed and crawled so. It was a veritable walking rats' nest, infested from within by verminous swarms.

"Ursola, throw one of your bombs at it!" the knight shouted to the dwarf. He had to defend himself as a pack of zombie rats rushed him. After his struggle with the undead wolf, it was almost absurd to be menaced by such vermin, but what the rats lacked in strength they made up for in numbers. Alaric's mail tightened around him as it was dragged down by the weight of rodents scrabbling at the chain.

"I don't have any dragon bile," Ursola yelled back, swatting a rat with her hammer and sending it to pelt the hulking beast that had once sheltered it.

"You don't need any," Alaric assured her. Perhaps the gigantic rat was too tough for normal fire to harm, but he knew the smaller rats weren't. The only question was whether they still retained any instinct for survival or if they were as mindless as human zombies.

Ursola drew away from the ratbomination. Ratbag helped keep the lesser vermin away from her as she caught up a torch and ignited one of her bombs. She let the fuse burn down. Alaric could see her calculating the time she'd need, the distance between herself and the monster.

The dwarf's arm crooked back and sent the firebomb sailing into the ratbomination. The incendiary engulfed the monster, crackling against its swollen, diseased hide. The squirming motion beneath the skin became frantic. The ratbomination's body looked like an angry sea, waves crashing and rippling across its bulk.

Then what Alaric had hoped for, what he'd prayed for, happened. The vermin inside the ratbomination, driven to a frenzy by the heat and flames, tried to escape. First a part of the beast's shoulder was ripped open, and a stream of rats boiled up through the hole, trying to plunge through the flames that enveloped the creature. Then another fissure opened across the monster's thigh as the rats in its leg chewed their way free. In a dozen places, the ratbomination was torn apart from within as the swarms it had played host to broke free.

The smaller rats still retained their fear of fire, but not the intelligence to escape it. By clawing and chewing their host to ribbons, they merely flung themselves upon the very thing they fought to escape. The flames ignited the desiccated bodies of the vermin, their fur flaring into tiny firebrands. As they spilled away from the ratbomination, the rodents collapsed and smoldered on the floor.

The beast itself sagged to the ground; its bulk far less imposing than it had been now that the rats inside were gone. Its neck mangled by the vermin escaping from its throat, the ratbomination crumpled to the ground, its head snapping free of its spine to roll across the floor.

Alaric limped over to join Ursola and Ratbag. Each of them had so many bites and scratches that their bodies looked like one open wound. The knight knew only his mail kept him from looking just as bad.

He turned his head and nodded at Drahoslav's crushed body. "You were a proud, boastful man," Alaric said, "but you died as valiantly as any knight I've been honored to fight beside."

Alaric gazed up at the ceiling and made a promise to the duelist's spirit. "Your sacrifice will not have been in vain."

CHAPTER TWENTY

"It's up to us to help Helchen," Hulmul told Gaiseric. He pointed out the blue flash of magic deeper in the cellar. He knew it was the effect of an arcane bolt and there was only one person other than himself in the cellar that could cast that spell. "We can't leave her to face Vasilescu on her own."

Gaiseric watched as Ratbag charged towards the sounds of combat ringing out from the other direction. They had no idea who was fighting over there, but it hadn't mattered to the orc. Hulmul could tell the thief was torn between which of his friends to help.

"You've seen my magic," Hulmul told him. "Consider that Vasilescu was my teacher." It was a bitter point to reflect on, accepting that his mentor was more capable than himself, but it was a reality he had to face… and one that might sway Gaiseric.

The thief nodded. "All right, what do we do?" He peered over the bench, studying the play of arcane light.

Hulmul spat, as though divesting himself of the last speck of affection he had for his mentor. "We kill him. No quarter. When a wizard goes bad, he's too dangerous to show mercy."

It was something a witch hunter might have said, and Hulmul was well aware of that bitter irony. Here he was, plotting the death of Vasilescu to save the life of Helchen. The gods certainly had a sense of humor.

Gaiseric nodded. "Best thing to do is come at him from behind. Hit him before he knows what happened and keep hitting him until there's not enough left to come back as a zombie." He looked across the cellar. There was a scattering of undead shifting about between themselves and where Vasilescu and Helchen must be. "I think he's over near that pillar," he said, pointing to a spot about a hundred yards away.

"I'm certain he is," Hulmul replied as a flash of blue light erupted from that area. If the traitor was still drawing on his magic, at least it meant Helchen was alive.

"Very well," Gaiseric sighed. "We do this as if we were breaking into a house. Fast and quiet and from different directions. That way, if Vasilescu spots one of us, the other one might still have a chance of surprising him."

Hulmul waved his staff. "I'll go left, you go right." He shook Gaiseric's hand. "Good luck," he told the thief.

"May fortune find you and the law lose you." Ducking down, Gaiseric dashed out from behind the bench and hurried toward a pillar twenty feet away.

Hulmul hurried off in the other direction. He didn't have the thief's knack for moving silently. Almost at once he noted a few zombies turn in his direction. The walkers he was certain he could outdistance. The danger was that their agitation would be noticed by Vasilescu and the villain would know someone was closing in on him.

The more immediate threat was a zombie wearing the cap

and apron of a baker. The creature wasn't one of the lumbering undead but moved with the ferocity of a fox that sights a hare. The runner hurtled toward the wizard with its mouth opened in a silent snarl.

Hulmul knew he couldn't risk using a spell to destroy the runner before it reached him. Just as Vasilescu's spells had betrayed his position, any magic he used would expose his own. He had to contend with the zombie the way Alaric or Drahoslav would. Strength and courage without the benefit of sorcery.

The wizard took up his staff in both hands and braced himself to meet the runner's attack. Upon closing with Hulmul, the zombie leaped at him, its clawed fingers ready to rend his flesh. Both hands clutching his staff, he brought it whipping around. The blow connected with such force that the staff cracked in half, the upper portion spinning away. The zombie was flung to the ground in a heap.

The terrific blow hadn't been enough to destroy the creature, however. Hulmul felt as if his heart had stopped when he saw the zombie jerk its head around and glare at him. Its ferocity undiminished, the runner lunged at him from the floor.

Hulmul stabbed at it with the broken stump of his staff, thrusting it at the zombie as though he held a pike. The splintered wood pierced the runner's breast, punching through the decayed flesh and breaking the ribs beneath. Even this wasn't a mortal wound, and the creature's clawed fingers raked the wizard's body, tearing his clothes and scratching his skin.

The wizard bit down on the cry of pain that rose up his

throat, reducing it to a guttural grunt that would have better suited Ratbag. Desperately he shifted the splintered staff around in the wound he'd made. Rancid blood and fragments of bone dribbled from the zombie's body as he worked to expand the damage he was inflicting, worrying the staff back and forth.

The runner tried to bite his shoulder, Hulmul could feel its teeth scrape against his skin. All the zombie got was a bit of his robe, the cloth snagging and hanging from the corner of its mouth as it came away in a jagged strip. Undaunted, the creature leaned in to try again.

Before it could, the hole Hulmul was boring in its chest finally impacted the zombie's heart. He could feel the shudder that passed through its body as the dark energies animating it were disrupted. Like a discarded puppet, the baker crumpled to the floor.

Hulmul looked up to see that the walkers had gotten much closer during his fight with the runner. He glanced ahead to the pillar where he was certain Vasilescu must be. An arcane bolt came flying from just behind the column, but this time it was aimed in a different direction!

Whether he'd killed Helchen or not, Vasilescu must have noticed Gaiseric and decided to target the thief. Hulmul saw the bright flash of light smash into Gaiseric as he was slinking toward a stack of old boxes about thirty yards from the necromancer. The man cried out as the spell slammed into him and knocked him down. After he fell, the thief scrambled to regain the cover offered by one of the columns. He might be hurt, but at least he was still alive.

Vasilescu sent a blast of flame at the column, the fire curling around the obstacle, but unable to reach the man directly behind it. Hulmul knew precisely where the traitor was, for he spotted the necromancer circling around to get a better angle, one from which the flames would reach Gaiseric.

To intervene directly might draw Vasilescu away from Gaiseric, but doing so would squander the opportunity to take the necromancer by surprise. Hulmul felt like a swine leaving the thief to fend for himself, but if he could only hold out a little longer the wizard would be in a position from which he could attack the traitor.

Hulmul darted around the walkers as the zombies tried to encircle him. He focused on the spot that would offer him the best vantage to unleash his magic against Vasilescu. He'd been hasty before, somehow missing the man with the wind gust that had struck Gogol. This time he'd be more careful. This time he'd be certain of hitting the traitor.

The wizard reached the spot he wanted, midway between several immense wooden kegs and barrels of raw grain. Hulmul glanced over the tower's supplies, which were but a sampling of the stores that stretched away into the unlit regions of the cellar. Anything might be hiding among the boxes and barrels, but he had no time to assure himself there were no zombies lurking nearby. If he was going to strike Vasilescu, he had to do it before he was discovered.

Hulmul focused his mind and stretched forth his hand. Since Vasilescu was so fond of fire, he decided to give the necromancer exactly what he was dealing out. The incantation sizzled off his lips and a gout of flame shot from his hand.

Only it didn't hurtle toward Vasilescu. Hulmul's head reeled as he watched the flame crackle against a column several yards away from the betrayer. The wizard couldn't understand the deviation. He'd been certain of his aim, positive the spell would slam into his enemy.

The capriciousness of magic! Hulmul refocused, this time pointing his finger and sending an arcane bolt flying at the necromancer. This time he noticed that his hand swayed at the last instant to send the attack well clear of Vasilescu.

The villain glanced back in his direction, a cruel smile on his face, then returned his attention to Gaiseric as the thief scurried to a new refuge a dozen feet farther back. The gout of magical fire Vasilescu sent chasing after the rogue singed his clothes and set them smoking.

Hulmul slumped behind the kegs and stared at his hands. What was happening? Why wasn't he able to fight his mentor?

Movement from among the boxes had him swing around. The necromancer knew where he was now, so Hulmul didn't have to show restraint. He readied a spell to annihilate whatever zombie dared to emerge, a receptacle for his mounting frustration. At the last second, the wizard banished the magic he was shaping into an arcane bolt. The figure that emerged from among the supplies wasn't a zombie.

"I saw you," Helchen said, as she scrambled over to join the wizard. "Why isn't your magic working?"

Hulmul slapped his fists together. "I don't know. Maybe he has some charm or talisman to protect him."

The witch hunter stared at Hulmul, doubt in her eyes. He could understand her suspicion. A wizard who conveniently couldn't fight against his mentor. If he were in Helchen's position, he'd be suspicious too.

Suddenly, Helchen reached forward and tugged at

Hulmul's torn sleeve, expanding the tear and exposing his shoulder. Before he could ask her what she was doing, she posed her own question. "It has to be! It *is* a witchmark! He put a witchmark on you when he was tending your injuries."

Understanding burned through Hulmul's mind. He turned his head and rolled his shoulder. Sight of the symbol that had been branded upon his skin confirmed his fear. "A witchmark," he snarled. He looked at Helchen. "You know what it means? The Order has used them often enough. I'm helpless to use my magic against the ones who tattooed this filth on my skin. So, this is how Vasilescu insults me," Hulmul growled, outrage rising with each word that left his lips. He ran his fingers around the blackish mark, feeling the scaly texture of the skin it stained. "In less civilized times, a wizard would protect himself from an apprentice by placing a witchmark. Someone bearing a wizard's witchmark is incapable of striking him with hostile magic." He ground his teeth together. For a practitioner of magic, such a violation was obscene.

Helchen looked around the edge of the keg. "He's sure to get Gaiseric. The rascal's running out of places to hide." She turned back to Hulmul. "Is there anything you can do to break Vasilescu's hold?"

"One way," Hulmul answered. He drew the dagger he carried from its sheath. His eyes studied Helchen. It was strange to think a witch hunter might hold him in higher regard than his old master. If that regard was enough to make him an exception to her prejudice against wizards, he'd have to hide the consequences of what he was going to ask her to do. If it wasn't… well, then he expected she wouldn't care about the consequences.

"You'll have to cut away the mark," Hulmul said, proffering her the dagger. When she took it from him, he ran his finger around the symbol. "You'll have to work fast and cut deep," he instructed. "If so much as a speck of it remains, you might as well leave it alone."

"I'll get it all," Helchen swore. She tossed aside her hat and set the point of the blade against his skin. Hulmul fixated on his anger, at the string of betrayals and abuses Vasilescu had inflicted on him. He couldn't let the pain overwhelm him as Helchen started cutting. He had to remain conscious.

He had work to do before the end.

Helchen bound Hulmul's arm as best she could. She was amazed the wizard had endured the brutal procedure. With time a critical factor, there hadn't been the luxury of being delicate. She'd pressed the edge of the dagger in, then shaved away the skin, scooping out a patch of flesh several inches wide and about half an inch deep.

The wizard's clothes were soaked in his blood. Trembling, he withdrew the books he'd saved from the vault and set them down. Hulmul glanced up at her. "Promise you won't burn these," he implored. "Something must be preserved."

She didn't like his tone. There was a fatalism there that sent an alarm through her. Her concern must have shown on her face, because Hulmul smiled and nodded.

"I can fight him now," the wizard said. He tensed as a spasm of pain rippled through him. "I have the ability now. I just don't know if I have the strength."

Helchen reached under her tunic, her hand tightening about her own claim from the Order's trove of relics. She drew it out and let Hulmul see the gruesome implement. It was a knife, several inches long and fashioned from a bone so old that it had turned to stone. Horrible, slithering letters writhed across its length, indecipherable carvings that nevertheless conveyed an impression of malevolent evil. It was far worse when you knew exactly what it was.

"Just keep his attention," the witch hunter told him. "Let me get close enough to use this."

"So that's what you took from the Order's trove." Hulmul couldn't take his eyes off the fossil blade but managed to nod in agreement. Helchen slipped away, creeping along the row of kegs until she was at the very edge. Vasilescu was still concentrating on Gaiseric, beckoning to his zombies to close in so the thief would have nowhere to run.

The witch hunter darted a last look back at Hulmul, then sprinted to the nearest column. She could see the cistern, its sides pitted and scored by Vasilescu's magic. The necromancer thought he'd killed her, for before he'd shifted targets, she'd set her crossbow on the ledge of the cistern as though taking aim at the blackguard. The answering barrage of spells had obliterated the weapon and much of the cistern. Pools of water and piles of rubble lay strewn about the vicinity.

Let her stay unnoticed only a little longer. Get near enough to use the profane relic she carried. Hulmul wasn't the only one ready to die to end Vasilescu's evil. If defeating the traitor marked the end of her, then Helchen would count it a reasonable trade.

She could feel the excitement of the knife in her hand, the upswell of its brooding malevolence. It was known as the Dragon's Kiss and had been found many years ago by a ranger who was exploring the shunned marshes far to the south, one Unger Ravengrave. It had lain, so the man later confessed, amid some blighted ruins half-submerged in the mud. Finding the knife had seemed so remarkable that he ignored the sinister aura it exuded and brought it back with him.

A reign of terror began months later, a trail of carnage that wove from village to town to city. Foul murders that left shriveled human husks in their wake, corpses that continued to rapidly decay even after they were found. Captain Dietrich was the one who finally tracked down the killer, running him to ground in Singerva. Ravengrave the ranger, the man who carried the Dragon's Kiss. Under interrogation he'd revealed the awful power of the knife, how it whispered to him as he slept, filling his dreams with red visions of slaughter until he was compelled to make these visions a reality. The Dragon's Kiss cried out for blood, and Ravengrave was incapable of denying it.

Helchen had heard about the gruesome relic while apprenticed to Dietrich. He'd described how the blade had been examined and found to possess tremendous power. Whether it could compel someone to murder or if Ravengrave had simply gone mad and imagined an outside force commanding him had never been resolved satisfactorily. The ranger had been taken in chains to lead an expedition into the cursed marshes to find the ruins. None of them had ever been seen again.

"Sometimes, you need a monster to fight a monster," Helchen whispered, staring at the fossil blade. It was a mantra of the witch hunters, an injunction against allowing compassion to restrain them from carrying out their obligations. The same wisdom applied here. She would use the Dragon's Kiss to kill Vasilescu. To use evil to bring good. The traitor might appreciate that irony.

Creeping toward the ruined cistern, Helchen watched as Hulmul stepped out from cover. His injured arm hung limp at his side, but he stretched out his hand and pointed at Vasilescu. A bolt of blue light sped from his finger and seared into the necromancer's back. The villain was spun around by the impact, his robe smoking where he'd been hit.

"Your dog no longer!" Hulmul shouted. Before Vasilescu could fully recover from his surprise, Hulmul forced his injured arm into motion. His hands curled into a pattern Helchen recognized. A blast of frost surged toward the necromancer.

Vasilescu recognized the spell as well. He quickly gestured with his hand, calling up a gout of fire and hurling it toward his former pupil. Flame and ice met in a searing collision. Steam rippled away from the sorcerous impact, each spell annihilating the other.

"Fool! My leash is still about your neck!" Vasilescu snarled. Helchen's hair swirled around her head as the villain conjured a fearsome tempest and sent it blowing down upon Hulmul. She saw the wizard strain to call up his own howling wind and set it striving against that invoked by his enemy. The two men strained against one other, each pouring his will into the gale. Helchen thought she could see a distortion where the spells collided. It seemed the point of conflict was slowly inching nearer to Hulmul. She could see the toll his magic was taking on the wizard. His visage had become as white as a sheet and the cut on his arm was bleeding fiercely.

There wouldn't be another chance. Though she'd hoped to get closer to Vasilescu before making her attack, Helchen abandoned the urge to caution. She lunged up from the rubble and charged toward the traitor.

Intent upon Hulmul, Vasilescu only noticed Helchen when she was a few feet away. The necromancer spun around, banishing the gale he'd called up. The witch hunter felt the air around her turn cold, felt ice forming on her armor and clothes.

Had Vasilescu been speedier, the witch hunter would have frozen solid, but the villain never had the chance to finish his conjuring. The Dragon's Kiss rasped across his chest, the fossil blade ripping through his robes and tearing into his flesh. Blood spurted across Helchen, sizzling as it splashed the frost forming around her.

Vasilescu's eyes were wide with horror when he saw the weapon Helchen held. "No... the Darkness shall not have me!" he moaned. He seemed to recognize both the blade and the power it possessed.

The necromancer set his hands against his wound. Helchen saw him try to work some sort of healing magic to stave off the force now tearing through his body. She stopped his conjuring with a second slash of the Dragon's Kiss, severing one of his hands.

Vasilescu staggered back and wailed in terror. The knife's destructive power now manifested in full. The traitor's body shriveled, flesh and muscle drying out until they were naught but a thin veneer covering his bones. His face fell in, curling around the contours of his skull. His eyes shrunk into hard beads of leathery tissue. The necromancer's screams trailed away into a shallow rasp.

Helchen felt sickened by the sight, but could not deny a sense of elation when the desiccated shell dropped to the floor. Life evaporated from the necromancer's body. The remains twitched and tried to rise. In drawing on the dark powers, Vasilescu was contaminated even more completely than scavenging crows and rats. In death his corpse tried to reanimate, but the effort only brought it to complete destruction. The zombified husk set its palm against the ground and tried to raise itself, but the withered arm shattered under the weight of its body. The corpse crashed back to the floor and rapidly crumbled to dust.

"Evil used to bring good." Helchen mocked the residue of Vasilescu's body. She looked at the fossil knife. She wanted to cast it away, to send the foul thing skittering away into the dark. Instead, she hid it beneath her armor once more.

Maybe she would need its terrible power again. Marduum forgive her.

Helchen turned away and glanced back at Hulmul. The wizard gave her a weary wave, then sagged against one of the kegs. She started toward him, but a cry from Gaiseric turned her back around. The thief had his back against a pillar, five zombies closing in on him. Setting aside her concern for the wizard, Helchen hefted her mace and hastened to Gaiseric's aid.

Between the two of them, Helchen and Gaiseric were able to vanquish the zombies without injury to themselves, though there was a nasty moment when one of the walkers got a choking grip on the rogue's neck. Even when the corpse's arm was severed, the dead hand retained its throttling clutch. Helchen had to break the fingers to finally remove it.

The moment the zombies were destroyed, Helchen and Gaiseric hurried back to Hulmul. The wizard was lying on the floor, his breathing reduced to shallow gasps. His pallor was such now that the zombies they'd recently fought looked more vital.

Hulmul pushed Helchen away when she crouched down and tried to minister to him. "There's nothing to be done," he told her. "The witchmark…"

"I cut it away," Helchen said. "It's gone." She was surprised to hear the catch in her voice. Fear for a wizard's life was the last thing a witch hunter expected to feel.

"The mark on the skin restrains," Hulmul said. "The mark on the soul binds. Vasilescu didn't lie. His leash was still upon me."

Sickness boiled inside the witch hunter when she heard Hulmul speak. She'd been unaware of that aspect of witchmarks, that their restraint went beyond the merely physical. But the wizard had known, and he'd defied its power anyway. Helchen motioned to Gaiseric. "Help me! We'll get him help!" The thief bent down to help her lift the wizard, but Hulmul shook his head.

"There's no help for me. I perish with Vasilescu." The wizard managed a thin smile. "I'm surprised I've lingered this long." The smile faded and he gripped Helchen's arm. "The books! If you'd help me, see that they're preserved. Not in a witch hunter's vault, but somewhere they can be studied. Somewhere they can bring some good into the world."

Hulmul slumped back against the kegs. Helchen could see the last flicker of life drain out of him. She leaned in and closed his sightless eyes. Part of her was shocked that she felt sorrow for any wizard, but another part of her saw him as a hero, someone who'd sacrificed himself for the sake of others. Even a witch hunter could mourn a hero.

"Gaiseric, you'll find the books he was talking about over there," Helchen said, waving her hand.

The thief hesitated. "What are you going to do?"

Helchen stood up and raised her mace. "What has to be done," she answered. She felt sick as she brought the bludgeon crunching down into Hulmul's skull. She quickly turned away when the deed was done.

"Let's see if anyone else survived," she told Gaiseric. "Let's see how much our victory has cost us."

EPILOGUE

Vasilescu's study had been appropriated by Alaric and his companions to hold a hasty conference. The room was more cramped than the knight would have liked, overstuffed with shelves of books and racks of scrolls, but Helchen had insisted on securing the place until she'd had a chance to go through and evaluate its contents. The witch hunter's discretion actually surprised him. He'd expected her to simply burn everything after learning that the wizard was, in truth, a necromancer.

"We've the run of the tower now, for what that's worth," Gaiseric said. The thief lounged in a high-backed chair with his feet propped up on the desk at the center of the room. "If taking responsibility for a few hundred refugees is your thing, that is."

Alaric limped around the desk and gave Gaiseric a stern look. "You think we should abandon them and leave Singerva?" The knight rapped the top of the desk with his finger. "This is a defensible position. We can hold it until help comes." He was angry at himself because of the lure Gaiseric's suggestion presented. He didn't *want* to stay in the tower.

What he wanted was to set out and hunt down Gogol...
wherever that trail might take him.

Yet, what he *needed* to do went against that desire. The
survivors had to have the help and guidance of someone with
a sense of tactics and strategy. Someone they'd accept as a
leader and follow in a crisis. Among his small group, he was
the only one suited to the task. Much as he didn't want the
role.

"If help comes," Ursola interjected. She rubbed at the
bandage that covered the half of her face that bore the bites
and scratches of rats. "From what you say, the province, even
the whole kingdom could be as bad off as Singerva is."

Helchen set down the book she'd been leafing through.
Alaric noted that it had joined the pile that contained
Arnault Kramm's tome. The pile that would be destroyed.
"There will be other survivors," she insisted. "The reach of
the necromancers can't be so complete. Nor do I think they
are as unified of purpose as they might seem. Vasilescu has
stores below that could sustain an entire army for months. He
certainly didn't gather that for his zombies."

Alaric took up the point she raised. "From what Vasilescu's
surviving servants tell us, their master intended to set himself
up as lord of Singerva. King of his own petty kingdom."

"Der goofz whot scrapin' fer der heel," Ratbag grumbled.
The orc's injuries were so numerous he was wrapped nearly
from head to toe in bandages. "Yer otta bump 'em. Der whol
caboodle."

"He thinks anyone who worked for Vasilescu isn't to be
trusted and should..." Gaiseric finished the translation by
drawing his finger across his throat.

Alaric sighed. It was a subject he didn't want to revisit. A few of Vasilescu's retainers had fought on after their master died, but most of them were quick to surrender, pleading for mercy and claiming ignorance of most of the wizard's plans. Helchen and Ratbag had been all for pitching them off the drawbridge and letting the zombies have them. Alaric felt there had been enough death already. Fortunately, Gaiseric and Ursola shared his viewpoint. Besides, the servants were the only ones who knew how to operate the pumps that fed the moat. While it developed that there were considerable stores of the incendiary elsewhere in the cellar, they still needed someone who knew how to operate the machine.

"Whatever Vasilescu's intentions, the defenses of his tower are genuine enough," Alaric said. "The pig lied about needing Kramm's book to keep the fires up. We can keep the moat ignited for months with the fuel stored below and we've secured the entrance to the catacombs." He wished he was as confident on that subject as he sounded, but the firetrap Ursola had the retainers excavate would at least thwart the impetus of any attack and give them time to react. "Whether he intended to use his tower as a refuge from the zombie hordes or not, we can make it into a sanctuary for anyone who's managed to survive this plague."

"As long as the supplies hold out," Gaiseric said. "As long as we can keep the zombies from getting inside." The thief slipped his legs away from the desk and came to his feet. "Why not tell us the real reason you want to stay here?" He waved his arm, taking in the room but indicating the rest of the tower. "You want to hunker down here because you think Gogol will come back."

"Is that true?" Helchen asked the knight, her gaze as piercing as any blade.

Alaric leaned against the desk. The accusation raised an air of doubt in his mind. Was that what truly motivated him? Not protecting others, but the idea that if he stayed here, he wouldn't have to seek out Gogol, but the necromancer would come to him? "If it is, it isn't the only reason," he conceded, trying to keep any doubt from his voice. "Whether Gogol comes back or not, it doesn't change that this is the best place for the people in our charge." He walked over to the narrow window on the west face of the tower. They'd taken pains to block much of it so no crows could get inside, but the little gap that remained still afforded him a view of the plaza below… and the undead horde that still infested it. "We can't take these people out into that. We're sure to lose the sick and the injured… which, incidentally, could describe us," he added, nodding at Ratbag.

"Gimme der good rumpuz." The orc grinned, flexing his fingers as though gripping a weapon.

"We could lose everyone if Gogol comes back," Gaiseric objected. "At least we could save some trying to strike out for the countryside."

"And what then?" Helchen shook her head. "We still need a safe place. Somewhere that could accommodate so many people." She raised her hand to cut off Ursola's suggestion. The same one she'd made several times now. "The hills are too far away and there's no guarantee that the dwarves would let humans into their halls."

Alaric thought there was another reason as well. They couldn't be certain that the dwarves had resisted the zombie plague. Certainly they'd seen evidence that Vasilescu had been experimenting with the undead, trying to expand and refine the scope of the contagion.

"There has to be something," Gaiseric said. "Fort, monastery, someplace that hasn't fallen."

"If there is, we have to find it before trying to take all of these people out of here." Alaric scowled as he felt pain rush up his leg. "Right now, we're in no shape to do much of anything. At least until we've healed up, we stay put."

Ursola nodded. "If we stay for a time, I'd like to have one of those jars of the incendiary for the moat." The dwarf smiled and rubbed her hands together. "I've a feeling I can make something special with that." She nodded at the window. "There's no lack of targets to test it on."

"She's got her bombs, I have these books to sort," Helchen said, setting a tome on the much smaller stack the witch hunter had decided to preserve. She arched an eyebrow when she looked at Gaiseric. "I dare say if you're worried about getting bored, you'll be able to find something to keep busy. I'm sure Vasilescu has some silverware lying about."

The jest brought a bestial chuckle from Ratbag and a smile from Ursola. Gaiseric, however, wasn't amused.

"Gogol *will* be back," Gaiseric emphasized. "He knows the strengths of this tower, so he'll also know how to bypass them."

"Or he'll know better than to try," Alaric countered, some disappointment creeping into his voice. "Because he knows how strongly Vasilescu built his defenses, Gogol might decide not to risk it."

A dour look came into the thief's face. "You didn't hear

them down there," Gaiseric said. He pointed at Ratbag. "Vasilescu was very interested in keeping him alive. Maybe they've been trying to figure out a way to spread this zombie plague to orcs."

Ratbag's eyes narrowed. He bared his teeth as he propped himself up on one elbow. "Der ain't naht noodlin' ter makin' orcz 'n goblinz inta cadavaz." He spat on the floor and clenched his hands into fists. "Yer naht lampin' whotz happnin' in der blight."

Alaric stared at the orc, then looked to Gaiseric for an explanation. Whatever Ratbag had said, it sent a shiver through the thief. He sank back in the chair and tried to compose himself before he translated. It seemed he was taking great care to relate exactly what was said.

The knight expected something bad, but he was unprepared for how bad.

"Ratbag says," Gaiseric paused and nervously licked his lips, "that the plague has already spread to the orcs and goblins. Their dead don't stay dead. The whole of the orclands are overrun." He shook his head. "Ratbag's one of the few among his people that wasn't turned into a zombie."

Alaric imagined the dreadful image, thought of the numberless encampments of orc warriors beyond the frontier. Tens of thousands of undead creatures, perhaps even now marching into the kingdom to bolster the necromancers' zombie hordes.

"A green horde," the knight said, his voice dropping to an awed whisper. "An army of death to sweep across the lands of the living."

Alaric turned back to the window and stared across

Singerva's desolation. If no other provinces in the kingdom had escaped the town's fate, what chance did they have? The undead orcs would flood down from the frontier and sweep away all that stood in their path.

Perhaps, Alaric reflected, there was nothing anyone could do. Nothing except try to survive.

ABOUT THE AUTHOR

C L WERNER is a voracious reader and prolific author from Phoenix, Arizona. His many novels and short stories span the genres of fantasy and horror, and he has written for Marvel's *Legends of Asgard*, *Warhammer's Age of Sigmar* and *Old World*, *Warhammer 40,000*, Warmachine's *Iron Kingdoms*, and Mantic's *Kings of War*.

WORLD EXPANDING FICTION

Do you have them all?

ARKHAM HORROR
- ☐ *Wrath of N'kai* by Josh Reynolds
- ☐ *The Last Ritual* by SA Sidor
- ☐ *Mask of Silver* by Rosemary Jones
- ☐ *Litany of Dreams* by Ari Marmell
- ☐ *The Devourer Below* ed Charlotte Llewelyn-Wells
- ☐ *Dark Origins, The Collected Novellas Vol 1*
- ☐ *Cult of the Spider Queen* by SA Sidor
- ☐ *The Deadly Grimoire* by Rosemary Jones
- ☐ *Grim Investigations, The Collected Novellas Vol 2*
- ☐ *In the Coils of the Labyrinth* by David Annandale
  (coming soon)

DESCENT
- ☐ *The Doom of Fallowhearth* by Robbie MacNiven
- ☐ *The Shield of Daqan* by David Guymer
- ☐ *The Gates of Thelgrim* by Robbie MacNiven
- ☐ *Zachareth* by Robbie MacNiven
- ☐ *The Raiders of Bloodwood* by Davide Mana
  (coming soon)

KEYFORGE
- ☐ *Tales from the Crucible* ed Charlotte Llewelyn-Wells
- ☐ *The Qubit Zirconium* by M Darusha Wehm

LEGEND OF THE FIVE RINGS
- ☐ *Curse of Honor* by David Annandale
- ☐ *Poison River* by Josh Reynolds
- ☐ *The Night Parade of 100 Demons* by Marie Brennan
- ☐ *Death's Kiss* by Josh Reynolds
- ☐ *The Great Clans of Rokugan, The Collected Novellas Vol 1*
- ☐ *To Chart the Clouds* by Evan Dicken
- ☐ *The Great Clans of Rokugan, The Collected Novellas Vol 2*
- ☐ *The Flower Path* by Josh Reynolds *(coming soon)*

PANDEMIC
- ☐ *Patient Zero* by Amanda Bridgeman

TERRAFORMING MARS
- ☐ *In the Shadow of Deimos* by Jane Killick
- ☐ *Edge of Catastrophe* by Jane Killick *(coming soon)*

TWILIGHT IMPERIUM
- ☐ *The Fractured Void* by Tim Pratt
- ☐ *The Necropolis Empire* by Tim Pratt
- ☐ *The Veiled Masters* by Tim Pratt *(coming soon)*

ZOMBICIDE
- ☐ *Last Resort* by Josh Reynolds
- ☐ *Planet Havoc* by Tim Waggoner
- ☑ *Age of the Undead* by C L Werner
- ☐ *All or Nothing* by Josh Reynolds *(coming soon)*